COLD DAYS

JIM BUTCHER

THE DRESDEN FILES

COLD DAYS

orbit

www.orbitbooks.net

ORBIT

First published in Great Britain in 2012 by Orbit

A CIP catalogue record for this book
is available from the British Library.

ISBN 978-0-356-50089-8

Printed and bound by CPI Group (UK) Ltd, Croydon CR0 4YY

Papers used by Orbit are from well-managed forests
and other responsible sources.

MIX
Paper from
responsible sources
FSC
www.fsc.org   FSC® C104740

Orbit
An imprint of
Little, Brown Book Group
100 Victoria Embankment
London EC4Y 0DY

An Hachette UK Company
www.hachette.co.uk

www.orbitbooks.net

For Chris Achterhof, writer of "Greed" (he'll know why after reading this), and all my old gaming buddies in the International Fantasy Gaming Society. You people are all silly, and you made the nineties a much brighter place.

1

Mab, the Queen of Air and Darkness, monarch of the Winter Court of the Sidhe, has unique ideas regarding physical therapy.

I woke up in softness.

What I probably should say was that I woke up in a soft bed. But . . . that just doesn't convey how soft this bed was. You know those old cartoons where people sleep on fluffy clouds? Those guys would wake up screaming in pain if they got suckered into taking one of those clouds after they'd been in Mab's bed.

The fire in my chest had finally begun to die away. The heavy wool lining coating my thoughts seemed to have lightened up. When I blinked my eyes open, they felt gummy, but I was able to lift my arm, slowly, and wipe them clear. I'd gone jogging on beaches with less sand than was in my eyes.

Man. Being mostly dead is hard on a guy.

I was in a bed.

A bed the size of my old apartment.

The sheets were all perfectly white and smooth. The bed was shrouded in drapes of more pure white, drifting on gentle currents of cool air. The temperature was cold enough that when I exhaled, my breath condensed, but I was comfortable beneath the bed's covering.

The curtains around the bed parted and a girl appeared.

She was probably too young to drink legally and she was one of the lovelier women I'd ever seen in person. High cheekbones, exotic almond-shaped eyes. Her skin was a medium olive tone, her eyes an almost eerie shade of pale green-gold. Her hair was pulled back into a simple tail, she wore pale blue hospital scrubs, and she had no makeup at all.

Wow. Any woman who could wear that and still look that good was a freaking goddess.

"Hello," she said, and smiled at me. Maybe it was just the bed talking, but the smile and her voice were even better than the rest of her.

"Hi," I said. My voice came out in a croak that hardly sounded human. I started coughing.

She placed a covered tray on a little stand beside the bed and sat down on the edge of it. She took the cover off the tray and picked up a white china cup. She passed it to me, and it proved to be filled with not quite scalding chicken noodle soup. "You do that every day. Talk before you've gotten anything down your throat. Drink."

I did. Campbell's. And it was awesome. I flashed on a sudden memory of being sick when I was very young. I couldn't remember where we'd been, but my dad had made me chicken noodle soup. It was the same.

"I think . . . I remember some of it," I said, after several sips. "Your name is . . . Sarah?" She frowned, but I shook my head before she could speak. "No, wait. Sarissa. Your name is Sarissa."

She lifted both eyebrows and smiled. "That's a first. It looks like you're finally coming back into focus."

My stomach gurgled and at the same time a roaring hunger went through me. I blinked at the sudden sensation and started gurgling down more soup.

Sarissa laughed at me. It made the room feel brighter. "Don't drown yourself. There's no rush."

I finished the cup, spilling only a little on my chin, and then murmured, "The hell there isn't. I'm starving. What else is there?"

"Tell you what," she said. "Before you do that, let's shoot for another first."

"Eh?" I said.

"Can you tell me your name?"

"What, you don't know?"

Sarissa smiled again. "Do you?"

"Harry Dresden," I said.

Her eyes sparkled and it made me feel good all the way to my toes. More so when she produced a plate that was piled with chicken and mashed potatoes and some other vegetables that I had little use for but which were probably good for me. I thought I was going to start drooling onto the floor, that food looked so good.

"What do you do, Harry?"

"Professional wizard," I said. "I'm a PI in Chicago." I frowned, suddenly remembering something else. "Oh. And I'm the Winter Knight, I guess."

She stared at me like a statue for several seconds, absolutely nothing on her face.

"Um," I said. "Food?"

She shivered and looked away from me. Then she took a quick breath and picked up an odd little fork, the kind they give to kids with motor control issues—it had lots of rounded edges—and pressed it into my hand. "If you're willing to go for three, we'll have had a really good day."

The fork felt weird and heavy in my fingers. I remembered using forks. I remembered how they felt, the slender weight of them, the precision with which I could get food from the plate to my mouth. This fork felt heavy and clumsy. I fumbled with it for a few seconds, and then managed, on the second try, to thrust it into the mashed potatoes. Then it was another chore to get the stupid thing to my mouth.

The potatoes were perfect. Just warm enough, barely salted, with a faint hint of rich butter.

"Ohmmgdd," I muttered around the mouthful. Then I went for more.

The second forkful was easier, and the third easier than that, and before I knew it the plate was empty and I was scraping the last of the remains into my mouth. I felt exhausted and stuffed, though it hadn't been all that much food. Sarissa was watching me with a pleased smile.

"Got it all over my face, don't I?" I asked her.

"It means you enjoyed the food," she said. She lifted a napkin to my face and wiped at it. "It's nice to know your name, finally, Harry."

There was the sound of light, steady footsteps coming closer.

Sarissa rose immediately, turned, and then knelt gracefully on the floor with her head bowed.

"Well?" said a woman's velvet voice.

My whole body shuddered in response to that voice, like a guitar's string quivering when the proper note is played near it.

"He's lucid, Your Majesty, and remembered my name and his. He fed himself."

"Excellent," said the voice. "You are dismissed for today."

"Thank you, Your Majesty," said Sarissa. She rose, glanced at me, and said, "I'm glad to see you feeling better, Sir Knight."

I tried to come up with something charming or witty and said, "Call me."

She huffed out a surprised little breath that might have been the beginning of a laugh, but shot a fearful glance the other way and then retreated. The sound of her sneakers scuffing on the hard floor faded into the distance outside the curtained bed.

A shadow moved across the curtains at the end of the bed. I knew whose it was.

"You have passed your nadir," she said in a decidedly pleased tone. "You are waxing rather than waning, my Knight."

I suddenly had difficulty thinking clearly enough to speak, but I managed. "Well. You know. Wax on, wax off."

She didn't open the curtain around the bed as much as she simply glided through, letting the sheer cloth press against her, outlining her form. She exhaled slowly as she reached my side, looking down at me, her eyes flickering through shades of green in dizzying cycles.

Mab, the Queen of Air and Darkness, was too terrifying to be beautiful. Though every cell in my body suddenly surged with mindless desire and my eyes blurred with tears to see her beauty, I did not want to come an inch closer. She was a tall woman, well over six feet, and every inch was radiance. Pale skin, soft lips the color of frozen raspberries, long silver-white hair that shone with opalescent highlights. She was dressed in a silk gown of deep frozen green that left her strong white shoulders bare.

And she was about six inches away from being in bed with me.

"You look great," I croaked.

Something smoldered in those almond-shaped eyes. "I *am* great, my Knight," she murmured. She reached out a hand, and her nails were all dark blues and greens, the colors shimmering and changing like deep opals. She touched my naked shoulder with those nails.

And I suddenly felt like a fifteen-year-old about to kiss a girl for the first time—excitement and wild expectation and fluttering anxiety.

Her nails, even just the very tips, were icy cold. She trailed them down over one side of my chest and rested them over my heart.

"Um," I said into what was, for me, an incredibly awkward silence. "How are you?"

She tilted her head and stared at me.

"Sarissa seems nice," I ventured.

"A changeling," Mab said. "Who once sought of me a favor. She saw Lloyd Slate's tenure as my Knight."

I licked my lips. "Um. Where are we?"

"Arctis Tor," she said. "My stronghold. In the Knight's suite. You will find every mortal amenity here."

"That's nice," I said. "What with my apartment burned to the ground and all. Is there a security deposit?"

A slow smile oozed over Mab's mouth and she leaned even closer to me. "It is well that you heal," she whispered. "Your spirit wandered far from your body while you slept."

"Free spirit," I said. "That's me."

"Not anymore," Mab murmured, and leaned down toward me. "You are shaking."

"Yeah."

Her eyes filled my vision. "Are you frightened of me, Harry?"

"I'm sane," I said.

"Do you think I am going to hurt you?" she breathed, her lips a fraction of an inch from mine.

My heart beat so hard that it actually hurt. "I think . . . you are who you are."

"Surely you have no reason to fear," she whispered, her breath tickling my lips. "You are mine now. If you are not well, I cannot use you to work my will."

I tried to force myself to relax. "That's . . . that's true," I said.

I hadn't seen her picking up the thick, fluffy pillow beside me while she held my eyes. So I was totally unprepared when she struck, as fast as any snake, and slammed the pillow down over my face.

I froze for half a second, and the pillow pressed down harder, shutting off my air, clogging my nose and mouth. Then the fear took over. I struggled, but my arms and legs felt as if they'd been coated in inches of lead. I tried to push Mab away, but she was simply too heavy, my arms too weak. Her hands and forearms were frozen steel, slender and immovable.

My vision went from red to black. Sensation began to recede.

Mab was cool. Unrelenting. Merciless.

She was Mab.

If I did not stop her, she *would* kill me. Mab couldn't kill a mortal, but to her I was no longer one of them. I was her vassal, a member of her court, and as far as she was concerned, she had every right to take my life if she saw fit.

That cold knowledge galvanized me. I locked my hands around one of her arms and twisted, straining my entire body. My hips arched up off the bed with the effort, and I wasn't even trying to push her away. There was no opposing the absolute force of her. But I did manage to direct her strength just a little to one side, and in so doing managed to push her hands and the smothering pillow past me, freeing my face enough to suck in a gasp of sweet, cold air.

Mab lay with her upper body across mine, and made no effort at all to move. I could feel her eyes on me, feel the empty intensity of her gaze as I panted, my head swimming with the sudden rush of blessed oxygen.

Mab moved very slowly, very gracefully. There was something serpentine about the way she slithered up my body and lay with her chest against mine. She was a cold, ephemeral weight, an incredibly feminine softness, and her silken hair glided over my cheeks and lips and neck.

Mab made a low, hungry sound in her throat as she leaned down, until her lips were almost touching my ear.

"I have no use for weakness, wizard." She shivered in a kind of slow, alien ecstasy. "Rest. Heal. Sleep. I shall most likely kill you on the morrow."

"You? A *Princess Bride* quote?" I croaked.

"What is that?" she asked.

Then she was gone. Just *gone*.

And that was day one of my physical therapy.

I could describe the next few weeks in detail, but as bad as they were, they did have a certain routine to them. Besides, in my head, they're a music video montage set to the Foo Fighters' "Walk."

I would wake in the morning and find Sarissa waiting for me, keeping a polite and professional distance between us. She would help me take care of the needs of my weakened body, which was rarely dignified, but she never spoke about herself. At some point after that, Mab would try to kill me in increasingly unexpected and inventive ways.

In the video in my head, there's a shot of me eating my own meal again—until, just as I finish, the giant bed bursts into flames. I awkwardly flop out of it and crawl away before I roast. Then, obviously the next day, Sarissa is helping me walk to the bathroom and back. Just as I relax back into bed, a poisonous serpent, a freaking Indian cobra, falls from the bed's canopy onto my shoulders. I scream like a girl and throw it on the floor. The next day, I'm fumbling my way into new clothes with Sarissa's help—until a small swarm of stinging ants comes boiling out of them onto my flesh, and I have to literally rip the clothes off of me.

It goes on like that. Sarissa and me on waist-high parallel bars, me struggling to remember how to keep my balance, interrupted by a tidal flood of red-eyed rats that forces us to hop up onto the bars before our feet get eaten off. Sarissa spotting me on a bench press, and then Mab bringing a great big old fireman's ax whistling down at my head at the end of my third set so that I have to block with the stupid straight bar. Me slogging my exhausted way into a hot shower, only to have the door slam shut and the thing start to fill with water. Into which freaking piranha begin to plop.

On and on. Seventy-seven days. Seventy-seven attempted murders. Use your imagination. Mab sure as hell did. There was even a ticking crocodile.

*   *   *

I had just gotten back from the small gym, where'd I'd hiked about four miles up and I don't know how many miles forward on the elliptical machine. I was sweaty and exhausted and thinking about a shower and then bed again. I opened the door to my quarters, and when I did, Mab opened fire with a freaking shotgun.

I didn't have time to think or calculate before she pulled the trigger. All I could do was react. I flung myself back, slammed my will out into the air ahead of me, coalescing it into a barrier of pure energy. The gun roared, deafening in the enclosed space. Buckshot slammed against the barrier and bounced, scattering everywhere, landing with pops and rattles. I hit the floor, keeping the barrier up, and Mab advanced, her eyes glittering through every shade of opal, wild and ecstatic and incongruous against her otherwise calm expression.

It was one of those Russian-designed shotguns with the big drum magazine, and she poured all of it into me, aiming for my face.

The second the gun went click instead of boom, I flung myself to one side in a swift roll, just in time to avoid the pounce of a silver-grey malk—a feline creature about the size of a bobcat with wicked claws and the strength of a small bear. It landed where my head had been, its claws gouging chips from the stone floor.

I kicked the malk with my heel and sent him flying across the hall and into the stone wall. He hit it with a yowl of protest. I whirled my attention back to Mab as she dropped one drum magazine on the floor and produced another.

Before she could seat it in the weapon, I slashed at the air with my hand and shouted, *"Forzare!"* Unseen force lashed out and ripped the magazine and the shotgun alike from her hands. I made a yanking motion, and the bouncing shotgun abruptly shot across the empty space between us. I grabbed it by the barrel (which was freaking *hot*) just as the malk recovered and leapt at me again. I swung the empty shotgun two-handed and slammed the malk in the skull, hard enough to knock it from the air and leave it senseless on the floor.

Mab let out a delighted silvery laugh and clapped her hands like a little girl who has just been told she's getting a pony. "Yes!" she said. "Lovely. Brutal, vicious, and lovely."

I held on to the shotgun until the stunned malk recovered and began slinking sullenly away, and only after it was out of sight around the corner did I turn to face Mab again.

"This is getting old," I said. "Don't you have anything better to do with your time than to play Grimtooth games with me?"

"Indeed, I do," she replied. "But why play games if not to prepare for challenges that lie ahead?"

I rolled my eyes. "Fun?" I suggested.

The delight faded from her face, replaced by the usual icy calm. It was a scary transformation, and I found myself hoping that I had not provoked her with my wiseassery.

"The fun begins when the games end, my Knight."

I frowned at her. "What is that supposed to mean?"

"That appropriate attire awaits you in your chambers, and that you are to get dressed for the evening." She turned to walk after the departed malk, her gown whispering on the stone of the floor. "Tonight, my wizard, shall be . . . fun."

2

Back in my room, I found my clothes waiting for me: a tux in dark silver and pearl. The first of two small paper envelopes proved to contain a pair of jeweled cuff links, the stones too blue and too brilliant to be sapphires.

The other one held my mother's amulet.

It was a simple silver pentacle, a battered five-pointed star bound within a circle, on a simple silver chain. The pentacle's center was filled with a small red stone, cut to size. I'd once fastened the gem into place with hot glue. Apparently Mab had sent it to a genuine jeweler to attach it with something more solid. I touched the stone gingerly, and could instantly sense the energy within it, the psychic journal of my late mother's travels.

I slipped the amulet on over my head and felt a sudden and profound sense of relief. I had thought it lost when my bullet-riddled self had fallen into the waters of Lake Michigan. I stood there with my hand over it for a moment, just feeling the cool metal press against my palm.

Then I got dressed in the tux and examined myself in a mirror the size of a pool table.

"Just a gigolo," I sang, off-key, trying to enjoy myself. "Everywhere I go, people know the part I'm playing."

The guy looking at me out of the mirror looked raw and hard. My cheekbones stood out starkly. I'd lost a lot of weight while I was in what amounted to a coma, and my rehabilitation had added only lean muscle back onto me. You could see veins tight against my skin. My brown hair hung down past my jawline, clean but shaggy. I hadn't cut it or asked for a barber. Things that know magic can do awful stuff to you if they get hold of a lock of your hair, so I'd decided to hang on to mine. I'd ditched the beard, though. Beards grow out so fast that if you shave every day, there isn't much of a window for anyone to use them against you—and shaved stubble is too diffuse to make a decent channel anyway.

I looked a little more like my brother with the long hair. Go figure. Long, lean face, dark eyes, a vertical line of a scar under the left one. My skin was absolutely pasty-pale. I hadn't seen the sun in months. Lots of months.

As I looked, the song just sort of faded out. I didn't have the heart for it. I closed my eyes.

"What the hell are you doing, Dresden?" I whispered. "You're being kept locked up like a goddamned pet. Like she owns you."

"Does she not?" growled a malk's voice.

Didn't I mention it? Those things can talk. They don't pronounce words too well, and the inhuman sound of it makes the hairs on the back of my everything stand up, but they talk.

I spun, lifting my hand in a defensive gesture again, but I needn't have bothered. A malk I didn't think I'd seen before sat on the floor of my chambers, just inside the door. His too-long tail curled all the way around his front feet and overlapped itself in the back. He was a huge specimen of the breed, maybe eighty or ninety pounds, the size of a young adult mountain lion. His fur was pitch-black, apart from a white spot on his chest.

One thing I'd learned about malks was that you didn't show them weakness. Ever. "These are my chambers," I said. "Get out."

The malk bowed its head. "I cannot, Sir Knight. I am under orders from the Queen herself."

"Get out before I get you out."

The very tip of the big malk's tail twitched once. "Were you not the bond servant of my Queen, and were I not obliged to show you courtesy, I should like to see you try it, mortal."

I squinted at him.

That was very unmalklike behavior. Apart from one, every malk I'd met had been a bloodthirsty little killing machine, primarily interested in what it could tear apart and devour next. They weren't much for small talk. They also weren't terribly brave, especially when alone. A malk might jump you in a dark alley, but you'd never see him coming.

This one . . . looked like it might like to see me put a chip on my shoulder.

I extended my senses cautiously and suddenly felt the nearly silent thrum of the malk's aura. Whoa. The thing had power. Like, lots of power. You couldn't usually feel a wizard's aura unless you were close enough to touch it, but I could feel his from across the room. Whatever that thing was, it only *looked* like one of the other furry, terminally ADD homicidal maniacs. I reeled in on the attitude.

"Who are you?"

The malk bowed his head once. "A faithful servant of the Queen of Air and Darkness. I am most often called Sith."

"Heh," I said. "Where's your red lightsaber?"

Sith's golden eyes narrowed. "When first your kind began scrawling knowledge upon stone and clay, my name was ancient. Walk carefully around it."

"Just trying to brighten the conversation with humor, Sithy. You need to cheer up."

Sith's tail twitched again. "Slicing your spine into coasters would cheer me. May I?"

"Gotta go with 'no' on that one," I said. Then I blinked. "Wait. You're . . . Cat Sith. *The* Cat Sith?"

The malk inclined its head again. "I am he."

Hell's bells. Cat Sith was a major figure in faerie folklore. This thing wasn't just a malk. It was the freaking monarch of the malks, their progenitor, their Optimus Prime. I'd taken on an ancient faerie creature like this one a few years back. It hadn't been pretty.

When Cat Sith had offered to slice my spine into coasters, he wasn't kidding. If he was anything like the ancient phobophage, he could do it.

"I see," I said. "Um. What are you doing here?"

"I am your batman."

"My . . ."

"Not the notional hero," Sith said, a bit of a growl in his voice. "Your batman. Your orderly."

"Orderly . . ." I frowned. "Wait. You work for me?"

"I prefer to think of it as managing your incompetence," Sith replied. "I will answer your questions. I will be your guide while you are here. I will see to it that your needs are met."

I folded my arms. "And you work for me?"

Sith's tail twitched again. "I serve my Queen."

Aha. Evasion. There was something he was avoiding. "You are to answer my questions, are you not?"

"Yes."

"Did Mab order you to obey my commands?"

Twitch, twitch, twitch went the tail. Sith stared at me and said nothing.

Silence could generally be taken as assent, but I just couldn't resist. "Get me a Coke."

Sith stared at me. Then he vanished.

I blinked and looked around, but he was gone. Then, maybe a second and a half later, there was the *snap-hiss* of a beverage can being opened. I turned and found Cat Sith sitting on one of the room's dressers. An opened can of Coke sat beside him.

"Whoa," I said. "How did . . . You don't even have *thumbs*."

Sith stared at me.

I crossed to the dresser and picked up the can. Sith's eyes tracked me the whole time, his expression enigmatic and definitely not friendly. I sipped at the drink and grimaced. "Warm?"

"You did not tell me otherwise," he said. "I shall be happy to similarly fulfill any such command you give me, Sir Knight, but for those that contravene the orders of my Queen."

Translation: *I don't want to be here. I don't like you. Give me commands and I will give you hell for it.* I nodded at the malk. "I hear you." I sipped at the Coke. Warm or not, it was still Coke. "So why the tux? What's the occasion?"

"Tonight is a celebration of birth."

"Birthday party, huh?" I said. "Whose?"

Sith said absolutely nothing for several seconds. Then he rose and leapt down to the floor, landing without a sound. He flowed past me to the door. "You cannot possibly be that stupid. Follow me."

My hair was still pretty messy. I slopped some water on it and combed it back, which was as close to neat as it was going to get, and then walked after Sith, my patent leather formal shoes gleaming and clicking on the stone floor.

"Who's going to be at this party?" I asked Sith when I caught up to him. I hadn't left my chambers in a while. My entire life had been eating, sleeping, and getting myself put back together. Besides, I hadn't wanted to go sightseeing around Arctis Tor. The last time I'd been there, I'd pissed off the faeries. Like, *all* of them. I hadn't fancied the idea of bumping into some hostile bogeyman looking for payback in a dark corridor. The door leading from my chambers opened by itself, and Sith walked through it with me behind him.

"The high and mighty among the Winter Sidhe," Sith said. "Important figures from the Wyld. There may even be a delegation from Summer there."

As we emerged into the capital of Winter, the corridors changed from what looked more or less like smooth, poured concrete to crystalline ice in every hue of glacial blue and green, the bands of color merging, intertwining. Flickers of light danced through the depths of the ice like lazy fireflies of violet and crimson and cold sky blue. My eyes wanted to follow the lights, but I didn't let them. I couldn't tell you why, but my instincts told me that would be dangerous, and I listened to them.

"Kind of a big event, huh?" I said. "Think there'll be a problem with the paparazzi?"

"One may hope," Sith said. "Dispatching the perpetrators of such an intrusion would be gratifying."

The air was arctic cold. I could feel the biting depth of the chill, but its fangs couldn't seem to break my skin. It wasn't exactly comfortable, but it didn't matter. I didn't shiver. I didn't shake. I chalked it up to the power Mab had given me.

Sith led me down a much dimmer corridor, and we passed in and out of patches of deep darkness and cold, sullen light. As we did, our shadows danced and stretched. After a few seconds, I noticed that Cat Sith's shadow was larger than mine. Like, seven or eight *times* larger than mine. I gulped.

"The last time I was at a supernatural shindig, I got poisoned and then everything there tried to kill me. So I burned the whole place to the ground," I said.

"An appropriate way to deal with one's enemies," Sith said. "Perhaps you will find Arctis Tor less flammable."

"I've never met a place I couldn't blow up, burn down, or knock over with enough motivation," I said. "Think anyone at the party wants to kill me?"

"Yes. I want to kill you."

"Because I annoy you?"

"Because I enjoy it." Sith glanced up at me for a moment. His billboard-size shadow on the wall mirrored the motion. "And you also annoy me."

"It's one of my gifts. Asking annoying questions is another. Other than you, is there anyone at the party I should make sure not to turn my back to?"

"You are of Winter now, wizard." His turned his golden eyes away from me again. "Don't turn your back to anyone."

3

Cat Sith led me down passages I had never seen on my previous visit to Mab's seat of power. Heck, back then I had thought it consisted entirely of a wall around a courtyard and a single turreted tower. I hadn't ever seen the complex beneath the ice of the courtyard. It was enormous. We walked for ten minutes, mostly in the same direction, before Cat Sith said, "That door."

The one he spoke of was made of ice, just like the walls, though it had a thick ring of what might have been silver hanging upon it. I grabbed the ring and tugged, and the door opened easily onto a small antechamber, a little waiting room complete with several easy chairs.

"Now what?"

"Go in," Cat Sith said. "Wait for instructions. Follow instructions."

"I'm not good at either of those things," I said.

Sith's eyes gleamed. "Excellent. I have orders to dispatch you if you disobey Mab's commands or undermine her authority in any way."

"Why don't you go ask Eldest Fetch how easy that one is, Mittens?" I said. "Scat."

Sith didn't vanish this time. He just sort of melted into shadow. His golden eyes remained behind for a few seconds, and then he was gone.

"Always stealing from the greats," I mumbled. "Lewis Carroll's estate should be collecting a licensing fee from that guy."

Unless, of course, it was maybe the other way around.

I went into the chamber and the door shut behind me. There was a table with what looked like handmade candies on it. I didn't touch them. Not because I was worried about my svelte figure, but because I was standing at the heart of wicked faerieland, and eating random candy seemed like a less than brilliant idea.

There was an old book on the table next to the candies, set carefully and precisely in place beside the dish. It was titled *Kinder- und Hausmärchen*. I leaned down and opened it. The text was in German. It was really old. The pages were made of paper of the finest quality, thin and crisp and edged in gold foil. On the title page, under the title, were the names Jacob and Wilhelm Grimm, and the year 1812.

It was autographed, and personalized, "For Mab." I couldn't read the text, so I settled for the illustrations. It was better than reading those stupid celebrity magazines in every other waiting room, and was probably more grounded in reality.

The door opened soundlessly while I looked at the book, and a vision came into the room. She wore a velvet dress the deep blue-purple of twilight. She glanced back toward the hallway behind her as the door closed, and I saw that the dress plunged low in the front. She had matching opera gloves that reached to halfway up her biceps, and there was a garland of periwinkles in her dark hair that complemented the dress gorgeously. Then she turned back to me and smiled. "Oh, my," she said. "You clean up nicely, Harry."

I rose politely to my feet, though it took me a couple of seconds to say, "Sarissa. Wow. You . . . barely look like you."

She quirked an eyebrow at me, but I saw a pleased tilt to her mouth. "My. That was almost a compliment."

"I'm out of practice," I said. I gestured toward a chair. "Would you care to sit?"

She gave me a demure smile and did, moving with an absolute and liquid grace. I offered her my hand to help her sit, which she didn't need. She gripped my fingers lightly anyway. Once she was seated, I sat back down myself. "Did you want a bit of candy?"

Her smile somehow contained gentle reproof. "I hardly think that would be wise. Do you?"

"Hell's bells, no," I said. "I just, uh . . . You make conversation when you're, uh . . . I'm not sure what to . . ." I picked up the priceless copy of the Grimms' tales and held it up. "Book."

Sarissa covered her mouth with one hand, but her eyes twinkled. "Oh, um, yes. I've seen it a few times. I've heard rumors that Her Majesty worked hard to make sure the tales were put into print."

"Sure," I said. "Makes sense."

"Why?" she asked.

"Oh, the Sidhe's influence had been waning as the Industrial Age gathered steam," I said. "By making sure the tales kept being told to mortal children, she made sure that she and her folk were never forgotten."

"And that's important?" Sarissa asked.

"If it wasn't, why else would she do it? I'm pretty sure that being forgotten is bad for beings that live with one foot in the mortal world and the other over here. Wouldn't shock me if she greased some wheels for Walt Disney, either. He did more than anyone else to bring those stories into modern times. Hell, he built a couple of fairylands in the mortal world."

"I hadn't ever thought about it that way," Sarissa said. She folded her hands in her lap and smiled at me. It was a completely calm and lovely expression—but I had the sudden instinct that she was concealing unease.

I might not have been able to tell a couple of months ago, but she'd been on the periphery of several of Mab's therapy sessions, and I'd seen her react to sudden fear and stress. There was that same sense of controlled tension in her now as there had been when a small avalanche of poisonous spiders—big ones—had come cascading out of the towel cupboard in the workout room. She'd been wearing capri pants and no shoes at the time, and she'd had to hold completely still while dozens of the things swarmed over her naked feet, until I could clear them off, gently and cautiously, so as not to threaten the little things into killing us.

That particular test had been all about regulating one's reaction to sudden fear. Sarissa had done it, refusing to let her anxiety control her. She'd waited, expressionless and almost calm, looking much then as she did right now.

It made my feet start to itch.

She was expecting spiders.

"So," I said. "To what do I owe the pleasure of your company? Do you need me to perform some last-minute yoga routines?"

"You took to yoga like a duck to vacuum," she said. "I know how much you love the routines, but I'm afraid I must disappoint you. Tonight I'm to be on your arm, by command of the Queen. I'm supposed to tell you the protocols for a gathering of the court and make sure you don't get too bored."

I leaned back in my chair and regarded her thoughtfully. "I can't remember the last time I had that problem. And gosh, walking around with someone as lovely as you all night sounds like torture."

She smiled and lowered her eyes.

"Can I ask you something?" I asked.

"Of course."

"I didn't use that like a rhetorical question," I said. "I'm serious. I'd like to ask you something, but if you would rather keep it to yourself, that's okay, too."

That put a crack in her mask. I saw her eyes flick up quickly to my face for a moment, and then back down. "Why wouldn't I want to answer your questions?"

"Because we've been working together every day for eleven weeks and I don't know your last name," I said. "I don't know what you do in the real world. I don't know your favorite color or what kind of ice cream you like best. I don't know if you have family. You're very, very good at talking about things that don't matter, and making it seem like the only conversation that could possibly have made sense."

She very carefully did not move or answer.

"Mab's got something on you, too, doesn't she? Just like she does me."

There was another moment of stillness. Then she said in a bare whisper, "Mab has something on everyone. The only question is whether they realize it or not."

"I get that you're afraid of me," I said. "I know you saw Lloyd Slate in action when he was the Winter Knight, and I know exactly what a peach of a human being he was. And I figure you think I'm going to be like him."

"I didn't say that," she said.

"It wasn't an accusation," I said, as gently as I could. "I'm not trying to trick you into saying something. I'm not hoping that you'll give me an excuse to do something to you. Okay? I'm not like Lloyd Slate."

"Neither was he," Sarissa whispered. "Not at first."

A cold little feeling wobbled through my guts.

See, that's the tragedy of the human condition. No one *wants* to be corrupted by power when they set out to get it. They have good, even noble reasons for doing whatever it is they do. They don't want to misuse it, they don't want to abuse it, and they don't want to become vicious monsters. Good people, decent people, set out to take the high road, to pick up power without letting it change them or push them away from their ideals.

But it keeps happening anyway.

History is full of it. As a rule, people aren't good at handling power. And the second you start to think you're better at controlling your power than anyone else, you've already taken the first step.

"This is the reality, Sarissa," I said quietly. "I'm the Winter Knight. I've got Mab's favor and blessing. I can pretty much do as I damned well please here, and I won't have to answer to anyone but her for it."

The young woman shivered.

"If I wanted it," I said quietly, "if I wanted y . . . to hurt you, I could do it. Right now. You couldn't stop me, and no one else would do a damned thing. I've spent a year on my back and now that I'm moving again, um . . . my various drives are clamoring for action. In fact, Mab probably sent you in here to see what I would do with you."

The pleasant mask faded from Sarissa's face, replaced with wary neutrality. "Yes. Of course she did." She switched her hands, moving the bottom one to the top, carefully, as if she worried about wrinkling her dress. "I know exactly what role she has in mind for me, Sir Knight. I am to"—her mouth twisted—"be at your convenience."

"Yeah, well," I said. "That isn't going to happen, obviously."

Her eyes widened slightly. She held completely still. "I'm sorry?"

"I'm not Lloyd Slate," I said. "I'm not one of Mab's pet monsters— and I'll die before I let her make me into one. You were kind to me and you helped me through a bad patch, Sarissa. I won't forget that. You have my word."

"I don't understand," she said.

"It isn't complicated," I said. "I won't take anything away from you. I won't force you to do anything you don't want to do. Period."

I couldn't interpret the expression on her face when I said that. There could have been anger in it, or suspicion or terror or skepticism. Whatever was going on in her head to make her face look like that, I couldn't translate it.

"You don't believe me," I said. "Do you?"

"I've lived a third of my life inside Arctis Tor," she said, and turned her face away. "I don't believe anyone."

In that moment, I didn't think I'd ever seen someone so entirely lovely look so utterly alone. A third of her life in Winter? And yet she could still be compassionate and friendly and caring. She'd probably seen things, had to face ugliness that few mortals ever did—the Unseelie were endlessly enthusiastic about their amusements, and they liked their games nasty and cruel.

But here she was, facing a fate she must have feared since she was a child—being given to a monster to be devoured. Facing it calmly. Staying in control of herself, and still managing to be warm to me, too. That told me she had a lot of strength, and strength has always been something I found attractive in a woman. So has courage. So has grace under pressure.

I could really get to like this girl.

Which, of course, was why Mab had chosen her—to tempt me, to make me convince myself to abandon the high road so that I could have her. Then, once I'd done one little thing, she'd start scattering new lures in front of me, until eventually I picked another one up. Mab was Mab. She had no intention of keeping a Knight with a conscience.

So she was planning on assassinating mine an inch at a time. Once I'd abused my power over the girl, Mab would use my guilt and self-loathing to push me to the next step, and the one after that.

Mab was one cold-blooded bitch.

I looked away from Sarissa. I was going to have to keep her safe—first and foremost from me.

"I understand," I told her. "Or at least I understand part of it. My first mentor wasn't exactly Officer Friendly, either."

She nodded, but it was an entirely noncommittal gesture, an acknowledgment that I had spoken, not a statement of agreement.

"Okay," I said. "Uncomfortable silence is uncomfortable. Why don't you tell me what I need to know for tonight?"

She collected herself and slipped back into her pleasant demeanor. "We'll enter next to last, just before the Queen. She will present you to the court, and then there will be a meal and entertainment. After the feast, you'll be expected to mingle with the court and give them a chance to meet you."

"That's the protocol? Thanksgiving dinner at the in-laws'?"

Something like a real smile brought a little light to her eyes, at the sight of which my glands did *not* go pitter-pat. At all.

"Not quite," she said. "There are two laws all must follow under pain of death."

"Only two? Man, how do Unseelie lawyers make a living?"

"First," Sarissa said, ignoring my wiseassery, "Blood may not be spilled upon the floor of the court without the Queen's express command."

"No murder without getting the nod first. Got it. Second?"

"No one may speak to the Queen without her express command."

I snorted. "Seriously? Because I'm not much for keeping my mouth shut. In fact, I'm pretty sure I physically can't. Probably because I was influenced at an impressionable age. Did you ever read any Spider-Man comics when you were—"

"Harry," Sarissa said, her voice suddenly tight. She put her hand on my arm, and her lean fingers were like heavy wires. "No one speaks to the Queen," she whispered intently. "No one. Not even the Lady Maeve dares disobey that law." She shuddered. "I've seen what happens. We all have."

I pursed my lips and studied her hand thoughtfully for a moment. Then I nodded. "Okay," I said. "I hear you."

Sarissa exhaled slowly and nodded.

Just then, a door I hadn't seen before opened in the center of what had looked exactly like a wall. Cat Sith stood on the other side of the door. He ignored me pointedly, turning his golden eyes to Sarissa. "It is time."

"Very well," Sarissa said. "We are ready."

I rose and offered Sarissa a hand up. She took it, and I tucked her arm into mine. Her fingers gave my forearm one quick squeeze, and then we turned to follow Cat Sith down another hallway.

Sarissa leaned a little closer to me and whispered, "You know what this is, don't you?"

I grunted quietly. "Yeah," I said. "It's my first day in the prison yard."

4

Sith led us down yet another passageway, this one darker than the others, until finally I couldn't see the malk at all in the dimness. Instead, a very dim phosphorescence in the shape of his paw prints began to rise from the floor, giving us just enough light to move by. I could feel Sarissa growing increasingly tense beside me, but she said nothing. Smart. If anything was going to jump up and eat us, our ears would tell us about it first.

The sound of our steps on the floor changed, and I realized that we had moved into a large open space. Just as I did, the glowing paw prints in front of us vanished.

I stopped at once, pulling Sarissa in closer against my side. Again, she remained completely silent, except for one sharp little inhalation.

Silent seconds went by.

"Sith," I said quietly. "You are a suck guide. I don't care how big your shadow is."

My voice echoed cavernously while I waited, but apparently Sith didn't have a comeback. After a few seconds, I reached up and tugged my amulet out of the tux.

I held it up and concentrated, sending a microcurrent of my will into the design, and an instant later it began to glow with a blue-white light. I held it aloft and looked around.

We were in another ice cave, this one filled with enormous, bizarre . . . structures, was the only thing I could think to call them. I might have

called them sculptures, except no one does sculptures the size of buildings these days, even in ice. I looked around the place slowly. There was
something odd about the structures, something almost . . .

Sarissa was looking, too. She seemed alert, but not frightened. "Are
those . . . giant pieces of furniture?"

. . . familiar.

The structures *were* sculpture, built on a scale of maybe one to eight,
of a couch, two easy chairs, a brick fireplace, bookshelves. . . . Mab had
re-created my old basement apartment in ice, right down to textured
carvings of all of my area rugs crafted into the ice of the floor.

I had about a second to take that in before the cavern exploded with
sound, color, and motion. A wave front of pure noise slapped against me
as a sudden horde of beings from every dark folktale ever told surged into
view at the edges of my light, their screams and cries coming from all
around me.

This was a worst-case scenario for a mortal wizard. We can do amazing things, but we need time to make them happen. Sometimes we get
that time by preparing well in advance—creating tools that help us focus
our abilities more quickly and with greater precision. Sometimes we get
the time by picking where and when to begin our battles. Sometimes we
do it by slinging the spell from a couple or a couple hundred miles away.
But I didn't have any of that going for me.

My convalescence with Mab had kept me way too busy recovering or
sleeping to have enough time to create new tools, and my amulet was all
I had. On the upside, Mab had given me a serious workout, magically
speaking. I'd been forced to use my abilities without any kind of tools or
crutch to help me, or else perish. I was better at wielding raw magic now
than I'd ever been in my life.

It just wasn't going to be enough to survive what was coming at me.

I moved without thinking, putting myself between Sarissa and as
many of them as I could, and bringing my will to bear upon my right
hand. Pallid blue-white fire suddenly engulfed my fingers as I let the
pentacle fall. I raised my hand—no time to think or aim or plan—deter-
mined to take someone down with me.

Sarissa's hand snapped out and she grabbed my wrist, jerking my arm down before I could unleash the spell, and I heard two things in the vast roar of sound:

First, Sarissa screaming, "No bloodshed!"

Second, I realized that everything else in the cavern was bellowing, "SURPRISE!"

The horde of all things dark and hideous stopped maybe twenty feet short of Sarissa and me, and the walls and floor and ceiling began to glow with light. Music began to play, a full symphonic freaking orchestra, *live*, somewhere on the other side of the giant replica of my old secondhand sofa. High up on the ceiling of the cavern, thousands of wisps of eerie light swarmed deep within the ice, swiftly forming up like a flotilla of synchronized swimmers until they formed the words: HAPPY BIRTH-DAY, DRESDEN.

I stood there with my heart beating too fast for several seconds and blinked at the entire place. "Uh. Oh."

Sarissa studied the ceiling for a moment and then looked up at me. "I didn't know."

"Neither did I, really," I said. "Is it Halloween already?"

"Just barely, I think," Sarissa said back.

It got weirder.

They started to sing.

They sang "Happy Birthday."

Remember when I said that a malk's voice made my skin crawl? It's nothing next to the cackling rasp of a swamp hag, or the freaky-weird whistling voice of a manticore. Goblins can't carry a tune if it has handles, and the huge bat things that served as Mab's air force shrieked in pitches that could barely be heard. Trolls, hideous giant thugs towering over ten feet tall, sound like laryngitic foghorns.

But layered all throughout that cacophony were voices that went to the other extreme, voices that carried the melody with such perfect, razor-edged clarity that it made me want to slash my wrists on it. People always equate beauty with good, but it just ain't so. Amongst the Winter Court were beings of haunting beauty, mesmerizing beauty, disarming beauty, flawless beauty, maddening beauty, bloodthirsty beauty. Even in the mortal world, a lot of predators are beautiful, and if you're quick and motivated enough, you can admire that beauty while they kill you and eat you. Like all the other things there, the Sidhe sang to me, and I could feel the weight of their attention on me like the pressure wave from an onrushing shark.

You don't listen to music like that. You survive it.

The voices ended abruptly, and left one crystalline alto singing, "And many more."

The crowd of creatures parted suddenly, and a girl stepped out of their ranks. She paused for a moment, for dramatic effect, and to give everyone time to admire her.

She'd changed her hair again. Now it was a kind of extra-wide Mohawk, long except for where it had been shaved completely away from the sides of her head, where the cut could show off the tips of her gently tapering ears. It was still colored in all glacial shades of blue and green and deep violet, and hung down over much of one side of her face, allowing her to borrow enough of Veronica Lake's vibe to give her wide, wide eyes a little extra hint of cheerily wicked mystery. She was tallish, for a girl, maybe five-ten, and built with that perfect balance of lean and lush proportions that some girls are lucky enough to have for maybe a year, the kind of look that gets girls that age in trouble with men who should be old enough to know better.

And she was naked. Gloriously, disconcertingly naked—and just as fresh and vibrant and unspoiled-looking as she'd been the first time I'd met her, most of ten years before.

Only, you know, she'd been less naked then.

Man, was I ever noticing that part.

"Here's the birthday boy!" Maeve said in a singsong voice, flinging both arms up. She started toward me in a slow and slightly exaggerated walk. Technically, she wasn't *entirely* naked. She had silver piercings at the tips of her breasts, beneath her lip, in her navel, and probably elsewhere. I didn't let myself look quite that close. Her flawless pale skin was also spangled with gemstones. I don't know how they'd been attached, but they clung to her and sent little flashes of color glittering around the cavern when she moved. They were concentrated most densely around her . . . well . . . She'd been, ah, vajazzled.

She came slinking over to me in the silence, her green eyes framed in a quasi-mask of gemstones and some kind of henna inking, and she absolutely smoldered with sex. Not that she'd never been suggestive before, but this was taking things to a whole new level.

"Look at you," she said, walking around me and eyeing me slowly and thoroughly. "Rumors of your death have been greatly exaggerated, it would seem."

"Hi, Maeve," I said. "You know, I almost wore that same outfit. Gosh, would our faces have been red."

The Winter Lady, Mab's successor and understudy, completed the circle and stopped in front of me, just oozing pure animal attraction. "It *is* a birthday. I wore a birthday suit." She took a deep breath, mostly for effect. "I hope you approve."

Hell, yes, I approved. Or at least everything south of my upper lip did—way more than it should have, really. She wasn't using some kind of magic on me; I had gone on alert to such a possibility the second I'd seen her. It must have been all the rest and the exercise and the good diet, most of which I'd successfully avoided back in the real world. It had resulted in a robust and healthy yet perfectly normal libido. Perfectly normal.

It wasn't me changing. Whatever Mab had done to me that had healed a broken spine, made me able to run at vampire speed, and given me the kind of reflexes that were capable of keeping up with the attack of a furious malk hadn't changed me on some fundamental level.

Everything was perfectly healthy and normal here in Denial Land.

Maeve's eyes met mine and she gave me a slow, slow smile. And, as when Mab had been near, I felt my whole body thrum in response to her, to her presence, her proximity, to her . . . everything. That smile contained something within it, something conveyed to me in a flashing instant—Maeve as she would look in ecstasy, beneath me, looking up at me with that lovely face mindless with sensation. And with that image came a hundred or a thousand others, each of them a single captured moment, the kind of moments that are the only one to survive a frenzied dream, frozen and layered atop one another, each of them a promise, a prediction, and every one of them aimed right at the most base, most primitive parts of my brain. It wasn't limited to visual imagery. Each layer of the flash had its own round of sensual memory, every one of them only partial but intense—touch, taste, scent, sound, and vision—dozens and dozens of dreams and fantasies compressed into that one instant of dark inspiration.

I've had *sex* that didn't feel as good as Maeve's smile.

You hear me, came Maeve's thoughts, along with the images. *You hear me now, because we are together now, just as you are with Mab. I felt you, you know, when you joined yourself to us. And I want to feel more. You are my Knight as well, Dresden. Let me welcome you. Come to me. Come with me. Walk by starlight and let me show you secret delights.*

It took me a couple of seconds to remember that I was still standing there in the icy hall, still wearing my clothes, still standing most of an arm's length away from Maeve. When I spoke, it was through clenched teeth. "Sorry. Already got a date for tonight, Maeve."

She dropped her head back and laughed. "Bring her," she said, her eyes both dancing and wild. Her eyes shifted to Sarissa, who took a short breath and went stiff beside me. "She's gorgeous, and I would love to . . . get to know her better."

Imagine the possibilities, my Knight. Another multisensory slide show hit my head, and every single image was something that I should have known better than to find intriguing, but that I could not bring myself to entirely ignore—only this time Sarissa was included. *I can show you pleasures you have never dreamed could be. Bring your lovely companion. I will give you her and many, many more besides.*

Again, my head lit up with lunatic pleasure-maybes, dizzying, electrifying, and I felt as if I were about to start tearing my way out of my clothes.

And, just for a second, I considered it.

I'm not really proud of that fact, but it's not like I'm beyond temptation, either. I'm just as stupid as the next guy, and for a second, I thought about seeing what was behind door number one. I knew it would be foolish—and fun, yeah, but mostly foolish. I knew that I'd be an idiot to go along, and yet . . .

One day, something is going to kill me. It might be some monster. It might be my own foolishness. It might be what gets most everyone in the end: simple, implacable time (although I wasn't betting on that one). I'd been closer to the idea of my own death lately, having been dead, or at least mostly dead, for a good while, and I wasn't any more comfortable with the idea. I didn't have any more desire to go out in an ugly, painful way than I did before.

And if you've gotta go, there are probably worse ways to do it than in a blaze of sybaritic glory.

Damn, Maeve had a great pitch.

Heh.

Everyone selling something to a sucker does.

The entire hall had gone completely silent, except for my own harsh breathing, and I suddenly became aware of the tension in the air. Every being there was waiting, and I suddenly realized that this was the second murder attempt of the evening. Maeve was trying to destroy me.

"You ever make Lloyd that offer?" I asked.

Maeve tilted her head, staring at me, her smile suddenly frozen.

"Cat got your tongue?" I asked in a louder voice. I put scorn into it. "Did you not hear the question?"

The frozen smile became something subarctic. "What did you say to me?"

"I said no, you psychopathic hosebeast," I answered, spitting out the words with every ounce of contempt I could muster up. "I saw how you treated Lloyd Slate. I saw how you treated the changelings of your court. I know what to expect from you, you arrogant, spoiled, self-involved, petty, cruel little queen-bee twit."

Maeve's expression changed, though not in any kind of focused way. She looked . . . startled.

Sarissa gave me a shocked look. Then she glanced around, as if hunting for a foxhole or bomb shelter or perhaps some kind of armored vehicle to throw herself into.

"You sent your last handmaiden to murder my friends on their wedding day, Maeve," I continued, in a voice loud enough to be heard by the entire hall. "Did you think I'd forgotten that? Or was it just too small and unimportant a fact for you to keep it from dribbling out of your alleged brain? Do you think I'm too stupid to understand that you set up this 'surprise' party in the hopes that you'd startle me into spilling blood at court, Darth Barbie? You tried to *murder* me just now, Maeve, and you think a little psychic porn is going to make me forget it? I can't decide if you're insane or just that stupid."

Maeve stared at me with her mouth dropping wide open.

"Now hear this," I said. "You're cute, doll. You're gorgeous. You inspire supernatural levels of wood. And so *what*? You're damaged goods. So turn around and move your naked little ass away from me—before I do it for you."

For a long moment, there was dead silence.

And then Maeve's face twisted up in fury. The seductive beauty of her features vanished, replaced by an animal's rage. Her eyes blazed, and the temperature in the air dropped suddenly, painfully, enough to cause icy frost crystals to start forming *on the ice*. The freaking *ice* iced over.

Maeve glared at me with naked hatred in her too-big eyes and then gave me a small bow of her head and a little smile. "It would appear we yet have a life to celebrate," she hissed. "Music."

From somewhere in the room, the symphony began playing again. The silent gang-circle ring of bedtime-story villainy broke up with fluid grace, and seconds later you would have thought you were at any kind of extremely wild, extremely posh costume party.

Maeve's eyes glittered and she spun once, displaying herself to me with a mocking little flick of her hair, and then vanished into the crowd.

I turned to Sarissa and found her staring at me with wide eyes. "You turned her down."

"Uh-huh."

"No one does that. Not here."

"Whatever," I said.

"You don't understand. The insult you've just given her is . . . is . . ." Sarissa shook her head and said, with masterful understatement, "You just earned a little payback, in her mind."

"That was going to happen sooner or later," I said. "What bugs me is her response."

"Music?" Sarissa asked.

"Yeah," I said. "And in a minute there might be dancing. Can't be good."

"It could be worse," she said. She took a deep breath and settled her arm in mine again. "You won the first round."

"I only survived it."

"Here, that *is* winning."

"So if we win the rest of the night, we'll be making a good start." I looked around us and said, "Come on."

"Where are we going?"

"Somewhere that isn't the middle of the floor," I said. "Somewhere I can put my back to a wall. And hopefully somewhere with snacks. I'm starving."

5

I'm never really comfortable at parties. Maybe I'm just not the partying type.

Even when they aren't full of lunatic elves, hulking monsters, and psychotic faerie queens, parties are kind of tough for me. I think it's because I'm never sure of what to do with myself.

I mean, there're drinks, but I don't like being drunk, and I'm pretty sure I don't get any more charming when I do get that way. More amusing, tops, and that isn't always in a good way. There's music, but I never really learned to dance to anything that involved an electric guitar. There are people to talk to and maybe girls to flirt with, but once you put all the stupid things I do aside, I'm really not all that interesting. I like reading, staying home, going on walks with my dog—it's like I'm already a retiree. Who wants to hear about that? Especially when I would have to scream it over the music to which no one dances.

So I'm there but not drinking, listening to music but not dancing, and trying to have conversations with near-strangers about anything other than my own stupid life, and they generally seem to have the same goals I do. Leads to a lot of awkward pauses. And then I start wondering why I showed up in the first place.

Hell's bells, the kind of party with monsters is actually easier for me. I mean, at least I have a pretty good idea of what to do when I'm at one of those.

The food table was set up over by the replica of the trapdoor that used to lead into my subbasement. It was open in the giant model, which meant that there was a gaping hole in the icy floor, and if you slipped at the wrong moment, you'd wind up falling down into Stygian darkness. I wondered whether the drop was to scale.

The table was loaded down with party food of every description, but apart from the sheer variety, it didn't look like anything but regular old food. I inhaled through my nose and felt absolutely certain about that— this was mortal chow, not the fabled ambrosia of faerie.

"Thank God," Sarissa said, picking up a pair of plates. "Food. I was afraid they'd have nothing but those flower trifles again."

"Wait," I said. "Are we sure this is food?"

"You can't smell it?" she asked. "I can always tell. Local cuisine is . . . not exactly subtle. Practically the first thing I learned here was how to tell the difference." She started loading up both plates, mostly with things I probably would have picked anyway. Well. She had basically been my dietitian for nearly three months. She'd know, by now, what I liked and didn't.

Weird. Would it be like that if I ever had, like . . . a wife or something?

Whoa, where the hell did *that* thought come from? All the recent, if entirely bent, domesticity? My heart did a weird little rabbitlike maneuver, beating way too fast for a few seconds. Hell's bells, had I just had a panic attack? At the very *notion* of calling some woman my wife? Though . . . now that I thought about it, I wasn't sure I had ever used that word in connection with myself and somebody else at the same time. Not explicitly, anyway.

I shook my head and filed the thought away to be examined later, when I didn't have a great big target drawn on my back.

I let Sarissa pick us some food while I kept an eye out for anyone or anything suspicious. After about twenty seconds of that, I decided that it was an impossibility, and dialed it back to watching for anyone who rushed us with a knife, screaming. I kept my defensive spells right on the tip of my mind, so to speak, and ready to erupt into reality at an instant's notice.

I spotted a good, quiet corner for us to stand in, over by the giant mantel above the giant fireplace. I took the plates from Sarissa, and we started that way.

A form that I recognized emerged from the crowd in our path, and I found myself smiling. The creature that came limping over to me wasn't much more than five feet tall, and leaned on a heavy, gnarled walking staff. He wore a hooded robe of undyed linen, belted with a length of soft-looking rope. Three folded strips of purple cloth were tucked into the belt—the formal stoles of senior members of the White Council of Wizards, taken after they fell to him in separate duels.

Oh, and he was a goat. Well, a very human-looking goat, anyway. He had the same long face as a goat, and curling ram's horns on his head. His eyes were golden, his beard long and white, and he looked pleased.

"Eldest Gruff," I said, smiling.

"Sir Knight," he replied, his basso a pleasant rumble. We exchanged small bows, which also seemed to please him. "Please do thou accept my best wishes on this day of your birth."

"Gladly," I said. "How did they rope you into showing up to this freak show?"

He sighed. "Obligation."

"Word." I nodded to Sarissa. "May I introduce Sarissa. She's been helping me recover from an injury. Sarissa, this is—"

"Lord Gruff," she said, giving him a courtesy that somehow seemed natural. "How lovely to meet you again, sir."

"It is pleasant to see thee, child," Eldest Gruff said. "Thou dost seem to thrive despite the climate."

"That may be a generous assessment," Sarissa replied.

"I prefer to think of it as a hopeful one," the Gruff said. "I see thou hast attached thyself to the new Knight."

"No," I said quickly. "No, she hasn't. There's been no . . . attaching. She's been doctoring me."

Sarissa arched an eyebrow at me, and then said to the Gruff, "It was Mab's price."

"Ah," the Gruff said. "A heavy burden obligation canst be, for Winter and Summer alike." He glanced aside at me. "Does he know of thine—"

"It hasn't come up," Sarissa said.

"Ah," Eldest Gruff said, raising his hands. He had weird nails. They were hoofy. "I will then follow the course of silence."

Sarissa inclined her head. "Thank you."

"Of course."

Two more figures approached us, both of them over seven feet tall. I'm not used to being the shortest person in any given conversation. Or even the shorter person. I can change lightbulbs without stretching. I can put the star on the Christmas tree without standing on tiptoe. I'm like the Bumble, but with way better teeth, and I didn't like feeling loomed over.

(Which probably should tell me about the kind of effect I might be having on other people, sort of generally speaking, and especially when I gave attitude to power figures who were shorter than me, but that kind of crystallized moment of enlightenment probably wouldn't be helpful in winning the evening.)

The first was depressingly familiar. He was dressed in hunter's leathers, all grey and green and brown. There was a sword with a hilt made from some sort of antler at his side. It was the first time I'd seen him wearing something other than a helmet. He had shaggy, grizzled light brown hair that fell to his shoulders. His features were asymmetrical but, though not handsome, contained a certain roguish charm, and his eyes were an unsettling shade of gold-green. I didn't know his name, but he was the Erlking, one of the beings of Faerie powerful enough to lead the Wild Hunt, and he was the reigning ruler of the goblins.

(Not like the big ugly dimwit in the Hobbit. Real goblins are like mutant Terminator serial killer psycho ninjas. Think Hannibal Lecter meets Jackie Chan.)

Oh, and I'd insulted him once by trapping him in a magic circle. Faeries large and small hate that action.

"Gruff," said the Erlking, tilting his head.

Eldest Gruff made a small bow in reply. "Lord Herne."

"Know you these children?"

"Aye," said Eldest Gruff. He began making polite introductions.

I studied the man standing beside the Erlking while he did. He was a sharp contrast. The Erlking was huge, but there was something about him that suggested agility and grace. It was like looking at a tiger. Sure, it might be standing there all calm and relaxed at the moment, but you knew that at any second it could surge with speed and terrible purpose and that it wouldn't give you any warning before it came at you.

This man wasn't a tiger. He was a bear. His shoulders were so broadly proportioned that he made Herne look positively slender by comparison. His forearms were nearly the size of his biceps, and he had the kind of thick neck that you see only in power lifters and professional thugs. There were scars all over his hands, and more on his face, all of them faded away to ancient white lines, like those you see on some lifelong bikers. He wore a coat of mail of some kind—a creature of Faerie couldn't abide the touch of iron, so it had to be made from something else.

Over the mail he wore a long, open coat of scarlet, trimmed in white fur. It was held in with a wide black leather belt. He had such a barrel of a chest that even a modest bit of stomach was a considerable mass on his huge frame. His gloves were made of black leather trimmed with more white fur, and they were tucked through the belt, right next to the very plain and functional hilt of an unadorned broadsword. His hair was short, white, and shining clean, and his white beard fell over his chest like the white breaker of a wave. His eyes were clean, winter sky blue.

I lost track of what Eldest Gruff was saying, because my mouth was falling open.

The second man noticed my expression and let out a low, rumbling chuckle. It wasn't one of those ironic snickers. It was a rolling, full-throated sound of amusement, and it made his stomach shake like . . . dare I say it?

Like a bowl full of jelly.

"And this," Eldest Gruff said, "is Mab's new Knight."

"Uh," I said. "Sorry. I . . . uh. Hi." I stuck my hand out. "Harry Dresden."

His hand engulfed mine as he continued to chortle. His fingers could have crushed my bones. "I know who you are, Dresden," he rumbled. "Call me Kringle."

"Wow, seriously? 'Cause . . . wow."

"Oh, my God, that's adorable," Sarissa said, smiling. "You are such a fanboy, Dresden."

"Yeah, I've just . . . I hadn't really expected this kind of thing."

Kringle let out another rumbling laugh. It absolutely filled the air around him. "Surely you knew that I made my home among the beings of Faerie. Did you think I would be a vassal of Summer, lad?"

"Honestly?" I asked. "I haven't ever really stopped to think it through."

"Few do," he said. "How does your new line of work suit you?"

"Doesn't," I said.

"Then why did you agree to it?"

"Seemed like the right thing to do at the time."

Kringle smiled at me. "Ah. I didn't much care for your predecessor."

"Ditto," I said. "So do you come to all of these?"

"It's customary," Kringle replied. "I get to visit folk I rarely see else-where." He nodded toward the Erlking and Eldest Gruff. "We take a few moments to catch up."

"And hunt," the Erlking said, showing sharp-looking teeth when he smiled.

"And hunt," Kringle said. He eyed Eldest Gruff. "Would you care to accompany us this year?"

Gruff somehow managed to smile. "You always ask."

"You always say no."

Eldest Gruff shrugged and said nothing.

"Wait," I said to Kringle. "You're going hunting?" I pointed at the Erlking. "With *him*? *You?*"

Kringle let out another guffaw and, I swear to God, rested his hands on his belly while he did it. "Why wouldn't I?"

"Dude," I said. "Dude. You're . . . freaking Santa Claus."

"Not until after Halloween," he said. "Enough is enough. I'm draw-ing a line."

"Hah," I said, "but I'm kinda not joking here."

He grunted, and the smile faded from his features. "Lad, let me tell you something here and now. None of us is what we once were. Everyone has a history. Everyone comes from somewhere. Each moves toward a destination. And in a lifetime as long as mine, the road can run far and take strange windings—something I judge you know something about."

I frowned. "Meaning?"

He gestured at himself. "This became the tale with which you are familiar only in fairly recent times. There are wizards enough alive today who knew of no such person when they were children awaiting the winter holiday."

I nodded thoughtfully. "You became something different."

He gave me a wink of his eye.

"So what were you before?"

Kringle smiled, apparently content to say nothing.

I turned to Sarissa, asking, "You seem to know these guys, mostly. What . . . ?"

She wasn't there.

I looked around the immediate area, but didn't see her. I moved my eyes back to Kringle and the Erlking. The two of them looked at me calmly, without expression. I darted a glance to Eldest Gruff, whose long, floppy right ear twitched once.

I glanced to my left, following the motion, and spotted Sarissa being led onto the dance floor underneath the replica of my original *Star Wars* poster. The poster was the size of a skyscraper mural now, the dance floor beneath it the size of a parking lot. For the most part, the Sidhe were dancing, all fantastic grace and whirling color, with the occasional glitter of jewellike feline eyes sparkling as they turned and swayed.

A young male Sidhe was leading her by the wrist, and from the set of her shoulders she was in pain. You couldn't have guessed it from her expression. The young Sidhe wore a black leather jacket and a Cincinnati ball cap, but I didn't get a look at his face.

"A fresh challenge, it would seem," the Erlking murmured.

"Yeah," I said. "Gentlemen, if you would excuse me."

"You know Mab's law at court, aye?" Kringle asked. "You know the price of breaking it?"

"Yep."

"What do you mean to do, lad?"

"Seems that what we have here is a failure to communicate," I said. "Think I'll go open up a dialogue."

6

Moving onto a dance floor full of Sidhe is like dropping acid.

Partly it's because they're just so damned pretty. The Sidhe maidens there were all in Maeve's league in terms of sheer physical attractiveness, and some of them were just about as barely dressed as she was, only in what must have been the latest trends in the Chicago club scene for the fashionably provocative. And, yeah, the boys were pretty, too, and tarting it up just as much as the girls, but they weren't nearly as much of a distraction to me.

Partly it's because of their grace. The Sidhe aren't human, even though they look like close relatives. When you see an Olympic gymnast or ice skater or a professional dancer performing a routine, you can't help but be impressed with the sheer, casual grace with which they move, as if their bodies are lighter than air. The clumsiest of the Sidhe operate at about that same level, and the exceptional leave the mortals eating dust behind them. It's hard to describe because it's hard for the brain to process—there's no frame of reference for what I saw, the motion, the balance, the power, the effortless subtlety. It was like suddenly discovering an entirely new sense with an enormous amount of input: I kept seeing things that made my brain scream at me to stop and watch so that it could catalog and process them properly.

And partly it's because of their magic. The Sidhe use magic the way the rest of us breathe, instinctively and without thinking about it. I'd fought them before, and their power was largely invoked through simple gestures, as if the spells had been hardwired into their motor reflexes. For them, movement was magic, and at no time so much as when they danced.

Their power didn't come after me, specifically—it was more like I had plunged into it, as if it were a pool of water occupying the same space as the dance floor. It subsumed my mind almost at once, and it was all I could do to grit my teeth and hang on. Ribbons of colored light flared in the air around the dancing Sidhe. Their feet struck the floor and their hands struck upon bodies, their own or otherwise, adding rippling layers of syncopated rhythm to the music. Gasps and cries joined with the beat and the melody, primal and fierce, echoing and challenging one another from all quarters, as if they'd practiced it. They hadn't. It was just what they were.

Sound and rhythm struck from either side, thrumming against my ears, disorienting me. Light danced and fluttered through the spectrum in subtle, seductive patterns. Bodies twisted and strained in inhuman artistry, their very grace an assault upon my reason. Part of me wanted to just stand there and drink it in, gawking like some ugly, clumsy behemoth among the Sidhe. Plenty of mortals had been lulled into tearful rapture by such dances—and generally speaking, it hadn't ended real well for them.

I put up every mental defense I could, reaching for that core of cold, clear power that had been within me since the night I'd murdered my predecessor with Medea's bronze dagger. I hadn't even realized what was happening to me at the time, since other things had been on my mind, but I now realized that the power had restored my shattered body, and given me strength and speed and endurance at the very limits of human ability—and maybe past them. I felt it only when I sought it out, but apparently my instinctive need to survive had been enough to tap into it back when I'd set out to rescue my daughter from the late Red Court of vampires.

Now it poured into my mind like an ice-cold breeze, and withered away the bedazzlement the Sidhes' dance had wrought on my thoughts. I started forward through the throng, and for a few feet I tried to skip and slip and duck my way through the moving crowd without hitting anyone. Then I realized that even with whatever I had gained from becoming the Winter Knight, I was still hopelessly dull-witted and slow-footed when compared to the Sidhe.

So I just started walking and left it up to them to get out of the way. It kinda fit my mood better, anyway. They did it, too. None of them were obvious about it, and some of them came within a fraction of an inch of striking me with whirling limbs, but none of them did.

The Sidhe are tall, generally speaking, but I'm NBA tall, and I could see over the crowd. I spotted the red ball cap and a flash of Sarissa's wide eyes and went after them. I caught up to them near the back wall of the cavernous chamber. The Sidhe who had grabbed Sarissa stood behind her, one of his arms wound around her neck, the other around her waist, holding her back against his chest. Her eyes were wide now. I could see deep red flushing on the skin of her wrist, where bruises were already starting to form in the shape of the Sidhe's fingers.

I found myself clenching my hands into fists and growling deep in my throat.

Without any evident forethought to it, the dance floor for ten feet all around any of the three of us became clear of moving bodies. The Sidhe had made room for the confrontation. Jewellike eyes glittered and watched intermittently while the dance continued.

"Sir Knight," said the Sidhe holding Sarissa. He had straight black hair beneath the cap, and cheekbones so high that they needed to wear oxygen tanks. He was smiling, and there was something particularly vulpine in it. His canines were just a little too large, a little too sharp. "What a pleasure it is to speak with you."

"You aren't going to think so in a minute," I said. "Let her go."

He leaned in closer to her and inhaled through his nose. "Odd," he said. "I don't smell you on her. You haven't claimed her as your own."

"She's not yours, either," I said. "Let her go. Don't make me say it again."

"She's just a mortal," he said, smiling. "A mortal of no station here in Arctis Tor, at court. This place is not meant for mortals. Her body, her mind, and her life are all forfeit, should we decide to take them."

"We just decided to let. Her. Go." I began walking toward him.

Something feverish came into his eyes and I could suddenly see every bone and tendon in his hand, tight against his skin. His nails seemed a little too long, a little too heavy, and a little too sharp to be normal. Sarissa tried to speak, but only made a choking sound and went silent.

"You keep coming," the Sidhe said, "and I'll keep squeezing. This game is terribly interesting. I wonder how hard I'll have to squeeze to crush her windpipe."

I stopped, because I knew the answer to his question: not very hard. It's only a little more pressure than you need to crush an empty beer can. It's sort of scary how easy it is to kill someone once you know how to get it done.

"What about Mab's law?" I said.

"I'll not shed a drop of her blood," he replied smoothly. "When I cut off her air or break her neck, she'll simply cease—which is a waste, but the law is the law."

And I got a sudden sinking feeling that the Sidhe in front of me, in his black leather jacket and his red cap, knew how to get it done. "You're not a Cincinnati fan, are you?"

"Ah!" the Sidhe said, smiling. "You see, Sarissa, he's worked it out. It took a while, but he got there."

"You're a redcap," I said.

"Not *a* redcap," he said, snapping annoyance in his voice. "*The* Redcap, little Knight."

The Redcap was one of those figures I had hoped was a story. According to what I knew of legend, he got his name by greeting travelers in a friendly fashion, and then murdering them horribly. Once that was done, he would dye his cap freshly scarlet by dipping it in their cooling blood. Odds seemed reasonable that he was a badass. Legend was about as reliable as every other rumor mill on the planet, but looking at the guy, I got the impression that he would smile and have an erection the whole time he murdered Sarissa. Or me.

He certainly *expected* me to react with fear and caution. Which just goes to show you that no matter how old something is, centuries don't necessarily make it all that bright.

"The big bad Redcap," I drawled. "And when you were picking a red cap for tonight to emblemize your power and skill, you went with Cincinnati over Philly? Or Boston? Seriously?"

The Redcap apparently didn't know what to make of that. He just stared at me, trying to decide whether he'd been insulted or not.

"Man, you Sidhe are a crowd of poseurs. Did you know that? You try to do and say the things you think will push our buttons—but you just don't get it, do you? Have you even *been* to a ball game? I caught one with Gwynn ap Nudd a few years back. Decent guy. Maybe you've heard of him."

"Do you think your allies frighten me, wizard?" the Redcap demanded.

"I think you're an opportunist," I said.

"A what?"

"You heard me. You jump people traveling alone, people who don't have a chance in hell of defending themselves against you. Especially not when you make nice and put them off their guard first." I gave him a toothy smile. "I'm not off my guard, Red. And I'm not someone who doesn't have a chance against you."

"Touch me and I will kill her," he snarled, giving Sarissa a little jerk by way of demonstration.

I looked at Sarissa and hoped that she could read deeper than the surface. "That's bad, but there's not much I can do about it if you decide to kill her now," I said. "Of course, after you do that . . . I don't really like your chances, Red. If she dies, you'll join her."

"You wouldn't break Mab's law," he sneered.

"You're right," I said. "So I figure I'll just open a Way back to the mortal world, drag you through it, and after that . . . well, I've always been partial to fire."

Evidently that line of possibility had not occurred to the Redcap. "What?"

"I know it's not thematically in tune with my new job and all, but I find it effective. Build a man a fire and he's warm for a day," I said. "But *set* a man on fire and he's warm for the rest of his life. Tao of Pratchett. I live by it. You wanted to face me down in front of everyone, get props for tweaking my nose on my first night here? Well, congratulations, Red. You're the man."

The Redcap's eyes narrowed, gleaming bright, and his foxlike smile widened. "You think I'm afraid of you."

"The last time somebody swiped my date to a party, it got a little messy," I said in a very mild voice. "Ask the Red Court about it. Oh, wait."

The Redcap actually laughed at that, and it was hurtful. Literally. My ears rang painfully at the sharpness of the sound. "It is nothing to me how many cockroaches or vampires you have ended, mortal. I am Sidhe."

"Whatever," I said. "Killed some of them, too."

"Yes," the Redcap said, and there was an ugly, hungry heat in his tone. "The Lady of Summer. I was in that battle, mortal. I saw her blood flow."

I nodded and said, "And what makes you think I won't do it again?"

The Redcap jerked his chin a little to one side and said, "They do."

I froze.

Dammit, Harry, I chided myself. *You're dealing with faeries. There is always a scam with faeries. There is always a sucker punch on the way.* I'd gotten too forward-focused. The Redcap hadn't been a challenger.

He was the bait.

As if on cue, the wild dancing turned to stillness. The music died. All motion in the chamber, as far as I could tell, ceased entirely, and suddenly I stood in a small glade within a forest of lean, wickedly beautiful figures and weirdly sparkling eyes.

Two beings emerged from that forest, shambling out from the crowd of Sidhe, one on either side of me, maybe fifteen feet away.

The first, on my right, was a huge figure, shuffling forward with its form doubled over beneath a tattered grey cloak that could have covered a small truck. Its legs took strides that were two or three times as long as mine, and when it came to a halt, its long arms spread out to either side of it and rested on the floor. Beneath its hood, I could make out a flat, broad head, as stark as a skull and colored red and glistening. Its arms ended in hands with only three fingers, but they were proportionally too thick and a couple of feet long. They, too, were red and glistening, as if something had been built on a bone framework with flesh and muscle added on over it, but then whoever had made it had forgotten to put the skin on. It dripped little patters of ichor onto the floor and stared at me with very wide, very white eyes that contained only tiny pinpoints of black.

I recognized the thing. It was a rawhead, a creature that assembled itself out of the discarded bones and flesh of slaughtered hogs and cattle. Then they started eating whatever they could catch, usually starting with pets, then working their way up to schoolchildren, and finally hunting down adults. If you caught them early, you should shut them down hard—but no one had caught this one.

As I watched, it rose, slowly, up to its full height of well over ten feet. Its jaws had come from more than a couple of different creatures, and they spread open in a slow, wide gape, into a mouth as wide as a water-slide tunnel. More liquid pattered down out of the rawhead's jaws onto the floor, and its breath rasped in and out in a slow, enormous wheeze.

On the left, the second figure drew back its hood. It was maybe only eight feet tall, and mostly human-looking, except for the thick coat of yellow-white fur that covered it. It was layered in so much muscle that it could be seen even through its pelt, and its eyes were burning, bloodshot orbs shining out from beneath a cavernous brow ridge. It was the Winter Court's version of an ogre, it was a great deal stronger than it looked, and if it wanted to, it could pick me up and drive my head *into* one of the icy walls, then hammer my spine in like a piton.

"I've been waiting to see that expression on his face all night," the Redcap said to Sarissa. "Isn't it priceless? What's going to happen next? I'm *so* interested."

Taking on a little friendly training and a grumpy malk was one thing, but going up against three of the nastier creatures in Faerie all at once was probably a losing proposition. Maybe I could survive it, if I was fast and good and a little bit lucky.

But Sarissa wouldn't.

I had only one real chance: instant and overwhelming aggression. If I could knock one of these bozos out of the fight before it even started, that changed the odds from impossible to merely daunting. It meant that there might be a chance of saving the girl.

Of course, it also meant that I would break Mab's law. I'd bragged about opening a Way, and if push came to shove, I probably could—but not before the rawhead and the ogre closed in on me.

Just then there was a sound: a shriek, a blast of cruel trumpets that sounded as if whoever blew them was being beaten with a salted lash. It took me a second to realize that no instruments were playing. Instead, high up on the constructed replica of my favorite chair, at my left shoulder, crystals were thrusting themselves up out of the ice, and screaming as the ice changed form. They rose into a half dome of spikes and frozen blades, and shuddered as the center of the new outgrowth shifted again. Wisps of arctic blue and green and purple buzzed and whirled within those sharp spikes, sending out a wild coruscation of colored light. The aurora was mesmerizing and blinding at the same time, and little disco balls hoped that they could grow up to be half as brilliant one day.

Mab stepped out of the solid ice as if passing through a gauzy curtain. She was in formal wear, a robe of opalescent white, belted with joined crystals of ice. A tall crown of more ice rose from her brow, and her white hair spilled down around her like snow atop a mountain. She was distant and cold, as pure and lovely and merciless as moonlit snow.

She stood for a moment, staring out at the cavern. Then she sat, the motion slow and regal, and the ice within the spiked dome reshaped itself into a seat beneath her. She settled onto it, and the ice screamed again, shrieking out a second tortured fanfare.

Every head in the cavern turned to her. The Sidhe all around me knelt at once, including the Redcap and his buddies. All over the chamber, other beings of the Winter Court did the same, and suddenly only a very few people were standing upright. I was one of them. So were the Erlking, Kringle, and Eldest Gruff, though each of them stood with his head bowed in acknowledgment of Winter's ruler. I took my cue from them, but kept my eyes open.

I spotted Maeve standing only forty or fifty feet away, on an icy deck that had been formed to look like a paperback that had fallen from one of my bookshelves. Maeve was in a perfect position to see the conflict between the Redcap crew and me, and she hadn't bowed either. She was sipping something ice blue from a champagne flute, and ignoring her mother's presence entirely—but I could feel her malice, burning toward me even though she wasn't looking directly at me.

Mab studied me and my playmates for a solid minute, saying nothing, and in that silence you could hear the fluid dripping from the rawhead's various bits onto the icy floor.

Maeve turned to her mother and sipped at her blue champagne. She said nothing, and her features were entirely smooth and relaxed, but you could just *smell* the way she was smirking on the inside.

And only then did I really get it. Maeve's first attempt to get me to start a fight at court had been a distraction, then. She'd wanted me to focus on her, to unnerve me with her high-voltage psychic sex moves. That way I wouldn't be thinking clearly enough to avoid it when the Redcap sprang *his* surprise.

Mab stared down at the Winter Lady for another silent minute. Then she smiled and bowed her head very slightly toward her daughter, the gesture one of acknowledgment.

"Well played," Mab murmured. She didn't raise her voice. She didn't have to. The ice rang with it.

Her eyes shifted to me, and though she was too far away for me to make out any details, I somehow knew exactly what the expression on her face meant: I had allowed myself to be drawn into this mess. I would have to be the one to get me out of it.

I was on my own.

Mab turned her gaze back to the rest of the room. "On this day of celebration of Our newest Knight's birth, We give you greetings one and all, you lords and ladies of Winter. Welcome again to Our home. We can see that the celebrations are already well under way." She settled back on her throne and placed one finger against her lips, as though she were fascinated with the scene before her. "We pray you, do not let Our entrance further disrupt them." She lifted a languid hand. "It is Our desire that you continue the festivities."

Oh, fun.

I turned back to face the Redcap, keeping his wingmen in my peripheral vision, and tried to think of something, anything, that would get both me and Sarissa out of this mess.

The rawhead gathered itself into a crouch again, clearly ready to pounce. Its mismatched set of claws and talons gouged at the floor in anticipation. The ogre flexed its hands open and closed once. It sounded like a popcorn popper. The Redcap already had his feet underneath him again, dragging Sarissa effortlessly up with him.

And I was wearing a tux.

Hell's bells.

Clearly, if I wanted us to survive the evening I had to step up my game.

Mab's voice came out as a throaty purr. "Music. Let Us see a dance."

7

The odds here were long. Way long. All three deadly faeries stood ready to move, and no matter which of them I took on first, Sarissa's outlook wasn't good. The music began, low and quiet, with a slowly, slowly rising presence.

I needed some kind of edge, a game changer.

In fact . . .

A game changer was *exactly* what I needed.

Faeries are always underhanded and tricksy, true, and I'd overlooked that a few moments before. But there's something else about faeries that runs absolutely bone deep: They love to play games.

"Why don't we make this interesting?" I said out loud. "I trust you wouldn't object to making a bit of a game of our dispute?"

Oh, the room got *intense* then, as maybe a thousand throats all inhaled at the same time. I could practically feel the air grow closer as all of those beings leaned very slightly toward me, their suddenly sharpened interest filling the cavern. The tempo of the music changed with it as well, now all suspended strings and muted percussion.

I felt a surge of emotion run through me, one that I knew was not my own—it was too pure, too primal, and it made my body do that thrumming thing again: Mab's approval was fierce.

"But, wizard," said the Redcap. "We're already playing a game. One cannot change the rules simply because one is losing."

"But one can change the stakes," I replied. "What if you could get more out of it?"

The Redcap narrowed his eyes. "What more could you have to lose than your life?"

I gave him what I hoped was a patronizing smile, and then said, "Wait. Why am I talking to the tool instead of the person holding it?" I turned my back on the Redcap, gulped, and faced Maeve. "I'm offering you a prize, Winter Lady. Are you willing to hear me out?"

Maeve's eyes sparkled more brightly than the jewels on her . . . midriff. She came to the edge of the platform and stood watching me.

"If he wins," I said, jerking my head back at the Redcap, "I'll go with you. Willingly."

Maeve tilted her head. "And if you win?"

"Sarissa goes free. You leave peacefully."

Maeve thrust out her lower lip. "Peacefully. That's hardly ever any fun." She lifted a hand and idly toyed with her hair. "As I see it, I already have a prize, mortal. I get to see Mother watch the steam rise from at least one fresh corpse, here in her own court."

"You're absolutely right, Maeve," I said. "And you've got me in a pickle, and it was cleverly done." I winked at her. "But what fun is the game you've already won? Why settle for so ephemeral a prize, however worthy, when you could take Mab's Knight from her in front of all of Winter?"

That one sank home. I could *feel* the sudden surge of ambitious lust that went racing through the Winter Lady, and the seething hatred that went along with a swift glance toward distant Mab on her throne.

Maeve's mouth curled up in an expression that bore as much resemblance to a smile as a shark does to a dolphin. She snapped her fingers, the sound almost as loud as a small-caliber gunshot, and two Sidhe hurried to her side escorting a dazed-looking athletic young man. Maeve didn't wait for him. She simply sat. The Sidhe shoved the young man to his hands and knees, and Maeve's slight weight settled across his broad back.

"I'll give you this much, Mother," she said, without looking toward Mab. "You do pick the most interesting mortals to serve you."

Mab's smirk said more than any words could have. Otherwise, she neither moved nor spoke.

"My lady . . ." began the Redcap, behind me.

"Hush," Maeve said absently. "I want to see what happens. What did you have in mind, wizard?"

In answer, I reached up and with a couple of quick tugs undid my tux's tie. It wasn't one of those preassembled ties. It was made out of a single band of pure silk, sized perfectly to wrap around my throat, with a couple of wider bits left over for handholds. I held it up, making a bit of drama out of it as I turned in a circle, and said, "Out of respect for our host and her law, there shall be no bloodshed."

Then I tossed the tie to the icy floor halfway between myself and the Redcap.

I looked up at Maeve and gave my chin an arrogant little lift. "'Sup, Princess. You game?"

Maeve lifted one hand and idly began tracing a fingertip over her lips, her eyes bright. She looked at Red and nodded.

"Okay, chucklehead," I said, turning to face him. "How about you let the yeti there hold the girl while you and I dance?" I gave him a broad grin. "Unless you're afraid of little old cockroach-swatting me."

Red's upper lip twitched. If he hadn't been one of the Sidhe, and at a party, and in front of all of his dearest frenemies, he would have snarled at me.

He beckoned the ogre with one hand, and the thing lumbered over to him. He thrust Sarissa into its huge, hairy, meaty arms. The ogre didn't get the girl around the neck. It simply wrapped its hand over her skull, like some hairy, spidery helmet, and held on. The smoky glass chopsticks in Sarissa's hair clattered to the ice, and her eyes got even wider.

"If the wizard uses his magic," the Redcap said, "break her neck." He eyed the ogre and said, "Without ripping it off."

"Yuh," the ogre said. Its beady eyes glared at me.

The Redcap nodded and turned to face me, his eyes narrowed.

Yowch. Nice move on Red's part. Though I'm not sure he needed to bother. I'd never been able to tag one of the Sidhe with a really solid hit with my magic. Their defenses against that kind of thing were just too damned good. But I'd been counting on using it indirectly to help out in the fight, and the Redcap had just taken that option away from me.

Sarissa gave the Redcap a glare that might have peeled paint from a wall, and then said, her voice rasping, "Harry, you don't have to do this for me. You can walk away."

"You kidding?" I said under my breath. "You think I'm going to go to all the trouble of finding a new PT guy? Hang tough."

She bit her lip and nodded.

I dismissed the girl from my thoughts, as much as I could, and tried to focus. I was still better off than I'd been a few moments ago. Now, instead of a three-versus-one fight that would probably kill me and certainly kill Sarissa, I had a pure one-on-one. If I lost, Sarissa wouldn't make it, and I would either be Maeve's chew toy or dead. (I was hoping for dead.) But if I won, Sarissa and I both got to walk away. It wouldn't keep something like this from happening again, but we'd live through the night, which was by definition victory.

Of course, now I had to win without using magic in a strangling-cord duel against a faerie who was faster than me, and who had centuries of experience in killing mortals. Oh, and I had to win it without drawing blood, or I'd be guilty of breaking Mab's law—and I knew how she would react to that. Mab wasn't evil, exactly, but she was Mab. She'd have me torn apart. The only mercy she would show would be by doing it all at once instead of spread over weeks.

Long story short, nobody there was going to help me. At times it sucks to be the lone hero guy.

I had one advantage: I was used to competing out of my weight class. I didn't have a whole ton of training in unarmed combat, but I did have considerable experience with being in dicey situations against homicide-oriented people and things that were bigger than me, stronger than me, faster than me, and motivated to end my life: I knew how to fight an uphill battle. The Redcap knew how to kill, but by maneuvering me out of using my magic, he'd tipped some of his hand: He was being cautious about me.

Sure, he was a predator, but in nature predators generally go after the weak, the sick, the aged, and the isolated. Solitary predators almost exclusively hunt by attacking from surprise, where they have every advantage in their favor. Hell, even great white sharks do that, and they're just about the biggest, oldest predators on the planet. I've seen a lot of things that hunted people in my time, and I regard them as a professional hazard, part of the job. I know how they operate. Predators don't like to pick fair fights. It runs counter to their nature and robs them of many of their advantages.

The Redcap had tried to limit what I could do in a bid to scrape together any advantage he could, as any predator does. That told me that he probably wasn't used to this kind of open confrontation.

He was nervous.

I was nervous, too—but I was on familiar psychological ground and he wasn't. Maybe I could use that.

I undid the top button of the shirt and shrugged out of the jacket as if nothing at all were about to happen, taking my time. I tossed it at one of the watching Sidhe. He caught it and folded it neatly over one arm, never looking away, while I calmly undid the cuffs of my shirt and rolled up the sleeves. I stowed the cuff links in a pocket.

I stretched and yawned, which might have been taking the pantomime over the top, but what the hell? In for a penny. I smiled at Maeve, inclined my head very slightly to Mab, and turned to face the Redcap.

"Ready," I said.

"Ready," the Redcap echoed.

The music abruptly stopped, and in the silence Mab's voice came from everywhere. "Begin."

I rushed forward faster than I ever could have done before I'd become Mab's Knight. It was damned close. The Redcap was quicker off the mark, but I had longer arms. He snatched the nearest end of the silk an instant before I grabbed my end. As my fingers closed, he snapped it back out of my grip, and then dropped his weight straight down, his back leg coming forward into a crescent-shaped sweep about six inches off the icy floor.

I turned my forward stumble into a forward roll. I went over the kick, tucked in tight, and came up to my feet smoothly—but the motion had carried me past him, and I knew that with his speed and grace, he'd already be leaping toward my back.

I spun to him, one hand at the level of my throat to intercept him if he was already close enough to get the tie around it, and lunged back toward him with my right arm raised to the horizontal, hoping to catch him across the neck in a clothesline.

I'd misjudged. He was moving so fast that all I got was motion blur, and he hadn't swept the silk tie at my neck—he'd aimed for my upraised left hand. The silk snaked around my wrist, and I caught it in my hand just in time for him to slip to one side, dragging my arm in close to his body. He used my forward momentum and my trapped arm to rob me of my balance and spin me in a circle, hauling at my arm with all his strength.

His strength was considerable, and his technique was sound. He suddenly reversed, using my own motion against me, and dislocated my arm from its shoulder socket with a loud pop and a flash of red-hot pain.

"Harry!" Sarissa screamed, grabbing uselessly at the ogre's wrist. It was as thick as her own leg, and the ogre didn't even seem to notice her struggling.

The Redcap kept hold of my arm, my wrist pulled up against his sternum and still trapped in the tie. He smiled broadly and walked backward in a small circle, the pain and the leverage forcing me to scramble along the floor in front of him. A gale of lovely, cold laughter went up from the Sidhe like a chorus of frozen chimes.

The Redcap took a miniature, mocking bow to the crowd and spoke to me. "I was worried for a moment, mortal. You're faster than you look."

He kicked me in the dislocated shoulder. He wasn't trying to kick my arm off. He was just doing it for the hell of it. It hurt a lot.

"You should see the look on your face, mortal," the Redcap said. "This is *fun*."

"You know what, Red?" I gasped. "We're all having fun."

I took my weight onto my knees and back, and slammed the heel of my right hand into the side of the jackass's knee.

I don't know how much stronger Mab's gift had made me, because I'd never been much of a weight lifter until I'd started therapy. I didn't know too much about how much weight lifters could, for example, bench-press. So I didn't have a very good idea how I stacked up against plain old me. Or plain old anybody. Plus the weights for the bench press were marked in metric units, and I kind of fell asleep the day we learned to convert them to pounds.

But I'm pretty sure four hundred kilos isn't bad.

The Redcap's knee popped like a balloon from the force of the strike, and bent *in* toward his other knee. He howled in startled agony and tried to throw himself away, but just as I hadn't been able to move for a few critical seconds after he'd injured me, his body wasn't responding properly either, and he fell next to me.

The left side of my body felt like it was on fire, but me and pain are old buddies. His grip on the tie had loosened, and I couldn't move my left arm enough to get it loose. So before he could recover, I punched him in the neck with my good hand. He gagged and thrashed, and I was able to unwrap the silk from my useless arm. I tried to pull the tie away from him, but he'd already shaken off the hits I'd given him and held on. I jerked on it as hard as I could, but I had only the one arm and was fresh out of leverage. I could feel the tie sliding through my fingers.

So I let go without warning and snapped my hand at a different target as he fell back.

He dropped into a backward roll and came up six feet away. He perched on one hand and a knee, still gripping the tie.

I casually settled his red ball cap onto my head, touched a forefinger to its brim, winked at him, and said, "You have hat hair."

Again there was a chorus of marrow-curdling laughter from the Sidhe. It wasn't any more pleasant to have them laughing *with* me than it had been to have them laughing *at* me.

The Redcap's face flushed a furious red, and I could *see* the blood vessels in his eyes bursting.

Hell's bells, the twit hadn't been particularly perturbed when I'd crippled his leg. But touch his *hat* and embarrass him in front of his peers and the dude flipped out. Nobody has their priorities straight anymore.

I made it to my feet before he simply leapt at me. He hit me before I could get my balance and we both went down. His eyes burning, he ignored the tie and latched onto my throat with both hands.

He was strong. I think I might have been stronger than he was, but I had only the one arm. I slammed it at his forearms—if he kept his grip on me, those nails would almost certainly draw blood. He hissed and jerked his hands away at the last second, and I slammed my knee against his injured leg. I bucked him off me while he screamed. I went after him.

We rolled a couple of times, and I cannot tell you how much it hurt both of us to do it. He had the use of both arms. I was able to use both legs to stabilize myself—but he was a hell of a lot squirmier than me, and in a blur of confusing motion he somehow managed to slither around to my back and get an arm across my throat. I got a few fingers underneath it, and started trying to pry him away. It wasn't a winning move. I managed to lessen the pressure, but I couldn't pull him off me, and my head started to pound.

Another group inhalation went up from the Sidhe, and I could feel them leaning closer, their interest almost frenzied, hundreds and hundreds of gemlike eyes sparkling like stars as the light started dimming. Sarissa stared at me with wide eyes, her expression horrified.

But . . . she'd lost one of her shoes.

I watched as she reached out with her toes and managed to pluck one of her fallen glassy chopsticks up off the floor. The freaking yeti holding her didn't notice. It was staring far too intently at the fight.

Sarissa passed the chopstick up to her hands, gripped it with both of them, and snapped it in the middle.

Shattered pieces of black glass fell away from a slender steel rod. Without looking, she simply lifted her hand and pressed the rod against the underside of the yeti's wrist.

Faeries, be they Sidhe or any other kind, cannot abide the touch of iron. To them, it's worse than molten plutonium. It burns them like fire, scars them, poisons them. There's a lot of folklore about cold iron, and it's a widely held belief that it refers only to cold-forged iron, but that's a bunch of hooey. When the old stories refer to cold iron, they're being poetic, like when they say "hot lead." If you want to hurt one of the fae, you just need iron, including any alloy containing it, to hurt them.

And man, does it ever *hurt* them.

The ogre's wrist burst into a sudden coruscation of yellow-white flame, as bright as that of an arc welder. The ogre howled and jerked its arm away from Sarissa's head as if he'd been a child experimenting with a penny and an electrical outlet.

Sarissa spun on her heel and slashed the little steel rod across the ogre's thigh.

It howled in primal fury and flinched back, sweeping one long arm at her in pure reflex.

Sarissa caught only a tiny fraction of the blow, but it was enough to send her staggering. She fell only a couple of feet away from me and looked up, her eyes dazed.

Her lower lip had been split wide-open.

A large ruby droplet fell from her lip and hung in the air, shining and perfect, and stayed there for half of forever. Then it finally splashed down onto the icy floor.

There was a shrieking hiss as the blood hit the supernatural ice, a sound somewhere between a hot skillet and a high-pressure industrial accident. The ice beneath the drop of blood shattered, as if the droplet had been unimaginably heavy, and a web of dark cracks shot out for fifty feet in every direction.

The music stopped. The Redcap froze. So did everyone else.

Mab rose out of her chair, and somehow in that instant of action she crossed the distance from her high seat, as though the simple act of standing up were what propelled her to the space nearby. As she came, the pallid finery of her dress darkened to raven black, as if the air had contained a fine mist of ink. Her hair darkened as well to the same color, and her eyes turned entirely black, sclera and all, as did her nails. The skin seemed to cling harder to her bones, making her beautiful features gaunt and terrible.

The Redcap flinched away from me and dragged himself back with his arms, getting clear. Give credit where it's due: He might have been a sadistic, bloodthirsty monster, but he wasn't a stupid one.

The furious, burned ogre wasn't bright enough to realize what was happening. Still smoldering, still enraged, it came stomping toward Sarissa.

"Knight," Mab said, the word a whipcrack.

Maeve came to the edge of the platform and clutched her hands into fists, her mouth twisted into a snarl.

I didn't get up off the ground. There wasn't time. Instead, I focused my will upon the advancing ogre and funneled my anger and my pain into the spell, along with the frozen core of power within me. I unleashed the energy as I thundered, *"Ventas servitas!"*

The ogre was only a couple of yards from Sarissa when the gale of arctic wind I'd called up slammed into the thing and lifted its massive bulk completely off the ground. It tossed the ogre a good ten feet away. It landed in a tumble, dug its claws into the ice, and fought its way back to its feet.

I rose from the ground, acutely conscious of Mab's black presence just over my left shoulder, of the watching eyes of the Winter Court.

I'd told Sarissa this was my first day in prison, and the yard was full of things that could and *would* kill me if they got the chance. It was time for an object lesson.

I reached down into the cold inside of me. It was painful to touch that power, like throwing yourself into icy water, like emerging from warm covers into the shuddering cold of an unheated apartment on a winter morning. I didn't like it, but I knew how to get it.

All I had to do was think about everyone I'd let down. Everyone I'd left behind back in Chicago. My brother, Thomas. My apprentice, Molly. My friends. My daughter. Karrin. I thought about them and it felt like something in my chest was starting to tear in half.

The Winter inside me was torment and agony—but at least when I was immersed in it, I couldn't *feel*.

I lifted my right arm, the side that projects energy, focused my will, and shouted, *"Infriga!"*

There was a flash of light, an arctic howl, a scream of air suddenly condensed into liquid, and an explosion of frost and fog centered upon the ogre. The air became a solid fog bank, a rolling mist, and for several seconds there was silence. I waited for the mist to disperse, and after several long seconds it began to clear away, swept along by the remnants of the gale I had called first.

When it cleared, the entire Winter Court could see the ogre, standing crouched just as it had been when I threw the spell at it.

I waited for a moment more, letting everyone see the ogre standing absolutely still in defiance of Mab's law.

Then I drew forth my will again, extended my hand, and snarled, "*Forzare!*" A lance of invisible power lashed out at the ogre—and when it struck, the frozen monster shattered into thousands of icy chunks, the largest of which was about the size of my fist.

The bits of the former ogre exploded over several hundred square yards of the dance floor, and grisly frozen shrapnel pelted the watching Sidhe and sent them reeling back with shouts of alarm. The Sidhe gathered themselves again, and every one of those bright eyes locked onto me, their expressions alien, unreadable.

From one of the back corners, I heard a deep, heartily amused chuckle rolling through the air. Kringle, I thought.

I turned to Mab and almost spoke—but then I remembered her other law and closed my mouth.

Mab's mouth twitched in an approving microsmile, and she nodded her head at me.

"If you consent, I would speak to them."

She stared at me with those black carrion-bird eyes and nodded.

First, I helped Sarissa to her feet, passing her a clean white handkerchief, which she immediately pressed to her mouth. I gave her what I hoped was a reassuring smile. Then I took a deep breath and turned to address the room, turning in a slow circle as I spoke to be sure I included everyone. My voice echoed throughout the whole chamber as clearly as if I'd been using a PA system.

"All right, you primitive screwheads. Listen up. I'm Harry Dresden. I'm the new Winter Knight. I'm instituting a rule: When you're within sight of me, mortals are off-limits." I paused for a moment to let that sink in. Then I continued. "I can't give you orders. I can't control what you do in your own domains. I'm not going to be able to change you. I'm not even going to try. But if I see you abusing a mortal, you'll join Chunky here. Zero warnings. Zero excuses. Subzero tolerance." I paused again and then asked, "Any questions?"

One of the Sidhe smirked and stepped forward, his leather pants creaking. He opened his mouth, his expression condescending. "Mortal, do you actually think that you can—"

"*Infriga!*" I snarled, unleashing Winter again, and without waiting for the cloud to clear, hurled the second strike, shouting, "*Forzare!*"

This time I aimed much of the force up. Grisly bits of frozen Sidhe noble came pattering and clattering down to the ice of the dance floor.

When the mist cleared, the Sidhe looked . . . stunned. Even Maeve.

"I'm glad you asked me that," I said to the space where the Sidhe lord had been standing. "I hope my answer clarified any misunderstandings." I looked left and right, seeking out eyes, but didn't find any willing to meet mine. "Are there any other questions?"

There was a vast and empty silence, broken only by Kringle's continued rumbles of amusement.

"Daughter," Mab said calmly. "Your lackey shamed me as the host of this gathering. I hold you accountable. You will return to Arctis Minora at once, there to await my pleasure."

Maeve stared at Mab, her eyes cold. Then she spun in a glitter of gems and began striding away. Several dozen of the Sidhe, including the Redcap and the rawhead, followed her.

Mab turned to Sarissa and said in a much calmer voice, "Honestly. Iron?"

"I apologize, my Queen," Sarissa said. "I'll dispose of it safely."

"See that you do," Mab said. "Now. I would have a dance. Sir Knight?"

I blinked, but didn't hesitate for more than an instant or three. "Um. My arm seems to be an obstacle."

Mab smiled and laid a hand upon my shoulder. My arm popped back into its socket with a silver shock of sensation, and the pain dwindled to almost nothing. I rolled my shoulder, testing it. If it wasn't exactly comfortable, it seemed to work well enough.

I turned to Mab, bowed, and stepped closer to her as the music rose again. It was a waltz. While the stunned Sidhe looked on, I waltzed with Mab to a full orchestral version of Shinedown's "45," and the smaller bits of our enemies crunched beneath our feet. Oddly enough, no one joined us.

Dancing with Mab was like dancing with a shadow. She moved so gracefully, so lightly that had my eyes been closed, I might not have been able to tell that she was there at all. I felt lumbering and clumsy beside her, but managed not to trip over my own feet.

"That was well-done, wizard," Mab murmured. "No one has lifted a hand to them that way since the days of Tam Lin."

"I wanted them to understand the nature of our relationship."

"It would seem you succeeded," she said. "The next time they come at you, they will not do it so openly."

"I'll handle it."

"I expect nothing less," Mab said. "In the future, try to avoid being at such a stark disadvantage. Sarissa may not be there to rescue you a second time."

I grunted. Then I frowned and said, "You wanted this to happen tonight. It wasn't just about me staring down your nobles. You're setting something into motion."

Her lips quirked slightly at one corner in approval. "I chose well. You are ready, my Knight. It is time for me to give you my first command."

I swallowed and tried not to look nervous. "Oh?"

The song came to a close with Mab standing very close to me, lifting her head slightly to whisper into my ear. The Sidhe applauded politely and without enthusiasm, but the sound was enough to muffle what she whispered into my ear.

"Wizard," she said, her breathy voice trembling. Every syllable bubbled with venom, with hate. "Kill my daughter. *Kill Maeve*."

8

Dancing with Mab was like rapidly downing shots of well-aged whiskey. Being that close to her, to her beauty, to her bottomless eyes, hit me pretty hard. The scent of her, cool and clean and intoxicating, lingered in my nose, a disorienting pleasure. I'd thrown around a lot of energy to pull off the pair of chunk-making combos, and between that and Mab's proximity, I was having a little trouble walking a straight line after the dance.

It wasn't like I had feelings for her. I didn't feel the kind of low pulse of physical attraction that I would around a pretty woman. I didn't particularly *like* her. I sure as hell didn't feel any love for her. It was simply impossible to be that close to her, to that kind of deadly power and beauty, to that kind of immortal hunger and desire, without it rattling the bars of my cage. Mab wasn't human, and wasn't meant for human company. I had no doubt whatsoever in my mind that long-term exposure to her would have serious, unpleasant side effects.

And never *mind* what she had just asked me to do.

The consequences of that kind of action would be . . . really, really huge. And only an idiot would willingly involve himself in direct action on a scale that significant—which really didn't say anything good about me, given how often I'd been the guy wearing the idiot's shoes.

After our dance, Mab returned to her high seat and surveyed the chamber through barely open eyes, a distant figure, now garbed in pure white and untouchable again. As my head came out of the cold, numb clarity of wielding Winter, the aches and pains the Redcap had given me began to resurface in a big way. Fatigue began piling up, and when I looked around for a place to sit down, I found Cat Sith sitting nearby, his wide eyes patient and opaque.

"Sir Knight," the malk said. "You do not suffer fools." There was the faintest hint of approval in his tone. "What is your need?"

"I've had enough party," I said. "Would it inconvenience the Queen for me to depart?"

"If she wished you to stay, you would be at her side," Cat Sith replied. "And it would seem that you have introduced yourself adequately."

"Good. If you do not mind," I said, "please ask Sarissa to join me."

"I do not mind," Cat Sith said in a decidedly approving tone. He vanished into the party and appeared a few moments later, leading Sarissa. She walked steadily enough, though she still had my handkerchief pressed to her mouth.

"You want to get out of here?" I asked her.

"It's a good idea," she said. "Most of the VIPs left after your dance. Things will . . . devolve from here."

"Devolve?" I asked.

"I don't care to stay," she said, her tone careful. "I would prefer to leave."

I frowned, and then realized that she was trying to get a read on me. I simultaneously became acutely aware of a number of Sidhe ladies who were . . . I would say "lurking" except that you don't generally use that word with someone so beautiful. There were half a dozen of them, though, who were staying nearby, and whose eyes were tracking me. I felt disconcertingly reminded of a documentary I'd once seen about lionesses involved in a cooperative hunt. There was something about them that was very similar.

One, a ravishing dark-haired beauty wearing leather pants and strategically applied electrical tape, stared hard at me and, when she saw me looking, licked her lips very, very slowly. She trailed a fingertip over her chin, down across her throat, and down over her sternum and gave me a smile so wicked that its parents should have sent it to military school.

"Oh," I said, understanding. Despite my fatigue, my throat felt dry and my heart revved up a bit. "Devolving."

"I'll go," Sarissa said. "I don't expect anything from you simply because we arrived together."

A Sidhe lady with deep indigo blue hair had sidled up to Miss Electrical Tape, and the two slid their arms around each other, both staring at me. Something inside me—and I'd be lying if I said that none of it was mine—let out a primal snarl and advised me to drag both of them back to my cave by the hair and do whatever I damned well pleased with them. It was an enormously powerful impulse, something that made me begin to shift my balance, to take a step toward them. I arrested the motion and closed my eyes.

"Yeah," I said. "Yeah, they look great, but that isn't a fantasy come true, Harry. That's a wood chipper in *Playboy* bunny clothing." I shook my head and turned deliberately away from temptation before I opened my eyes again. "We'll both go," I said to Sarissa. "It'd be a bad idea to stay." I offered her my arm.

She frowned thoughtfully at me for a moment before she put her hand on my arm. We left, again preceded by Cat Sith. Once we were in the icy hallways, she asked me, "Why?"

"Why what?"

"Leave," she said. "You wanted to stay. And . . . let's just say that the, ah, appetite of Sidhe ladies has never been overstated. And nothing excites them more than violence and power. There are men who would literally kill to have the opportunity you just passed up."

"Probably," I said. "Morons."

"Then why turn it down?" she asked.

"Because I'm not a goddamned sex doll."

"That's a good reason to avoid attention that is forced on you," she said. "But that isn't what happened. Why pass up what they were offering?"

We walked for a while before I answered. "I've already made one choice that . . . that took everything away from me," I said. "I don't know how much longer I'll be around, or how much of a life I can make for myself now. But I'm going to live as much of it as I can as my own man. Not somebody's prison bitch. Not the flavor of the day."

"Ah," she said, and frowned faintly.

I blinked several times and suddenly realized what she'd been trying to find out. "Oh. You're wondering if I turned them down because I was planning to have *you* instead."

She gave me an oblique look. "I wouldn't have phrased it that way."

I snorted. "I'm not."

She nodded. "Why not?"

"Does it matter?" I asked.

"Why always matters."

It was my turn to give Sarissa an appraising look. "Yeah, it does."

"So, why not?"

"Because you aren't a goddamned sex doll, either."

"Even if I were willing?" she asked.

My stomach jumped a little at that. Sarissa was attractive as hell, and I liked her. I'd made her smile and laugh on occasion. And it had been a while.

Man, story of my life. It seems like it's almost always been a while.

But you have to think about more than what is going to happen in the next hour.

"You're here because Mab ordered you to be here," I said. "Anything we did would have an element of coercion to it, no matter how it happened. I'm not into that."

"You saved my life just now," Sarissa said. "Some people might think you'd earned my attentions."

"People think stupid things all the time. The only opinion that matters is yours." I glanced at her. "Besides, you probably saved me right back. Toting steel into the heart of Winter. Using it right in front of Mab herself? That's crazy."

She smiled a little. "It would have been crazy not to tote it," she said. "I've learned a few things in my time here."

We had reached the doors to my suite, which still felt awkward to say, even in my own head. My suite. Guys like me don't have suites. We have lairs. Cat Sith had departed discreetly. I hadn't seen him go.

"How long has it been?" I asked.

"Too long," she said. She hadn't taken her hand off of my arm.

"You know," I said, "we've been working together for a while now."

"We have."

"But we haven't ever talked about ourselves. Not really. It's all been surface stuff."

"You haven't talked about you," she said. "I haven't talked about me."

"Maybe we should change that," I said.

Sarissa looked down. There were points of color in her cheeks. "I . . . Should we?"

"You want to come in?" I asked. "To talk. That's all."

She took a moment to choose her words. "If you want me to."

I tried to think about this from Sarissa's point of view. She was a beautiful woman who had to be constantly aware of male interest. She was a mortal living in a world of faeries, most of whom were malicious, all of whom were dangerous. Her introduction to the office of the Winter Knight had been Lloyd Slate, who had been one monstrous son of a bitch. She had some kind of relationship with Mab herself, a being who could have her destroyed at any moment she was displeased with Sarissa.

And I was Mab's hatchet man.

She'd been targeted for death for no better reason than that she happened to be my date at the party. She'd nearly died. Yet she'd taken action to save herself—and me, too—and now here she was standing calmly beside me, not showing the least anxiety. She'd spent months helping me get back on my feet again, always gentle, always helpful, always patient.

She was wary about extending me any trust. She'd been holding herself at a careful distance. I could understand why. Caution was a critical survival trait in Winter, and as far as she was concerned, I was most likely a monster in the process of being born. A monster she'd been *given* to, no less.

Thinking about it, even if I had saved her life, it wouldn't have needed saving had she not been with me. I figured that between that and every-thing else she'd done for me, I was well in her debt.

But I couldn't help her if I didn't know more about her.

"For a couple of minutes," I said. "Please."

She nodded, and we went inside. I had a little living room outside of my bedroom. I read somewhere that in general, women tend to be more comfortable with someone sitting beside them, rather than across from them. Men tend to be the opposite. Facing each other has undertones of direct physical conflict—in which a generally larger, stronger person would have an advantage. I didn't know whether it was true or not, but she was already keyed up enough, and I didn't want to add anything to it. So I seated her at one end of the couch, and then seated myself at the opposite end, out of arm's reach.

"Okay," I said. "We haven't talked, I guess, because I've never told you anything about myself. Is that about the shape of it?"

"Trust has to go both ways," she said.

I huffed out a short laugh. "You've been hanging around Mab too much. She's not big on answering simple yes-or-no questions either."

Sarissa's mouth twitched at the corners. "Yes."

I laughed again. "Okay," I said. "Well, when in Rome. Maybe we should exchange questions and answers. You can go first."

She folded her hands, frowning, and then nodded. "I've heard a lot of stories about you. That you've killed a lot of people. Are they true?"

"I don't know what you've heard," I said. "But . . . yeah. When bad things came after people in my town, I made it my business to get in the way. And I've been a Warden of the White Council for a while now. I fought in the war against the Red Court. I've done a lot of fighting. Sometimes people get killed. Why are you in Mab's debt?"

"I . . . have a form of congenital dementia," she said. "I watched what it did to my older sister and . . ." She shuddered. "Doctors can't help me. Mab can. Have you ever killed anyone who wasn't trying to kill you?"

I looked down at my shoes. "Twice," I said quietly. "I cut Lloyd Slate's throat to become the Winter Knight. And—"

A flash of memory. A ruined city full of howling monsters and blood.

Flashes of light and roaring detonations of magic tearing asunder stone and air alike. Dust everywhere. Friends fighting, bleeding, desperate. A stone altar covered in a thick coating of dried blood. A terrified little girl, my daughter. Treachery.

A kiss pressed against the forehead of a woman I was about to murder. *God, Susan, forgive me.*

I couldn't see through the blur in my eyes, and my throat felt like the Redcap might be garroting me again, but I forced myself to speak. "And I killed a woman named Susan Rodriguez on a stone altar, because if I hadn't, a little girl and a lot of good people would have died. She knew it, too." I swiped a hand at my eyes and coughed to clear my throat. "What were the terms of your bargain with Mab?"

"That as long as I remained myself, and sane, I would attend her and do as she bade me for three months out of every year. Summer vacation, when I was in school. Weekends, now, except for lately. Taking care of you meant that I'd have months and months off to make up for it." She fidgeted with the bloodied handkerchief. Her split lip had stopped bleeding, and a line of dark, drying blood marred it. "The whole time we worked on your therapy, I think you said something about having a dog and a cat once. But you never spoke about any friends or family. Why not?"

I shrugged. "I'm not sure," I said. And then I realized that I was lying to everyone in the room. "Maybe . . . maybe because it hurts to think about them. Because I miss them. Because . . . because they're good people. The best. And I'm not sure I can look them in the eye anymore, after what I've done. What about you? Do you have any friends?"

"There are people I sometimes do things with," she said. "I don't . . . I'm not sure I'd call them friends. I don't want to make friends. I have the attention of some dangerous beings. If I got close to anyone, I could be putting them in danger. Don't you ever worry about that?"

"Every day," I said. "I've buried friends who died because they were involved with my work, and my life. But they wanted to be there. They knew the dangers and chose to face them. It isn't my place to choose for them. Do you think it's better to be alone?"

"I think it's better for *them*," Sarissa said. "You're healthy now. Are you going to go home? To your friends and family?"

"Home isn't there anymore," I said, and suddenly felt very tired. "They burned my apartment down. My books, my lab. And my friends think I'm dead. How do I just walk back in? 'Hi, everyone. I'm back, and did you miss me? I'm working for one of the bad guys now, and what good movies came out while I was gone?' " I shook my head. "I'm making fresh enemies. Nasty ones. I'd be pulling them in all over again. I know what they'd say—that it didn't matter. But I don't know what I'm going to do yet. Mab seems to trust you. What is it that you do for her, exactly?"

Sarissa smiled faintly. "I'm sort of her humanity Sherpa," she said. "For all of her power and knowledge, Mab doesn't always understand people very well. She asks me questions. Sometimes we watch television or go to movies or listen to music. I've taken her to rock concerts. We've gone ice skating. Shopping. Clubbing. Once we went to Disneyland."

I blinked. "Wait. Your job is . . . You're BFFs with *Mab*?"

Sarissa let out a sudden torrent of giggles, until her eyes started to water a little. "Oh," she said, still giggling. "Oh, I've never thought of it like that, but . . . God, it applies, doesn't it? We do something every weekend." She shook her head and took a moment to compose herself. Then she asked me, "Is there anyone special for you? Back home?"

Karrin.

But I didn't dare use her name. No telling what other ears might be listening.

"Maybe," I said. "It was . . . sort of starting up when I left. I'm not sure where it would have gone. I'd like to think that . . ." I shrugged. "Well. It was bad timing on an epic level. You?"

"Nothing more than casual," she said. "If I was close to someone, well . . . it would create a target for Mab's enemies, which I sometimes think is practically everybody in Faerie. Killing the lover of Mab's pet mortal would be an insult while remaining oblique enough to not allow her room to respond." She took a deep breath and looked at her hands. "I saw you speaking to her on the dance floor. I saw your face. Who did she tell you to kill?"

I hesitated. "I . . . I'm pretty sure I shouldn't say. It's information that could get you into trouble."

I looked up in time to see the wariness returning to Sarissa's features. "Ah," she said. "Well, I suppose our little exchange is over, then." She bit her lower lip and asked, quite calmly, "Was it me?"

That one caught me off guard. "Uh, what? No. No, it wasn't you."

She didn't move for several heartbeats. "I . . . see." Then she looked up, gave me a pleasant and false smile, and said, "Well, it's late. And you should still try to rest as much as you can."

"Sarissa, wait," I began.

She rose, her back straight, her shoulders tense. "I think I'm going to my bed. Um. Unless you'd prefer . . ."

I stood up with her. "Don't think that I'm against the idea, as a general principle. You're smart, and I like you, and you're gorgeous. But no. Not like this."

She chewed on her lip again and nodded. "Thank you for that. For understanding."

"Sure," I said. I offered my arm and walked her back to the door of my lair.

("Lair" worked so much better in my head than "suite.")

At the door, she looked up at me. "May I ask you a question?"

"Of course."

"Are you going to obey Mab?"

My brain started gibbering and running in circles at the very thought of what Mab had asked me to do. But I forced it to sit down and start breathing into a paper bag, and then I thought about it for a second. "Maybe. Maybe not."

"Why?" she asked.

I rocked back onto my heels. It felt like that one little word had thumped me between the eyes with a Wiffle ball bat. Sarissa had hit exactly upon what most bothered me about Mab's command.

Why? Why now instead of six months ago, or a year ago, or a hundred years ago? Why today instead of tomorrow? Hell, why should I do it in the first place? The whole reason Winter and Summer *had* a Knight was because the Queens of Faerie themselves were forbidden from directly killing any mortal, and they needed a hit man to make it happen. But Maeve wasn't a mortal. As far as Mab was concerned, Little Miss Spanglecrotch was fair game.

Why?

"I'm not sure yet," I said. "But I'm damned well going to find out."

9

"Cat Sith," I called, once Sarissa had left.

From behind me, a voice said, "Yes, Sir Knight?"

I twitched and didn't whirl around like a frightened teenager. I turned in a very urbane and James Bondian fashion, in keeping with my tux, eyed him, and said, "Hell's bells. Do you always come in like that?"

"No," the malk replied. He was sitting on the back of the sofa Sarissa and I had recently vacated. "Generally I do not speak. I simply proceed."

"Are you aware of my orders?" I asked.

"I am aware that you have been given orders. I am to facilitate your ability to comply with them."

I nodded. "I need to get back to Chicago. Right now. And I need a car."

Cat Sith turned and padded down the hallway, toward my bedroom. He stopped in the hall at the door to the linen closet and lashed his tail once, then looked at me. "Very well."

I frowned at him. Then I went to the closet and opened the door.

Autumn air, humid and smothering compared to that of Arctis Tor, flooded into my lair. Brilliant lights shone on the other side of the door, and it took me a few seconds of blinking against them to adjust, and realize that I was being blinded by simple streetlights. Inside my closet, there was a bit of sidewalk and then Michigan Avenue stretching out to the storefront opposite.

I blinked several times. Sith had opened a Way between Faerie and Chicago.

The spirit world, the Nevernever, is vast almost beyond imagining. Faerie is but one part of it, for the most part occupying the realms of spirit that lie most adjacent to the mortal world. The geography of the spirit world isn't like that of the real world. Different places in the spirit world will connect with places with a similar energy in the real world. So dark, spooky parts of the Nevernever hook up with dark, spooky places in the mortal world.

And my freaking linen closet in Arctis Tor hooked up to Chicago— specifically to Michigan Avenue, to the Gothic stone building across the street from the Old Historic Water Tower. It was night. Cars went by occasionally, but no one seemed to take notice of the open portal to the heart of Winter. Arctis Tor was isolated in the Nevernever, difficult to reach without inside help. Even traveling by Ways takes at least some time, and I'd expected a hike back to the real world.

"How?" I asked quietly.

"Her Majesty had it made," Sith said.

I whistled. Intentionally forming a connection from a specific place to a specific place took amounts of energy so enormous that even the White Council of Wizards could rarely manage it—I'd seen it done only once in my lifetime, the year before, in Chichén Itzá. "She had it made? For me?"

"Indeed," Sith said. "In fact, this is, for the time being, the only way in or out of Faerie."

I blinked several times. "You mean Winter?"

"Faerie," Sith stated. "All of it."

I choked. "Wait. You mean all of Faerie is on lockdown?"

"Indeed," Sith said. "Until dawn."

"Why?" I asked.

"One presumes it was done to give you a head start." With that, Sith walked calmly through the door and onto the sidewalk. "Your car, Sir Knight."

I stepped through the door into the Chicago air, and it slugged me in the face with a legion of scents and sensations and sounds that were as familiar to me as my own breathing. After the cool, dry silence of Arctis Tor, I felt like I'd leapt into the middle of an active circus. There were too many sounds, scents, too much color, too much motion. Arctis Tor was as still as the deepest night of winter, twenty-four/seven. Chicago is . . . well, Chicago.

I found myself blinking my eyes very rapidly.

Home.

I know. It's corny. Especially since Chicago is what a polite person would call a colorful place. It's a den of crime and corruption. And it's a monument to architecture and enterprise. It's violent and dangerous, and an epicenter of music and the arts. The good, the bad, the ugly, the sublime, monsters and angels—they're all here.

The scents and sounds triggered a mental avalanche of memories and I shivered at the intensity of it. I almost didn't notice the car that pulled up to the curb beside me.

It was an ancient hearse, a Caddy that must have been built sometime in the years immediately following World War II, complete with rounded tail fins. It had been painted dark, dark blue, and given a flame job in shades of electric purple. It wavered and bobbed drunkenly down the avenue, turned a bit too sharply toward the curb, lurched ahead with a roar of the engine, and then skidded to a halt with the brakes locked, missing the posts along the edge of the road, and the chains that hung between them, by maybe an inch.

"Will there be anything else, Sir Knight?" Cat Sith asked.

"Not right now," I said warily. "Um. Who is driving that thing?"

"I recommend it be you," Sith said with unmistakable contempt, and then with a swish of his tail, he vanished.

The engine roared once more, and the car lurched but didn't move from its rest. The lights went on and then off, and then the wipers swept on a few times before the engine dropped to an idle and the brake lights shut off.

I approached the car warily, leaned across the chains, and rapped on the driver's-side window.

Nothing happened. The windows were tinted a little, enough to make the dark interior invisible on the well-lit street. I couldn't see anyone inside. I opened the door.

"Three cheers, boys!" piped a tiny cartoon-character voice. "Hip, hip!"

"Hip!" shrilled maybe a dozen more tiny voices.

"Hip, hip!"

"Hip!"

"Hip, hip!"

"Hip!" That was followed by a heartfelt chorus of "Yay!"

Sitting in the driver's seat of the hearse were a dozen tiny humanoids. Their leader, the largest of them, was maybe eighteen inches tall. He looked like an extremely athletic youth, drawn down to scale. He was dressed in armor made from castoff bits of garbage and refuse. His breastplate had been made from a section of aluminum can, a white one bearing a Coca-Cola logo. The shield on his left arm was made from the same material, this one sporting Coke's seasonal Christmas polar bears. Part of a plastic toothpaste travel container had been fixed to his belt, and what looked like a serrated butter knife was thrust into it, its handle wrapped in layers of duct tape and string. His hair was violet, a few shades of blue darker than the lavender I remembered, silky, and nearly weightless, drifting around his head like dandelion down. Wings like a dragonfly's hung from his back like an iridescent cloak.

He was standing atop a formation of smaller sprites stacked up in a miniature human pyramid, and his hands rested on the wheel. Several weary-looking little wee folk were leaning against the gearshift, and several more were on the floor, holding the brake down in a dog pile of tiny bodies. They were all dressed in similar outfits of repurposed garbage.

The leader gave me a sharp salute, beaming. "Major General Toot-toot of the Sir Za Winter Lord Knight's Guard reporting for duty! It is good to see you, my lord!" His wings buzzed and he fluttered out of the hearse to hover in front of my face, spinning in circles. "Look, look! I got new gear!"

"We're all Winter and stuff!" piped up one of the smaller members of the guard. He brandished his shield, which was made out of a section of plastic that had come from a solid-stick deodorant container, bearing the words "Winter Clean."

"Go, Winter!" shouted Toot, thrusting a fist into the air.

"Go, pizza!" echoed the others.

Toot spun around and scowled at them. "No, no, no! We practiced this!"

"GO, PIZZA!" they bellowed, louder and more in unison.

Toot-toot sighed and shook his head. "This is why you're all kernels and I'm a major general. 'Cause you got corn silk in your ears."

Toot and company were kind of my minions. I'd gotten along well with the Little Folk over the years, mostly by virtue of bribing them with pizza. A few snitches and stool pigeons had developed into a band of cute little moochers, and then into an army—and at some point after that, Toot had somehow gotten the idea to make them into a real army. And they tried—they honestly did—but it's tough to form a disciplined military when most of the guys in it have an attention span about twenty seconds long. Discipline is boring.

"Guys, guys," I said. "Break it up and shove over. I'm in a hurry."

The wee folk complied at once, all of them scrambling into the passenger seat or over into the rear compartment. I got in as quickly as I could and shut the door behind me.

I buckled in and pulled out into the sparse traffic. The big Caddy moved out with a satisfied rumble and way more power than I was used to in an automobile. My last car had been a vintage VW Bug with an engine about the size of a deck of cards.

"Toot," I said, "have you grown?"

"Yes," Toot said, disgusted. "Even though I stand around with weights on my head for, like, twenty whole minutes every day. I even got laundered. Twice! And nothing!"

"I think you look dashing," I said.

He settled down at the center of the dashboard, his legs hanging off and kicking idly. "Thank you, my lord!"

"So the pizza came on schedule while I was, uh, away?"

"Yes, my lord! The Lady Leanansidhe provided it in your stead!" Toot lowered his voice and talked from between clenched teeth. "If she hadn't, these knuckleheads would have deserted!"

"Well, we do have a deal," I said. "That's what a deal means, right?"

"Right," Toot said firmly. "We trust you, Harry. You're barely like a human at all!"

I knew he meant it as a compliment, but something chilly slithered down my back at the statement. My faerie godmother, the Leanansidhe, had covered my obligations at home while I was gone? Man, that could get complicated. Among the Sidhe, favors are hard currency.

But I was glad to see Toot and his gang. They were damned handy, and could be far more dangerous and capable than most, even in the supernatural world, I realized.

"I never doubted you or the guard for a second, Major General."

Which was true: I had no doubt at all that as long as the pizza kept flowing, I'd have their absolute loyalty.

Toot beamed at the compliment, and his body pulsed with a gentle aura of cool blue light. "How can the guard serve you, my lord?"

They'd started off the evening nearly crashing the car, but it was impressive they'd managed it at all. "I'm on a case," I said seriously. "I'll need someone to watch my back."

"Lean forward a little, my lord," Toot said instantly, and shouted, "Hey, Kernel Purpleweed! Come watch the Za Winter Lord Knight's back!"

I fought not to smile. "No, that's a metaphor," I said.

Toot frowned and scratched his head. "I don't know what it's for."

Mustn't laugh. Mustn't. It would crush his little feelings. "In a minute, I'm going to pull over and go into a building. I want guards to stay inside and around the car, and I want a couple more to go with me and make sure no one sneaks up on me when I'm not looking."

"Oh!" Toot said. "That's easy!"

"Good," I said, as I pulled the car over. "Make it so."

Toot saluted, leapt into the air, and zipped back to the rear compartment, piping orders as he went.

I set the old Caddy's parking brake and got out, wasting no time. I didn't hold the door open any longer than I would have if I'd been alone. The Little Folk do not need that kind of coddling. They're not always bright, but they're fast, tough, and resourceful. I'd have had trouble keeping them in the car if I wanted to.

Once I was out and moving, I was to all appearances alone. Whoever Toot had sent to watch my back would be silent and nearly invisible, and I didn't bother rubbernecking around to try to spot them. One thing about the Little Folk that held as well with every faerie—when they made a deal, they stuck to it. They'd had my back before, and they had it now. Heck, since I was committing a felony, they probably thought it was fun to come along for the ride.

It's tough to get one of the Little Folk to care about discipline. On the other hand, they really aren't terribly impressed with danger, either.

I walked about a block to the right apartment building, a brownstone blockhouse that had all the flair and imaginative design of a brick of baking chocolate. It wasn't an upscale place like where my brother lived, but it wasn't one of the projects at their worst, either. It didn't have a doorman, and the security wouldn't be top-of-the-line, and that was, for now, the important thing.

I got a little bit lucky on the way in—a resident, a man in his twenties who had apparently been out drinking, opened the door on his way home, and I called out, "Hold that, please?"

He did. He probably shouldn't have, but guys in tuxes, even without a tie, don't strike anyone as a criminal upon first impression. I nodded to him and thanked him with a smile. He muttered something bleary and turned down a side hallway. I hit the elevators and took one up.

Once I was on the right floor, the rest wasn't too tough. I walked calmly down the hallway to the proper door and leaned against it.

A ripple of gooseflesh washed up my arm, beginning on the back of my hand, and I jerked my fingers back in pure instinct. Huh. There were wards on the door, magical defenses. I hadn't expected that. Wards can do all kinds of things to an intruder, from suggesting that he turn around and leave, to giving him a stiff push away, to frying him like a bug zapper.

I took a moment to study the wards. They were a smooth patchwork of enchantment, probably the result of several lesser talents working together. Somebody like me can put up a ward that is like a huge iron wall. This was more like a curtain of tightly interwoven steel rings. For most purposes, both would serve fairly well—but with the right tool, the latter kind of wall is easily dealt with.

"And I'm the tool," I muttered. Then I thought about it, sighed, and shook my head. "One day," I told myself, "one brave and magnificent day, I will actually be cool."

I rested my fingertips lightly on the door and went over the wards in my thoughts. Aha. Had I tried to break in, the wards would have set off an enormous racket and a bunch of smoke, along with a sudden, intense sensation of claustrophobia. Fire alarms would have gone off, and sprinklers, and the authorities would have been summoned.

That was a nominally effective defense all by itself, but the claustrophobia bit was really masterful. The noise would trip off an instinctive adrenaline response, and that combined with the induced panic of the ward would send just about anything scurrying for the exit rather than take chances in what would have been a very noisy and crowded environment. That kind of subtle manipulation always works best amidst a flurry of distractions.

Washington's been doing it like that for decades.

I cut the wards off from their power source one at a time, trying to keep the damage to a minimum so that it would be easy to fix. I already felt bad enough over what I was about to do. Then, once the wards were off-line, I took a deep breath and leaned against the door with a sudden thrust of my legs and body. I'd been working out. The doorframe splintered and gave way, and I slipped quickly and quietly into Waldo Butters's apartment.

It was dark inside, and I didn't know it well enough to navigate without light. I left the door a little bit open so that the light from the hall would leak in. This was the dangerous part. If someone had heard the noise, they'd be calling the cops. I needed to be gone in the next five minutes.

I crossed the living room to the short hallway. Butters's bedroom was on the right, his computer room on the left. The bedroom door was closed. There was a faint light in the computer room. I entered. There were several computers set up around the walls of the room, which I knew Butters and company used for some kind of group computer game-related thingy they all did together. The computers were all turned off except for one, the biggest one in the corner, which sat facing out into the room. Butters called it the captain's chair. He sat there and coordinated some kind of game activity. Raids, I think they were called, and they went on into the wee hours. His job required him to work nights, and he claimed it helped him keep circadian rhythm to play video games on his off nights.

That monitor was on, and in the reflection in the glass of the room's single window, I could see that the screen had been divided into maybe a dozen sections, and every single one of them was playing a different pornographic scenario.

A human skull sat on the table, facing the monitor, and faint orange flickers of light danced in its eyes. Despite its utter inability to form any expression, it somehow gave the impression of a happily glazed look.

I'd been in the room for about two seconds when the computer made an awful sound, coughed out a little puff of smoke, and the monitor screen went black. I winced. My fault. Wizards and technology don't get along so well, and the more advanced the technology is, the sooner something seems to go wrong—especially with electronics. Butters had been cobbling together a theory to explain why the world worked like that, but I'd drawn the line at covering my head in a tinfoil hat in the name of science.

The skull let out a startled, disappointed sound, and after several disoriented flickers, its eyelights panned around the room and landed on me.

"Harry!" said the skull. It didn't move its jaws to form the words or anything. They just came out. "Hell's bells, you're back from the dead?"

"From the mostly dead," I replied. "You made it out of Omaha Beach, huh?"

"You kidding?" Bob said. "The minute you were clear, I ran like a bunny and hid!"

"You could have taken that jerk," I said.

"Why would I want to?" Bob asked. "So when do we set up the new lab? And can I have broadband?" His eyes gleamed with avarice or something near it. "I *need* broadband, Harry."

"That's a computer thing, right?"

"Philistine," Bob the Skull muttered.

Bob wasn't a skull, per se. He was a spirit of air, or intellect, or one of any of a great many other terms used to describe such beings. The skull was the vessel that he inhabited, kind of like a djinni's bottle. Bob had been working as an assistant and adviser to wizards since before crossbows had gone out of style, and he'd forgotten more about the ins and outs of magical theory than I knew. He'd been my assistant and friend since I'd first come to Chicago.

I hadn't realized, until I actually heard his voice, how much I'd missed the demented little perv.

"When do we get to work?" Bob asked brightly.

"I am working," I said. "I need to talk to you."

"I'm all ears," Bob said. "Except for the ears part." Bob blinked. "Are you wearing a tux?"

"Uh, yeah."

"Tell me you did not get married."

"I didn't get married," I said. "Except for the whole Mab thing, which is creepy and weird. She spent the last three months trying to kill me once a day."

"Sounds like her style," Bob said. "How'd you get out of it?"

"Um," I said.

"Oh," Bob said. "Uh . . . oh. Maybe you should go, Harry."

"Relax," I said. "I know you've had your issues with Mab, but I'm the only one here."

"Yeah. That's kinda the part that bothers me."

I scowled at him. "Oh, come on. How long have you known me?"

"Harry . . . you're *Mab's hit man*."

"Yeah, but I'm not here to hit you," I said.

"You could be lying," Bob said. "Maybe the Sidhe can't lie, but you can."

"Hell's bells, I'm not lying."

"But how do I *know* that?"

"Because I haven't hit you already?" I frowned at him. "Wait a minute. . . . You're *stalling* me, aren't you?"

"Stalling you?" Bob asked brightly. "What do you mean?"

There was no warning. None at all. The door to Butters's bedroom exploded outward, sending splinters of cheap plywood sailing every-where. A missile of living muscle hit me in the back at almost the same instant, shoving my chest forward and whiplashing my head back. My spine lit up like a casino, and I felt myself driven hard to the ground.

Something powerful and snarling and terribly strong came down on top of me, and I felt claws and fangs begin to rake at me.

Guess I used up all my evening's luck on the front door guy.

10

Claws shredded my tux, raking over my back, my buttocks, and the backs of my legs. Jaws would have bitten into my neck if I hadn't gotten my hands in the way, clamping them over the back of my neck and squeezing them as tight as I could, hoping that a finger wouldn't come up and be nipped off. Pain came in, hot and high, but the claws didn't dig as deep as they would have if this had been a malk or a ghoul, and I had to hope the damage wouldn't be too serious—unless the fight went on long enough for blood loss to weaken me.

Some analytical part of my head was going over those facts in a detached and rational fashion.

The rest of me went freaking berserk with anger.

I got one arm beneath me to brace myself and threw the other elbow back in a heavy strike that slammed into something soft and drew a startled yelp out of my attacker. The teeth vanished for a second and the claws slowed. I rolled, shoving with a broad motion of that same arm, and threw a wolf the size of a Great Dane off of my back. It hit one of the computer tables with a tremendous racket, sending bits of equipment tumbling.

I got my feet underneath me, seized a computer chair by its back, and lifted it. By the time the wolf with dark red fur was getting back onto its feet, the chair was already halfway through its swing, and I was snarling in incoherent fury.

Only at the last second did I recognize my attacker through my rage and divert the arc of the descending chair. It broke into about fifty pieces when it hit the floor just in front of the wolf, plastic and metal tumbling in every direction.

The wolf flinched back from the flying bits, and lifted its eyes toward mine. It froze in what was an expression of perfect shock, and in a pair of seconds the wolf was gone, its form melting rapidly into the shape of a girl, a redhead with generous curves and not a stitch of clothing. She stared at me, gasping in short breaths, her expression pained, before she whispered, "Harry?"

"Andi," I said, standing straighter and trying to force my body to relax. The word came out in a snarl. Adrenaline still sang along my arms and legs, and more than anything in the whole world, at that moment I wanted to punch someone in the face. Anyone. It didn't matter who.

And that was *not* right.

"Andi," I said, forcing myself to quiet and gentle my voice. "What the hell are you doing here?"

"Me?" she breathed. "I . . . I'm not the one who's *dead*."

The night is young, thought the furious part of me, but I fought it down. "Rumors, death, exaggerated," I said instead. "And I don't have time to chat about it."

I turned toward Bob at his desk, and heard Andi open a drawer behind me. The sound an automatic makes when someone racks the slide and pops a round into the chamber is specific and memorable—and gets your attention as effectively as if it were also really, really loud.

"Get your hands away from the skull," said Andi's shortened, pained voice, "or I put a bullet in you."

I paused. My first impulse was to cover the floor of the computer room with frozen chunks of Andi, and what the hell was I *thinking*? It was the anger that kept on rolling through me in cold waves that was pushing for that, for action, for violence. Don't get me wrong; it's not like I exactly have an allergy to either of those things—but I'd always done a reasonably good job of keeping my temper under control. I hadn't felt like this in years, not since the first days I'd nearly been killed by the White Council.

I fell back on what I'd learned then. I closed my eyes and took a few deep breaths, reminding myself that the anger was just anger, that it was a sensation, like feeling hot or cold. It didn't mean anything by itself. It wasn't a reason to act. That's what thinking was for.

The old lessons helped, and I separated myself from the fury. I put my hands slowly out to my sides, making sure they were visible. Then I turned to face Andi. She stood with a pistol in a solid Weaver stance, like she'd learned how from someone who knew.

I could deflect bullets if I had to do it, but I couldn't *stop* them. And we were in a building full of innocent bystanders. "You know about the skull?" I asked.

"Kind of hard not to," she said. "Since I live here."

I blinked several times. "You and . . . Damn. Way to go, Butters."

Andi stared steadily down the sights of her gun. She was holding herself a little hitched, as if her right side pained her. That elbow I'd thrown must have caught her in the ribs. I winced. I don't mind a little of the rough-and-tumble when necessary, but I don't hit my friends, I don't hit women, and Andi was both.

"Sorry about that," I said, nodding toward her. "I didn't know it was you."

"And I still don't know if it's you," she replied. "Especially with you dead and all. There are plenty of things that might try to look like Harry."

"Bob," I said over my shoulder. "Tell her it's me."

"Can't," Bob said in a dreamy tone. "Boobs."

Right. Because Andi was naked. I'd seen her that way before, because that was one of the hazards of being a werewolf. I knew several, and they'd been my friends. When they change form, clothes and things don't go with, so when they change back, they're stark naked.

I'll give Bob this much—the little creep had good taste. Changing into a wolf must be a really fantastic exercise regimen, because Andi and naked went really well together. Although at the moment, I was mostly impressed with her great big, slightly heaving gun.

"*Bob*," I said more urgently. I put my hand out, trying to get it between the skull and Andi without actually reaching for it.

"Hey!" Bob demanded. "Dammit, Harry! It's not like I get much of a chance to see 'em!"

Andi's eyes widened. "Bob . . . is it really him?"

"Yes, but he works for the bad guys now," Bob said. "It's probably safest to shoot him."

"Hey!" I said.

"Nothing personal," Bob assured me. "What would *you* advise a client to do if the Winter Knight broke into her place, fought with her, and cracked two of her ribs?"

"Not to shoot," I said. "The bullet's going to bounce and there are way too many people in the apartments around us."

At that, Andi took her finger off the trigger, though she left it extended and pressed against the guard. She exhaled slowly. "That's . . . more like what I would expect from . . . from you, Harry." She swallowed. "Is it really you?"

"Whatever's left of me," I said.

"We heard about your ghost. I could even sort of . . . sort of smell you, when you were near. I knew. We thought you were dead."

"Wasn't really my ghost," I said. "It was me. I just sort of forgot to bring my body along with me." I coughed. "Think you could maybe point that somewhere else?"

"My finger's not on the trigger," she said. "Don't be such a baby. I'm thinking." She watched me for a moment and said, "Okay, let's assume it's really you. What are you doing here?"

"I came for the skull," I said.

"I'm invaluable!" Bob piped.

"Useful." I scowled at him. "Don't get cocky."

"I know you came for the skull," Andi said. "Why now? In the middle of the night? Why break in? Harry, all you had to do was ask."

I ground my teeth. "Andi . . . I don't have a lot of time. So I'm going to give you the short answer. Okay?"

"Okay."

"When I break in here and *take* something from Butters, he's my victim and of no particular consequence. If I come here and *ask* him for help, he's my accomplice, and it makes him a target for the people I'm working against."

She frowned. "What people?"

I sighed. "That's the kind of thing I'd tell an accomplice, Andi."

"Um," she said, "isn't that kind of what we are?"

"It's what you *were*," I said, with gentle emphasis. "Bob's right. I'm not exactly on the side of the angels right now. And I'm not taking you and Butters down the drain with me."

"Say, Harry," Bob asked, "who *are* you up against?"

"Not in front of the eye-stander-bey," I said.

"Just trolling for info like a good lackey," Bob said. "You understand."

"Sure," I said.

Andi frowned. "Bob isn't . . . Isn't he supposed to be yours?"

"I'm not the present owner of the skull," I said. "Whoever has the skull has Bob's loyalty."

"Services," Bob corrected me. "Don't get cocky. And right now I'm working for Butters. And you, of course, toots."

"Toots," Andi said in a flat voice. "Did you really just say that?" Her gaze shifted to me. "Bystander?"

"If you don't know anything," I said, "there's no reason for anyone to torture you to death to find it."

That made her face turn a little pale.

"These people think the *Saw* movies were hilarious," I said. "They'll hurt you because for them, it feels better than sex. They won't hesitate. And I'm trying to give you all the cover I can. You and Butters both." I shook my head and lowered my hands. "I need you to trust me, Andi. I'll have Bob back here before dawn."

She frowned. "Why by then?"

"Because I don't want the people I work for to get hold of him either," I said. "He's not the same thing as a human—"

"*Thank* you," Bob said. "I explain and explain that, but no one listens."

"—but he's still kind of a friend."

Bob made a gagging sound. "Don't get all sappy on me, Dresden."

"Andi," I said, ignoring him. "I don't have any more time. I'm gonna pick up the skull now. You gonna shoot me or what?"

Andi let out a short, frustrated breath and sagged back against the table. She lowered the gun, grimaced, and slipped one hand across her stomach to press against her ribs on the other side.

I didn't look at what that motion did to her chest, because that would have been grotesquely inappropriate, regardless of how fascinating the resulting contours may or may not have been.

I picked up the skull, an old, familiar shape and weight in my hand. There was a flitter in the flickering eyelights, and maybe a subtle change of hue in the flames.

"Awright!" Bob crowed. "Back in the saddle!"

"Pipe down," I said. "I've got backup with me. The other team might have surveillance on me that is just as invisible. I'd rather they didn't listen to every word."

"Piping down, O mighty one," Bob replied.

When I turned back to Andi, she looked horrified. "Oh, God, Harry. Your back."

I grunted, twisted a bit, and got a look at myself in the reflection in the window. My jacket was in tatters and stained with blots of blood. It hurt, but not horribly, maybe as much as a bad sunburn.

"I'm sorry," Andi said.

"I'll live," I said. I walked over to her, leaned down, and kissed the top of her head. "I'm sorry about your ribs. And the computers. I'll make up the damages to you guys."

She shook her head. "Don't worry about it. Whatever, you know. Whatever we can do to help."

I sighed and said, "Yeah, about that. Um. I'm sorry about this, too."

She frowned and looked up at me. "About what?"

I was going to deck her, clip her on the chin and put her down for a few moments while I left. That would do two things. First, it would prevent her from getting all heroic and following me. Second, if I was currently being observed, it would sell the notion that I had stolen Bob from her. It was a logical, if ruthless move that would give her an extra layer of protection, however thin.

But when I told my hand to move, it wouldn't.

Winter Knight, Mab's assassin, whatever. I don't hit girls.

I sighed. "I'm sorry I can't deck you right now."

She lifted both eyebrows. "Oh. You think you'd be protecting me, I take it?"

"As screwed up as it is to think that—yeah, I would be."

"I've been protecting myself just fine for a year, Harry," Andi said. "Even without you around."

Ouch. I winced.

Andi looked down. "I didn't . . . Sorry."

"No worries," I said. "Better call the police after I'm gone. Report an intruder. It's what you'd do if a burglar had broken in."

She nodded. "Is it all right if I talk to Butters about it?"

This whole thing would have been a lot simpler if I could have kept anyone from getting involved. That had been the point of the burglary. But now . . . Well. Andi knew, and I owed her more than to ask her to keep secrets from Butters, whom I owed even more. "Carefully," I said. "Behind your threshold. And . . . maybe not anyone else just yet. Okay?"

"Okay," she said quietly.

"Thanks." I didn't know what else to say, so I added another "I'm sorry."

Then I took the skull and hurried back out into the night.

11

Once I was in the hearse again, I started driving. I had a silent and nearly invisible squadron of the Za Lord's Guard flying in a loose formation around the car, except for Toot, who perched on the back of the passenger seat. Bob's skull sat in the seat proper, its glowing eye sockets turned toward me.

"So, boss," Bob said brightly, "where we headed?"

"Nowhere yet," I said. "But I'm operating on the theory that a moving target is harder to hit."

"That's a little more paranoid than usual," Bob said. "I approve. But why?"

I grimaced. "Mab wants me to kill Maeve."

"*What?*" Bob squeaked.

Toot fell off the back of the passenger seat in a fit of shock.

"You heard me," I said. "You okay, Toot?"

"Just . . . checking for assassins, my lord," Toot said gamely. "All clear back here."

"That doesn't make any sense," Bob said. "Tell me everything."

So I did.

"And then she told me to kill Maeve," I finished, "and I decided to come looking for you."

"Wait, wait, wait," Bob said. "Let me get this straight. Mab gave you a whole girl, all to yourself, and you didn't even get to first base?"

I scowled. "Bob, can you focus, please? This isn't about the girl."

Bob snorted. "Making this the first time it hasn't been about the girl, I guess."

"Maeve, Bob," I said. "What I need to know is why Mab would want her dead."

"Maybe she's trying to flunk you intentionally," Bob said.

"Why do you say that?"

"Because you *can't* kill Maeve, Harry."

"I don't want to do it," I said. "I'm not even sure if I'm going to."

"You're too busy wrestling with your stupid conscience to listen to me, boss," Bob said. "You *can't* kill her. Not might, not shouldn't. *Can't.*"

I blinked several times. "Uh. Why not?"

"Maeve's an immortal, Harry. One of the least of the immortals, maybe, but immortal all the same. Chop her up if you want to. Burn her. Scatter her ashes to the winds. But it won't kill her. She'll be back. Maybe in months, maybe years, but you can't just *kill* her. She's the Winter Lady."

I frowned. "Huh? I killed the Summer Lady just fine."

Bob made a frustrated sound. "Yeah, but that was because you were in the right place to *do* it."

"How's that?"

"Mab and Titania *created* that place specifically to be a killing ground for immortals, a place where balances of power are *supposed* to change. They've got to have a location like that for the important fights— otherwise nothing really gets decided. It's a waste of everyone's time and cannon fodder."

I'd seen part of that place being created—with my Sight, no less—and it was burned indelibly into my memory. I saw the surging energy the two Queens of Faerie were pouring out, power on a level that defied description. And of course I had, in some sense, been in that place when I murdered Lloyd Slate and took his job as Mab's triggerman.

Memory. The ancient stone table, stained with blood. Stars wheeling above me, dizzying in their speed and clarity. Writhing, cold mist reaching up over the edges of the table, clutching at my bare skin, while Mab bestrode me, her naked beauty strangling me, raking my thoughts out through my eyes. Power surging through me, into me, from the blood in the swirling grooves of the table, from Mab's hungry will.

I shuddered and forced the memory away. My hands clenched the wheel.

"So I can't kill her," I said quietly.

"No," Bob said.

I glowered out at the road. "What is the point of telling me to do something she knows is impossible?" I wondered aloud. "You're sure about this, Bob? There's no way at all, without the stone table?"

"Not really," Bob said, his eyes flicking around the car. "And not in most of the Nevernever, either."

"Hey," I said. "What's with the shifty eyes?"

"What shifty eyes?" Bob asked.

"When you said 'Not really,' your eyes got all shifty."

"Uh, no, they didn't."

"Bob."

The skull sighed. "Do I have to tell you?"

"Dude," I said. "Since when has it been like that between us?"

"Since you started working for *her*," Bob said, and somehow managed to shudder.

I tilted my head, thinking as hard as I could. "Wait. This has to do with your feud with Mab?"

"Not a feud," Bob says. "In a feud, both sides fight. This is more like me screaming and running away before she rips me apart."

I shook my head. "Man, Bob. I know you can be an annoying git when you want to be one—but what did you *do* to make Mab mad at you?"

"It isn't what I do, Harry," Bob said in a very small voice. "It's what I know."

I lifted an eyebrow. It took a lot to make the skull flinch. "And what is that, exactly?"

The lights in the eye sockets dwindled to tiny pinpoints, and his voice came out in a whisper. "I know how to kill an immortal."

"Like Maeve?" I asked him.

"Maeve," Bob said. "Mab. Mother Winter. Any of them."

Holy crap.

Now, *that* was a piece of information worth killing for.

If the skull knew how to subtract the *im* from *immortal*, then he could be a source of danger to beings of power throughout the universe. Hell, he was lucky that gods and demons and supernatural powers everywhere hadn't formed up in a safari and come gunning for him. And it meant that maybe I wasn't looking at an impossible mission after all.

"I'd like you to tell me," I said.

"No way," Bob said. "No way. The only reason I've been around this long is that I've kept my mouth shut. If I start shooting it off now, Mab and every other immortal with an interest in this stupid planet are going to smash my skull to powder and leave me out to fry in the sun." The eyelights bobbed toward the rear compartment. "And there are too many ears around here."

"Toot," I said, "get everybody out of the car. I need privacy. Make sure no one gets close enough to eavesdrop."

"Aw," Toot complained from the rear compartment. "Not even me?"

"You're the only one I can trust to keep those other mugs from doing it, Major General. No one overhears. Got it?"

I could practically hear the pride bursting out of his voice: "Got it!" he piped. "Will do, my lord!"

He rolled down a window and buzzed out. I rolled it back up and took a look around the hearse with both normal and supernatural senses, to be sure we were alone. Then I turned back to the skull.

"Bob, it's just you and me talking here. Think about this. Mab sends me off to kill Maeve, something that would be impossible for me to do on my own—and she *knew* that you know how to do it. She knew the first thing I would do is come back *here* as the first step in the job. I think she meant for me to come to you. I think she meant for you to tell me."

The skull considered that for a moment. "It's indirect and manipulative, so you're probably onto something. Let me think." A long minute went by. Then he spoke very quietly. "If I tell you," he said, "you've got to do something for me."

"Like what?"

"A new vessel," he said. "You've got to make me a new house. Somewhere I can get to it. Then if they come after this one, I've got somewhere else to go."

"Tall order for me," I said soberly. "You've basically got your own little pocket dimension in there. I've never tried anything that complicated before. Not even Little Chicago."

"Promise me," Bob said. "Promise me on your power."

Swearing by one's power is how a wizard makes a verbal contract. If you break your word, your ability with magic starts to fray, and if you keep doing it, sooner or later it'll just wither up and die. A broken promise, sworn by my power, could set me back years and years in terms of my ability to use magic. I held up my hand. "I swear, on my power, to construct a new vessel for you if you tell me, Bob, assuming I survive the next few days. Just . . . don't expect a deluxe place like you have now."

The flickering eyelights flared up to their normal size again. "Don't worry, boss," Bob said with compassion. "I won't."

"Wiseass."

"Right, then!" Bob said. "The only way to kill an immortal is at certain specific places."

"And you know one? Where?"

"Hah, already you're making a human assumption. There are more than three dimensions, Harry. Not all places are in space. Some of them are places in *time*. They're called conjunctions."

"I know about conjunctions, Bob," I said, annoyed. "When the stars and planets align. You can use them to support heavy-duty magic sometimes."

"That's one way to measure a conjunction," said the skull. "But stars and planets are ultimately just measuring stakes used to describe a position in time. And that's one way to *use* a conjunction, but they do other things, too."

I nodded thoughtfully. "And there's a conjunction when immortals are vulnerable?"

"Give the man a cookie; he's got the idea. Every year."

"When is it?"

"On Halloween night, of course."

I slammed on the brakes and pulled the car to the side of the road. "Say that again?"

"Halloween," Bob said, his voice turning sober. "It's when the world of the dead is closest to the mortal world. Everyone—everything—standing in this world is mortal on Halloween."

I let out a low, slow whistle.

"I doubt there are more than a couple of people alive who know that, Harry," Bob said. "And the immortals *will* keep it that way."

"Why are they so worried?" I asked. "I mean, why not just not show up on Halloween night?"

"Because it's when they . . ." He made a frustrated noise. "It's hard to explain, because you don't have the right conceptual models. You can barely count to four dimensions."

"I think the math guys can go into the teens. Skip the insults and try."

"Halloween is when they feed," Bob said. "Or . . . or refuel. Or run free. It's all sort of the same thing, and I'm only conveying a small part of it. Halloween night is when the locked stasis of immortality becomes malleable. They take in energy—and it's when they can add new power to their mantle. Mostly they steal tiny bits of it from other immortals."

"Those Kemmlerite freaks and their Darkhallow," I breathed. "That was Halloween night."

"Exactly!" Bob said. "That ritual was supposed to turn one of them *into* an immortal. And the same rule applies—that's the only night of the year it actually can happen. I doubt all of *them* knew that it had to be that night. But I betcha Cowl did. Guy is seriously scary."

"Seriously in need of a body cast and a therapist, more like." I raked at my too-long, too-messy hair with my fingers, thinking. "So on Halloween, they're here? All of them?"

"Any who are . . . The only word I can come close with is 'awake.' Immortals aren't always moving through the time stream at the same rate as the universe. From where you stand, it looks like they're dormant. They aren't. You just can't perceive the true state of their existence properly."

"They're *here*," I said slowly. "Feeding and swindling one another for little bits of power."

"Right."

"They're trick-or-treating?"

"Duh," Bob said. "Where do you think that comes from?"

"Ugh, this whole time? That is creepy beyond belief," I said.

"I think it was the second or third Merlin of the White Council who engineered the whole Halloween custom. That's the real reason people started wearing masks on that night, back in the day. It was so that any hungry immortal who came by might—might—think twice before gobbling someone up. After all, they could never be sure the person behind the mask wasn't another immortal, setting them up."

"Halloween is tomorrow night," I said. A bank sign I was passing told me it was a bit after two a.m. "Or tonight, I guess, technically."

"What a coincidence," Bob said. "Happy birthday, by the way. I didn't get you anything."

Except maybe my life. "'S okay. I'm kinda birthdayed out already." I rubbed at my jaw. "So . . . if I can get to Maeve on Halloween night, I can kill her."

"Well," Bob hedged. "You can try, anyway. It's technically possible. It doesn't mean you're strong enough to do it."

"How big a window do I have? When does Halloween night end?" I asked.

"At the first natural morning birdsong," Bob replied promptly. "Songbirds, rooster, whatever. They start to sing, the night ends."

"Oh, good. A deadline." I narrowed my eyes, thinking. "Gives me a bit more than twenty-four hours, then," I muttered. "And all I have to do is find her, when she can be anywhere in the world *or* the Nevernever, then get her here, then beat her down, all without her escaping or killing me first. Simple."

"Yep. Almost impossible, but simple. And at least you know the when and the how," Bob said.

"But I'm no closer to why."

"Can't help you there, boss," the skull said. "I'm a spirit of intellect, and the premise we're dealing with makes no sense."

"Why not?"

"Because there's no *reason* for it," Bob said, his tone unhappy. "I mean, when Maeve dies, there will just be another Maeve."

I frowned. "What do you mean?"

Bob sighed. "You keep thinking of the Faerie Queens as specific individuals, Harry," Bob said. "But they aren't individuals. They're mantles of power, roles, positions. The person in them is basically an interchangeable part."

"What, like being the Winter Knight is?"

"Exactly like that," Bob said. "When you killed Slate, the power, the mantle, just transferred over to you. It's the same for the Queens of Faerie. Maeve wears the mantle of the Winter Lady. Kill her, and you'll just get a new Winter Lady."

"Maybe that's what Mab wants," I said.

"Doesn't track," Bob said.

"Why not?" I asked.

"Because the mantle changes whoever wears it."

My guts felt suddenly cold.

(*I'm not Lloyd Slate.*)

(*Neither was he. Not at first.*)

"Doesn't matter who it is," Bob prattled on. "Over time, it changes them. Somewhere down the line, you wouldn't be able to find much difference between Maeve and her successor. Meet the new Maeve. Same as the old Maeve."

I swallowed. "So . . . so Lily, who took the Summer Lady's mantle after I killed Aurora . . ."

"It's been what? Ten years or so? She's gone by now, or getting there," Bob said. "Give it another decade or two, tops, and she might as well *be* Aurora."

I was quiet for a moment. Then I asked, "Is that going to happen to me, too?"

Bob hedged. "You've . . . probably felt it starting. Um, strong impulses. Intense emotions. That kind of thing. It builds. And it doesn't stop." He managed to give the impression of a wince. "Sorry, boss."

I stared at my knuckles for a moment. "So," I said, "even if I frag this Maeve, another one steps up. Maybe not for decades, but she does."

"Immortals don't really care about decades, boss," Bob said. "To them, it's like a few weeks are to you."

I nodded thoughtfully. "Then maybe it's about the timing."

"How so?"

I shrugged. "Hell if I know, but it's the only thing I can think of. Maybe Mab wants a less Maeve-ish Maeve for the next few years."

"Why?" Bob asked.

I growled. "I already have one why. I don't need you adding more." I drummed my fingers on the steering wheel. "Why doesn't Mab do it herself?"

"Oh, I see. It's okay if *you* add more whys. You have complicated rules, Harry."

I ignored that with the disdain it deserved. "I'm serious. Mab has the power. What's stopping her from tearing Maeve to shreds?"

"Something?" Bob suggested.

"I can't believe I got my tux shredded for brilliant analysis like that," I said.

"Hey!" Bob said. "I just told you something so valuable that it could save your life! Or get you killed!"

"Yeah." I sighed. "You did. But it isn't enough. I need more information."

"You do know a few people around here," Bob said.

I growled. "My physical therapist, who I've known for three whole months, nearly died tonight because she showed up at a party with me— and that was with Mab looking over my shoulder as a referee."

"How is that any different from the last time you played with faeries?"

"Because now I know them," I said. It was actually sort of scary looking back at the me from a decade ago. That guy was terrifying in his ignorance. "Aurora and her crew were basically a decent crowd. Misguided, yeah. But to them, we were the bad guys. They were tough, but they weren't killers. Maeve's different."

"How?" Bob asked.

"She doesn't have limits," I said.

"And you figure you're up against her."

"I know I am," I said. "And she's grown powerful enough to challenge Mab in her own court. I also know more about Mab now, and all of it scares the crap out of me." I snorted, and felt a tremble of winged insects in my midsection. "And apparently Maeve is a *threat* to her. And I'm supposed to deal with it."

Bob whistled. "Well. Maybe that explains it."

"Explains what?"

"Why Mab was so hell-bent on getting *you* to be the new Knight," Bob said. "I mean, you're kind of an avatar of the phrase 'Things fall apart.' Mab has a target she wants to be absolutely sure of. You're like . . . her guided missile. She can't know exactly what's going to happen, but she knows there's going to be a great big boom."

"I'm a missile, huh?"

"Her big, dumb bunker buster," he said cheerily. "Of course, you know the thing about missiles, Harry."

"Yeah," I said, as I put the Caddy back in gear again. "They're expendable."

"Buck up, little camper. At least you had a hot redhead jump your bones tonight. Not the *right* bone, but you can't have everything."

I snorted. "Thanks, Bob."

"Andi totally got the drop on you. Where was your tiny secret service team?"

"I forgot to invite them past the threshold," I said. "Besides, I think she'd hit me before anyone could have shouted a lookout anyway."

"You ever think about replacing them with some real bodyguard goons, Harry? I know a thing that knows a thing."

"Screw that. Toot and his gang aren't exactly gangstas, but I trust them. That means more."

"That means you're a sucker!" Bob said. "Did *The X-Files* teach you nothing? Trust no one."

I grunted. "Cat Sith gave me almost the same advice."

"Ack," Bob said. "That guy. He still got the attitude?"

"I feel safe in assuming that he does."

"I don't like him, but he's no dummy," Bob said. "At least he gives good advice."

"Mathematically, maybe," I said. "But trust isn't one of those things that lends itself well to math."

"Sure it does," Bob said. "You trust somebody, they betray you, you get a negative value. You never trust, they can never disappoint you, you break even."

I laughed. "Or you trust, it's vindicated, and you're better off."

"Shah," Bob said. "Like that happens."

"Life's about more than breaking even," I said.

Bob snorted. "Which is why the first thing you did, when you got back to town, was call all of your friends and immediately tell them you needed their help, and trust them to help you."

I scowled out at the road.

"It wasn't like the first thing you did was abuse one of your friends and inflict property damage on his house and steal a powerful magical counselor whose loyalties are transferrable to whoever happens to be holding an old skull—presumably so that you'd have a lackey who would agree with whatever you said instead of give you a hard time about it. And the only beings you're allowing to help you are a bunch of tiny faeries who worship the ground you walk on because you buy them pizza." Bob made a skeptical sound. "I can see how important trust is to you, boss."

"That's why I got you, clearly," I said. "Because I wanted a yes-man and you're so good for that."

"Hey, I'm just a mirror, boss. Not my fault you're ambivalent."

"I'm not ambivalent."

"You know better, but you're being a moron about it anyway," Bob said. "If that ain't ambivalence, maybe Mab's getting to you. Because it's a little crazy." He sniffed. "Besides, if you weren't of two minds about it, I wouldn't be giving you this kind of crap, now, would I?"

I was going to say something sarcastic, but the red glare of a stoplight suddenly appeared about ten feet in front of the old Caddy's nose. I stared at the light for a fraction of a second, and then mashed the brakes down. I had an instant to see that it wasn't a traffic signal, but Toot-toot, his aura glaring brilliant scarlet, frantically waving his arms at me. As the Caddy lumbered forward, I saw him take a couple of steps forward, running up the windshield, and up out of sight above me.

As the heavy old piece of Detroit iron began to slide on the asphalt,

I saw an object tumble out of the air in front of me and hit the street, turning over and over. I had another instant to recognize a plain black nylon duffel bag.

And then the world went white and a hammer the size of the Chrysler Building slammed me back against the old Caddy's seat.

12

The bomb might have been fifty feet away when it exploded.

Mab's therapy had paid off. On raw instinct, I'd already begun to form a defensive shield in front of me when everything went boom. I hadn't had time to build much of a shield, but what little I could do probably kept me conscious.

Explosions are unbelievably loud. If you haven't been near one, there's no way to convey the sheer violence of it. It doesn't really register as a sound, the way a gunshot will. There's just this single, terrible *power* in the air, a sudden hammer blow of disorienting pressure, as if you've been hit by a truck made of pillow-top mattresses.

Your hearing goes. There's a familiar, high-pitched tone, only no one is telling you that this is a test of the Emergency Broadcast System. There's dust and smoke everywhere, and you can't see. Your muscles don't all work right. You tell them to move and it's iffy. Maybe they do; maybe they don't. It's hard to tell which way is down. Not that you don't know it rationally, somewhere in your head—but your body just seems to forget its natural awareness of gravity.

Even if something sharp and fast doesn't go flying through some of your favorite organs, a nearby explosion leaves you half-blind, deaf, and drunkenly impaired.

Vulnerable.

One moment the Caddy was screeching and sliding toward that black duffel bag. The next, I was staring at a cloud of dust and the dim image of a brick wall at the end of the Caddy's nose. The windshield had been splintered into a webwork of cracks that made it hard to see. My chest hurt like hell.

I picked fitfully at it, my fingers clumsy, and thought to myself that the car Sith had provided must have had armored glass, or there would be windshield mixed in with my intestines. Lights danced and darted in my vision. My eyes wouldn't focus enough to track them. Smells were incredibly sharp. The air was acrid, thick with smoke, laced with the scents of things it is unhealthy to burn. I smelled gasoline nearby. There were wires hanging down from something in the corner of my vision, outside the car, spitting white sparks.

None of it seemed normal, but I couldn't quite remember the right word to describe it.

Danger.

Right. That was it. Danger. I was in danger.

A moving target is harder to hit.

I pushed open the passenger door and stumbled out of the car, choking on dust. Another car wreck? Man, Mike was going to charge me a small fortune to fix the *Blue Beetle* this time. Did I have the money in the bank? I couldn't remember whether I'd deposited my last stipend check from the Wardens.

No, wait. The car I'd just gotten out of wasn't the *Blue Beetle*, my trusty old Volkswagen Bug that had died in the line of duty. It was the creepy Herman Munster hot rod my boss had gotten m—

My brain finished rebooting, and things snapped back into focus; someone had just tried to bomb me back into the Stone Age.

I shook my head, gagging on dust, then dragged the Redcap's hat down off my head and over my mouth as a dust mask. The Caddy was up on the curb and had hit a building. The building had gotten the worst of it. One of the Caddy's headlights was out, its front fender crumpled a bit, and the passenger door had been thrown open, but otherwise the car was fine. Maybe ten or twelve square feet of brick wall had fallen out, some of it onto the hood, some of it onto the sidewalk. I looked around. It was hard to see through the dust. There were a lot of busted-up walls. Several small fires. A streetlight had come swinging down from the line that supported it—that was where the sparking cables came from.

Lights still darted and flickered randomly, and I blinked, trying to clear the stars away. But stars in the vision were usually white and silver. These were orange and red, like the embers of a fire.

Then one of those lights pivoted in midair and flashed toward my eyes. I jerked away from it, still clumsy, and a sudden spike of agony burned through my face.

I screamed and staggered to one knee. Something had gone through my cheek and was still there, tacking the damned Cincinnati cap to my face. I reached for it on instinct, but before I could get to it, pain exploded from my back, from the fresh wounds there, from my bruised hands, from my throat where the Redcap had nearly crushed it.

That *did* put me on the ground. It was too much to process, much less ignore. I reacted on blind animal instinct, swiping at the most intense source of pain with my paw. There was another flash of agony, and suddenly the hat came away from my face. A bloodied nail a good four inches long fell away with the hat, its last two inches bloodied, its other end swathed in duct tape.

The instant it came free, I felt my pain recede again, back to the dull background annoyance it had been a few moments before. My thoughts cleared as the agony retreated.

Someone had shot me? With a freaking nail gun? What the hell was going on here?

No sooner had I thought that than another light flashed toward me, and before I could react, a second round of utterly ridiculous levels of pain slammed through me, starting at my leg. The other pains resurfaced, with the fresh addition of my throbbing face. I screamed and swatted, and tore a second nail, much like the first, from the flesh of my right quadriceps. Again that cold power flooded into me, making pain distant, making thoughts more clear.

The ember-colored lights were coming at me too fast. There was no time to get a defensive spell up, not in my condition, and my body, Winter Knight or not, wasn't fast enough to dodge or swat them out of the way. Even as I processed those thoughts, a third nail hit me in the left arm, and I had to scream and thrash my way out of another spike of pure agony. I felt utterly helpless, and stunned at my inability to overcome so tiny a foe.

And I suddenly knew how the late Summer Lady, Aurora, had felt at the end.

"Get up, Harry," I panted, fighting through the disorientation, the polar shifts in pain. "Get up before they nail you."

Nail you. Get it?

But I always joke when I'm afraid, and I was terrified. Whatever these things were, if they got more than one of those nails into me, I doubted I would be able to hold my thoughts together long enough to get them out again. I had a gruesome vision of myself stretched in lifeless, agonized rigor on the sidewalk, nails sticking out of every square inch of my skin.

I tried to scramble, to evade, but compared to the darting motes of light, I was moving in slow-motion replay. Half a dozen more of the glimmering things came arrowing toward me out of the night, zooming at me in a flying V formation, and I knew things were about to get really bad.

Then someone blew on a coach's whistle, a sound I heard even through my stunned ears, and a tiny, distant voice piped, "To the Za Lord!"

Half a dozen little cool blue spheres of light flashed toward my attackers, intercepting them only a couple of feet from my body. Six explosions of sparks and glowing motes lit the night, various colors swirling and spinning, as the tiny soldiers of the Za Lord's Guard closed to battle with my attackers.

Toot soared in from directly overhead, his heels landing hard on my stomach. For somebody the size of a chicken, he was strong, and my breath huffed out as I was knocked back to the ground. He planted his feet wide, a snarl on his tiny face, his shield hefted up to a defensive position, his table-knife sword in hand. "Stay down, my lord! Wait until we clear a path for escape!"

A path? I took a second to look around. I saw one of Toot's "kernels" go by, flying sideways, wielding a spear made of a straight pin and a pencil against another of the Little Folk, a humanish figure dressed in what looked like actual black armor made of some kind of shaped plastic or maybe carapace, and carrying another of the too-familiar nails. The enemy faerie was wounded, and glowing motes of scarlet and sullen orange light dribbled from a straight pin–inflicted wound on his tiny leg.

Sullen and chill spheres of light darted *everywhere*, dozens of them, all spinning and diving and looping at once. There was no way to track all of that motion. Even if I'd been completely clearheaded, I would have done well to follow a tenth of it.

Five or six more enemy fae, larger and brighter than the others, dived down at me bearing a nail sword in each hand. They let out shrill, eerie little cries as they came at me—and at Toot-toot.

Okay, I've thought a lot of things about Toot-toot over the years. I've compared him to a lot of really humorous stuff, and occasionally to people I didn't admire too much. I've made jokes at his expense, though never when I thought it would hurt him. But if you'd asked me for a perfect parallel for the little guy a year ago, I would never, ever, *ever* have said, "King Leonidas."

Toot let out a high-pitched roar and leapt into the air. He smashed his shield into the black-armored fae in the center of the enemy formation, spinning as he did, to send the luckless faerie careening into the companion on his left. Toot's sword lashed out, and a single dragonfly wing went fluttering free of the body it had been attached to. The little fae went spinning out of the air to crash into a pile of fallen bricks and rubble.

Two got through.

Agony.

The next thing I knew, Toot was pulling a nail from the muscle over my abdomen, and fresh hits there and in my left pectoral muscle had added their toll of pain to my evening. Toot, gripping the nail carefully by its duct-tape handle, turned and flung it at a pair of dueling fae, striking the orange-lit enemy with the broad side of the steel nail. There was a flash of white light, and the hit fae let out a shriek that started at the edge of human hearing and went up into dog frequencies, and darted away, the guard in hot pursuit.

"They're breaking!" Toot bellowed. Well. As much as someone who can fit in a bread box can bellow. "After them, kernels!"

Sullen lights slithered away in panic, while bright balls of blue buzzed after them.

"Permission to pursue those jerks, my lord?" Toot shouted.

I finally had a couple of seconds to get my head together. I shook it violently. It didn't help, but the simple act of putting together recognition of a problem, consideration of a solution, and taking action to fix it had gotten my mental house in some kind of order.

"It's a feint," I said, looking around. "They're luring the guard away."

There. High up. Way the hell high up, maybe twenty stories. A blob of ember-colored light suddenly plunged off of a balcony and began to fall toward us. As it came closer, the blob broke apart into dozens of angry little spheres. They began to bob and interweave, picking up more and more speed, the patterns dizzying, confusing. Streaking lights peeled off from the main cloud in every direction.

Toot, once more perched on my stomach, stared up at them, his mouth open. His left arm sagged, his shield dropping down to his side. "Uh-oh." He gulped. "Um. I'm not sure I can get them all, my lord."

I sat up, forcing him off my stomach, and gained my feet. "You did good, Toot," I growled. "Okay, small fry. Wizard time."

A couple of years back, me and my apprentice, Molly, had been studying air magic as part of her basic grounding in the elemental forces. She hadn't ever picked up the knack for using blasts of wind as weapons, but she had managed to develop a spell that did a passable imitation of a blow-dryer.

I lifted my right hand, summoned my will, and readied the blow-dryer spell.

Only I turned it to eleven.

"*Ventas reductas!*" I thundered, unleashing my will, and an arctic gale came howling and shrieking from my outstretched hand. It condensed the damp October air into mist, too, bellowing out from my hand in a cone the size of an apartment building. Frost formed on every surface in the immediate area. It struck the cloud of diving Little Folk and sent them tumbling in every direction. Little orange lights went spinning and wobbling, their complex formation shattered.

I saw them begin to gather to one side, trying to re-form, but I poured on the wind and altered the direction of the blast, scattering them again.

Molly's spell was more efficient than anything I'd come up with when I had her level of experience, but there's no free lunch. That much wind takes a lot of energy to whip up, and I wasn't going to be able to hold it forever.

Abruptly, Toot flashed away from me, diving through the air, his wings a blur. He vanished behind the nose of a parked car on the other side of the street, brandishing his sword.

A brawl spilled out from the tail end of the car an instant later. One of the enemy Little Folk went tumbling in a windmill of arms and legs and fetched up against the corpse of the traffic signal. Two went darting away in obvious panic, their flight erratic and swift, dropping their nail swords as they fled.

And then there was a flash of sparks as steel struck steel, and Toot came out from behind the truck, frantically defending himself from another of the Little Folk almost as tall as he was. The foe was dressed in black armor covered in spikes made from the tips of freaking fishhooks, even the helmet, and he fought with what seemed to be an actual sword designed to size, a wavy-bladed thing that I think was called a flamberge.

As I watched, the enemy champion's blade sheared half an inch of aluminum from the top of Toot's shield, and he followed up with a series of heavy two-handed blows meant to divide Toot in half.

Toot bobbed and weaved like a reed, but the assault was ferocious, the foe as fast as he was. He got the flat of the shield in front of another blow, stopping it, but on the next strike the flamberge's wavy blade caught on the edge of the shield and sliced through it again, leaving it little more than a rectangle of aluminum strapped to Toot's arm. Toot took to the air, but his opponent matched him, and they darted and spun around a light pole, the enemy's sword meeting Toot's improvised blade in flashes of silver sparks.

I wanted to intervene, but, like it always does, size mattered. My target was tiny and moving fast. The pair of them were darting around so much that even if I got lucky and hit someone, I probably had as much chance of taking out Toot as I did Captain Hook over there. My evocation magic was more focused and precise than it had ever been, thanks to

Mab, but my control still wasn't up to the task of being *that* discriminating. And besides—I still had to keep my giant leaf blower going against the rest of Hook's goons. All I could do was watch.

Hook swung at Toot's head, but Toot ducked in the nick of time, and the flamberge caught briefly in the metal of the streetlight's post.

"Aha!" Toot said, and slammed his table knife down onto Hook's armored hand.

The other fae reeled, obviously in pain, and the flamberge fell to the ground.

"Surrender, villain!" Toot cried. "Face the justice of the Za Lord!"

"Never!" answered another piping voice from within the helmet, and Hook produced a pair of toothpick-slender daggers. He made a scissor shape of them and caught Toot's next attack in it, flicking the table knife aside and whipping his dagger at Toot's throat. Toot recoiled, but took a long cut across his chest, the knife shearing through his armor just as the flamberge had done.

My major general screamed in pain, recoiling.

It was the opening I'd needed, and I twisted my leaf blower around to slam into Hook. It caught the little fae as he was starting to move toward Toot-toot, sending him tumbling into the side of a building, while the back blast of wind actually threw Toot clear. He managed to recover in midair, wings blurring, and shot unsteadily toward me. I caught him in my free hand, drawing him in close against my side, and turned partly away from Hook, sheltering Toot.

The cloud of hostile fae was still swirling and wobbling around. They obviously lacked any kind of leadership, and were still disordered by the gale-force winds with which I'd hit them—but I was almost out of energy, and about two seconds after they got their act together, I was a dead man.

"Feets don't fail me now," I muttered.

I kept the leaf blower on Hook, who I suspected was their leader, and strode forward, toward the car. I checked it with several quick glances. The gasoline smell wasn't coming from the Caddy, but from a half-smashed car that had been close to the exploding duffel bag.

I gave the leaf blower one last surge of power and lunged into the Caddy, slamming the door behind me. I dumped Toot down next to Bob as gently as I could.

"What's happening?" Bob shouted blearily from where he'd landed, sideways, in the well of the passenger seat.

"I'm getting my ass kicked by tiny faeries!" I shouted back, fumbling to start the car. "They've got my freaking number!"

There was a loud pop, and a slender miniature steel dagger slammed through the passenger window, transforming it into a broken webwork, as difficult to see through as a stained-glass window.

"Ack!" I said.

Bob started laughing hysterically.

The dagger vanished and then the same thing happened on the driver's side.

Holy crap, Hook was way too bright for someone the size of a Tickle Me Elmo. He was blinding me.

I got the Caddy into reverse and rumbled back off the sidewalk onto the street, shedding bricks and debris as I went. Just as I bounced down onto the street proper, the front windshield exploded into a web of cracks, too, so I just kept driving backward, turning to look over my shoulder. That went well for a few seconds, and then the rear window broke, too.

I gritted my teeth. Under normal circumstances, the next move would be to roll down the window and stick my head out of it. Tonight, I was pretty sure I'd get a miniature dagger in the eye if I tried.

Sometimes you have to choose between doing something stupid and doing something suicidal. So I kept driving blind and backward through the middle of Chicago while Bob chortled his bony ass off.

"Tiny faeries!" He giggled, rolling a bit as the Caddy weaved and jounced. "Tiny faeries!"

My plan worked for about ten seconds—and then I slammed into a parked car. I was lucky that it wasn't a large one. I mean, I couldn't see it, but it bounced off the Caddy like a billiard ball struck by the cue ball. It also knocked the wheel out of my hands, wrenching it from my fingers and sending the Caddy onto another sidewalk. It smashed through a metal railing and then the back tires bounced down into a sunken stairwell.

I struggled to get the Caddy clear, but there was nothing for the tires to grab onto.

End of the line.

I let out a heartfelt curse and slammed a fist against the steering wheel. Then I made myself close my eyes and think. *Think, think, don't react in panic. Keep your head, Dresden.*

"Major General," I said. "You okay?"

"It's not bad, my lord." He gasped. "I've had worse."

"We've got to move," I said.

"Run away!" Bob giggled. "Run away! Tiny faeries!"

I growled in frustration and popped the Redcap's hat down over Bob. "Stop being a jerk. This is serious."

Bob's voice was only barely muffled. It sounded like he couldn't breathe. "Serious! Tiny! Faeries! The m-m-mighty wizard Dresden!"

"You are not as funny as you think you are," I said severely. "Toot, you got any ideas?"

"Trap them all in a circle?" Toot suggested.

I sighed. Right. I'd just need to get them all to land in the same place at the same time, inside of a magic circle I had no means to create.

Toot's a great little guy. Just . . . not really adviser material.

Orange light began to bathe the broken windows, highlighting the webwork of cracks in them. A lot of orange light.

"Crap," I gasped. "I am *not* going to be known as the wizard who used his death curse thanks to a bunch of bitty nail guns."

Then there was a very sinister sound.

Toward the rear of the Caddy, someone opened the lid to the fuel tank.

It wasn't hard to work out what would happen next. Fire.

"Hell, no," I said. I recovered the ball cap, turned a still-giggling Bob upside down, and then popped Toot into the skull. He sprawled in it, arms and legs sticking out, but he didn't complain.

"Hey!" Bob protested.

"Serves you right, Giggles," I snapped. I tucked the skull under my arm like a football.

I knew I didn't have much of a chance of getting away from that swarm of fae piranha, but it was an infinitely larger chance than I would have if I stayed in the car and burned to death. Hell's bells, what I wouldn't give to have my shield bracelet. Or my old staff. I didn't even have an umbrella.

I wasn't sure how much more magic I had left in me, but I readied my shield spell, shaping it to surround me as I ran. I wouldn't be able to hold it in place for long—but maybe if I got very, very lucky, I would survive the swarm long enough to find another option.

I took several sharp and completely not-panicked breaths, then piled out of the Cadillac, bringing my shield up with a shout of *"Defendarius!"*

The Little Folk started hitting my shield almost instantly. I once rode out a hailstorm in a dome-shaped Quonset hut made of corrugated steel. It sounded like that, only closer and a hell of a lot more lethal.

I went into a sprint. Between the still-present dust, the shroud of mist my leaf-blower spell had billowed forth, and the swarm of hostile fae, I could barely see. I picked a direction and ran. Ten steps. Twenty steps. The enemy continued pounding against the shield, and as I kept pouring my will into it to keep it in place, my body began to feel heavier and heavier.

Thirty steps—and I stepped into a small pothole in the sidewalk, stumbled, and fell.

Falling in a fight is generally bad. You tend not to get up again. I mean, there's a reason that the phrase "He fell" was synonymous with death for a bunch of centuries.

I fell.

And then I heard the most beautiful sound of my life. Somewhere nearby, a cat let out an angry, hissing scream.

The Little Folk live in mortal dread of *Felis domesticus*. Cats are observant, curious, and fast enough to catch the little fae. Hell, the domestic cat can stalk, kill, and subsist upon more species than any other land predator in the world. They are peerless hunters and the Little Folk know it.

The effect of the scream was instantaneous. My attackers recoiled on pure reflex, immediately darting about twenty feet into the air—even Hook. I got a chance to look up and saw a large brindle tomcat leap from the top of a trash can onto the sidewalk beside me.

"No!" shouted Hook from inside his helmet. "Slay the beast! Slay them all!"

"What? What did I ever do to *you*?" Bob protested, indignant. "I'm not even supposed to be here today!"

The fae all looked at Hook and seemed to begin gathering their courage again.

A second cat screamed nearby. And a third. And a fourth. Cats started prowling out of alleys and from beneath parked cars. Cats began pacing along building ledges twenty feet from the ground. Glowing eyes reflected light from the deep shadows between buildings.

Even Hook wasn't willing to put up with that action, I guess. The little fae champion let out a frustrated scream, then turned and darted up, up, and away, vanishing into the night. The others followed Hook, flowing away in a ribbon of emberlight.

I lay there for a second, exhausted and panting. Then I sat up and looked around.

The cats were gone, vanished as if they'd never been there.

I heard someone walk out of the alley behind me, and my body went tense and tight, despite my weariness. Then a young woman's voice said, in a passable British accent, "The Little Folk are easily startled, but they'll soon be back. And in greater numbers."

I sagged in sudden, exhausted relief. The bad guys hardly ever quote *Star Wars*.

"Molly," I breathed.

A tall young woman dressed in rather shabby secondhand clothing crouched down next to me and smiled. "Hey, boss. Welcome home."

13

"Grasshopper," I said, feeling myself smile. "Illusion. Very nice."

Molly gave me a little bow of her head. "It's what I do."

"Also good timing," I said. "Also, what the hell? How did you know I was . . . ?"

"Alive?"

"Here, but sure. How did you know?"

"Priorities, boss. Can you walk?"

"I'm good," I said, and pushed myself to my feet. It wasn't as hard as it really should have been, and I could feel my endurance rebuilding itself already, the energy coming back into me. I was still tired—don't get me wrong—but I should have been falling-down dizzy and I wasn't.

"You don't look so good," Molly said. "Was that a tux?"

"Briefly," I said. I eyed the car. "Feel like driving?"

"Sure," she said. "But . . . that's pretty stuck, Harry, unless you brought a crane."

I grunted, faintly irritated by her tone. "Just get in, start it, and give it gas gently."

Molly looked like she wanted to argue, but then she looked down abruptly. A second later, I heard sirens. She frowned, shook her head, and got into the car. The motor rumbled to life a second later.

I went down the stairwell where the car's tires were stuck, set down Bob's skull, and found a good spot beneath the rear frame. Then I set my feet, put the heels of my hands against the underside of the Caddy, and pushed.

It was hard. I mean, it was really, really gut-bustingly hard—but the Caddy groaned and then shifted and then slowly rose. I was lifting with my legs as much as my arms, putting my whole body into it, and everything in me gave off a dull burn of effort. My breath escaped my lungs in a slow groan, but then the tires were up out of the stairwell, and turning, and they caught on the sidewalk and the Caddy pulled itself the rest of the way.

I grabbed the skull, still with the mostly limp Toot-toot inside it, staggered back up out of the stairwell and into the passenger side of the car. I lifted my hand and sent a surge of will down through it, muttering, *"Forzare,"* and the overstrained windshield groaned and gave way, tearing itself free of the frame and clearing Molly's vision.

"Go," I grated.

Molly went, driving carefully. The emergency vehicles were rolling in past us, and she pulled over and drove slowly to let them by. I sat there breathing hard, and realized that the real effort of moving that much weight didn't hit you while you were actually moving it—it came in the moments after, when your muscles recovered enough to demand oxygen, right the hell now. I leaned my head against the window, panting.

"How's it going, buddy?" I asked a moment later.

"It hurts." Toot sighed. "But I'll be okay, my lord. The armor held off some of the blow."

I checked the skull. The eyelights were gone. Bob had dummied up the moment Molly was around, as per my standing orders, which had been in place since she had first become my apprentice. Bob had almost unlimited knowledge of magic. Molly had a calculated disregard for self-limitation when she thought it justified. They would have made a really scary pair, and I'd kept them carefully separate during her training.

"We need to get off the street," I said. "Someplace quiet and secure."

"I know a place just like that," Molly said. "What happened?"

"Someone tossed a gym bag full of explosives at my car," I growled. "And followed it up with the freaking pixie death squadron from hell."

"You mean they picked *this* car out of all the other traffic?" she asked, her tone dry. "What are the odds?"

I grunted. "One more reason to get off the street, pronto."

"Relax," she said. "I started veiling the car as soon as we passed the police. If someone was following you before, they aren't now. Catch your breath, Harry. We'll be there soon."

I blinked, impressed. Veils were not simple spells. Granted, they were sort of a specialty of Molly's, but this was taking it up a notch. I didn't know whether I could have covered the entire Caddy with a veil while driving alertly *and* carrying on a conversation. In fact, I was pretty sure I couldn't.

Grasshopper was growing up on me.

I studied Molly's profile while she drove. Stared, really. I'd first met her years ago, when she was a gawky little kid in a training bra. She'd grown up tall, five-ten or a little more. She had dark blond hair, although she had changed its color about fifty times since I'd met her. At the moment, it was in its natural shade and cut short, hanging in an even sheet to her chin. She was wearing minimal makeup. The girl was built like a particularly well-proportioned statue, but she wasn't flaunting it in this outfit—khaki pants, a cream-colored shirt, and a chocolate brown jacket.

The last time I'd seen Molly, she'd been a starved-looking thing, dressed in rags and twitching at every sound and motion, like a feral cat—which was hardly surprising, given that she'd been fighting a covert war against a group called the Fomor while dodging the cops and the Wardens of the White Council. She was still lean and a little hyperalert, her eyes trying to watch the whole world at once, but that sense of overly coiled spring tension was much reduced.

She looked good. Noticing that made things stir under the surface, things that shouldn't have been, and I abruptly looked away.

"Uh," she said. "Harry?"

"You look better than the last time I saw you, kiddo," I said.

She grinned, briefly. "Right back atcha."

I snorted. "It'd be hard to look worse. For either of us, I guess."

She glanced at me. "Yeah. I'm a lot better. I'm still not . . ." She shrugged. "I'm not exactly Little Miss Stability. At least, not yet. But I'm working on it."

"Sometimes I think that's where most of us are," I said. "Fighting off the crazy as best we can. Trying to become something better than we were. It's that second bit that's important."

She smiled, and didn't say anything else. Within a few moments, she had turned the Caddy into a private parking lot.

"I don't have any money for parking," I said.

"Don't need it." She paused and rolled down the cracked window to wave at an attendant operating the gate. He glanced up from his book, smiled at her, and pushed a button. The gate opened, and Molly pulled the Caddy into the lot. She drove down the length of it, and pulled the car carefully into a covered parking spot. "Okay. Come on."

We got out of the car, and Molly led me to a doorway leading into an adjacent apartment building. She opened the door with a key, but instead of moving to the elevators, she guided me to another doorway to one side of the entrance. She unlocked that one too, and went down two flights of stairs to a final door. I could sense magical defenses on the doors and the stairs without even making an effort to open myself up to it. That was a serious bunch of security spells. Molly opened the second door and said, "Please come in." She smiled at Toot. "And your crew with you, of course."

"Thanks," I said, and followed her inside.

Molly had an apartment.

She had an apartment big enough for Hugh Hefner's birthday party.

The living room was the size of a basketball court, and it had eleven-foot ceilings. There was a little bar separating the kitchen from the rest of the open space. She had a fireplace with what looked like a handmade living room set around it in one corner of the room, and a second section of comfy chairs and a desk tucked into a nook lined with built-in bookshelves. She had a weight bench, too, along with an elliptical machine, both of them expensive European setups. The floors were hardwood, broken up by occasional carpets that probably cost more than the floor space they covered. A couple of doors led off from the main room. They were oak. Granite countertops. A six-burner gas stove. Recessed lighting.

"Hell's bells," I said. "Uh. Nice place."

Molly shrugged out of her jacket and tossed it onto the back of a couch. "You like?" She walked into the kitchen, opened a cabinet door, and pulled out a first-aid kit.

"I like," I said. "Uh. How?"

"The svartalves built it for me," she said.

Svartalves. They were some serious customers in the supernatural scene. Peerless artisans, a very private and independent folk—and they tolerated absolutely no nonsense. No one wants to get on the bad side of a svartalf. They weren't exactly known for their generosity, either. "You working for them?" I asked.

"No," she said. "This is mine. I bought it from them."

I blinked again. "With what?"

"Honor," she said. She muttered something and flicked a hand at a chandelier hanging over the table in the little dining area. It began to glow with a pure white light as bright as any collection of incandescent bulbs. "Bring him over here, and we'll see if we can't help him."

I did so, transferring Toot from the skull to the table as gently as possible. Molly leaned down over him, peering. "Right through the breastplate? What hit you, Toot-toot?"

"A big fat jerk!" Toot replied, wincing. "He had a real sword, too. You know how hard it is to convince any of you big people to make us a sword we can actually use?"

"I saw his gear," I said. "I totally liked yours better, Major General. Way cooler and more stylish than that stupid black-knight look."

Toot gave me a brief, fierce grin. "Thank you, my lord!"

Toot got out of his ruined armor with effort, and with Molly's cautious, steady-fingered help I managed to clean the wound and bandage it. It looked ugly, and Toot was anything but happy during the process, but he was clearly uncomfortable and weary, rather than being badly hurt. Once the wound was taken care of, Toot promptly flopped onto the table and went to sleep.

Molly smiled, got a clean towel out of a cabinet, and draped it over the little guy. Toot seized it and curled up beneath it with a sigh.

"All right," Molly said, picking up the first-aid kit. She beckoned me to follow her to the kitchen. "Your turn. Off with the shirt."

"Not until you buy me dinner," I said.

For a second, she froze, and I wondered whether that had come out like the joke it had sounded like in my mind. Then she recovered. Molly arched her eyebrow in a look that was disturbingly like that of her mother (a woman around with whom a wise man will not mess) and folded her arms.

"Fine," I said, rolling my eyes. I shrugged my way out of the ruined tux.

"Jesus," Molly said softly, looking at me. She leaned around me, frowning at my back. "You look like a passion play."

"Doesn't feel so bad," I said.

"It might if one of these cuts gets infected," Molly said. "Just . . . just stand there and hold still. Man." She went to the cabinet and came back with a big brown bottle of hydrogen peroxide and a couple of kitchen towels. I watched her walking back and forth. "We'll start with your back. Lean on the counter."

I did, resting my elbows on the granite, still watching her. Molly fumbled with the supplies for a second, then bit her lower lip and began to move with purpose. She started dribbling peroxide onto the cuts on my back in little bursts of cold liquid that might have made me jump before I'd spent so much time in Arctis Tor. It burned a little, and then fizzed enthusiastically.

"So, not one question?" I asked her.

"Hmmm?" She didn't look up from her work.

"I come back from the dead, I sort of expected . . . I don't know. A little shock. And about a million questions."

"I knew you were alive," Molly said.

"Yeah, I sort of figured. How?" She didn't answer, and after a moment I realized the likely answer. "My godmother."

"She takes her Yoda-ing seriously."

"I remember," I said, keeping my tone neutral. "How long have you known?"

"Several weeks," Molly said. "There are so many cuts here, I don't think I have enough Band-Aids. We'll have to wrap it, I guess."

"I'll just put a clean shirt over them," I said. "Look, it isn't a big deal. Little marks like that are going to be gone in a day or two."

"Little . . . Winter Knight stuff?"

"Pretty much," I said. "Mab . . . kinda gave me the tour during my recovery."

"What happened?" she asked.

I found my eyes wandering to Bob's skull. Telling Molly what was going on would mean that she was involved. It would draw her into the conflict. I didn't want to expose her to that kind of danger—not again.

Of course, it probably wasn't my sole decision. And besides, Molly had intervened in an assassination that had been really close to succeeding. Whoever was behind the swarm of piranha pixies had probably seen it. Molly was already in the fight. If I started keeping things from her now, it would only hinder her chances of surviving it.

I didn't want her involved, but she'd earned the right to make that choice for herself.

So I gave it to her, straight, succinct, and with zero editing except for the bit about Halloween. It felt sort of strange. I hardly ever tell anyone that much truth. The truth is dangerous. She listened, her large eyes steadily focused on a point around my chin.

When I finished, all she said was, "Turn around."

I did, and she started working on the cuts on my chest, arms, and face. Again, cleaning the wounds was a little uncomfortable, but nothing more. I watched her tending me. I couldn't read her expression. She didn't look up at my eyes while she worked, and she kept her manner brisk and steady, very businesslike.

"Molly," I said, as she finished.

She paused, still not looking up at me.

"I'm sorry. I'm sorry that I had to ask you to help me . . . do what I did. I'm sorry that I didn't make you stay home from Chichén Itzá. I never should have exposed you to that. You weren't ready."

"No kidding," Molly said quietly. "But . . . I wasn't really taking no for an answer at the time, either. Neither of us made smart choices that night."

"Maybe. But only one of us is the mentor," I said. "I'm supposed to be the one who knows what's going on."

Molly shook her head several times, a jerky motion. "Harry—it's over. Okay? It's done. It's the past. Let it stay there."

"Sure you want that?"

"I am."

"Okay." I picked up a paper towel and dabbed at a few runnels of peroxide bubbling their way down my stomach. "Well. Now all I need is a clean shirt."

Molly pointed at one of the oak doors. "In there. There are two dressers and a closet. Nothing fancy, but I'm pretty sure it will all fit you."

I blinked several times. "Um. What?"

She snorted and rolled her eyes. "Harry . . . duh. I knew you were alive. That meant you'd be coming back. Lea told me to keep it to myself, so I got a place ready for you." She took a quick step back into the kitchen, opened a drawer, and came back with a small brass key. "Here, this will get you past the locks, and past the svartalves' wards and past my defenses."

I took the key, frowning. "Um . . ."

"I'm not asking you to shack up with me, Harry," Molly said, her tone dry. "It's just . . . until you get back on your feet. Or . . . or just as long as you're in town and need a place to stay."

"Did you think I couldn't take care of it myself?"

"Of course not," Molly said. "But . . . you know. I guess I think that maybe you shouldn't have to?" She looked up at me uncertainly. "You were there when I needed you. I figured it was my turn now."

I looked away before I got all emotional. The kid had gotten this place together, made some kind of alliance with a very suspicious and cautious supernatural nation, furnished a room for me, *and* picked me up a wardrobe? In just a few weeks? When she'd been living in rags on the street all the time for the better part of a year before that?

"I'm impressed, grasshopper," I said. "Seriously."

"This isn't the impressive part," she said. "But I don't think we have time to get into that right now, given what you've got going."

"Let's survive Halloween," I said, "and then maybe we can sit and have a nice talk. Molly, you shouldn't have done this for me."

"Ego much?" she asked, the ghost of her old, irreverent self lurking in her eyes. "I got this place for *me*, Harry. I lived my whole life in one home. Living on the street wasn't . . . wasn't a good place for me to put myself back together. I needed someplace . . . someplace . . ." She frowned.

"Yours?" I suggested.

"Stable," she said. "Quiet. And mine. Not that you aren't welcome here. While you need it."

"I suppose you didn't get those clothes for my sake, either."

"Maybe I started dating basketball teams," Molly said, her eyes actually sparkling for a moment. "You don't know."

"Sure I do," I said.

She started putting the kit away. "Think of the clothes as . . . as a birthday present." She looked up at me for a second and gave me a hesitant smile. "It's really good to see you, Harry. Happy birthday."

"Thanks," I said. "I'd give you a hug, but I'd bleach and bloodstain your clothes at the same time."

"Rain check," Molly said. "I'm, uh . . . Working up to hugs might take a while." She took a deep breath. "Harry, I know you've got your hands full already, but there's something you need to know."

I frowned. "Yeah?"

"Yeah." She rubbed her arms with her hands as though cold. "I've kind of been visiting your island."

In the middle of the southern reaches of Lake Michigan lies an island that doesn't appear on any charts, maps, or satellite images. It's a nexus point of ley lines of dark energy, and it doesn't like company. It encourages people who come near it to get lost and wander away. Planes fly over the thing all the time, but no one sees it. A few years back, I'd bound myself to the island, and the world-class genius loci that watched over it. I'd named it Demonreach, and knew relatively little about it, beyond that it was an ally.

When I'd been shot and plunged into the dark waters of Lake Michigan, it had taken Mab and Demonreach both to preserve my life. I'd woken up from a coma in a cavern beneath the island's surface with plants growing into my freaking veins like some kind of organic IV line. It was a seriously weird kind of place.

"How did you get there?" I asked.

"In a boat. Duh."

I gave her a look. "You know what I mean."

She smiled, the expression a little sad. "After you've had someone like the Corpsetaker pound your mind into pomegranate seeds, a psychic No Trespassing sign seems kinda slow-pitch."

"Heh," I said. "Point. But it's a dangerous place, Molly."

"And it's getting worse," she said.

I shifted my weight uneasily. "Define 'worse.'"

"Energy is building up there. Like . . . like steam in a boiler. I know I'm still new at this—but I've talked with Lea about it and she agrees."

God, she was dragging this out, making me wonder what she knew. I hate that. "Agrees with *what*?"

"Um," Molly said, looking down. "Harry. I think that within the next few days, the island is going to explode. And I think that when it does, it will take about half the Midwest with it."

14

"Of course it is," I said. I looked around and grabbed the first-aid kit, then started stomping toward the indicated guest bedroom. "I *swear*, this *stupid* town. Why does every hideous supernatural thing that happens happen *here*? I'm gone for a few months and *augh*. Be right back. Grrssll frrrsl rassle mrrrfl."

There was a light switch in the bedroom and it worked. The lightbulb stayed on and everything. I scowled up at it suspiciously. Normally when I'm in a snit like this, lightbulbs don't survive eye contact, much less my Yosemite Sam impersonation. Evidently, the svartalves had worked out a fix for technological grumpy-wizard syndrome.

And the room . . . well.

It reminded me of home.

My apartment had been tiny. You could have fit it into Molly's main room half a dozen times, easy. My old place was almost the same size as her guest bedroom. She'd furnished it with secondhand furniture, like my place had been. There was a small fireplace, with a couple of easy chairs and a comfortable-looking couch. There were scuffed-up old bookshelves, cheap and sturdy, lining the walls, and they contained what was probably meant to be the beginning of a replacement for my old paperback fiction library. Over toward where my bedroom used to be was a bed, though it was a full rather than a twin. A counter stood where my kitchen counter had been, more or less, and there was a small fridge and what looked like an electric griddle on it.

I looked around. It wasn't home, but . . . it was in the right zip code. And it was maybe the single sweetest thing anyone had ever done for me.

For just a second, I remembered the scent of my old apartment, wood smoke and pine cleaner and a little bit of musty dampness that was inevitable in a basement, and if I squinted my eyes up really tight, I could almost pretend I was there again. That I was home.

But they'd burned down my home. I had repaid them for it, with interest, but I still felt oddly hollow in my guts when I thought about how I would never see it again. I missed Mister, my cat. I missed my dog. I missed the familiarity of having a place that I knew, that was a shelter. I missed my life.

I'd been away from home for what felt like a very long time.

There was a closet by the bed, with a narrow dresser on two sides. It was full of clothes. Nothing fancy. T-shirts. Old jeans. Some new underwear and socks, still in their plastic packaging. Some shorts, some sweatpants. Several pairs of used sneakers the size of small canoes, and some hiking boots that were a tolerable fit. I went for the boots. My feet are not for the faint of sole, ah, ha, ha.

I ditched the tux, cleaned up and covered the injuries on my legs, and got dressed in clothes that felt familiar and comfortable for the first time since I'd taken a bullet in the chest.

I came out of the bedroom holding the bloodied clothes, and glanced at Molly. She pointed a finger at the fire. I nodded my thanks, remembered to take the bejeweled cuff links out of the pockets of the pants, and tossed what was left into the fire. Blood that had already been soaked up by cloth wouldn't be easy to use against me, even if someone had broken in and taken it somehow, but it's one of those things best not left to chance.

"Okay," I said, settling down on the arm of a chair. "The island. Who else knows about it?"

"Lea," Molly said. "Presumably she told Mab. I assumed word would get to you."

"Mab," I said, "is apparently the sort of mom who thinks you need to find things out for yourself."

"Those are real?"

I grunted. "Have you had any contact with Demonreach?"

"The spirit itself?" Molly shook her head. "It . . . tolerates my presence, but it isn't anything like cordial or friendly. I think it knows I'm connected to you."

"Yeah," I said. "I'm sure it does. If it wanted you off the island, you'd be gone." I shook my head several times. "Let me think."

Molly did. She went into the kitchen, to the fridge. She came out with a couple of cans of Coca-Cola, popped them both open, and handed me one. We tapped the cans together gently and drank. I closed my eyes and tried to order my thoughts. Molly waited.

"Okay," I said. "Who else knows?"

"No one," she said.

"You didn't tell the Council?"

Molly grimaced at the mention of the White Council of Wizards. "How would I do that, exactly? Given that according to them, I'm a wanted fugitive, and that no one there would blink twice if I was executed on sight."

"Plenty of them would blink twice," I said quietly. "Why do you think you're still walking around?"

Molly frowned and eyed me. "What do you mean?"

"I mean that Lea's clearly taught you a lot, Molly, and it's obvious that your skills have matured a lot in the past year. But there are people there with *decades'* worth of years like the one you've had. Maybe even centuries. If they really wanted you found and dead, you'd be found and dead. Period."

"Then how come I'm not?" Molly asked.

"Because there are people on the Council who wouldn't like it," I said. "My g— Ebenezar can take anyone else on the Council on any given day, if he gets mad at them. That's probably enough—but Ramirez likes you, too. And since he'd be the guy who would, theoretically, be in charge of capturing you, anyone else who did it would be walking all over his turf. He's young, too, but he's earned respect. And most of the young guns in the Wardens would probably side with him in an argument." I sighed. "Look, the White Council has always been a gigantic mound of assorted jerks. But they're not inhuman."

"Except sometimes," Molly said, her voice bitter.

"Humanity matters," I said. "You're still here, aren't you?"

"No thanks to them," she said.

"If they hadn't shown up at Chichén Itzá, none of us would have made it out."

Molly frowned at that. "That wasn't the White Council."

True, technically. That had been the Grey Council. But since the Grey Council was mostly made up of members of the White Council working together in secret, it still counted, in my mind. Sort of.

"Those guys," I said, "are what the Council should be. And might be. And when we needed help the most, they were *there*." I sipped some more Coke. "I know the world seems dark and ugly sometimes. But there are still good things in it. And good people. And some of them are on the Council. They haven't been in contact with you because they can't be—but believe me, they've been shielding you from getting in even more trouble than you've already had."

"You assume," she said stubbornly.

I sighed. "Kid, you're going to be dealing with the Council your whole life. And that could be for three or four hundred years. I'm not saying you shouldn't get in their faces when they're in the wrong. But you might want to consider the idea that burning your bridges behind you could prove to be a very bad policy a century or two from now."

Molly looked like she wanted to disagree with me—but she looked pensive, too. She drank some more of her Coke, frowning.

Damn. Why couldn't I have figured out that particular piece of advice to give to myself when I was her age? It might have made my life a whole lot simpler.

"Back to the island," I said. "How sure are you about the level of energy involved?"

She considered her answer. "I was at Chichén Itzá," she said. "It's all pretty blurry, but I remember a lot of fragments really well. One of the things I remember is the tension that had built up under the main ziggurat. Do you remember?"

I did, though it had been pretty far down on my list of priorities at the time. The Red King had ordered dozens, maybe hundreds of human sacrifices to build up a charge for the spell he was going to use to wipe me and everyone connected to me by blood from the face of the earth. That energy had been humming inside the very stones of the city. Go to a large power station sometime, and stand near the capacitors. The air is full of the same kind of silently vibrating potential.

"I remember," I said.

"It's like that. Maybe more. Maybe less. But it's really, really *big*. It's scaring the animals away."

"What time is it?" I asked.

Molly checked a tall old grandfather clock, ticking steadily away in a corner. "Three fifteen."

"Ten minutes to the marina. An hour and change to the island and back. Call it an hour for a service call." I shook my head and snorted. "If we leave right now, that puts us back here in town right around sunrise, wouldn't you say?"

"More or less," she agreed.

"Mab," I said, in the same tone I reserved for curse words.

"What?"

"That's why the lockdown," I said. Then clarified. "Mab closed the border with Faerie until dawn."

Molly was no dummy. I could see the wheels turning as she figured it out. "She's giving you time to deal with it unmolested."

"Relatively unmolested," I corrected her. "I'm starting to think that Mab mainly helps those who help themselves. Okay. Once Maeve gets to start moving pieces in and out of Faerie in the morning, things are going to get busy, fast. Also, I don't want to be working with the magical equivalent of a reactor core the next time Hook and his band of minipsychos catch up with me. So."

Molly nodded. "So we go to the island first?"

"We go to the island *now*."

Molly had the apartment building's security call us a cab on the theory that it would be slightly less noticeable than the monster car now in the parking lot. They took her orders as if she were some kind of visiting dignitary. Whatever she'd done for the svartalves, they had taken it very,

very seriously. I left Toot sleeping off the fight, with some junk food left out where he would find it when he woke up. Bob was in a cloth messenger bag I had slung over one shoulder, still buttoned up tight. Molly glanced at the bag, then at me, but she didn't ask any questions.

I felt like wincing. Molly hadn't ever exactly been shy about pushing the boundaries of my authority in our relationship as teacher and apprentice. Her time with my faerie godmother, the Leanansidhe, Mab's girl Friday, was starting to show. Lea had firm and unyielding opinions about boundaries. People who pushed them got turned into dogs—or something dogs ate.

The marina was one of several in the city. Lake Michigan provided an ideal venue for all kinds of boating, sailing, and shipping, and there was a nautical community firmly established all around the shores of the Great Lake. I'm not really part of it. I say "wall" instead of "bulkhead," and I'm not quite sure if port is left, or if it's something best left until after dinner. I get the terms wrong a lot. I don't care.

Marinas are parking lots for boats. Lots of walkways were built on piers or were floating pontoon bridge–style in long, straight rows. Boats were parked in individual lots much like in any automobile parking lot. Most of the boats showed signs of being prepared for winter—November can be a dangerous time for pleasure boating on Lake Michigan, and most people pack it in right around Halloween. Windows and hatches were covered, doors closed, and there were very few lights on in the marina.

Which was good, because I was breaking and entering again.

I'd had a key to the marina's locks at one time, but I'd lost track of it when I got shot, drowned, died, got revived into a coma, haunted my friends for a while, and then woke up in Mab's bed.

(My life. Hell's bells.)

Anyway, I didn't have a key or any time to spare, so when I got to the locked gate to the marina, I abused my cool new superstrength and forced the chain-link gate open in a low squeal of bending metal. It took me about three seconds.

"*Cool*," Molly murmured from behind me. "Wait. Did you do the car, too?"

I grunted, a little out of breath from the effort.

"Holy cow," Molly said. "You're like Spider-Man strong."

"Nah," I panted. "Spider-Man can press ten tons. I can do sets with four hundred kilos."

"Kilos," Molly said.

"I inherited the last guy's weight set," I said. "It's this fancy European thing. Not sure exactly how heavy that is in English."

"In England they use kilos," Molly said wryly. "But it would also be around sixty or sixty-five stone."

I stopped and looked at her.

She smiled sweetly at me.

I sighed and kept on walking out to the boat.

It's called the *Water Beetle*. It could be the stunt double for the boat of the crusty old fisherman in *Jaws*, except that it had been freshly painted and refinished and it looked a little too nice. I stopped on the dock in front of it.

There. I'd been standing right there, looking out toward the parking lot when it happened. My chest didn't actually feel a pang of agony, but the memory of it was so sharp and clear that I might as well have re-experienced it—it hadn't hurt at the time, not until I'd been in the water for a while, but it had been pure fire once Mab and Demonreach had succeeded in keeping my soul and body knit together.

And to think, I'd had to call in a solid to get the guy to come shoot me. It seemed like kind of a waste, at this point. I'd been sure that if I had managed to win the day, thanks to my deal with Mab, that I would be a monster in need of a good putting down. I'd scheduled my own assassin, and Molly had used her unique talents to help me forget that it was coming. Once the day had been safely saved, the plan had been to circumvent the evolution of monster-Harry by way of high-powered rifle.

Except I'd survived. Next, I guess, came the monster-Harry part.

I had it on good authority that it didn't have to end with me going all nutty and villainous—assuming an archangel was trustworthy, which I didn't. I also had it on good authority that it would end like that anyway. So at the end of the day, I really didn't know what was going to happen to me in the future.

Heh. Why should I be any different?

The *Water Beetle* was definitely not battened down for winter, not yet. She was a sturdy, tough little craft—not fast, but not afraid of much of anything nature would throw at her, either. Her gangplank was down, and "batten" and "gangplank" are about the only boat words I'm comfortable with. I moved up it without hesitation, even in the shadowy dimness of late night on the marina. I was familiar with the boat. I'd visited the island on it on multiple occasions.

I went aboard and up onto the roof of the wheelhouse, where the driver's position was. I flicked on a couple of tired old bulbs and checked the gauges. Fuel, oil, good. She had more than enough for the trip out to the island and back. The key wasn't in the ignition—it would be in the small safe down in the boat's cabin, but I knew the combination.

"We're good," I called softly. "Come on."

Molly came up the gangplank while I went down into the cabin.

I got no warning whatsoever, no sound, no visible motion, nothing. One second I was going down the stairs, and the next my face and chest were being crushed against the wall and something extremely sharp was pressing against my neck, just beneath my right ear. Cool, iron-strong fingers were spread over my whole head, pressing it to the wall. The message was clear—if I struggled or made any sound, something pointy would go into my brain.

I froze. It seemed smart. If my attacker wanted me dead, I wouldn't still be able to reason that he could already have killed me.

"Hello, precious," murmured a man's very soft voice. "I think you're on the wrong boat."

I sagged suddenly in relief. "Stars and stones," I breathed. "Thomas, you scared the hell out of me."

The power of the cold fingers against my head did not falter in the slightest, but there was a short, stunned silence. Then the pressure against my skull became furious. "Do you think this is funny?" my half brother said, his voice becoming louder, fairly boiling with anger. "Do you think I am amused by this kind of prank?"

"Thomas," I said. "It's *me*."

"Sure it is," Thomas snarled, the pressure against me surging for a second. "Harry Dresden is *dead*."

I thought my eyeballs were trying to squeeze their way out of their sockets. "Glurk!"

"Now," he growled. "I'm going to give you exactly three seconds to start telling me the truth, or I swear to God they will never find enough pieces of you to identify the body."

He meant it, Hell's bells. He was furious. If I were the kind of guy who ever got scared by anything, ever, which of course I am not, I would have been feeling extremely nervous at that moment.

"Mab!" I ground out. "Dammit, Thomas, you lunatic. It was Mab!"

"Mab sent you?" Thomas demanded.

"Mab *saved* me!" I rasped. "Hell's bells, man, it's *me*!"

Thomas growled, lower, but he didn't pancake my skull or stick something sharp and metal into my brain. Thomas was strong—stronger than me. A vampire of the White Court can bring out that kind of strength only on special occasions, but Thomas was a very well-fed vampire. I knew that if he wanted to do it, Winter Knight steroids or no, he could twist me like a congressman's logic.

"Molly!" he called out. "I know you're out there. I can smell you."

A few seconds later, there were soft steps on the gangplank, and then the shadows moved at the door. "I'm here."

"What the fuck is *this*?" he demanded.

"I'm not sure," Molly said. "It's dark. But if I could see, I'd tell you that I try not to put myself between two siblings when they're fighting. It never seems to help."

Two or three flabbergasted seconds passed. Then the pressure against my skull was gone so fast that I all but fell over. I grabbed myself before I could and shook my head. "Ow. Nice to see you again, too, man."

He moved silently across the cabin and something clicked. A battery-powered tap light came to life, bringing a dim if adequate level of light to the compartment.

My brother was a hair shy of six feet tall. He looked much as I remembered him: dark, glossy hair fell to his shoulders. His skin was even paler than mine. His eyes were storm-cloud grey, though they looked brighter than that now, glinting with little metallic flecks that revealed his anxiety and anger. He and I shared a similar scowl, all dark brows and intense eyes, and his mouth was twisted into a silent snarl as he stared at me. He was wearing a pair of jeans, and that was it. The cabin's bunk had been folded down and slept in. I'd woken him when I came aboard. In his right hand he held a metal tent stake. There was both dirt and rust on it. Can you get gangrene in your brain?

"Oh," Molly said. She stared at Thomas for a moment. "Oh, um. My."

Oh, I forgot to mention it: My brother is the kind of man whom women stalk. In cooperative *packs*. I'd say he was model pretty, except that as far as I could tell, there weren't any models as pretty as he was. He had muscles that rippled even when he was motionless and relaxed, and it was utterly unfair.

And . . . I didn't do a lot of appraising myself in the mirror, typically, but I suddenly realized that sometime in the past few years, Thomas had stopped looking like my older brother. He looked younger than me. Wizards can live a long time, but we don't look youthful while we do it. Thomas was a vampire. He'd look this good until he stopped breathing.

The guy barely works out, eats whatever he wants, and gets to look that good *and* that young his whole life. How is that fair?

"You can't be my brother," Thomas said, staring hard at me. "My brother is dead. You know how I know?"

"Thomas," I began.

"Because my *brother* would have contacted me," Thomas snarled. "If he were alive, he would have gotten in *touch* with me. He would have let me know."

Molly winced and looked away as though she'd just heard a very loud and very unpleasant sound. I'm not sensitive to the emotions of others the way Molly is, but I didn't need to be to know that Thomas was boiling over in reaction to seeing me there.

"I'm sorry, Harry," Molly said. "I can't . . . It hurts."

"Go," I said softly.

She nodded and withdrew onto the deck of the boat, shutting the door behind her.

My brother stayed where he was, staring at me. "All this time," he said. "And not a word."

"I was dead," I said quietly. "Or the next-best thing to it. Maybe it was more like a coma. Hell, I thought I was dead."

"When did you wake up?" he asked. His voice was carefully neutral.

"About three months ago," I said. "Wasn't in good shape. I've been recovering since then."

"Three months," he said. "No phones there?"

"No, actually. I was in a cave on the island for a while. Then Arctis Tor."

"No way for you to make contact?" he asked calmly. *"You?"*

Silence fell heavily. Thomas knew the kinds of things I could do. If I want someone to get a message, I can generally make sure it gets done—one way or another.

"What do you want me to say, man?" I responded. "I sold out, Thomas."

"Yeah, when you hurt your back. You told us. For Maggie. To get her home safe."

"Right."

He was silent for a second. Then he said, "Empty night, why didn't I put that together . . . ?" He sighed. "Let me guess. You tried to kill yourself after she was home safe, right?"

I snorted through my nose. "Something like that."

He shook his head in silence for several seconds. Then he took a deep breath, looked up at me again, and said, "You. *Moron.*"

"Hey," I said.

"You. *Idiot.*"

"Dammit, Thomas," I said. "I haven't lived my life the way I have to watch myself get turned into—" I broke off suddenly, and looked away.

"Into what, Harry?" he asked. "Say it."

I shook my head.

"No, you don't get a pass on this one, little brother," Thomas said. "Say it."

"Into a monster," I snapped.

"Right," Thomas said. "A monster. Like me."

"That isn't what I meant."

"It is exactly what you meant," he spat, angry. "You arrogant . . ." He flung the tent spike in a fit of pure frustration. It tumbled end over end once, and sank two inches into a wooden beam. "You were going to be tempted, eh? Going to have to deal with monstrous urges? Going to have to face the possibility that you might change if you lost focus for a minute? Lose control of yourself? Maybe hurt somebody you care about?" He shook his head. "Cry me a fucking river, man. Boo-fucking-hoo."

I couldn't look at him.

"You'd rather be *dead* than be like me," he said. "That's one hell of a thing to say to your brother."

"It wasn't about that," I said.

"It kind of was," he snapped back. "Dammit, Harry."

"I can't go back and change it," I said. "Maybe I would if I could. But it's done. I'm sorry, but it is."

"You should have talked to me," he said.

"Thomas."

"You should have *trusted* me," he said. "Dammit, man."

The memory of those desperate hours hit me hard. I felt so helpless. My daughter had been taken away from her home, and for all the times I had gone out on a limb for others, no one had seemed willing to do the same for me. The White Council for whom I had fought a war had turned its back on me. Time had been running out. And the life of a little girl who had never known her father was on the line.

"Why?" I asked him tiredly. "What would it have changed? What could you possibly have said that would have made a difference?"

"That I was your brother, Harry," he said. "That I loved you. That I knew a few things about denying the dark parts of your nature. And that we would get through it." He put his elbows on his knees and rested his forehead on his hands. "That we'd figure it out. That you weren't alone."

Stab.

Twist.

He was right. It was just that simple. My brother was right. I had been self-involved and arrogant. Maybe it was understandable, given the pressures on me at the time, but that didn't mean that I hadn't made bad calls of colossal proportion.

I should have talked to him. Trusted him. I hadn't even tried to consider anyone other than Maggie, hadn't even thought to start seeking support from my family. I'd just moved right along to the part of the plan where I hired one of the world's premier supernatural assassins to whack me. That probably said something about the state of despair I'd been in at the time.

But it didn't say as much as I had about my brother. He was right about that, too. It wasn't something I had ever consciously faced before, but I had told Thomas, with my actions, that it was better to be dead than a monster—a monster like him. And actions speak far more loudly than words.

I always thought it would get easier to be a person as I aged. But it just gets more and more complicated.

"I'm sorry. I should have talked to you then," I said. My voice sounded hoarse. "I should have talked to you three months ago. But I couldn't because I made the wrong call. I didn't think I should contact anyone."

"Why not?" he asked, looking up.

"Because I didn't deserve to do it," I said quietly. "Because I sold out. Because I was ashamed."

He came to his feet, angry. "Oh, absolutely, I get that. I mean, you had to stay away. Otherwise we all would have known that you *aren't perfect*, you gawking, stupid, arrogant, egotistical . . ."

He hit my chest and wrapped his arms around me so hard that I felt my ribs creaking.

". . . clumsy, short-tempered, exasperating, goofy, useless . . ."

I hugged my brother back and listened to a steady string of derogatory adjectives until he finished it.

". . . asshole."

"Yeah," I said. "I missed you, too."

15

Thomas got us to the island navigating by the stars.

I kept checking the ship's compass. Not because I didn't trust my brother, but because I had no freaking idea how he managed to keep the *Water Beetle* on course without one. Molly had spent the first part of the trip down in the cabin, wrapped up in some blankets: It was a chilly night out on the lake. Thomas and I were comfortable in shirts. I suspected my apprentice was still feeling the aftereffects of standing too close to my reunion with Thomas.

I filled Thomas in on recent events on the way out, omitting only the details on the immortal-killing thing. I had a sinking feeling that knowing something that important about beings that powerful was an excellent way to get yourself killed horribly on any night of the year that *wasn't* Halloween.

"Yeah, yeah, yeah," Thomas said, when I finished the briefing. "Have you seen her yet?"

I scowled. "Seen who?"

"You tell me," he said.

"Just you and Molly," I said.

He gave me a look of profound disappointment, and shook his head.

"Thanks, Dad," I said.

"You're alive," he said. "You owe it to her to go see her."

"Maybe when this is done," I said.

"You might be dead by then," he said. "Empty night, Harry. Didn't your little adventure in the lake teach you a damned thing?"

I scowled some more. "Like what?"

"Like life is short," he said. "Like you don't know when it's going to end. Like some things, left unsaid, can't ever be said." He sighed. "I'm a freaking vampire, man. I rip out pieces of people's souls and eat them, and make them happy to have it happen."

I didn't say anything. That was what my brother was. He was more than that, too, but it would have been stupid to deny that part of him.

"I'm mostly a monster," he said. "And even I know that she deserves to hear you tell her you love her. Even if she never gets anything more than that."

I frowned. "Wait. Who are we talking about here?"

"Either," he said. "Stop being an idiot. Stop flagellating yourself about how you endanger her by being in her life. You're the only you *in* her life, Harry. Believe me. They don't make replacements for a guy like you."

"They don't make replacements for anybody," I said tiredly. "We'll see."

Thomas looked at me like he wanted to push. But he didn't.

"So what about you?" I asked. "Justine and her playmate keeping you company?"

"Playmates," Thomas said absently. "Plural."

Totally not fair.

"Hmph," I said.

He frowned. "Hey. How did you know about that?"

"Ghost me was there the night Justine decided she'd had enough of you moping," I said.

"Ghost you was there for how long, exactly?" he asked.

"I left before it got to an NC-17."

He snorted. "Yeah, well, Justine . . . has sort of become a dietitian."

"Uh, what?"

He shrugged. "You are what you eat, right? Same principle applies to vampires. Justine thinks I'm sad, she brings home someone happy. She thinks I'm too tense, someone laid-back and calm." He pursed his lips. "Really . . . it's been kind of nice. Balanced, like." His eyes narrowed and flickered through a few paler shades. "And I get to be with *Justine* again. Even if it was hell, that would make it worthwhile."

"Dude," I said, making the word a disgusted sound. "Single guys everywhere hate you. Starting with me."

"I know, right?" he asked, nodding and smiling. Then he looked ahead and pointed. "There, see it?"

I peered ahead into the black and found a giant block of more solid black. We were at the island.

The cabin door opened and Molly emerged, the blanket still wrapped around her shoulders. Her face still looked drawn, but not as pale as it had before we left the marina. She came up the steps to the top of the wheelhouse and stood beside me. "Thomas," she asked. "Why were you down at the boat tonight?"

Thomas blinked and looked at her. "What do you mean?"

"I mean why were you sleeping on board?"

"Because you didn't tell me what time you'd be there, and I got sleepy," he said.

Molly glanced aside at Thomas, and then at me. "I asked you to do it?"

"Uh, yeah," Thomas said, snorting. "You called around ten."

Molly kept looking at me, frowning. "No. No, I didn't."

Thomas promptly cut the throttle on the boat. The *Water Beetle* began coasting to a halt, and the sound of the water hitting her hull resurfaced as the rattle of her engines died.

"Okay," Thomas said. "Uh. What the hell is going on, then?"

"Molly," I said, "are you sure?"

"None of my issues have included memory loss or unconscious actions," she said.

Thomas squinted back at her. "If they had, how would you know it?"

Molly frowned. "Valid point. But . . . there's been no evidence of that, to my knowledge. I'm as confident about that as anything else I perceive."

"So if Molly didn't call me . . ." Thomas began.

"Who did?" I finished.

Water slapped against the hull.

"What do we do?" Molly asked.

"If someone set us up to be here," Thomas said, "it's a trap."

"If it's a trap, they sure as hell didn't try very hard to hide it," I said. "All we really know is that someone wanted us here."

Molly nodded. "Do you think . . . ?"

"Mab's work?" I asked. "Having my ride prepared? Yeah, maybe."

"If your new boss wanted you on the island, wouldn't she just have told you to go there?" Thomas asked.

"Seems like," I said. "Taking her orders is pretty much my job now."

Molly snorted softly.

"Maybe I'll grow into it," I said. "You don't know."

Thomas snorted softly.

More water sounds.

We didn't have a lot of choice, really. Whether or not we'd been manipulated into showing up, there was still a giant potential problem with the island, something that had to be addressed as soon as possible. If I waited, dawn would be upon us, and it was entirely possible I'd be too busy—or dead—to fix the problem before it went boom. Which meant that the only time I had to take real action was right now.

"Just once," I growled, "I'd like to save the goddamned day without a shot clock. You know?"

"The monster business is an easier gig," Thomas said, nodding. "Way, way easier."

Which was my brother's backhanded way of telling me what he thought of me.

"I think we all know I'm not smart enough for that," I said. "Eyes open, everyone. Thomas, pull her up to the dock. Let's see who's waiting for us."

The island had once been host to a small town, back in the late nineteenth century. It had been home to docks, warehouses, and what might have been a fishery or cannery or something. Probably no more than a couple of hundred people had lived there, at most.

But the people weren't there anymore. And what was left of the town was like some kind of skeleton lying among the trees that had grown up through the floorboards. I don't know what happened to the town. Stories from the time mention only mysterious events in the lake, and an influx of new customers to what passed for a psychiatric care facility of the day. The town itself had been expunged from any records, and not even its name remained to be found. The island, likewise, had vanished from the official record—though if I had to guess, I would say that the reigning authorities at the time decided that covering up the island's existence was the best way to protect people from exposure to it.

Actually, knowing what I know now, I'd guess that the island *made* them come to that conclusion. The island I'd named Demonreach was very much alive.

Most of the world is, actually. People think that civilization and organized religion have somehow erased the spirits that exist in nature, in all the world. They haven't. People aren't the omnipotent force for destruction that we arrogantly believe we are. We can change things, true, but we never really destroyed those old spirits and presences of the wild. We aren't that powerful. We *are* very loud and very self-involved, though, so most people never really understand when they're in the presence of a spirit of the land, what the old Romans called a genius loci.

So, naturally, they also didn't understand when they were in the presence of a truly powerful spirit of the land—a potent spirit like that of, say, Vesuvius.

Or Demonreach.

I'd been to the island on most weekends up until I got shot, and Thomas had often come with me. We'd used some fresh lumber, some material salvaged from the ruined town, and some pontoons made from plastic sheathing and old tractor-tire inner tubes to construct a floating walkway to serve as a dock, anchored to the old pilings that had once supported a much larger structure. Upon completion, I had dubbed it the Whatsup Dock, and Thomas had chucked me twenty feet out into the lake, thus proving his utter lack of appreciation for reference-oriented humor.

(And I'd thrown him *forty* feet out with magic, once I got dry. Because come on, he's my brother. It was the only thing to do.)

The *Water Beetle* came drifting slowly into the dock, and bumped it gently. You had to be a little bit nimble to get over the side of the boat and onto the floating dock, but fortunately for me you didn't need to be a gymnast. We'd limned the outer boards of the floating dock in phosphorescent paint, and in the darkness it was a gently glowing, clearly visible outline. I hit the dock and secured the first line on the ring we'd installed, then walked down the dock and caught the second when Thomas threw it to me. Once the boat had been made fast, Thomas lowered the gangplank (a pirate's life for me!), and Molly padded down it. Thomas came last, buckling on his gun belt, which was currently hung with his ridiculously huge Desert Eagle, just in case we were attacked by a rabid Cape buffalo, and a big old bolo-style machete.

Watching him put the weapons on, I started to feel a little bit naked. I didn't have any of my usual gear, and I'd survived a bunch of nasty situations because I'd had it. I rubbed my hands against the thighs of my jeans, scowling, and tried not to think of how the only gear I had now consisted of a messenger bag and a talking skull.

Thomas noticed. "Oh. Hey, you need a piece, man?"

"They're just so fashionable," I said.

He slipped back aboard and came out with a freaking relic. He tossed it to me.

I caught it, frowning. It was a repeating rifle, a Winchester, complete with the large rounded hoop handle on the lever action. It was seriously heavy, with an octagonal barrel, walnut wood fixtures, and shining brass housing. Elkhorn sights. The gun had a certain comforting mass to it, and I felt like even if it ran out of ammunition, I would still be holding a seriously formidable club. Plus, whatever it was chambered in, a gun that heavy would hardly kick at all. It'd be more like handling a shotgun that pushed against your shoulder, rather than trying to jar it off.

"What am I?" I complained. "John Wayne?"

"You aren't that cool," Thomas said. "It's quick, easy to instinct-shoot, and good to way out past the effective range of a handgun. Lever action, it'll be reliable, keep working right through the apocalypse."

Which was a point in its favor, the way my life had been lately. "Rounds?"

"Traditional, forty-five Colt," he said. "Knock a big man down in one hit and keep him there. Catch."

He tossed me an ammo belt heavy with metallic shells that were nearly as big around as my thumb. I slung the belt across my chest, made sure the chamber was empty, but with a shell ready to be levered into it, and balanced the heavy gun up on one shoulder, keeping one hand on the stock.

Molly sighed. "Boys."

Thomas hooked a thumb back at the boat. "I got a machine gun you can have, Molly."

"Barbarian," she said.

"I don't rate a machine gun?" I asked.

"No, you don't," Thomas said, "because you can't shoot. I just gave you that to make you feel better."

"You ready?" I asked them.

Molly had her little wands out, one in each hand. Thomas swaggered down the gangplank and looked bored. I nodded at them, turned, and took several quick steps off the dock and onto the stony soil of the island.

My link with the island was an extremely solid and powerful bond—but it existed only when I was actually standing on it. Now that I was, knowledge flooded into me, through me, a wave of absolute information that should have inundated my senses and disoriented me entirely.

But it didn't.

That was the beauty of intellectus, pure universal knowledge. While I stood on the island, I understood it in a way that was breathtakingly simple to experience and understand, but practically impossible to explain properly. Knowledge of the island just flowed into me. I could tell you how many trees stood upon it (17,429), how many had been taken down by the summer's storms (seventy-nine), and how many of the apple trees currently bore fruit (twenty-two). I didn't have to focus on an idea, or wrest the knowledge from the island. I just thought about it and *knew*, the way I knew what my fingers were touching, the way I knew what scents belonged to what foods.

We were alone on the island. That much I knew. But I could also sense a profound unease in the place. Molly's description had been perfectly accurate. Something was wrong; some kind of horrible strain was upon the island, a pressure so pervasive that the trees themselves had begun to lean away from the island's heart, stretching their branches toward the waters of the lake. Without my heightened awareness of the island, I never would have been able to sense the shift of inches across thousands and thousands of branches, but it was real and it was there.

"We're clear," I said. "There's no one else out here."

"You're sure?" Thomas asked.

"I'm certain," I said. "But I'll stay alert. If I sense anyone showing up, I'll fire off a shot."

"Wait," Thomas said. "Where are you going?"

"Up the hill," I told him. "Uh . . . up to the tower, I think."

"Alone? You sure that's smart?" he asked.

Molly was standing at the end of the dock. She crouched down, reaching a hand out toward the dirt of the island. She brushed her fingers against it and then jerked them away with a shudder. "Ugh. Yes. We don't want to step off the dock. Not tonight."

I could hear Thomas's frown in his voice. "Island's got its panties in a bunch, eh?"

"I think something bad would happen to us if we tried to go with him," Molly said, her voice troubled. "Whatever's happening . . . Demonreach only wants Harry to see what's going on."

"Why doesn't it just marry him?" Thomas muttered under his breath.

"It sort of did," I said.

"My brother the . . . geosexual?"

I snorted. "Look, think of it as a business partner. And be glad it's on our side."

"It isn't on *our* side," Molly said quietly. "But . . . I think it might be on yours."

"Same thing," I said warningly, out at the island in general. "You hear that? They're my guests. Be nice."

The thrumming tension in the island didn't change. Not in the least. It went on with a kind of glacial inevitability that didn't give two shakes for the desires of one ephemeral little mortal, wizard or not. I got the feeling that *nice* simply wasn't in Demonreach's vocabulary. I'd probably have to be satisfied with it refraining from violence.

"We'll talk," I said to the island, trying to make it a threat.

Demonreach didn't care.

I muttered under my breath, bounced the Winchester on my shoulder, and started walking.

Walking on the island is an odd experience. I'd say it's like walking through your house in the dark, except I've never known a house as well as I knew that island. I knew where every stone lay, where every branch stuck out in my path, knew it without being warned by any senses at all. Walking in the dark was as easy as doing it in broad daylight—easier, even. I'd have had to pay at least a little attention to use my eyes. But here, every step was solid, and every motion I made was minimal, efficient, and necessary.

I made my way through unbroken brush in the dark, hardly making a sound, never tripping once. As I did I noted that Molly had been right about another thing: The clash of energies in the air had created enough dissonance to drive away most of the animals, the ones that had the capacity to readily escape. The deer were gone. Birds and raccoons were gone, and so were the skunks—though that would be one hell of a long swim to the nearest stretch of lakeshore, animals had been known to swim farther. Smaller mammals, mice and squirrels and so on, remained, though they had crowded into the ten yards or so nearest the shoreline all around the island. The snakes were having a field day with that, and evidently weren't bright enough to know that there was a bigger problem brewing.

I found the trail to the top of the hill, the high point on the island, and started up it. There were irregular steps cut into the hillside to make the ascent easier. They were treacherous if you didn't walk carefully, or if you didn't have near-omniscience about the place.

At the top of the hill is a ruined lighthouse made of stone. It's basically just a chewed-up silo shape now, having collapsed long ago. Next to the ruined tower, someone cobbled together a small cottage out of fallen stones. When I first saw it, it had been a square, squat little building with no roof. Thomas and I had been planning on putting the roof back on, so that I could overnight on the island someplace where I could build a fire and stay warm, but we hadn't gotten that far yet when everything had gone sideways. The cottage just sat, empty and forlorn—but a soft golden glow bathed the interior wall I could see from my position. There was the scent of wood smoke on the air.

Someone had built me a fire.

I made my way forward cautiously, looking around with both my awareness and my eyes, just in case my omniscience was in actuality nigh-omniscience, but I couldn't sense any threat. So I went into the cabin and looked around.

There was a fire in the fireplace and a folding table stacked with thick plastic boxes containing jars of food that would stay good for months at a time. The boxes would resist the tampering of critters. There were some camp implements stored in another box, and I took the time to break out a metal coffeepot, went out to the little old iron pump just outside the front door, and filled it. I tossed in a couple of handfuls of coffee grounds, hung it on the swivel arm by the fireplace, and nudged it over the fire.

Then I broke out the skull and set him down on the table. "Okay, Bob," I said. "We have work to do. You been listening?"

"Yeah, yeah," Bob said, his eyelights flickering to life. "Island go boom or something."

"We're on a mission to find out what it's going to do, and why, and how we can stop it."

"Gosh, I'd never have thought of that myself, Harry."

"This is top secret stuff," I said. "Anything you learn here is for me and you only. You go to someone else, I want this whole evening locked away someplace nice and tight. And don't go splitting off another per-sonality on me, like you did with Evil Bob."

"Entirely confidential, check," Bob said. "And it would take a lot more than one night working with *you* to build up enough momentum to spin off a whole new me. I have to actually learn things to make that happen."

"Less insult, more analysis," I said.

The beams from the skull's eye sockets grew brighter. They swept left and right, up and down, panning around like prison searchlights. Bob made thoughtful noises.

I tended the coffeepot. After it had been boiling for a few minutes, I took it off the fire, added a splash of cold water from the pump to settle the grounds, and poured myself a cup. I added a little powdered creamer and a bunch of sugar.

"Might as well drink syrup," Bob muttered.

"Says the guy with no taste buds," I said. I sipped. "Been meaning to have you out here to take a look at the place anyway."

"Uh-huh," Bob said absently.

"So?" I asked.

"Um," Bob said. "I'm still working on the surface layer of spells on the stones of this cottage, Harry."

I frowned. "Uh. What?"

"You know there're symbols there, right?"

I sipped coffee. "Sure," I said. "They kinda lit up when—"

Nauseating, mind-numbing horror and pain flashed over my thoughts for a couple of seconds. I'd used my wizard's Sight to look at the wrong being a couple of years ago, and that isn't the kind of mistake you ever live down. Now the memory of seeing that thing's true being was locked into my noggin, and it wouldn't go away or fade into the past—not ever.

That's bad. But the really bad part is that I've gotten used to it. It just caused a stutter step in my speech.

"—the naagloshii tried to get inside. It didn't seem to like them much."

"I should fucking think not," Bob said, his voice nervous. "Um, Harry . . . I don't know what these are."

I frowned at him. "Uh. What?"

"I don't *know*," he repeated. He sounded genuinely surprised. "I don't *know* what they are, Harry."

Magic is like a lot of other disciplines that people have recently begun developing, in historic terms. Working with magic is a way of understanding the universe and how it functions. You can approach it from a lot of different angles, applying a lot of different theories and mental models to it. You can get to the same place through a lot of different lines of theory and reasoning, kind of like really advanced mathematics. There's no truly right or wrong way to get there, either—there are just *different* ways, some more or less useful than others for a given application. And new vistas of thought, theory, and application open up on a pretty regular basis, as the Art develops and expands through the participation of multiple brilliant minds.

But that said, once you have a good grounding in it, you get a pretty solid idea of what's possible and what isn't. No matter how much circumlocution you do with your formulae, two plus two doesn't equal five. (Except maybe very, very rarely, sometimes, in extremely specific and highly unlikely circumstances.) Magic isn't something that just makes things happen, poof. There are laws to how it behaves, structure, limits—and the whole reason Bob was created was so that those limits could be explored, tested, and charted.

I could count on the fingers of no hands how many times Bob had come up completely dry. He *always* knew something. The skull had been working with wizards for centuries. He'd run into damned near everything.

"Uh, what?" I said. "Seriously? Nothing?"

"They're powerful," he said. "I can tell you that much. But they're also complex. I mean, like, Molly on her best day could not come close to weaving together something this crazy. You on your best day could not sling around enough power to juice up one of the smallest stones. And that's just the first *layer*. I think there are more. Maybe a *lot* more. Uh, like hundreds."

"On each *stone*?"

"Yeah."

"That's . . . It isn't . . . You can't put that much magic into that little space," I protested.

"No, no, I can't," Bob said. "And, no, you can't. Because it's impossible. But, um. Someone doesn't care."

"How did they do it?"

"If I knew that, it wouldn't be impossible," Bob said, an edge to his voice. "But I can tell you this much: It predates wizardry as we know it."

I would have said, *What?* but I felt like I'd been saying that a lot already. So I sipped coffee and scowled interrogatively instead.

"This work, the actual spells on the stone, comes from before even the predecessors to the White Council. I'm conversant in the course and

application of the Art since the golden age of Greece. This stuff, whatever it is? It's older."

"You can't lay out spells that last that long," I mumbled. "It isn't possible."

"Lot of that going around," Bob said. "Harry . . . you're . . . we're
talking about a whole different level, here. One that I didn't even know
existed. Uh. Do you get what that means? In round terms, at least?"

I shook my head slowly.

"Well, at least you're smart enough to know that," Bob said. "Um,
okay. You know the old chestnut about how sufficiently advanced science
could be described only as magic?"

"Right," I said.

"Well, I'm going to use the same model right now: As a wizard, you're
pretty good at making wooden axles and stone wheels. These spells?
They're an internal combustion engine. You do the math from there. On
your metaphorical abacus, I guess."

I blew out a very long, very slow breath.

Hell's bells.

I suddenly felt very young and very arrogant, and not terribly bright.
I mean, I'd known I was going to be out of my depth when I first hooked
up with the island, but I thought I'd at least be in the same freaking *ocean*.
Instead, I was . . .

I was in uncharted space, wasn't I?

And the *best* part of this whole conversation? Those spells that had
stymied one of the most advanced research tools known to wizardry and
baffled the collected knowledge of centuries? Those were just the *ruined*
part of the island.

What the hell was I going to find in the part that was *working*?

One second I was alone in the ruined cottage, and the next, there was
a presence filling the doorway, looking down at me through the empty
space where the roof should have been. It was huge, maybe twelve feet
tall, and roughly humanoid in shape. I couldn't see much of it. It was
covered in what looked like a heavy cloak that covered it completely. Two
points of green fire burned from within the cloak's hood. It simply stood,

unnaturally still, staring down at me, though the cool night breeze over the lake stirred the edges of its cloak.

Demonreach. The manifested spirit of the island.

"Uh," I said. "Hi."

The burning eyes shifted from me to Bob on the table. And then Demonreach did something it had never done before.

It spoke.

Out loud.

Its voice was a rumble of heavy rocks scraping together, of summer thunder rolling in from over the horizon. The voice was *huge*. Not loud. That didn't do it justice. It just came from everywhere, all at once. The surface of my partly drunk coffee buzzed and vibrated at the all-pervasive sound. "ANOTHER ONE."

"Meep," Bob squeaked. The lights vanished from the eye sockets of the skull.

I blinked a bunch of times. "You . . . you're talking now?"

"NECESSITY."

"Right," I said. "Um. So . . . you're having some trouble, I guess?"

"TROUBLE," it said. "YES."

"I came to help," I said, feeling extremely lame as I did. "Um. Is that even possible?"

"POTENTIALLY," came the answer. Then the vast form turned. It took a limping step. The ground didn't so much tremble at the weight as shift slightly beneath the sheer, overwhelming presence of the ancient spirit. "FOLLOW. BRING THE MEMORY SPIRIT."

". . . meep . . ." Bob whimpered.

I grabbed the skull in shaking hands and stuffed it into the messenger bag. I grabbed a chemical light from the storage boxes on the table, snapped it, and shook it to life as I hurried to catch up. I had an instinct about where we were headed, but I asked to be sure. "Uh. Where are we going?"

Demonreach kept walking, slow paces that nonetheless forced me to scurry to keep up. "BELOW."

The spirit walked to the ruined circle of the lighthouse and lifted a shadowy arm in a vague gesture. When it did, the ground of the circle

rippled and quivered, and then what had appeared to be solid stone began to run down, pouring itself into a hole like sand falling through an
hourglass. In seconds, an opening the size of the trapdoor to my old lab
had formed in the stone, and stairs led down into the darkness.

"Oh," I said. I'd known there were caves beneath the island, but not
how I had gotten there or where I could find them. "Wow. What's the
game plan here, exactly?"

"THE WELL IS UNDER ATTACK," came the surround-sound
answer. "IT MUST BE DEFENDED." Demonreach started toward the
stairs. There was no way it should have fit down them, but it moved as
though that wasn't going to be an issue.

"Wait. You want *me* to fight off something *you* can't stop?" I asked.

"IT IS TIME FOR YOU TO UNDERSTAND."

"Understand *what*?"

"OUR PURPOSE, WARDEN," it said. "FOLLOW ME."

Then it went down the stairs and vanished into the unknown.

"Here there be monsters!" Bob whispered, half hysterically. "Run!
Run already!"

"Think it's a little late for that," I said.

But for a second there, I thought about taking his advice. Some part
of me wondered what Tibet looked like this time of year. For a minute,
it seemed like an awesome idea to go find out.

But only for a minute.

Then I swallowed, gripped the plastic glow stick in fingers that felt
very slippery for some reason, and followed Demonreach down into the
dark.

16

I don't know how far down those stairs went.

I'm not even kidding. I'm not taking poetic license. The stairs went down twelve steps, took a right angle, and went down twelve more, took another right-angled turn, and went down twelve more, and so on. I stopped counting in the low two hundreds and resorted to my awareness of the island to feel out the rest of them. Duh. Seventeen hundred and twenty-eight—twelve cubed.

The stairs were about eight inches each, which meant eleven hundred feet and change, straight down. That was *well* below the water level of the lake. Hell, it was below the *bottom* of the lake. The staircase echoed with deep, groaning sounds pitched almost too low to be heard. In the wan light of the chemical glow stick, the place took on a kind of amusement-park fun-house atmosphere, where you suddenly realize that you've been routed into a circle with no apparent way out.

"Down, down to goblin town you go, my lad!" I sang in a hearty, badly pitched baritone. I was panting. "Ho, ho, my lad!"

Demonreach's glowing eyes flicked toward me. Maybe irritated.

"Oh, come on," I said. "You never saw the Rankin-Bass animated version of *The Hobbit*? The one they made before they did the movies in New Zealand?"

It didn't answer.

"Harry," Bob muttered at me. "Stop trying to piss it off."

"I'm bored," I said. "And I'm not looking forward to coming back *up*.

I get that we're going a long, long way down, but couldn't we use an elevator? Ooh, or a fireman's pole. Then it'd be like going down to the
Batcave. Way more fun." I raised my voice a little. "And more efficient."

Maybe it was my imagination, but when I said that last, I thought I
saw Demonreach's steady pace slow for a thoughtful second or two.

Nah.

"Hey, how come you called me Warden?" I asked. "I mean, I've been
a Warden, but there are a lot of other guys who are better at it than me.
I'm not exactly the poster child."

"WARDEN," Demonreach said. "NOW THERE ARE MANY.
FIRST THERE WAS ONE."

I counted down the last ten steps out loud, stopped at two, and
jumped over the last one to the floor beneath with both feet. My hiking
boots clomped on the stone.

We had reached a small chamber, the floor and walls lined in the
same stone used in the lighthouse and cottage. I put a hand on them and
could feel them quivering with power, with the dissonance of conflicting
energies. Actually, looking back, I saw that at some point, the walls of the
stairway, and the stairs themselves, had begun to be constructed of the
same material—every single stone of it invested with impossible amounts
of power and skill.

"Uh," I said. "Question?"

Demonreach had stopped at a stone doorway shape in the wall. It was
surrounded with larger stones covered in intricate carving. The burning
eyes turned toward me.

"Um. Who made this place?"

It didn't speak. It pointed to the door. I looked. There was a sign in
the middle of it, a sigil. It wasn't something I recognized as part of any
set of runes that I knew, but I knew I'd seen it somewhere before. It took
me several seconds of sorting through memories to run it down—I'd
seen it on the spine of a very, very, *very* old journal on my mentor's book-
shelf.

"Merlin," I said quietly. "That's whose sign that is, isn't it?"

Demonreach did not respond. Why say YES when silence will do?

I swallowed. The original Merlin was the real deal, Arthur and Excalibur and everything. Merlin had, according to legend, created the White Council of Wizards from the chaos of the fall of the Roman Empire. He plunged into the flames of the burning Library of Alexandria to save the most critical texts, helped engineer the Catholic Church as a vessel to preserve knowledge and culture during Europe's Dark Ages, and leapt tall cathedrals in a single bound. There were endless stories about Merlin. Popular theory among contemporary wizards was that they were more apocryphal than accurate. Hell, I'd always figured it that way, too.

But staring around at this place, I suddenly felt less sure.

"WATCH."

Demonreach stretched out one long arm, still shadowy and indistinct in the feeble light of my glow stick. It touched one of the stones framing the door, and the stone erupted into emerald light.

I hissed and shielded my eyes against it, and took note of the fact that the air suddenly crackled with power.

Demonreach touched a second stone, which also began to glow. When it did, the sense of building energy was palpable in the air, and the hairs on my arms began to stand up. That was when I got what was happening here: Demonreach had wards around whatever was beyond the door—much like the wards that had been put into position around Butters's apartment. Only they had to be fueled with freaking mystic plutonium or something to generate this much ambient energy simply from being *bypassed*.

The giant spirit reached for another stone, but paused before touching it.

"REMEMBER."

The stones. They were like a security keypad. Demonreach was giving me the combination to its security system. And given how much dangerous energy was in the air right now, it stood to reason that if I ever got the combination wrong, well . . . you'd need a bloodhound, a Ouija board, a forensic anthropologist, and a small army of Little Folk to find what was left of me.

I took *careful* note of which stones the spirit had indicated. Really careful note. Demonreach touched the last stone, and the granite doorway in front of us didn't move, exactly—it simply stopped being there.

The leashed violence in the air, that angry, watchful energy dwindled and vanished, and Demonreach moved forward through the doorway. I followed.

We emerged into a familiar cavern, and once again my chest lit up with phantom remembered pain.

It was surprisingly well lit, for a subterranean chamber. When I'd last been there, I hadn't been in any shape to go over the details, but I could now see that several glimmering clusters of crystal in the floor, some kind of pale green quartz maybe, gave off a dim glow. No single patch of them really provided adequate illumination, but as a whole they filled most of the cavern with wan green-white light.

Roots burrowed down into the cavern through its ceiling, though I had no idea how in the hell they'd gotten there. No plant sent roots down as deep beneath the surface as this chamber. No normal, earthly plant did, anyway. Water dripped slowly down from above, and where it fell from the ceiling was where the patches of crystal lay.

Over to one side of the chamber was a hollowed-out section of soft earth no deeper than a very shallow bathtub, about seven feet long. I recognized it, even without seeing the withered vines that lay strewn forgotten all around the area. It was my sickbed, where my body had lain for months while Mab and Demonreach exerted themselves to keep the pumps working while my mind and spirit were doing a Casper impersonation.

My chest panged again and I looked away. Waking up from that particular nap had been one of the top two or three most painful moments of my life. Something inside me had changed. Not because of the pain of the experience—though that had been profound. Staring at that place, I felt as if the pain had been a side effect of a deeper and more significant shift in the way I thought of myself, saw myself, and how I should interact with my world.

Fire isn't always an element of destruction. Classical alchemical doctrine teaches that it also has dominion over another province: change. The fire of my tribulations had not simply been pain to be endured. It had been an agent of transformation. After all that I'd been through, I'd changed.

Not for the worse, I was pretty sure—at least, not yet. But only a moron or a freaking lunatic could have faced the things I had and remained unfazed by them.

I blinked myself out of my reverie to find Demonreach watching me. There was something intense about its eyes.

"MEMORY," it said, "REFLECTION."

I frowned. "What do you mean?"

"THIS PLACE."

I pondered that one for a minute. "Are you saying that I just went into an internal monologue because I came in here?"

Demonreach did not seem to feel a need to clarify. "MEMORY. REFLECTION."

I sighed. "Well, if I ever need to mull things over, I know just where to go, I guess." It was chilly in the cavern, and damp, and the air was thick with musty, earthy smells. I turned a slow circle, surveying the entire chamber. "What do you call this place?"

Demonreach said nothing and did not move.

"Right," I said. "You don't call it anything at all, I guess." I scrunched up my nose, thinking. "What is this chamber's purpose?"

"CONTAINMENT."

I frowned. "Uh. Of what?"

"THE LEAST."

"The least *what*?" I asked, feeling exasperated.

Demonreach just watched me.

"Uh, Harry," Bob said in a small voice. "Maybe you should look at the crystals?"

I glanced down at the skull, shrugged, and walked over to the nearest formation. I stood over it for a moment. It was a large clump, maybe twelve feet long and four or five across. And . . . and the shadows passing through the translucent crystals seemed to indicate that the floor beneath it had been hollowed out, much the same as my own recovery bed. In fact . . .

I frowned, leaning closer. There was a form beneath the crystals, an outline. The image of whatever it was got to me only after being refracted through multiple crystals, so it was awfully blurry, but I peered at it, trying to unfocus my eyes and look past it, the way you do those magic paintings at the mall.

The image suddenly snapped into disjointed clarity. The form beneath the crystal was a lean creature of basically human shape, maybe nine or ten feet tall and lithe, covered in shaggy hair of golden brown. Its arms were too long for its body. Its hands were too big for its arms. Its fingers were too long for its hands, and were tipped with vicious claws.

And its yellow-gold eyes were open, aware, staring at me in naked, undisguised hatred.

"Fuck me!" I shouted, staggering back in pure, panicked reflex. "That's a naagloshii! That's a fucking naagloshii!"

Naagloshii were bad news. Serious bad news. Originally divine messengers of the Dine's Holy People, they had turned their backs on their origins and become the legendary skinwalkers of the American Southwest. I went up against one of them once. It killed one of my friends, tortured my brother half-crazy, and left me with permanent psychic scars before beating the ever-loving snot out of me. The only reason I had survived was that the wizard who was the greatest shape-shifter I'd ever seen had intervened. Listens-to-Wind had taken on the naagloshii head-to-head. Even then, it had been close, and the naagloshii had escaped to fight another day.

I've run into cruel and dangerous beings before. But the naagloshii were quite simply among the most evil creatures it had ever been my displeasure to encounter. And one of the damned things was *staring* at me from beneath a fragile layer of quartz I could have smashed with a wrench, its eyes burning like it was going to eat me whole.

I got a sudden sinking feeling.

And I turned to the next mound of quartz. And the next.

I'm a lucky guy. I didn't have one of the most nightmarish fiends in circulation lying on the floor within pouncing distance.

I had *six* of them.

There were more shapes beneath more crystal mounds. I didn't recognize them. I'm pretty sure I was extremely happy that I didn't.

"The least," I said, my voice shaking. "You're telling me that a *naa-gloshii* is one of the *least*." I felt like sitting down, so I did, sort of abruptly, onto the floor. "What . . . what else is in here?"

Demonreach turned to a wall. It lifted an arm and the stone of the wall faded into nonexistence, revealing a hallway maybe fifty feet across. I got back up onto my shaky legs again to take a look. The tunnel sloped down gently, and was lit by the wan glow of the crystals.

Lots of crystals.

Lots and lots and *lots* of crystals.

The tunnel stretched into the distance. Maybe it was a mile long. Maybe two. Maybe it ran all the way down to Hell. Mounds of crystals dotted the tunnel at regular intervals. Some of them were the size of buildings. Some of the individual crystals had to be the size of freaking trees. I had barely gotten my gawk on when a flood of energy smashed into me, as though opening the door had released liquid held back under pressure. The energy had no physical presence—but I felt a nauseating wave of greasy cold flooding through me, the dark power of the ley lines that converged upon the island breathing across me like a cloud of invisible smog.

"THE WELL," Demonreach said. The spirit turned, slowly, and eleven more doorways to tunnels almost identical to the first one sighed into existence. Eleven more of them. Because one infinite tunnel full of horrors obviously wasn't enough. *I had twelve.*

The dark energy from them hissed and oozed through the air, as if sheer malice and vicious will had been distilled into an unseen mist.

"And . . . and everything down there makes a naagloshii look like small change?" I asked.

"CORRECT."

"Of course. Naturally," I said, staring down the first hall. "What are they? What's down there?"

"NIGHTMARES. DARK GODS. NAMELESS THINGS. IM-MORTALS."

"Holy crap," I whispered. And that was when I understood why the place was called the Well. "This is *why* the island is the source of all those ley lines. It's like a great big bubbling geyser of bad."

Bob let out an awed whistle. "Uh. Wow, boss, yeah. That's exactly it. The energy in those ley lines . . . it's the body heat these things give off."

I felt a giggle coming up. "Man. Containment. Hell's bells, containment." I tried to stuff the giggles back down and addressed Demonreach. "This isn't a magical stronghold," I said. "It's a *prison*. It's a prison so hard that half a dozen freaking *naagloshii* are in *minimum security*."

"CORRECT," Demonreach answered, "WARDEN."

17

"I don't guess this job pays anything, does it?" I asked.

The spirit just regarded me.

"Didn't think so," I said. "So . . . when you call me Warden, you're speaking literally."

"INDEED."

"And you are what? The guard?"

"THE GUARD. THE WALLS. THE BARS. I AM ORDER."

"You are not the first law-person I would want to be involved with," I said. I raked my fingers back through my hair. "Okay," I said, wincing. "The things in here. Are they dangerous where they are?"

"THEY ARE ALWAYS DANGEROUS. BUT THEY HAVE THE LEAST OPPORTUNITY TO EXPRESS IT HERE."

I blinked. Those were some of the longest, most nuanced, and most complex sentiments the spirit had expressed to me. Which meant that we were speaking about something important—which only made sense. Demonreach didn't care about friends or enemies or the price of tea in China. It cared about its inmates, period. Anything else, *everything* else, would be judged based upon its relevance to that subject.

"But can they get loose?"

"NOT WITHOUT OUTSIDE INTERVENTION," Demonreach said, "OR YOUR AUTHORIZATION."

"Meep," I breathed. "Uh. You mean I could turn these things loose?"

"YOU ARE THE WARDEN."

I swallowed. "Is it possible for me to communicate with them?"

"YOU ARE THE WARDEN."

"Oh, Hell's bells, this is bad."

I had just inherited myself a world of trouble.

Having experienced a naagloshii up close and personal, there wasn't any way I was letting one of those hideous things loose. I doubted I was going to like anything *else* that was being held prisoner here any better. In fact, I had no intention, for the time being, of even *looking* at them, much less finding out who and what the inmates were—and forget about actually *talking* to them. Not going to happen. Things that old and powerful could be deadly with only a few carefully chosen words dropped at the right place—and I'd learned that one the hard way, too.

But none of that really mattered.

I'd just been handed what amounted to a great big ugly weapon of mass destruction and potential havoc. To the various powers of the supernatural world, it wouldn't matter that I would never use it. All that would matter was that I *had* it to use. Really, Officer, I know that's a rocket launcher in my trunk, but I'm only holding it so that someone *bad* won't use it. Really. Honest.

The guys in the White Council who didn't like me were going to turn purple and start frothing at the mouth when they found out. And every foe the White Council ever had would start looking at me like a gift from Heaven—someone with knowledge of the inner workings of the Council, with enormously concentrated personal power, who was almost certain to frighten the Council enough to make them suspect, isolate, and eventually move against him. That guy would be an awesome asset in any struggle against the wizards of the world.

And boy, wouldn't the White Council know it?

Like I didn't have enough recruiters aiming for me already.

And hey, the very best part? *I didn't actually have a real, usable super-weapon.* I just had the key to a great big box full of pain and trouble for a whole lot of people.

No wonder my grandfather had looked stunned when he'd seen what I had done with Demonreach. Or maybe less "stunned" than "horrified."

My head was starting to ache again. Dammit, this was all I needed.

Over the past few years, my headaches had grown steadily worse, to the point where sometimes they all but knocked me unconscious. I could function through it, to some degree—you don't spend most of your life learning to manipulate the powers of the universe without racking up a considerable amount of self-discipline and tolerance for pain. But it was just one more freaking stone being added to the baggage I had to carry while I tried to get out of the tightest corner I had ever been in.

Demonreach growled. In all capital letters.

And the headache vanished.

One second, my scalp was tightening up as two separate ice picks dug into my skull in the same places they always did, and the next the pain was utterly gone. The endorphins my body had started pumping got to the scene to find no pain there and threw a party instead. I didn't fall over in a dazed stupor, because of my universe-manipulating chops, but it was close.

"Whoa," I breathed. "Uh . . . what did you just do?"

"I WARNED IT."

I blinked several times. "You . . . warned away my headache?"

"THE CREATURE CAUSING IT. THE PARASITE."

I stared stupidly for a second, and then sorted through my memories again. That's right. Right here in this chamber, the last time I'd been here, either Mab or Demonreach had said something about the division of labor keeping my body alive while the rest of me was elsewhere. They'd said that the parasite kept my heart running. I glowered at Demonreach and said, "Tell me about this parasite."

"I WILL NOT."

I made an exasperated sound. "*Why* not?"

"IT BARGAINED."

"With *what*?"

"YOUR LIFE, WARDEN."

I thought about that one for a few seconds. "Wait. . . . You needed its help to save me? And its price was that you don't tell me about it?"

"INDEED."

I exhaled slowly and ran my fingers over my head. Something was running around in there, giving me migraines. "Is it a danger to me?"

"IN TIME."

"What happens if it stays in there?" I asked.

"IT BURSTS FORTH FROM YOUR SKULL."

"Aglck!" I said. I couldn't help it. My skin was crawling. I'd seen those *Alien* movies at a formative age. "How do I get it out?"

Demonreach seemed to consider that for a moment. Then it said, "ASK GRASSHOPPER."

"Molly? Uh, seriously? You know she's new, right?"

It just looked at me.

"How long do I have to take care of it?" I asked.

"SOON."

"Soon? How soon is soon? What do you mean, soon?"

It just stared at me.

Right. Immortal, inhuman, wholly-focused-on-holding-evil-horde-still-forever sorts of creatures don't have a real solid grasp of the concept of time. From what I've seen and heard over the years, I've begun to understand that linear time is a uniquely mortal perspective. Other things aren't attached to it nearly as tightly as we are. There were bushes on the island older than me. There were trees there older than Chicago. Demonreach was not compatible with stopwatches or day planners.

"Okay," I said. "Okay, priorities: Put the skull-bursting-parasite issue aside for the moment. That leaves me in charge of a veritable doomsday machine that the White Council and everyone else is gonna flip out about. But they aren't going to flip out about it today, because presumably they don't even know I'm alive yet, and if I don't stay focused on the next twenty-four hours, I might not live long enough to have all that fun. So we forget about that for now, too."

"SENSIBLE PRIORITIES."

"I'm glad you approve," I said. I was pretty sure something that didn't understand minutes and seconds wouldn't be big on getting sarcasm either. "You've still got a problem. I need you to explain it to me."

"YOU ARE TOO LIMITED," Demonreach said. "IT WOULD DAMAGE YOU, AS IT DAMAGED YOUR SPIRIT."

I held up both my hands and half flinched. "For God's sake, don't *think* it at me. You think way too loud."

The glowing eyes looked somehow disgusted. "THIS MEANS OF CONVEYANCE OF IDEAS IS INEFFICIENT AND LIMITED."

"Words, words, words," I said. "Tell me about it. But it's what we've got, unless you can draw me a picture."

Demonreach was still for a moment—and then vines abruptly twined up out of the floor. I almost jumped, but stopped myself. It clearly hadn't done me any harm, apart from what I'd done to myself, and if it wanted to hurt me, I wasn't going to be able to stop it anyway. So I waited.

The vines twined up into my bag and came out wrapped around Bob's skull.

"Harry!" Bob squeaked.

"He's one of mine," I said in a hard voice. "You hurt him and you can forget me helping you."

"LITTLE ENTITY," Demonreach said. "YOU ARE FAMILIAR WITH THE WARDEN. YOU WILL TRANSLATE. YOU WILL NOT BE DAMAGED."

"Hey!" I said, and took a step between Demonreach and Bob. "Did you hear me, Hopalong? Put down the skull."

"Harry!" Bob said again. "Harry, wait! It heard you!"

I scowled and turned to look at Bob. He looked like the same old Bob. "Yeah?"

"Yeah," the skull said. The eyelights were flicking everywhere, as if watching dozens of screens at once. "Man, this thing is big! And old!"

"Is it hurting you?"

"Uh, no . . . no, it isn't. And it could if it wanted to. It's just . . . kind of a lot to take in. . . ." Then the skull quivered in the grip of the tendrils and said, "Oh!"

"Oh, what?" I asked.

"It's explaining the problem," Bob reported. "It had to take it through several levels of dumbing-down before I was able to get it."

I grunted and relaxed a little. "Oh. So what's the problem?"

"Hang on. I'm trying to figure out how to dumb it down enough for *you* to get it."

"Thanks," I growled.

"I got your back, boss." Then Bob bounced up and down in the ten-drils a few times. "Hey, Hopalong! Turn this thing around this way!"

Demonreach glowered at the skull.

Bob jiggled a little more. "Come on! We're on a schedule here!"

I blinked at that. "Damn. You went from scared to wiseass pretty quick there, Bob."

Bob snorted. "'Cause as big and bad as this thing is, it needs me to talk to you, and that makes me important. And it knows it."

"LESSER BEINGS ONCE KNEW TO RESPECT THEIR EL-DERS," Demonreach said.

"I respect the crap out of you," Bob complained. "You want me to help, and I'm telling you how. Now turn me around."

A sudden breeze passed through the cavern in a long, enormous sigh. And the vines stirred and twisted the skull toward the nearest wall.

Bob's eyelights brightened to brilliance and suddenly cast double cones of light on the wall. There was a scratchy sound that seemed to emanate from the skull itself, a blur of a sound like an old film sound track warming up, and then the old spotlight-sweeping 20th Century Fox logo appeared on the wall, along with the pompous trumpet-led symphony theme that often accompanied it.

"A movie?" I asked. "You can play *movies*?"

"And music! And TV! Butters gave me the Internet, baby! Now hush and pay attention."

The opening logo bit faded to black and then familiar blue lettering appeared. It read: A LONG TIME AGO, PRETTY MUCH RIGHT HERE . . .

"Okay, come on," I said. "You're going to buy me a lawsuit, Bob."

"Hush, Harry. Or you'll go to the special hell."

I blinked at that, confused. I'm not supposed to be the guy who doesn't get the reference joke, dammit.

On the wall, the black gave way to a star field that panned down to a blue-and-green planet. Earth. Then it zoomed in and in and in until I recognized the outline of Lake Michigan and the other Great Lakes, and came closer still until it got to the outline of the island itself.

Bob is invaluable, but man, he loves his wisecracks and his drama.

The image sank down until it showed a familiar landing point, though it had no ruined town and no Whatsup Dock and no row of wooden piles in the water. It was just a little beach of dirt and sand and heavy, brooding forest growth.

Then a ribbon of light maybe eight feet long split the air vertically. The light broadened until it was maybe three feet wide, and then a figure appeared through it. I recognized the signs—someone had opened a Way, a passage from the Nevernever to the island. The figure emerged, made a gesture with one hand, and the Way closed behind it.

It was a man, fairly tall, fairly lean. He wore ragged clothing in many shades of grey. His grey cloak had a deep hood on it, and it shadowed his features, except for the tip of his nose and a short grey-white beard covering a rather pointy chin.

(Letters appeared at the bottom of the screen. They read: MERLIN.)

"Wait? You saw Merlin?" I asked Bob.

"Nah," Bob said, "but I cast Alec Guinness. Looks good, right?"

I sighed. "Could you get to the point, please?"

"Oh, come on," Bob said. "I wrote in this romance triangle subplot and cast Jenna Jameson and Carrie Fisher. There's a love scene you're gonna *really*—"

"Bob!"

"Okay, okay. Fine. Sheesh."

The movie shifted into fast motion. The grey-clad figure became a blur. It walked about waving its arms, and directed oceans of energy here and there, settling them all in and around the substance of the island itself.

"Wait. Did Demonreach tell you how he did that?"

"No," Bob said, annoyed. "It's called artistic license, Harry."

"Okay, I get it. Merlin built the island. However he did it. Get to the part with the problem."

Bob sighed.

Merlin walked into the woods in comically fast motion and vanished. Then time passed. The sun streaked by hundreds and then thousands of times, the shadows of the island bowing and twisting, the trees rising, growing, growing old, and dying. At the bottom of the screen, words appeared that read, A LOT OF TIME PASSES.

"Thank you for dumbing that down for me," I said.

"*De nada.*"

Then the camera slowed. Again, Merlin appeared. Again, oceans of power rose up and settled into the island. Then Merlin vanished, and more years passed. Maybe a minute later, he appeared again—looking exactly the same, I might add—and repeated the cycle.

"Hold on," I said. "He did it again? Twice?"

"Ah," Bob said, as a fourth cycle began on the screen. "Sort of. See, Harry, this is one of those things that you're going to have trouble grabbing onto."

"Go slow and try me."

"Merlin didn't build the prison five times," Bob said. "He built it once. In five *different* times. All at the same time."

I felt my brows knit. "Uh. He was in the same place, doing the same thing, in five different times at once?"

"Exactly."

"That does not make any sense," I said.

"Look, a mortal jail is built in three dimensions, right? Merlin built this one in four, and probably in several more, though you can't really tell whether or not he built it in a given dimension until you go there and measure it, and the act of measuring it will change it, but the point is: This is really advanced stuff."

I sighed. "Yeah. I'm getting that. But what's wrong?"

The shot zoomed out, rising up to give a top-down view of the island, which became a blurry shape. A familiar five-pointed star blazed itself across the surface of the lake, its lines so long that the pentagon shape at its center enfolded the island entirely. Within the pentagon, a second pentacle formed, like the first one drawn in the manner to preserve and protect. The camera tightened in, and I saw that the second pentagon enfolded the entire hilltop where the cottage and ruined tower lay. The camera tightened more, and I saw more pentacles drawn, this time not flat but at dozens of intersecting angles, their centers encircling the dozen tunnels full of evil beings beneath the island.

"These," Bob said, "represent the original enchantments on the island. This is vastly simplified, of course, but the basic star-and-circle architecture is the same as the work you do, Harry."

Then the design blurred and increased, growing denser and more delicate and more brilliant in power, until something twinged in my brain and I had to look away from the diagram.

"Yeah, sorry about that, boss. This is meant to represent the entanglement of the spells being delivered at different times."

"No wonder it was so complicated," I muttered.

"And it's even worse than this," Bob said. "I'm filtering it down for you. And here's the problem."

I forced myself to look back at the projection, and saw those millions upon millions of spells resonating with one another, spreading and interlocking into an impenetrable barrier. It was, I thought, somehow like watching crystals grow. The spells powering the actual construction of it hadn't been, alone, too much stronger than some of the work I had done—but when they'd been interconnected with their counterparts across time, they'd fed upon one another, created a perfect resonance of energy that had become something infinitely greater than the sum of its parts.

Then I saw the dissonance appear. Bob had chosen to show it as a sullen red light that began to pulse lightly at the westernmost edges of the great design. It began as something faint, but then, like an oncoming headache, started to throb into something larger and more noticeable. Where scarlet and blue light touched, there were ugly flares of energy—flares that I had been sensing ever since I'd gotten to the island. Before long, that scarlet pulse had spread to half the island, and then, abruptly, the screen went white.

Text at the bottom read, NOVEMBER 1.

"By tomorrow," I said. "Super. But I still don't see what is *wrong*, Bob."

"Energy hits it," Bob said. "A directed burst of energy, a whole lot of it. It unravels the whole containment spell Merlin laid down and triggers the fail-safe."

"FIRE," rumbled Demonreach.

"I figured that one out, thanks," I said. "But nothing has actually happened to the spells yet?"

"Nope," said Bob. "That tension that's building? It's . . . Well, think of it as cause and effect, only backward."

"Huh?"

"What the island is experiencing now is the echo of the moment that burst of energy strikes it," Bob said. "Only instead of the echo happening after, it's happening first."

I stopped and thought. "You're telling me that the reason the island is about to blow up is . . . because it's about to blow up?"

Bob sighed. "Someone hits the island with energy, Harry. But they've figured out *how* Merlin put this place together. They aren't attacking it in three dimensions. They're attacking in *four*. They're sending power through *time* as well as through space."

"So . . . I have to stop them from attacking the island tomorrow?"

"No," Bob said, exasperated. "You have to stop them from attacking whenever it is that they actually *attack*."

"Uh . . ."

"Look, the rock they're throwing hits tomorrow," Bob said. "But you have to stop them from throwing it at whatever point they're standing when they throw it."

"Oh," I said, blinking. "I get that."

Bob turned to look at Demonreach. "Do you see what I have to work with here? I had to take *that* down to throwing a *rock* before it got through."

"HIS UNDERSTANDING IS LIMITED," Demonreach agreed.

"Okay, I've had just about enough from both of you," I said. "If you're so smart, how come *you* don't stop it from happening?"

"THE EXPLANATION WOULD DAMAGE YOU, WARDEN."

Bob made an impatient sound. "Because that spirit *is* the island, Harry. The spells, the Well, the physical island, all of it. Demonreach *does not exist* outside this island. It has *no* ability to reach beyond itself. The attack is coming from *outside* the prison. That's why it needs a Warden in the first place."

I scowled. "It talked to me in the graveyard last year."

"It bullied Mab into helping it," Bob said.

"I DID NOT BULLY. I BARGAINED."

"Okay, okay," I said. "I'll add that to my list, then. Find whoever it is, wherever they are, and stop them from doing something they haven't done yet."

"Unless they have," Bob said. "In which case, well. Kinda too late."

"Right," I said tiredly.

I had my own private purgatory full of sleeping monsters.

I had a parasite in my brain that was fixing to burst my skull on its way out of me.

My little island paradise was about to explode with enough energy to cook dark gods and Lord only knew what else hanging around under the island. That meant we were talking about a release of energy in the gigaton range. And if I didn't stop someone from doing it, the continental shelf was about to have a very bad day.

Oh, right. And I was supposed to kill an insane immortal—or else face the wrath of her mother.

And I had to do it all in the next twenty-four hours. Maybe a little less.

"And the sad part is, this actually feels like having my life back. How bent is that?"

"Harry," Bob said. "Sunrise in one hour."

"Right." I sighed and picked up the skull. I tucked him away into the messenger bag and said to Demonreach, "I'm on it."

"GOOD."

I muttered darkly under my breath and turned for the stairs, then started jogging back up them, thinking of all the problems arrayed against me.

Good thing I'd been working out.

18

Okay, for the record: That is one *hell* of a lot of stairs to go up.

Also for the record: I did them two and three at a time, at a run, and went to the top without stopping.

From there, I went pounding down the hillside, my feet never slipping or faltering, until I got back to the beach, moving at an easy run. The sun was rising behind me, but the solid mass of Demonreach kept it blotted out in shadow, and I could tell only by the light beginning to fill the sky.

Thomas came to his feet as I left the woods, his hands moving to his weapons automatically. I shook my head at him, never slowing down, and said, "Let's get this tub moving!"

"What did you find out?" he called. He started untying the lines and then leapt nimbly up to the deck of the *Water Beetle*. Molly appeared from the cabin, looking as though she'd been sleeping a few seconds before.

I ran down the dock and hopped up to the ship's deck. "A bunch of people are gonna be mad at me, I've got some kind of medical issue that's going to kill me in a while if I don't deal with it, oh, and the island's blowing up tomorrow and taking a whole lot of the country with it if I don't fix it."

Thomas gave me a steady look. "So," he said. "Same old, same old."

"I think it's nice that there are some things in this world you can rely on," I said.

My brother snorted and started the *Water Beetle*'s engines. We backed away from the dock, and then he turned, gunned it, and headed back toward town. Like I said before, the boat isn't a racing machine, but it's got some horsepower in it, and as the sun rose properly, we were zooming over the orange-gold water, leaving a huge V-shaped wake behind us, while I stood at the front of the boat, my hands on the railing.

I felt it when the dawn broke, the way you almost always can if you stop to pay attention. Something subtle and profound simply shifted in the air around me. Even if I'd been blindfolded, I would have felt the transition, the way that the winds and currents of energy broadly known as magic began to gust and shift, driven by the light of the oncoming sun.

I wasn't close enough to any of the Ways to the realms of Faerie to be able to sense whether they had been reopened, but it made sense that they would be. Sunrise tends to disperse and dissolve patterns of magical energy—not because magic is inherently a force of the night so much as because the dawn is inherently a force of new beginnings and renewal.

Every sunrise tended to erode ongoing enchantments. A spell spread so wide that it curtained the whole of Faerie away from the mortal world would by necessity be rather thin and fragile. When the sun hit it, it would be like about a zillion magnifying glasses focusing light on old newsprint. It would blacken and wither away. My mind treated me to a gruesome little collage of images—the darkest beings of Faerie suddenly pouring forth from every creepy shadow and unsettling alley and dangerous-looking old abandoned building in the city. You'd think my mind would find better things to do, like fantasize about improbably friendly women or something.

Molly came up and stood with me, facing ahead. I looked at her obliquely. The rising sun behind us painted her hair gold but left her face lightly veiled in shadow. She didn't look young anymore.

I mean, don't get me wrong; it wasn't like her hair had gone grey and her teeth fell out. But there had always been a sense of energy and life and simple joy welling up from the grasshopper. It had been her default setting, and I hadn't realized how much I had loved that about her.

Now her blue eyes looked weary, wary. She wasn't looking at the beauty in life as much as she once had. Her eyes scanned for dangers both nearby and farther down the road, heavy with caution and made wise by pain—and they had far, far more steel in them than I had ever seen there before.

Months of training with the Leanansidhe while fighting a street war will do that.

Maybe if I'd been tougher on the grasshopper early on, it wouldn't have come as such a shock to her. Maybe if I'd focused on different aspects of her training, she would have been better prepared.

Maybe, maybe, maybe, but I was kidding myself. Molly's eyes were always going to end up like that sooner or later—just like mine had.

This business doesn't play nice with children.

"I told you," Molly said, never looking toward me. "It's in the past. Leave it there."

"You listening to my head, kiddo?"

Her mouth twitched. "Only when I want to hear the roar of the ocean."

I grinned. I liked that *so* much better than all the "Sir Knights" I'd been getting lately.

"How much can you tell me?" she asked.

I looked at her eyes for a moment while she stared ahead and made a decision.

"Everything," I said quietly. "But not right this second. We've got priorities to focus on first. We can get into the details after we've dealt with the immediate threat."

"Maeve?" Molly asked.

"And the island." I told her about the danger to Demonreach without going into specifics about the island's purpose. "So if I don't stop it, boom."

Molly frowned. "I can't imagine how you can stop an event from happening if you don't know who is going to do it, and both where and when it's going to happen."

"If the problem was simple and easy, it wouldn't require wizards to fix it," I said. "The impossible we do immediately. The unimaginable takes a little while."

"I'm serious," she said.

"So am I," I replied. "Be of good cheer. I think I know the right guy to talk to about this one."

Half the sun was over the horizon when Chicago's skyline came into sight. I just basked in that for a minute. Yeah, I know, stupid, but it's my town and I'd been gone for what felt like a lifetime. It was good to see the autumn sun gleaming off of glass and steel.

Then I felt myself tense, and I pushed myself up from where I'd been leaning on the forward rail. I took a moment to look around me very carefully. I didn't know what had set off my instincts, but they were doing the same routine they'd learned to do every time Mab had been about to spring her daily assassination attempt, and I couldn't have ignored them if I'd wanted to.

I didn't see anything, but then I heard it—the humming roar of small, high-revolution engines.

"Thomas!" I shouted over the snorting of the *Water Beetle*'s motor. I gestured toward my ear and then spun my hand in a wide circle.

It wasn't exactly tactical sign language, but Thomas got the message. From his vantage point in the wheelhouse atop the cabin, he swept his gaze around warily. Then his gaze locked on something northwest of us.

"Uh-oh," I breathed.

Thomas spun the wheel and rolled the *Water Beetle* onto a southwesterly course. I hustled over to the ladder up to the wheelhouse and stood on the top rung, which put my head about level with Thomas's. I shielded my eyes from the glare of the oncoming sun with one hand and peered northwest.

There were five Jet Skis flying toward us over the water. Thomas had altered course enough to buy us a little time, but I could see at a glance that the Jet Skis were moving considerably faster than we were. Thomas opened the throttle all the way and passed me, I kid you not, a shiny brass telescope.

"Seriously?" I asked him.

"Ever since those pirate movies came out, they're everywhere," he said. "I've got a sextant, too."

"Any tent you have is a sex tent," I muttered darkly, extending the telescope.

Thomas smirked.

I peered through the thing, holding myself steady with one hand. Given the speed and bounce of the boat, it wasn't easy, but I finally managed to get a prolonged glimpse of the Jet Skis. I couldn't see much in the way of detail yet—but the guy on the lead Jet Ski was wearing a bright red beret.

"We've definitely got a problem," I said.

"Friends of yours?"

"The Redcap and some of his Sidhe buddies, it looks like," I said, lowering the telescope. "They're Winter muscle, but I think they're mostly medieval types. That gives us a couple of minutes to—"

There was a sharp hissing sound and something unseen slapped the telescope out of my hand, sending it spinning through the air in a whirl of torn metal and tiny shards of broken glass.

The report of a gunshot followed a second later.

"Holy crap!" I sputtered, and dropped down to lie flat on the deck. There was another hiss and a loud cracking sound as a round smacked into the wall of the cabin above me.

"Medieval? Are you sure you know what that means?" Thomas demanded. He heeled the boat about a bit and then snaked it back in the original direction, following a serpentine course. That would make us a harder target—but it also meant that we were going slower, cruising in a zigzag while our pursuers were rushing forward in a straight line.

But even with the maneuvers, the rounds kept coming in. At that distance, with the relative movements of the vehicles, a purely human marksman could have hit us only through something that went well past good luck and began approaching divine intervention. But the Redcap and his cronies weren't human. The grace I'd seen the Sidhe displaying on the dance floor had been all precise, subtle elegance and flawless grace. Both of those things transitioned well into marksmanship.

I still had my shiny, gleaming cowboy rifle, but it was worse than useless in this situation. The .45 Colt round would be killer at conventional gunfight distances, most of which happened at about twenty feet—but it would lose a lot of effectiveness shooting at targets that distant. Coincidentally, the guy holding the gun would also lose effectiveness shooting at targets that distant. So blazing away at them seemed like a stupid plan.

"Hey!" I shouted toward my brother. "If I take the wheel, can you pick them off from here?"

"If we drive straight, maybe!" he called back.

A round tore a chunk of wood off the corner of the boat's dashboard. Thomas stared hard at it for a second. Six inches to the left and it would have hit him in the lower back.

"Uh," he said, continuing to veer and swerve the boat. "Plan B?"

"Right," I muttered. "Right. Plan B."

I thought furiously while the fusillade continued. Rounds hit the side of the ship in sharp, angry whacks. Surely they didn't have the ammunition to keep this kind of thing up for very long. Though, thinking about it, I had no idea how rapidly they were going through the ammo. For all I knew, one guy was shooting at us, and getting more and more successful at judging the shot over the surface of the water. And the Sidhe were closing. Their accuracy seemed to be increasing as they did. Once they got into optimal range, where they were close enough to land rounds but we weren't capable of replying in kind, all they had to do was maintain the distance and kill us to death.

I could start throwing magic at them, but Mab's training had a gap in it: Everything had been right up in my grille. I'd never engaged her or one of her proxies at more than twenty feet or so, and without a properly prepared staff or blasting rod, I'd never be able to reach out far enough to hit those clowns. Odds were good that they knew it, too. They'd hold the distance.

A weakness. I had to exploit a weakness. The Sidhe hated iron, but even if I found some, how did I get it to them? I mean, a gun shooting jacketed rounds would really screw them up, but for it to work I'd have to hit them. There was a box of nails in the toolbox. I could throw those, maybe, but again there was the issue of actually hitting them. Which wasn't going to happen as long as they were way out there.

I needed to lure them in closer.

"Grasshopper!" I shouted.

The cabin door swung open and Molly belly-crawled onto the deck until she could see me. "Who started shooting at us?"

"Bad guys!" I cringed as another round hit the side of the boat and peppered me with wooden splinters. "Obviously!"

"Can we outrun them?"

"Not happening," I said. "Ideas?"

"I could veil us?"

"Going to be hard to hide the boat's wake, isn't it?"

"Oh. Right. What do we do?"

"I need mist," I said. "A bunch of it. Gimme."

"Oh, ow, I don't know Harry. I'd have to move an awful lot of fire to give you even a little. You know that's not my thing."

"It doesn't have to be *real* mist," I said.

"Oh!" Molly called. "That is *exactly* my thing!"

"Attagirl!"

"Fuck!" Thomas snarled. I looked up to see him stagger, holding on to the boat's wheel with his right hand, his face twisted in pain. He'd taken a bullet in his left arm, just above the elbow, and he held it clenched in tight against his body, teeth bared. Slightly too pale blood trickled down his elbow and dribbled to the deck. "Plan B, Harry! Where the hell is plan B?!"

"Go, go, go!" I told Molly.

My apprentice closed her eyes and clenched her fists. I saw her focus, felt the slight stirring in the air as she gathered her will and power. Then she moved her hands in a complicated little gesture, whispering something. She continued making the gesture, and I realized that the motion was duplicating that of weaving three lines into a braid.

From between her fingers a thick white mist began to appear. First it came as a trickle, but as I watched it thickened to a stream. Then Molly bowed her head in concentration and muttered words beneath her breath, and a sudden plume of white mist bigger than the *Water Beetle* itself began jetting from her hands and spreading out to blanket the surface of the water over the boat's wake, shutting the pursuing Sidhe away from view.

For a long minute we raced across the water, a wall of white mist spreading out to cover our wake. The enemy fire continued for a few seconds, but then dropped off to nothing. Hell, if we could keep this up, maybe we could make it back to shore without doing anything more. I checked Molly. Her face was pale, twisted into a grimace of concentration, and already the plume of illusory mist was beginning to wane. Mist isn't a hard illusion to pull off, and it's usually the first thing an apprentice learns to do with that kind of magic, but Molly was spreading the illusion out over an enormous area, and brute-force approaches were not her strong point in magic. We wouldn't make it back to shore that way.

Fine, then.

"Thomas!" I shouted. "Throttle down! Let them catch up to us and then gun it!"

Thomas slowed the boat abruptly, and the sound of screaming Jet Ski engines rose up over the *Water Beetle*'s motor, growing higher-pitched as they approached.

"Molly, drop it on my signal!"

"'Kay," she gasped.

My brother stood at the wheel with his eyes closed, focused intently on the sound. Then, abruptly, he gunned the *Water Beetle*'s engines again.

"Molly, now!"

Molly let out a groan and the illusionary cloud of white mist vanished as if it had never existed.

The formation of oncoming Jet Skis was only about fifty yards away, charging hard after us over the water, and they were moving so much more swiftly than us that within seconds they were almost on top of the *Water Beetle*. Jet Skis started swerving left and right to avoid a collision with our boat.

All except for the Redcap. He was guiding the Jet Ski with one hand and held a military carbine in the other. His eyes widened as the vehicle rushed closer, but rather than swerving to one side, he broke out into a wild smile, swung the gun around to point toward me, and *accelerated*.

Before he could shoot, I unleashed my gathered will into a burst of completely unfocused magical energy, shouting, "*Hexus!*"

I think I mentioned before how technology doesn't get along with wizards. Put any kind of intricate machine in a wizard's presence, and suddenly everything that *might* go wrong with the machine *does* go wrong. And that's when we're not even *trying* to make it happen. Electronics generally get hit the hardest, like poor Butters's computers, but that particular law of magical forces is good across the spectrum.

Jet Skis, especially the brand-new ones, are intricate machines. They focus tremendous power and energy into a tiny space, and their systems are regulated by little computers and so on. They're a gathering of tiny, nearly continuous explosions in a box, moving water under intense pressure—and a world of things can go wrong with them.

The Redcap's Jet Ski suffered an abrupt, catastrophic engine failure. There was a hideous sound of tearing metal, a flash of flame, and the handlebar twisted abruptly from his hands. The Jet Ski's nose plunged down into the water, flinging the Redcap off of it at full speed. He'd been doing maybe sixty when I hit him, and he skipped twice across the water's surface before he slammed into a swell from the *Water Beetle*'s wake and vanished under the surface.

Thomas, meanwhile, had seized another opportunity. As the Jet Skis split off to swing around us, he whirled the steering wheel, turning the *Water Beetle* sharply to her left. I heard one scream, and a crunching sound accompanied by a heavy reverberation in the deck beneath my feet as a Jet Ski slammed into our boat's nose—with results very similar to a deer slamming into a speeding semi.

"Hexus!" Molly shouted from where she was crouched on the deck. Her aim was good, even if her hex wouldn't carry the same kind of raw power mine did. The Jet Ski Thomas had missed suddenly began billowing smoke, and its roaring engine cut away to a gasping, labored rattle.

I spun to face the other direction, pitching another hex at the two Jet Skis passing on the far side of the ship. They were at the edge of my range and racing away, so my hex didn't convince their engines to tear themselves apart, the way the short-range, focused curse had the Redcap's vehicle—but one of the Jet Skis abruptly began coasting to a stop, and the other took a sharp right turn and then simply went on turning in a furious, continuous circle.

Thomas opened up the throttle all the way, and the *Water Beetle* left the lamed flotilla of would-be assassins bobbing in her wake.

I didn't relax until I'd swept the ship's exterior with my eyes and magical senses alike to make sure no one was hanging on to a rail or something. Then, just to be certain, I double-checked the cabin and hold, until I was certain that no one had infiltrated the boat in the chaos.

And then I sank down in relief on a chair in the cabin. But only for a second. Then I grabbed the first-aid kit and went up to the bridge to see to Thomas.

Molly was sprawled on the deck in the morning sunshine, exhausted from her efforts, and obviously asleep. She snored a little. I stepped over her and went up to my brother. He saw me and grunted. "We should be pulling into port in another fifteen minutes," he said. "I think we're clear."

"That won't last," I said. "How's your arm?"

"Through and through," Thomas said. "Not too bad. Just stop the leak."

"Hold still," I told him. Then I started working on his arm. It wasn't bad, as bullet wounds go. It had entered the lean muscle at the bottom of his triceps in back and come out the other side, leaving a small hole. That had probably been the Redcap, then—the rounds from his M4 would be armor-piercing, metal-jacketed military rounds, specifically designed to punch long, fairly small holes. I cleaned it up with disinfectant, got a pressure bandage positioned over the holes, and taped it down. "Okay, you can stop complaining now."

Thomas, who had been silent the whole time, gave me a look.

"You can have your harem change out the bandages later," I said. "How busy are you today?"

"Oh," he mused. "I don't know. I mean, I've got to get a new shirt now."

"After that," I asked, "would you like to help me save the city? If you don't already have plans."

He snorted. "You mean, would I like to follow you around, wondering what the hell is going on because you won't tell me everything, then get in a fight with something that is going to leave me in intensive care?"

"Uh-huh," I said, nodding, "pretty much."

"Yeah," he said. "Okay."

19

We took Thomas's car back to his apartment.

"You got the Hummer fixed," I said approvingly.

He snorted. "After I let you ride in it, it went undamaged for what, about thirty minutes?"

"Come on," I said, stretching out my legs. There was room. "It was at least an hour. How you doing back there, Molly?"

From the backseat, Molly snored. I smiled. The grasshopper had shambled to the truck and flung herself down on the backseat without saying a word.

"She okay?" Thomas asked.

"She pushed it today," I said.

"With that mist thing? She does illusions all the time, I thought."

"Dude," I said. "It was hundreds of yards long and hundreds of yards across. That's a huge freaking image to project, especially over water."

"Because water grounds out magic?" Thomas asked.

"Exactly right," I said. "And be glad it does, or the Sidhe would have been chucking lightning bolts at us instead of bullets. Molly had to sustain her image while the energy from which it was made kept on draining away. And then she hexed one of the Jet Skis. For her, that's some serious heavy lifting. She's tired."

He frowned. "Like that time you collapsed at my dad's place?"

"More or less," I said. "Molly's still relatively new at this. The first few times you hit your wall, it just about knocks you out. She'll be fine."

"So how come the Sidhe didn't hex up their own engines? I mean, I'm guessing a Jet Ski would run for about ten seconds with you on it."

"I'd give it ten or fifteen minutes," I said. "And it worked for the Sidhe because they aren't human."

"Why should that make a difference?"

I shrugged. "No one really knows. Ebenezar thinks it's because human beings are inherently conflicted creatures. Magic responds to your thoughts and to your emotions—and people's thoughts and emotions are constantly conflicting with one another. The way he figures it, that means that there's a kind of turbulence around people with magical talent. The turbulence is what causes mechanical failure."

"Why?"

I shrugged again. "It's just the way things are. The specific effects this turbulence causes tend to change slowly over time. Three hundred years ago, it made cream turn sour, disturbed animals, and tended to encourage minor skin infections in wizards. Gave them blemishes and moles and pockmarks."

"Fun," Thomas said.

"Yeah, I'm not upset about missing out on that kind of fun," I said. "Then sometime between then and now, it segued into triggering odd flashes of hallucination in the people who hung around in close proximity to us. You know the whole ergot theory of history? People with talent, especially people who didn't even know they had it, probably had a lot to do with that. Now it mucks around with probability where machines are concerned."

Thomas eyed me. Then he carefully powered off his truck's stereo.

"Funny," I said. After a moment I added, "I don't mean to do it. I mean, I try not to do it, but . . ."

"I don't mind if you break my stuff," Thomas said. "I'll just make Lara buy me new stuff."

Lara, Thomas's half sister, was the power behind the throne of the White Court of vampires. Lara was gorgeous, brilliant, and sexier than a Swedish bikini team hiking up a mountain of money. As a potential enemy, she was a little scary. As an occasional ally, she was freaking terrifying.

I wasn't ever going to tell Thomas this, but when I'd been arranging my own murder, Lara had been the runner-up on my list of possible administrators of my demise. I mean, hey, if you're going to go, there are worse ways to do it than to be taken out by the freaking queen of the world's succubi.

"How's Lara doing?" I asked.

"She's Lara," Thomas said. "Always doing business, planning plans, scheming schemes."

"Like the Brighter Future Society?" I asked. The BFS was an alliance of unlikely bedfellows of the supernatural scene in Chicago, headquartered out of a small but genuine castle, guarded by hired guns from Valhalla.

Thomas bared his teeth in a smile. "That was Lara's idea, actually. Marcone imported that freaking castle and had it rebuilt over your old boardinghouse. Lara says it's impregnable."

"The Death Star was impregnable," I said. "So Lara got in bed with Marcone?"

"She tried," Thomas said, "but Marcone kept it purely business. That's two men who have turned her down in the same century. She was annoyed."

I grunted. I'd been the other guy. John Marcone was the crime lord of Chicago. He could buy and sell United States congressmen, and had the establishment in Chicago completely wired. He was also the first regular mortal to sign on to the Unseelie Accords, and according to them, he was the baron of Chicago.

"I was sort of hoping she'd kill him," I said.

"I was sort of hoping for the other way around," Thomas said. "But with the Fomor trying to muscle in on everyone's territory, they need each other—for now."

"The Fomor are that bad?" I asked. They were a crew of bad guys whose names were known primarily in old mythology books, the survivors of a number of dark mythoi across the world, the worst of the worst—or at least the most survival-minded of the worst.

"They're ruthless," Thomas said. "And they're everywhere. But between Marcone's hired goons, Lara's resources, and Murphy's people, they haven't gotten a solid foothold here. Other cities, it's bad. Los Angeles, Seattle, San Francisco, Miami, and Boston are the worst off. They're grabbing anyone with a lick of magical ability and carrying them away. Thousands of people."

"Hell's bells," I muttered. "What about the White Council?"

"They're busy," Thomas said. "Word is that they're operating around the coasts of Europe, especially in the Mediterranean, fighting the Fomor there. Lara's people have been sharing a little information with the Council, and vice versa, but there's nothing like an alliance."

"They aren't working in the U.S. at all?" I asked.

Thomas shrugged. "Your Warden buddies are trying," he said. "Ramirez got hurt pretty bad last year. I don't think he's back in action yet. But the Wardens in Baltimore and San Diego are holding out, and the kid in Texas is giving them hell."

"Good for Wild Bill," I said. "So how come other cities haven't gone down?"

"Lara," Thomas said simply. His voice altered subtly and I could recognize the precise, enunciated tones that marked his sister's voice. "We labored for centuries to cultivate this herd. I will *not* abide a horde of toady, has-been poachers."

"She's a sweetheart," I said.

"She's done a lot," he said. "But she wouldn't have been able to do it without the Paranet."

"Wow. Seriously?"

"Knowledge is power," Thomas said. "There are tens of thousands of people on the Paranet. Eyes and ears in every city, getting more experienced every day. Something happens, one of the Fomor moves, and the entire community knows about it in minutes."

I blinked. "They can do that?"

"Internet," Thomas said. "The Netters are all low-grade talents. They can use computers and cell phones without hexing them up. So something starts happening, they tweet about it, and Lara dispatches a ready team."

"And she just happens to get to find out more about the magical talents in other cities. The ones who can't really defend themselves. In case she gets hungry later."

"Yeah," Thomas said. "But it's not like the Netters have a lot of choice in the matter." He paused for a couple of blocks and then said, "Lara's getting scary."

"Lara was always scary."

Thomas shook his head. "Not like this. She's getting involved in government."

"She was always doing that," I said.

"City officials, sure. A few key state bureaucrats. And she kept it gentle and invisible—manipulation, influence. But now she's going for something different."

"What?"

"Control."

It's funny how chilling one little word can be.

"I'll stick her on my to-do list, then," I said.

Thomas snorted.

"Not like that," I said. "Pervert."

"Yeah. Because you think she's hideous."

"She's too scary to be pretty," I lied.

"If she knew I'd told you even that much, bad things would happen," Thomas said.

"To you?"

"Not me. I'm family." His jaw tensed. "To Justine."

"No, it won't," I said. "Because if she tries it, we'll protect Justine."

My brother looked at me. "Thanks," he said quietly.

"Whatever," I said. "It's getting cloying in here. Are we there yet?"

He smiled. "Jerk."

"Wuss."

"Jackass."

"Pansy."

"Philistine."

"Dandysprat."

"Butthead."

"Whiner . . ."

Thomas had just pulled the Hummer into a parking space in a garage across from his apartment building in the Loop when a gold SUV roared

up and came to a sudden halt behind the Hummer. Thomas and I traded
a fast look, and we were both thinking the same thing. A car meant that
an attacker would probably be a mortal, using mortal weapons. That
meant guns. That meant that if they started shooting at us while we were
still in the car, Molly, asleep in the backseat, wouldn't have a prayer.

Both of us rolled out of the front seat, getting clear of the Hummer
as fast as possible. Thomas had his handgun with him. I took the Winchester with me.

The occupants of the gold SUV didn't come leaping out with guns
blazing. The engine stopped. Then, several seconds later, the driver's
door opened, and someone got out. He walked calmly around the front
of the SUV.

It was a slender man, a bit below average height. His hair was a blond
so pale that it was nearly white. He wore faded blue jeans and a green silk
shirt. He had a gun belt a lot like Thomas's number, fitted with an automatic pistol on one hip and a sword on the other. He wasn't a particularly
good-looking man, and he didn't carry himself aggressively, but his jaw
and his eyes were both hard. He stopped at a point where he could see
both of us and stood there, his arms akimbo, his hands not *quite* entirely
relaxed by his sides—and near his weapons.

"Harry," he said quietly.

"Fix," I said. I knew him. He was my opposite number on the Summer side of things. His predecessor had been murdered by *my* predecessor.

"I heard that Mab had recruited you to be the new Winter Knight,"
he said. "I was sure that it was a wild rumor. The man I knew would never
have bowed to a creature like Mab."

"I had my reasons," I said.

He looked me up and down, slowly. Then he said, "You've been given
instructions."

"Maybe," I said.

"You have," he said. "Mab's sent you to kill someone, hasn't she?"

"It's none of your concern," I said quietly.

"The hell it isn't," Fix said. "The Winter Knight exists to execute
people Mab can't kill herself. You think I don't know that?"

"I think that there's an awful lot of glass in your house, Fix," I said. "You're in the same business as me."

"Never," Fix said. "The Summer Knight's job isn't to do Titania's killing."

"No? What is it, then?"

"To stop you," he said simply. "Not even Mab should get to decide who lives and who dies, Harry. Life is too precious to be wasted that way. So when she sends you to kill someone, someone gets in the way. That's me."

I didn't say anything for a minute. I had assumed that the Summer Knight would have the same job I did, just for a different crew. I hadn't really thought about actually crossing swords with Fix—metaphorically or otherwise. Ten years ago, that possibility wouldn't have fazed me. But Fix wasn't the same guy he had been back then. He was the Summer Knight, and he was currently standing up to a champion of the White Court and the Winter Knight without batting an eye. I recognized the calm in him, the stillness that was almost like serenity—it was focus and confidence. He knew the danger, he didn't want to fight, but he was quietly ready for it, and ready to accept whatever consequences it might bring.

It's generally a really bad idea to fight guys who are in that particular mental space.

"You want me to run him off?" Thomas asked.

Fix's eyes didn't move from me, but he directed his words at Thomas. "Come try it, vampire."

"Stars and stones." I sighed. I took the Winchester and put it gently back into the Hummer. "Fix, can we stop the *High Noon* routine? I'm not going to fight *you*."

He frowned slightly. "That sort of remains to be seen."

"Thomas," I said, "get back in the truck, please."

"What?"

"I want to talk to Fix, and it isn't going to be a real productive conversation if he has to keep one eye on each of us and his fingers by his gun in case you draw on him."

Thomas grunted. "Suppose he draws and shoots you as soon as I'm not backing you up."

"If that happens, and if it'll make you feel better, you can come fight him, I suppose." I regarded Fix for a moment and then said, "But he won't."

"Harry," Thomas said.

"He won't," I said quietly. "I know him. He won't."

Thomas let out a low growling grumble—but he got back into the Hummer and shut the door.

Fix eyed me warily, and checked his surroundings quickly, as though expecting some kind of ambush.

I sighed and sat down on the rear bumper of the Hummer. "Fix," I said. "Look, I've been doing this job for about six hours now. I haven't gone all dark side. Yet."

Fix folded his arms. His fingers were still close to his weapons, but a little farther away than they'd been a moment before. "You've got to understand. Lloyd Slate was a real monster, man."

"I know."

"You don't know. Because you never had to face him without power, the way we did."

I spread my hands. "I didn't always have power, Fix. And even with it, there are plenty of big, scary things out there that I'm just as helpless against. I know."

"Then you know what my problem is," he said.

"Let's assume for a moment that I'm sometimes an idiot," I said. "What's your problem?"

He gave me a brief smile. "You were dangerous enough without Mab's hand on you. Now? You can make Lloyd Slate look like a grade-school bully."

"But I haven't," I said.

"But you could."

"Maybe I won't."

"Maybe you will."

"If I'm as powerful as you seem to think," I said, "then what makes you think you can stand up to me?"

He shrugged. "Maybe I can't. But at least I have a chance. The people behind me wouldn't."

"Ah," I said. We both sat for a moment. Then I said, "So I guess it won't be enough for me to assure you that I'm not up to no good."

"You know how you could tell when Slate was lying?"

"How?"

"His lips were moving."

I smiled briefly. "Well. It seems to me you've got a couple of choices."

"Oh?"

"You do the math. You see what I have the potential to do, and you plan for what I *could* do, rather than what you think I *will* do."

"Might be smart," Fix said. "Von Clausewitz would say so."

"If this was a war and I was the enemy, sure."

"What else do you think I could do?"

"Extend a little trust, maybe," I said. "That's the illusion here, man. As far as I'm concerned, we don't need to be enemies. We don't need to be at war."

Fix pursed his lips. Then he said, "Here's the problem with that. You belong to Mab. I like Harry. Maybe I could even trust him. But I know what Mab is like—and Harry belongs to Mab now."

"The hell I do," I said. "Just because I took this job doesn't mean I'm all cozy with her."

"You, uh, looked kinda cozy, man. With Mab. On the stone table."

Sealing a contract like the one with Mab isn't something you do with an impersonal handshake. I felt my cheeks heat up. "Oh. You saw that."

"All of Faerie did," Fix said.

"God, that's humiliating," I muttered.

"I know what you mean," he said. "At least it wasn't on pay-per-view."

I snorted.

"Okay," I said finally. "I'm under some time pressure here, so I think you need to make a decision."

"Yeah?"

I nodded. "Who is going to make this call? You? Or von Clausewitz?"

Fix looked away. Then he said, "I hate this kind of crap. This is the first time I've had a job I've held down for more than six months."

"I hear you."

He gave me another brief smile. "I want to believe you," he said.

Then he took a steadying breath and faced me, lowering his arms to his sides again. "But there are people depending on me to keep them safe. I can't afford to do that."

I stood up, very slowly and reluctantly. "Fix, I don't want this fight."

"And you'll get a chance to avoid it," he said. "I'm going to give you until noon to get out of town, Harry. If I see you after that, I'm not going to spend any more time talking, and I'm not going to challenge you to a fair fight. If you're really serious about being your own man, if you really want to keep the peace between us—you'll go."

"I don't think I can do that," I said.

"I didn't think you could," he said quietly. "You have until noon."

We exchanged a nod. Then he moved back to his SUV, never taking his eyes off me. Once he was in, he started it and drove away.

I sank back down onto the Hummer's back bumper again and closed my eyes.

Great.

One more thing.

I liked Fix. He was a decent guy. He'd become the Summer Knight, and as far as I knew, he'd never abused his power. People in the supernatural community liked and respected him. I'd even seen him in action once. He was a hell of a lot more formidable than he'd been as the scared young man I'd first met.

I didn't want to fight him.

He might not give me a choice.

Mab was not about puppies and kittens, and I'd known that when I signed on. Even if she wasn't evil, exactly, she was vicious, violent, and ruthless. I had no doubt that Mab had done for a number of decent people in her time, one way or another. There were stories about the Winter Knight stretching back for centuries, and various vile personalities had held the title. Some of them had even been famous. Gilles de Rais. Andrei Chikatilo. John Haigh. Fritz Haarmann. If I were in Fix's shoes, and he were in mine, I might well have pulled the trigger without thinking twice.

I leaned my head back against the truck with a little thunk.

Thomas sat down next to me, and the Hummer settled a little more. "Well?"

"Well, what?"

"He going to back off?"

"Doesn't matter," I said.

"Sure it does."

I shook my head. "It doesn't matter because he's a decent guy, and I'm not going to hurt him."

"He might not give you much choice."

"There's always a choice," I said. "That's the thing, man. There's always, *always* a choice. My options might really, truly *suck*, but that doesn't mean there isn't a choice."

"You'd let him kill you?" Thomas asked.

I looked up at him. "No. But I won't hurt him."

My brother gave me a tight-lipped look and then got up and walked away.

There was a shimmer in the air, and Molly appeared, standing about ten feet behind what had been Fix's position during our conversation. She watched Thomas go with an unhappy expression.

I blinked at her. "How long have you been standing there?"

"I got out of your side of the car when Thomas got in," she said. "You know. Just in case something happened. It seemed like a good idea to make sure he went down quick if a fight broke out, so you wouldn't have to kill him."

I smiled at her. "Totally unfair."

"I had this teacher who kept telling me that if I was ever in a fair fight, someone had made a mistake," she said.

"Sounds like a jerk."

"He has his moments," she said. She squinted after Thomas and said, "He's just afraid, you know. He doesn't want to lose his brother twice."

"I know," I said.

"But I'm really proud of you, boss," she said, her voice quieter. "I mean . . . I know you've had some hard calls to make lately. But my dad would say that you were right about this one. There's always a choice."

I grunted. "If I get into it with Fix," I said, "I don't want you to get involved."

"Why not?"

"Because faeries keep score," I said. "And they'll never leave a score unsettled."

"If I told you that, you'd tell me that wasn't my choice to make."

"And I'd be right," I said, and sighed. "But I have enough worries already, grasshopper. Leave it alone. For me."

She looked like I'd just asked her to swallow a bug. "I'll try," she said.

"Thanks," I said, and extended my hand.

She helped me up. "What's next?"

"A phone call. Let's go."

20

"I don't care how busy he is," I said into the phone. "I need to talk with him. Period."

We were in Thomas's living room. Thomas was sprawled on a recliner. The hideous high-tech brushed-steel look that had been the place's trademark had been softened with window dressings and various bits of decoration—Justine's touch. Thomas, like most men, regarded a throw pillow as something to throw.

One bounced off of my chest. "Way to turn on the charm, Harry," he murmured.

I covered the phone's receiver with one hand. "Polite gets you nowhere with these people. Trust me." I turned back to the phone. "No," I said. "Not over this line. It's bugged. Just tell him that Doughnut Boy needs to speak to him or an informed high-level operative in person, within the hour."

Thomas mouthed the word *operative* at me, his fingers spread in a gesture meant to convey spooky importance. I kicked the pillow back at him.

"Don't give me excuses," I said. "He can get here if he damned well wants to and we both know it. Call me back at this number." I thunked the phone down.

"Earlier today," Molly said, from where she sat on the floor, "someone said something to me about not burning my bridges. Let me think. Who was that?"

"Ixnay," I growled. "I know what I'm doing." I turned to Thomas. "How many bugs does Lara have on this place?"

"Harry," Thomas said in a scandalized tone—one that was just a little bit too well projected to be meant for me. "I'm her brother. She would never behave that way toward her own flesh and blood, her own kin, her own dear sibling."

I growled. "How many?"

He shrugged. "It changes. New ones come in sometimes when I'm not home."

I grunted. I put the phone on the counter, unplugged it, and grabbed a pepper shaker. I put a circle of pepper around the phone, and sealed it with a gentle effort of will. "You're set for money, right?"

"With Lara's money, yes."

"Good," I said, and then I unleashed a burst of will with a mutter of, "Hexus," that burned out every bit of electronics within fifty feet. The apartment's lightbulbs all winked out at the same instant.

Thomas groaned, but he didn't otherwise complain.

"Grasshopper," I said.

"On it," Molly said. She rose to her feet, frowning, her eyes mostly closed, and began walking slowly around the apartment.

While she did that, I broke the circle of pepper with a brush of my hand and plugged the phone back in.

"If you were going to do that," Thomas asked, "why not do it before you made the phone call that absolutely did set off every flag Lara's security teams have to wave?"

I held up a hand for silence, until Molly had wandered down the hall and back. "Nothing," she said.

"No spells?" Thomas asked.

"Right," I said. "Anyone who came in uninvited wouldn't be able to make that kind of spell stick. And no one you've invited in has . . ." I frowned. "Molly?"

"I didn't," she said quickly.

". . . has planted a spell to listen in on you," I finished. "And I wanted Lara's people to know who I contacted. When they try to follow up on it, they'll betray their presence and he'll be alerted to how they operate."

"It was a payment," Thomas said.

I shrugged. "Call it a friendly gesture."

"At my sister's expense," Thomas said.

"Lara's a big girl. She'll understand." I considered things for a moment and then said, "Everyone be cool. Something might happen."

Thomas frowned. "Like what?"

"Cat Sith!" I called in a firm voice. "I need you, if you please!"

There was a rushing sound, like a heavy curtain stirred by a strong wind, and then, from the fresh, dark shadows beneath Thomas's dining table, the malk's alien voice said, "I am here, Sir Knight."

Thomas jerked in reaction, despite my warning, and produced a tiny semiautomatic pistol from I knew not where. Molly drew in a sharp, harsh breath, and backed directly away from the source of the voice until her shoulder blades hit a wall.

It was just possible that I had understated how unsettling a malk sounds when it speaks. I'd clearly been hanging around creepy things for way too long.

"Take it easy," I said, holding a hand out to Thomas. "This is Cat Sith."

Molly made a sputtering noise.

I gave her a quelling glance and said to Thomas, "He's working with me."

Cat Sith came to the edge of the shadows so that his silhouette could be seen. His eyes reflected the light from the almost entirely curtained windows. "Sir Knight. How may I assist you?"

"Empty night, it talks," Thomas breathed.

"How?" Molly asked. "The threshold here is solid. How did it just come *in* like that?"

Which was a reasonable question, given that Molly didn't know about my former cleaning service and how it had interacted with my old apartment's threshold. "Beings out of Faerie don't necessarily need to be invited over a threshold," I said. "If they're benevolent to the inhabitants of the house, they can pretty much come right in."

"Wait," Thomas said. "These freaks can walk in and out whenever they want? Pop in directly from the Nevernever? And you didn't tell us about it?"

"Only if their intentions are benign," I said. "Cat Sith came here to assist me, and by extension you. As long as he's here, he's . . ." I frowned and looked at the malk. "Help me find the correct way to explain this to him?"

Sith directed his eyes to Thomas and said, "While I am here, I am bound by the same traditions as would apply were I your invited guest," he said. "I will offer no harm to anyone you have accepted into your home, nor take any action which would be considered untoward for a guest. I will report nothing of what I see and hear in this place, and make every effort to aid and assist your household and other guests while I remain."

I blinked several times. I had expected Sith to hit me with a big old snark-club rather than actually answering the question—much less an-swering it in such detail. But that made sense. The obligations of guest and host were almost holy in the supernatural world. If Sith truly did regard that kind of courtesy as the obligation of a guest, he would have little choice but to live up to it.

Thomas seemed to digest that for a few moments and then grunted. "I suppose I am obliged to comport myself as a proper host, then."

"Say instead that I am under no obligation to allow myself to be harmed, or to remain and give my aid, if you behave in any other fash-ion," Sith corrected him. "If you began shooting at me with that weapon, for example, I would depart without doing harm, and only then would I hunt you, catch you outside the protection of your threshold, and kill you in order to discourage such behavior from others in the future."

Thomas looked like he was about to talk some smack at the malk, but only for a second. Then he frowned and said, "It's odd. You sound like . . . like a grade-school teacher."

"Perhaps it is because I am speaking to a child," Cat Sith said. "The comparison is apt."

Thomas blinked several times and then looked at me. "Did the evil kitty just call me a child?"

"I don't think he's evil so much as hyperviolent and easily bored," I said. "And you started it. You called him a freak."

My brother pursed his lips and frowned. "I did, didn't I?" He turned to Cat Sith and set his gun aside. "Cat Sith, the remark was not directed specifically at you or meant to insult you, but I acknowledge that I have given offense, and recognize that the slight puts me in your debt. Please accept my apologies, and feel free to ask a commensurate service of me should you ever have need of it, to balance the scales."

Cat Sith stared at Thomas for a moment, and then inclined his head. "Even children can learn manners. Done. Until such time as I have need of you, I regard the matter as settled, Thomas Raith."

"You know him?" I asked.

"And your apprentice, Molly Carpenter," Sith said, his voice impatient, "as well as the rest of your frequent associates. May I suggest that you get on with the business at hand, Sir Knight? *Tempus fugit.*"

One of Winter's most dangerous creatures—most dangerous *hunters*—knew all about my friends. That was something that a smart man would be concerned about. I reminded myself that just because someone is courteous, it does not necessarily mean that they aren't planning to vivisect you. It just means that they'll ask whether the ropes holding you down are comfortable before they pick up the scalpel. Cat Sith might be an ally, for the moment, but he was *not* my friend.

"In a few minutes, we're going to be leaving," I said. "I've got a hunch that we'll be under observation, and I don't want that. I want you to distract anyone who has us under direct surveillance."

"With pleasure."

"Without killing them or causing significant bodily harm," I said. "For all I know there's a cop or a PI watching the place. So nothing permanent."

Cat Sith narrowed his eyes. His tail twitched to one side, but he said nothing.

"Think of it as a compliment," I suggested. "Any idiot could murder them. What I ask is far more difficult, as befits your station."

His tail twitched the other way. He said nothing.

"After that," I said, "I want you to get word to the Summer Lady. I want a meeting."

"Uh, what?" Thomas said.

"Is that a good idea?" Molly asked at the same time.

I waved a hand at both of them, and kept talking to Sith. "Tell her it's got to happen before noon. Can you contact her?"

"Of course, Sir Knight," said Sith. "She will wish to know the reason for such a meeting."

"Tell her that I'd prefer not to kill her Knight, and I'd like to discuss how best to avoid it. Tell her that I'll meet her wherever she pleases, if she promises me safe conduct. Bring me her answer."

Sith eyed me, then said, "Such a course is unwise."

"I'm not asking you to do it. What do you care?"

"The Queen may be less than pleased with me if I break her newest toy before she's gotten sufficient use from it."

"Gosh," I said.

Sith flicked an ear and managed to do it contemptuously. "I will bear this message, Sir Knight. And I will . . . distract . . . those who hunt you. When will you be departing?"

Behind me, Thomas's phone began to ring.

"Tell you in a second," I said. I answered the phone. "Go for Doughnut Boy."

A woman with a voice cold enough to merit the use of the Kelvin scale spat, "He will meet you. Accorded Neutral Ground. Ten minutes."

"Cool," I said. "I haven't had a beer in forever."

There was a brief, perhaps baffled silence, and then she hung up on me.

I turned back to Thomas and Molly and said, "Let's go. Sith, please be—"

The eldest malk vanished.

"—gin," I finished, somewhat lamely.

Thomas swung to his feet and slipped the little automatic into the back of his pants, then pulled his shirt down over it. "Where are we going?"

"Accorded Neutral Ground," I said.

"Oh, good," Molly said. "I'm starving."

21

In the lobby, we found the doorman sitting on the ground grimacing in pain. A CPD patrol officer was next to him with a first-aid kit. As we passed, I saw several long, long slices in the back of one of the doorman's legs, running from just above his heel to the top of his calf. His slacks and socks alike were sliced in neat, parallel strips. The wounds were painful and bloody, but not life-threatening.

Both men were both too preoccupied to pay an instant of attention to the three of us as we calmly left the building.

I winced a little as we went by them. Dammit. I hadn't wanted to turn even the gentlest of Cat Sith's attentions upon any of my fellow Chicagoans, but I hadn't worded my command to him tightly enough. Of course, that was a rabbit hole I didn't want to start down—experience has taught me that you do *not* win against supernatural entities at lawyering. It just doesn't happen. I didn't even want to think about what Sith might have done if I hadn't forbidden him the use of deadly force.

Maybe this was the malk's way of telling me to beware the consequences if I kept giving him commands like a common servant. Or maybe this *was* his idea of playing nice. After all, he hadn't slashed up the cop and every passerby. For all I knew, he thought he'd been a perfect gentleman.

Molly checked out the parking garage from beneath a veil while Thomas and I waited. Once she pronounced the garage villain-free, we got into my brother's troop transport and left.

*   *   *

In Chicago, you can't swing a cat without hitting an Irish pub (and angering the cat), but McAnally's place stands out from the crowd. It's the favored watering hole for the supernatural scene of Chicago. Normals never really seem to find their way in, though we get some tourists once in a while. They rarely linger.

Morning traffic was roaring at full steam, and even though Mac's wasn't far, it took us a little time to get there. Clouds had swallowed up the bright dawn, thick and grey. A light rain was falling. Occasionally I could see flashes of distant lightning glowing through the clouds overhead, or hear a subtle growl of low thunder.

"And it was supposed to be nice today," Molly murmured.

I smiled a little, but didn't say anything.

Thomas pulled into the little parking lot adjacent to Mac's, parking his Hummer next to an old white Trans Am. He stopped, frowning at it.

"I thought Mac usually opened up at noon," he said.

"Eleven," I said. My old office building hadn't been far away. I'd eaten many a lunch at Mac's place. "Guess he came in early today."

"That's handy," Thomas said.

"Where does that saying come from?" I asked.

"Uh," Thomas said. "Handy?"

I blinked as we walked. "Well, yeah, that one, too, but I was thinking of the phrase, 'You can't swing a cat without hitting something around here.'"

Thomas gave me a steady look. "Don't you have important things to be thinking about right now?"

I shrugged. "I wonder about these things. Life goes on, man. If I stop thinking about things just because some psycho or crew of psychos wants me dead, I'll never get to think about *anything*, will I?"

Thomas bobbed his head to one side in acknowledgment of my point.

About thirty feet from the door, Molly abruptly stopped in her tracks and said, "Harry."

I paused and looked back at her.

Her eyes were wide. She said, "I sense . . ."

I narrowed my eyes. "Say it. You know you want to say it."

"It is *not* a disturbance in the Force," she said, her voice half-exasperated. "There's a . . . a presence here. Something powerful. I felt it in Chichén Itzá."

"Good," I said, nodding. "He's here. Seriously, neither of you guys knows where that saying comes from? Damn."

I hate not knowing things. It's enough to make a guy wish he could use the Internet.

Mac's pub was all but empty. It's a place that looks pretty spacious when empty, yet it's small enough to feel cozy when it's full. It's a study in deliberate asymmetry. There are thirteen tables of varying sizes and heights scattered irregularly around the floor. There are thirteen wooden columns, placed in similarly random positions, their faces carved with scenes from old-world nursery tales. The bar kind of meanders, and there are thirteen stools spaced unevenly along it. Just about everything is made from wood, including the paneled walls, the hardwood floors, and the paneled ceiling. Thirteen ceiling fans hang suspended from the ceiling, ancient things that Mac manages to keep running despite the frequent presence of magical talents.

The decor is a kind of feng shui, or at least something close to it. All that imbalance is intended to scatter the random outbursts of magical energy that cause problems for practitioners. It must work. The electric fans and the telephone hardly ever melt down.

Mac stood behind the bar, a lean man a little taller than average, his shaven head gleaming. I've patronized his establishment for most of my adult life and he still looked more or less like he had when I first met him: neat, dressed in dark pants, a white shirt, and a pristine white apron that proved its ongoing redundancy by never getting messy. Mac was leaning on the bar, listening to something the pub's only other occupant was saying.

The second man was well over six feet tall, and built with the kind of broad shoulders and lean power that made me think of a long-distance swimmer. He wore a dark grey business suit, an immaculate European number of some kind, obviously custom-made. His hair was the color of old steel, highlighted with sweeps of silver, and his sharp chin and jawline were emphasized by the cut of a short silver-white beard. The man wore a black eye patch made of silk, and even against the backdrop of that suit, it gave him a piratical aura.

The man in the eye patch finished saying whatever it was, and Mac dropped his head back and let out a short, hefty belly laugh. It lasted only a second, and then it was gone, replaced with Mac's usual calm, genial expression, but the man in the suit sat back with an expression of pleasure on his face at the reaction.

"It's him," Molly said. "Who is that?"

"Donar Vadderung," I told her.

"Whoa," Thomas said.

Molly frowned. "The . . . the security company guy?"

"CEO of Monoc Securities," I said, nodding.

"Empty night, Dresden," Thomas said. "You just demanded that *he* come to see *you*?"

"Is that bad?" Molly asked him.

"It's . . . glah," Thomas said. "Think of doing that to Donald Trump or George Soros."

Molly winced. "I'm . . . not sure I can do that."

Thomas glared at me. "You set up Lara's surveillance crew to go up against *his* guys?"

I smiled.

"Balls," Thomas said. "She's going to rip mine off."

"Tell her it wasn't your fault. You couldn't have stopped me. She'll get it," I said. "You guys sit down; get some food or something. This shouldn't take long."

Molly blinked, then looked at Thomas and said, "Wait a minute. . . . We're his *flunkies*."

"You, maybe," Thomas said, sneering. "I'm his *thug*. I'm way higher than a flunky."

"You *are* high if you think I'm taking any orders from you," Molly said tartly.

The two of them went to a far table, bickering cheerfully, and sat down, passing by the real reason we were meeting here—a modest

wooden sign with simple letters burned into it: ACCORDED NEU-
TRAL TERRITORY.

The Unseelie Accords had supported the various supernatural political
entities over the past few turbulent decades. They were a series of agreements that, at the end of the day, were basically meant to limit conflicts
between the various nations to something with a definite structure. They
defined the rights of those lords who held territory, as well as the infrac-
tions that could be committed against those lords by other lords. Think of
them as the Geneva Conventions of the spooky side. That's kind of close.

Mac had somehow gotten his place declared neutral ground. It meant
that whenever any signatory of the Accords was here, he was obligated to be
a good guest, to offer no harm or violence to any other signatory, and to take
any violence that might erupt outside. It was a meeting ground, where there
was at least a fair chance that you might actually get to finish a meal without
being murdered by someone who might otherwise be a mortal enemy.

Vadderung watched Molly and Thomas sit and then transferred his
attention back to me. His single eye was an icy shade of blue, and unsettling. As I approached him, I had an instinctive impression that he could
see more of me than I could of him.

"Well, well, well," he said. "Rumors of your death, et cetera."

I shrugged. "I'm sure it isn't an uncommon play among wizards," I
said.

Something in his eye flashed, an amused thought that went by almost
before I could see it. "Fewer try it than you might think," he said.

"I didn't try anything," I said. "It just happened."

Vadderung reached out and lazily collected a cup of coffee. He sipped
it, watching me. Then he leaned forward slightly and said slowly, "Nothing that significant just happens, Dresden."

I squinted at him. Shrugged. Then I said, "Mac, can I get a beer?"

Mac had sauntered a discreet distance down the bar. He eyed me, and
then a slowly ticking clock on the wall.

"I haven't had a drink in a lifetime," I said. "If I go all nutty about it,
you can sign me up for AA."

Mac snorted. Then he got me a bottle of one of his microbrewed ales.

They are nectar and ambrosia. He opened it and passed me the bottle (since he knew I rarely drink beer out of a glass), and I tilted it toward him before drinking some.

"Pretty early for that, isn't it?" Vadderung asked.

"I can smell the whiskey in yours from here," I said, and held up my bottle.

He smiled, lifted his coffee cup toward me in salute, and took a long sip as I put back some more ale. Then we both set our drinks down.

"What do you need?" Vadderung asked.

"Advice," I said. "If the price is right."

"And what do you think a sufficient price would be?"

"Lucy charges a nickel."

"Ah," Vadderung said. "But Lucy is a psychiatrist. You realize that you've just cast yourself as Charlie Brown."

"Augh," I said.

Vadderung smiled. "You found it lonely where you were, I see."

"Why would you say that?"

"The banter. The talk. Unnecessary companions. Many would say that now is the time for rapid, decisive action. But you have spent precious time reconnecting with your allies." He tilted his head slightly. "Therefore, if you have such a driving need for it, I can logically assume that you have spent your recent time apart from such company. Does that seem reasonable to you?"

"Arctis Tor isn't much of a vacation spot," I said.

"No? What is it?"

I narrowed my eyes. "Wait. Are you trying to shrink me?"

He sipped his coffee. "Why would you ask me that question?"

"Because you keep asking questions," I said. "Joke's on you, Lucy. I don't have a nickel." I regarded my bottle. "I've got time for banter. Just not for games."

Vadderung set his coffee down and spread his hands. "I don't work for free," he said.

"I haven't earned enough money in my entire lifetime to afford your fees," I said. "But you don't need more money."

He waited.

"I'll owe you one," I said.

That seemed to amuse the hell out of him. Wrinkled topography appeared at the corner of his eye. "Given the caliber of your talents for making enemies, I hope you'll understand if I don't consider what you offer a sound long-term value."

I smiled and sipped some beer. "But it's worth a few minutes of your time—or you wouldn't have come here in the first place."

That drew a quick flicker of an amused smile. "I will accept your offer of one favor—and a nickel."

"I told you. I don't have a nickel."

He nodded gravely. "What do you have?"

I rummaged in my pockets and came out with the jeweled cuff links from my tux. I showed them to him.

"Those aren't a nickel," he said soberly. He leaned forward again, as he had a moment before, and spoke slowly. "What do you have?"

I stared at him for a second. Then I said, "Friends."

He sat back, his blue eye all but throwing off sparks, it was so bright.

"Thomas," I called. "I need a nickel."

"What?" Thomas asked. "In cash?"

"Yeah."

Thomas reached into a pocket and produced a bunch of plastic cards. He fanned them out and showed them to me. "What about these?"

"Those aren't a nickel," I said.

"Oh, for goodness' sake." Molly sighed. She reached into a pocket and produced what looked like a little old lady's coin purse. Then she flicked a nickel toward me.

I caught it. "Thanks. You're promoted to lackey."

She rolled her eyes. "Hail, Ming."

I slid the nickel across the bar to Vadderung. "There."

He nodded. "Talk to me."

"Right," I said. "Um. It's about time."

"No," he said, "it's about your island."

I eyed him warily. "What do you mean?"

"What I mean," he said, "is that I know about your island. I know where it came from. I know what it does. I know what's beneath it."

"Uh," I said. "Oh."

"I'm aware of how important it is that the island be well managed. Most of the people who came to your party in Mexico are."

By which he meant the Grey Council. Vadderung was a part of it. It was a group of folks, mostly wizards of the White Council, who had joined together because it seemed like the White Council was getting close to meltdown, and they wanted to save it. But since the rats were in the walls, the only way to do it was covertly, working in cells. I wasn't sure who, exactly, was a member, except for my grandfather and Vadderung. He had come along with the rest of the mostly anonymous Grey Council when I'd gone to take my daughter back from the Red Court, and seemed to fit right in.

Of course, I was pretty sure he wasn't a wizard. I was pretty sure he was a lot more than that.

So I broke it down for him, speaking very quietly. I told him about the attack being aimed at the island from across time. Hard lines appeared in his face as I did.

"Idiots," he breathed. "Even if they could defeat the banefire . . ."

"Wait," I said. "Banefire?"

"The fail-safe," Vadderung said. "The fire the island showed you."

"Right. It'll kill everything held there rather than let them escape, right?"

"It is the only way," Vadderung said. "If anyone managed to set free the things in the Well . . ."

"Seems like it would be bad," I said.

"Not bad," Vadderung said. "The end."

"Oh," I said. "Good to know. The island didn't mention that part."

"The island cannot accept it as a possibility," Vadderung said absently.

"It should probably put its big-girl pants on, then," I said. "The way I understand it, it might already be too late. I mean, for all I know, someone cast this spell a hundred years ago. Or a hundred years from now."

Vadderung waved a hand. "Nonsense. There are laws that govern the progression of time in relation to space, like everything else."

"Meaning what?"

"Meaning that the echoes caused by the temporal event are proportionately greater than the span of time that was bridged," he said. "Had the attack been launched from a century ago, or hence, the echoes of it would have begun far, far in advance of the event—centuries ago. These echoes have appeared only within the past few days. I would guess, roughly, that the attack must originate only hours from the actual, real-time occurrence."

"Which is tomorrow," I said. "So it's happening sometime today or sometime tomorrow."

"Most likely not tomorrow," Vadderung said. "Altering one's past is more than mildly difficult."

"The paradox thing?" I asked. "Like, if I go back and kill my grandfather, how was I ever born to go back and kill my grandfather?"

"Paradox is an overrated threat. There is . . . a quality similar to inertia at work. Once an event has occurred, there is an extremely strong tendency for that event to occur. The larger, more significant, or more energetic the event, the more it tends to remain as it originally happened, despite any interference."

I frowned. "There's . . . a law of the conservation of history?"

Vadderung grinned. "I've never heard it phrased quite like that, but it's accurate enough. In any event, overcoming that inertia requires tremendous energy, will, and a measure of simple luck. If one wishes to alter the course of history, it's a far simpler matter to attempt to shape the future."

I grunted. "So if I go back in time and kill my grandfather, what happens?"

"He beats you senseless, I suspect," Vadderung said, his gaze direct.

Oh, man. Vadderung *knew* about Ebenezar. Which meant that either he was higher in the old man's circle of trust than I was, or he had access to an astoundingly scary pool of information.

"You know what I mean," I said. "Paradox? Universe goes poof?"

"If it works like that, I've never seen it, as evidenced by the fact that . . ." He spread his hands. "Here it is. I suspect a different form of apocalypse happens."

I frowned. "Like what?"

"A twinned universe," Vadderung said. "A new parallel reality, identical except for that event. One in which you never existed, and one in which you failed to kill your grandfather."

I pursed my lips. "That . . . doesn't really end well for me in either case."

"An excellent reason not to meddle in the natural course of time, wouldn't you say? Meddling with time is an irrationally, outrageously, catastrophically dangerous and costly business. I encourage you to avoid it at all costs."

"You and the White Council," I said. "So it's going to happen sometime today or tonight."

Vadderung nodded. "And nearby."

"Why?"

"Because the energy requirements are astronomical," he said. "Bridging a temporal gap of any length is something utterly beyond the reach of any mortal practitioner acting alone. Doing such a thing and then trying to project the spell over a distance as well? The difficulty of it would be prohibitive. And do not forget how much water surrounds the island, which will tend to mitigate any energy sent toward it—that's one reason the Well was built there."

I nodded. All of that hung together, based upon everything I knew of magic. People always assume that magic is a free ride—but it isn't. You can't pull energy from nowhere, and there are laws that govern how it behaves.

"So this . . . time bomb. It has to come from how close?" I asked.

"The shores of the lake, I suspect," Vadderung said. "The island itself would be the ideal location, but I doubt that it will cooperate with any such effort."

"Not hardly," I agreed. "And you can't just scribble a chalk circle and pull this spell out of your hat. It's got to have an energy source. A big one."

"Precisely," Vadderung said.

"And those things tend to stand out."

He smiled. "They do."

"And whoever is trying to pull this off, if they know enough about futzing with time to be making this attempt, they know that the echoes will warn people that it's coming. They'll be ready to argue with anyone who tries to thwart them."

"They most certainly will." He finished his coffee.

I had made the right call here. Vadderung's advice had changed the problem from something enormous and inexplicable to something that was merely very difficult, very dangerous, and likely to get me killed.

"Um," I said. "Don't take this the wrong way, but . . . this is a high-stakes game."

"The highest, yes," he agreed.

"I'm thinking that maybe someone with a little more experience and better footing should handle it. Someone like you, maybe."

He shook his head. "It isn't practical."

I frowned. "Not practical?"

"It must be you."

"Why me?"

"It's *your* island," Vadderung said.

"That makes no sense."

He tilted his head and looked at me. "Wizard . . . you have been dead and returned. It has marked you. It has opened doors and paths that you do not yet know exist, and attracted the attention of beings who formerly would never have taken note of your insignificance."

"Meaning what?" I asked.

There was no humor at all in his face. "Meaning that now more than ever, you are a fulcrum. Meaning that your life is about to become very, very interesting."

"I don't understand," I said.

He leaned forward slightly. "Correct that." He looked at his watch and rose. "I'm afraid I'm out of time."

I shook my head, rising with him, blocking him. "Wait. My plate is already pretty full here, and if you haven't noticed, I'm barely competent to keep myself alive, much less to prevent Arkham Asylum from turning into the next Tunguska blast."

Vadderung met my eyes with his and said in a growl, "Move."

I moved.

I looked away, too. I'd seen too many things with my Sight already.

And I had a bad feeling that trading a soulgaze with Vadderung would not improve my performance over the next day or so.

"Where are Hugin and Munin?" I asked.

"I left them at the office," he said. "They don't like you, I'm afraid."

"Birdbrains," I muttered.

He smiled, nodded to Mac, and walked to the door.

"Can I do this?" I asked his back.

"You can."

I made an exasperated sound. "How do you know?"

Odin turned to look back at me with his gleaming eye, his teeth bared in a wolf's smile, the scar on either side of his eye patch silver in the light coming through the door. "Perhaps," he murmured, "you already have."

Then he opened the door and left.

I scowled at where he'd been standing, and then slouched back on my barstool. I grabbed my beer, finished it, and set it down a little harder than I had to.

Mac was back at the grill, making some of his famous steak sandwiches for Thomas and Molly. I waved at him, but before I could say anything, he had already added another steak to the first two. My stomach growled as I got up and went to Molly and Thomas's table.

Perhaps you already have.

Now, what the hell had he meant by that?

22

I filled Molly and Thomas in on what I had learned from Vadderung while we ate. Mac's steak sandwiches were too awesome not to eat, even if it was more or less breakfast time.

Molly blinked as I finished. "Uh. Who *is* that guy?"

Thomas gave me an even look. My brother had figured it out. He tilted his head microscopically toward Molly.

"A friend, I think," I said. "When you work it out, you're ready to know."

"Ah." Molly frowned and toyed with a few crumbs, pushing them around with a forefinger. She nodded. "Okay."

"So what's next?" Thomas asked.

I finished the last few bites of my sandwich in a hurry. Man, that tasted good. I washed it down with some more of Mac's excellent beer. Normally, a couple of bottles along with a meal would leave me ready for a nap. Today they felt about as soporific as Red Bull.

"Molly," I said, "I want you to go talk to Toot. I need the guard to gather up and be ready to move when I give the word."

"Scouts?" she guessed.

I nodded. "While you're doing that, I'm going to go figure out the potential sites for the time bomb spell so we know where to aim the guard. Order some pizza; that will gather them in."

"Okay," she said. "Um . . . money?"

I looked at Thomas. "She already came through for me once. Your turn."

Thomas snorted and slipped a white plastic card out of his pocket. It was utterly unmarked except for a few stamped numbers and a magnetic strip. He flicked it across the table to Molly. "When you get your pizza, have them run that."

Molly studied the card, back and front. "Is this a Diners Club card or something?"

"It's a Raith contingency card," he said. "Lara hands them out to the family. Once they ring up the first charge on the card, it'll be good for twenty-four hours."

"For how much?" Molly asked.

"Twenty-four hours," Thomas repeated.

Molly lifted her eyebrows.

Thomas smiled faintly. "Don't worry about amounts. My sister doesn't really believe in limits. Do whatever you want with it. I don't care."

Molly took the card and placed it very carefully in her secondhand coin purse. "Okay." She looked at me. "Now?"

I nodded. "Get a move on."

She paused to draw a pen from her purse. She scribbled on a napkin and passed it to me. "My apartment's phone."

I glanced at it, read it, and memorized it. Then I slid it to Thomas, who tucked the napkin away in a pocket. "You're going to just send her out there alone?"

Molly regarded Thomas blankly. Then vanished.

"Oh," Thomas said. "Right."

I stood up and crossed the room to the door. I opened it and glanced out, as though scanning suspiciously for anyone's approach. I felt Molly slip out past me as I did. Then I closed it again and came back inside. Thunder rumbled over the lake, but no rain fell.

"I noticed," my brother drawled, "that you didn't leave her a way to contact you."

"Did you?"

He snorted. "You think Fix would hurt her?"

"I think she won't give him much choice," I said. "She's come a long way—but Fix is exactly the wrong kind of threat for her to mess with. He's used to glamour, he can defend against it, and he's smart."

"Molly's not too shabby herself," Thomas said.

"Molly is my responsibility," I said.

I hadn't meant for the words to come out that cold, that hard. The anger surprised me, but it bubbled and seethed still. Some part of me was furious at Thomas for questioning *my* decision regarding *my* apprentice. Molly was *mine*, and I would be damned if some chisel-jawed White Court pretty boy was going to—

I closed my eyes and clenched my jaw. Pride. Possession. Territoriality. That wasn't me. That was the mantle of Winter talking through me.

"Sorry," I said a moment later, and opened my eyes.

Thomas hadn't reacted in any way, to my snarl, my anger, or my apology. He just studied me. Then he said, quietly, "I want to suggest something to you. I'm not trying to make you do anything. You just need to hear it."

"Sure," I said.

"I'm a predator, Harry," he said. "We both know that."

"Yeah. So?"

"So I recognize it in others when I see it."

"And?"

"And you're looking at Molly like she's food."

I frowned at him. "I am not."

He shrugged. "It isn't all the time. It's just little moments. You look at her, and I can see the calculations running. You notice every time she yawns."

I didn't want what Thomas was saying to be true. "So what?"

"When she yawns, she's showing us that she's tired. It makes us take notice because tired prey is easy prey." He leaned forward, putting one arm on the table. "I know what I'm talking about."

"No," I said, my voice getting cold again. "You don't."

"I tried going into denial like that when I was about fifteen. It didn't work out too well."

"What?" I asked him. "You think I'm going to attack her when she goes to sleep?"

"Yeah," he said. "If you don't recognize what's motivating you and control it, you will. Maybe not today, maybe not tomorrow. But eventually. You can't just ignore those instincts, man. If you do, they'll catch you off guard some night. And you *will* hurt her, one way or another."

I wasn't sure what to say to that. I frowned down at my empty bottle of ale.

"She trusts you," Thomas said. "I think some part of you knows that. I think that part sent her away from you for a damned good reason. Take this seriously, Harry."

"Yeah," I said quietly. "I'll . . . try. This stuff keeps catching me off guard."

"Nature of the beast. You've always been good at keeping things right between the two of you, even though she's carrying a torch the size of a building. I admire you for that. I'd hate to see it come apart."

I rubbed at my eyes. My brother was right. I'd been forcing myself to look away from Molly all morning. That had never been an issue before. That was part of Winter, too—hunger and lust, a need for heat in the darkness. It had driven Lloyd Slate, just as it had several other Winter Knights over the years.

It had driven them insane.

I had to learn to recognize that influence before someone got hurt.

"Yeah, okay," I said. "When I get done sprinting from one forest fire to the next, I'll . . . I'll figure something out. Until then, feel free to slap me around a bit if you think I need it."

Thomas nodded very seriously, but his eyes sparkled. "I'm your brother. I pretty much always feel free to do that."

"Heh," I said. "I'd like to see you . . ."

I trailed off, glancing at Mac, who was staring at the door to the pub, frowning. I followed his gaze. The glass on the top half of the door was faceted and partly frosted, but it was clear enough to give you a blurry image of whoever was standing outside the door. Or at least, it would have been if the exterior hadn't been blanketed by a thick grey mist.

Thomas noticed me, and looked. "Huh," he said. "Uh. Doesn't the fog usually burn off in the morning?"

"We didn't have any this morning," I said.

"So . . ." Thomas drawled. "That isn't right."

"No," I said. "No, it isn't."

There just weren't all that many reasons someone would blanket an area with mist—to conceal an approach. We both stood up and faced the door.

Behind us, Mac reached under the bar and came out with a pistol-grip shotgun made of black composite material. It had a folding stock and barely enough of a barrel to qualify as a hunting piece.

"This is crazy," Thomas said. "Nobody attacks Mac's. It's neutral ground."

"What about these Fomor I've heard about?"

"Not even them," Thomas said. "Every time they've gotten close to this place, the BFS came down on them like an avalanche. It's practically the only thing they've really agreed on."

I blanked for a second and then said, "Oh, Brighter Future Society."

"It isn't the faeries, is it?" Thomas asked.

"They're called the Unseelie Accords," I said. "Winter equals Unseelie. Anyone in Winter who violated Mab's treaty would be thrilled to die before she was through with them."

"Summer, then?"

"It isn't noon yet," I said.

The sounds of the city outside had vanished. An unnatural hush fell. I could hear three people breathing a little harder than they normally would, a creaky ceiling fan, and that was about it.

"Definitely magic," I said. "Someone doesn't want anybody seeing or hearing what happens in here."

There was a sharp sound, a sudden motion, and a stone sailed through one of the faceted panes of glass on the door. Thomas produced his pistol, and Mac's shotgun snapped up to his shoulder. Some broken glass tinkled to the floor, and the stone tumbled down and bounced off of my foot before it came to rest on the floor. It was a rounded piece of glassy black obsidian about the size of an egg.

Tendrils of mist came through the broken pane of glass, and the stone on the floor abruptly quivered and began to buzz. Thomas and I both took several wary steps away from it, but the buzzing increased and warped until it became an eerie, quavering voice, like something you'd hear on an old, worn-out vinyl record.

"Sssssend out the wizzzzard," it hummed, each word slow and drawnout. "Sssssend him to ussssss and all othersssss may ssssstay."

"I know a good place for you to pound sand, you gutless fu—" Thomas began helpfully.

I held up a hand. "No," I told him quietly. "Wait."

"For what?"

"This is neutral territory," I said in a voice pitched to carry outside the door. "If you want to talk, come on in. You won't be attacked."

"Sssssend him to usssss."

That wasn't creepy or anything. "My schedule is kind of full today," I called. "How's next Tuesday for you?"

"Thrice we assssk and done," hissed the voice. "Sssssend him to ussssss. Now!"

I took slow, steady breaths to keep the fear at bay and think. I was pretty sure that whatever was out there, it wasn't interested in talking. I was also pretty sure that I didn't want to toddle out onto that narrow, mist-clouded stairway to start a fight. But I wasn't the only one in the room. I looked back at Mac.

"I don't want to bring any trouble into your place, Mac," I said. "You're my host here. I'll take it outside if you want me to."

In answer, Mac made a growling sound and worked the action on the shotgun, pumping a shell into the chamber. Then he reached under the counter, produced a heavy-caliber automatic pistol, and put it on the bar within easy reach.

Thomas showed his teeth in a predatory grin. "I'm leaving bigger tips from now on."

"Right," I muttered. I gestured at Thomas to move a few steps back, and made sure that neither of us was standing in Mac's line of fire to the door. I focused on the black stone. It would start there. "Hey, creep!" I called, lifting my left hand. "You heard the man. Kissssss my asssssss!"

"Sssso be it," hissed the voice from the stone.

And the black stone exploded.

I was ready for it, though. I'd already prepared the defensive spell, and I poured my will into a thick wall in the air in front of me as fragments of glossy black stone flew around the room. They bounced off my shield and went zinging, shattering one of my empty beer bottles on the table, slamming into the wooden columns, and gouging wood out of the walls. None of them got to Thomas, Mac, or me. I'd put the shield between us and the black stone while our attackers wasted time in negotiation. It wasn't as good as the shield I could have thrown up if I had managed to replace my old shield bracelet, and I couldn't hold it up anywhere near as long, but I didn't need to.

Once the explosion had passed, I dropped the shield, already focusing my will upon my other hand, gathering a cannonball of raw force, and at the first flicker of motion outside the door's glass, I snarled, *"Forzare!"* and sent it hurtling forth.

Force hammered into the door, and turned maybe fifty pounds of leaded glass into a cloud of razor-sharp shards. The stairwell down to Mac's place was sunken—there was no way any of the shrapnel could fly out at street level.

An instant later, the bottom half of the door exploded into flying daggers of wood. My shield stopped anything heading toward Mac, but I couldn't catch them all. One of them clipped my left cheekbone broadside—if it had tumbled for another fraction of a second, the sharp end would have driven right into my brain. As it was, it hit me like a baseball bat, stunning me and knocking me down.

The world did that slow-motion echo-chamber thing that happens sometimes with a head blow, and I saw our attacker come in.

At first, I couldn't translate what I was seeing into something that made sense: It looked something like those giant spinning, whirling tubes covered in strips of soft cloth at an automated car wash, the ones that actually shampoo your car. Except it wasn't a tube; it was a sphere, and it wasn't at a car wash; it was rolling in through Mac's doorway.

Mac's shotgun went off, the sound of it slapping me in the back. Those things are *loud* in an enclosed space. Dust and bits of scrap cloth flew out of the attacker, but it didn't slow down. The giant rag ball hurtled toward me, until Thomas dashed in from the side and smashed it with a roundhouse swing of one of Mac's heavy oak tables.

Quick bar fighting tip for you—in real life, when you hit a guy with furniture, it doesn't break into pieces the way it does in the movies. It breaks whoever you hit with it. There was a meaty sound of impact and the rolling shape's forward momentum was instantly converted into a perpendicular line drive. It streaked across the room, trailing streamers of grey-brown cloth like a ragged comet, the cloth flapping and snapping with unnatural volume until it hit the wall with a solid thwack.

Another fighting tip for you: Don't stay on the ground. If you don't know exactly what you're up against, if you aren't sure that the guy you're fighting doesn't have a buddy coming along who might help, you can't afford to be down and relatively motionless. My body was already moving, though I wasn't sure how it was doing that, pushing me back to my feet.

Mac put a hand on the bar and vaulted up onto it like he did it all the time. The attacker bounced off the wall, rolled across a tabletop, and fell to the floor in a heap. Mac took a pair of quick steps to get a better line of fire, and *boom* went the shotgun again. Another cloud of scrap cloth and dust flew up from the attacker.

The room lurched back into normal speed. Dozens of strips of the dark sackcloth came flying off of the thing, twining in an instant around chairs and tables. A chair flew at Thomas, knocking the table out of his hands, and he was forced to dodge to one side instead of closing in. Mac's shotgun bellowed three more times, and I hurled another lance of force at the thing. Mac's shells did nothing but create puffs of debris, and my own arcane strike split and flowed around the thing, shattering a chair and smashing in a portion of the wall behind it.

And it laughed.

Furniture exploded out from it, flung with superhuman force. My shield barely caught the narrow edge of a table that had been flung like a Frisbee. Thomas's legs were scythed out from under him by a flying bar stool, and he hit the floor with a huff of expelled breath. Mac had already thrown himself down behind the bar—but when another table hit it, there was an enormous cracking sound, and several pieces of wood broke under the impact.

A shape stirred in the writhing mass of ash-colored sackcloth and rose, its outline veiled but not entirely obscured by the cloth. It was lanky-tall, and had to stand hunched over to avoid the lazily spinning blades of the ceiling fans. It was more or less human-shaped, and I was suddenly struck by the realization that I was looking at a humanoid who was wearing some kind of enormous, ungainly garment made of all those restless, rustling strips.

It lifted its head slowly and focused on me.

It didn't look at me—it didn't have any eyes, just smooth skin laced with scars where they had once been. Its skin was pearly grey lined with darker stripes that made me think of a shark. Its mouth was gaping open in a wide grin that reinforced the impression. It didn't have teeth—just a single smooth ridge of bone where teeth would have been on a human. Its lips were black, and its mouth smudged with more of it. Twin trails of saliva drooled from the corners of its mouth, leaving black streaks to down past its chin. There wasn't a hair to be seen on its head.

"Wizard," it said, and its voice was the same as had come through the glossy stone. "Your life need not end this day. Surrender and I will spare your companions."

I could hear Mac reloading behind me. Thomas had his gun in his hand, behind his back, and was prowling silently around the room to force Sharkface to turn to keep an eye on him.

Except it didn't have eyes. Whatever this thing was using to keep track of us, I had a feeling that just standing in an inconvenient spot wasn't going to net us much of an advantage.

"Surrender," I said, as though trying to place where I'd heard the word before. "Yeah, um. I'm not so sure I want any surrenders today. There was a sale on surrenders last week, and I missed it, but I don't want to rush out and buy another one at the regular price right away. I'm afraid the sale might come back a week later, and then, I mean, come on. How stupid would I feel then?"

"Levity will not change the course of this day," Sharkface said. Its buzzing, twisting voice was distinctly unpleasant in my ears, the aural equivalent of the stench of rotting meat. Which was appropriate, because the rest of him *did* smell like rotting meat. "You *will* come with me."

"Isn't that what Mab said, Harry?" Thomas quipped.

I kept my hand shielded from Sharkface with my body and gave my brother the finger. "Look, Spanky," I said to Sharkface. "I'm a little busy to be tussling with every random weirdo who is insecure about his junk. Otherwise I would just love to smash you with a beer bottle, kick you in the balls, throw you out through the saloon doors, the whole bit. Why don't you have your people contact my people, and we can do this maybe next week?"

"Next week is your self-deprecation awareness seminar," Thomas said.

I snapped my fingers. "What about the week after?"

"Apartment hunting."

"Bother," I said. "Well, no one can say we didn't try. See you later."

"Harry," said a strange voice. Or rather, it wasn't strange—it was just strange to actually *hear* it. Mac isn't much of a talker. "Don't chat. Kill it."

Mac's words seemed to do what none of my nonsense had—they made Sharkface pissed off. It whirled toward Mac, dozens of sackcloth strips flicking out in every direction, grabbing whatever objects were there, and its alien voice came out in a harsh rasp. "You!" Sharkface snarled. "You have no place in this, *watcher*. Do you think this gesture has meaning? It is every bit as empty as *you*. You chose your road long ago. Have the grace to lie down and die beside it."

I think my jaw might have hung a little loosely for a second. "Uh. Mac?"

"Kill it," Mac repeated, his voice harder. "It's only the first."

"Yes," Sharkface said, tilting its head almost to the perpendicular. "Kill it. And more will come. Destroy me and they will know. Leave me and they will know. Your breaths are numbered, wizard."

As it spoke, I could feel a horrible, hopeless weight settling across my heart. Dammit, hadn't I been through enough? More than enough? Hadn't my life handed me enough misery and grief and pain and loneliness already? And now I was going to be up against something else, something new and scary, something that came galumphing at me by the *legion*, no less. What was the point? No matter what I did, no matter how much stronger or smarter or better connected I got, the bad guys just kept getting bigger and stronger and more numerous.

Behind me, I heard Mac let out a low groan. The shotgun must have fallen from his fingers, because it clattered on the floor. On my left, I saw Thomas's shoulders slump, and he turned his face away, his eyes closed as if in pain.

The people who stayed near me got hurt or killed. As often as not, the bad guys got away to come embadden my life another day. Why deal with a life like that?

Why did I keep on doing this to myself?

"Because," I growled under my breath. "You're Charlie Brown, stupid. You've got to try for the damned football because that's who you are."

And just like that, the psychic assault of despair that Sharkface had sent into my head evaporated, and I could think clearly again. I hadn't felt the cloying, somehow oily power slithering up to me—but I could sure as hell feel it now as it recoiled and pulled away. I'd felt it before—and I suddenly knew what I was dealing with.

Sharkface jerked its head toward me, and its mouth opened in shock. For a frozen instant, we stared at each other across maybe fifteen feet of cluttered pub. It seemed to last for hours. Thomas and Mac were both motionless, reaching out for physical supports as though drunk or bearing a heavy burden. They wouldn't be able to get themselves out of the building in their current condition—but I didn't have any choice.

Sharkface and its sackcloth cloak flung half a ton of furniture at me about a quarter of a second after I raised my right hand and snarled, "*Fuego!*"

I hadn't used much fire magic lately, obviously. You don't go messing around conjuring up flame when you're at the heart of Winter. There are things there that hate that action. But fire magic has always been my strongest suit. It was the first fully realized spell I ever mastered, and on a good day I could hang around in the same general league as any other wizard in the world when it came to fire magic.

On top of that, I tapped into the latent energy a particularly meddlesome angel had bestowed upon me whether I wanted it or not—an ancient source of the very energy of Creation itself known as soulfire. Soulfire was never meant for battle—but its presence could infuse my battle spells with significant energy and momentum, making them far more difficult to counter. I had to be careful with it—burn too much in too short a time and it would kill me. But if I didn't live to walk out of the pub, it wouldn't matter how much soulfire I had stored up for a rainy day.

I expected a roar of flame, a flash of white and gold light, the concussion of superheated air suddenly expanding, right in Sharkface's ugly mug.

What I got was an arctic-gale howl and a spiraling harpoon of blue-white fire burning hotter than anything this side of a star.

Sharkface hurled furniture at me, trying to shelter behind it, but the fire I'd just called vaporized chairs and tables in the instant it touched them. They shattered with enormous, screaming detonations of thunder, and every impact made sounds that by all rights should have belonged to extremely large and poorly handled construction vehicles.

Sharkface crossed its bony grey forearms before it in a last-ditch effort to deflect the spell. If I'd been focused on it, concentrating on pushing the spell past its defenses, maybe it would have burned right through Sharkface and its stupid cloak. But that wasn't the plan. Instead, I sprinted across the distance between us, through the hideous heat of my spell's thermal bloom. It was like running through an oven. I saw my spell splash against Sharkface's crossed forearms, and the thing managed to deflect almost all of the spell away—but not all of it. Fire scorched across one of its cheeks and splashed over its right shoulder, setting a large mass of sackcloth strips aflame.

It screamed in pain, a sound that raked at my ears, and began to lower its arms to retaliate.

The second it did, I drove my right fist into its stupid, creepy face.

Man, the yahoos I scrap with never seem to anticipate that tactic. They all assume that what with me being a wizard and all, I'm going to stand back and chuck Magic Missiles at them or something, then scream and run away the second they get close enough to let me see the whites of their eyes.

Okay, granted, that *is* how a lot of wizards operate. But all the same, you'd think they would remember that there's no particular reason why a wizard can't be as comfortable with physical mayhem as the next guy.

Two things happened.

First, as my fist sailed forward, there was a sudden thrill that flowed up my arm from my hand, something delicious and startling. I had barely processed that when I heard a crackling noise, and then saw glacial blue and green ice abruptly coating my fist.

Second, I hit Sharkface like a freaking truck, starting right on the tip of its chin and driving straight toward South America. The ice coating my fist shattered into tiny shards that laced and sliced, but I barely felt it. Sharkface flew back as if I'd slugged it with a sledgehammer, and hit the wall with enough violence to crack and splinter the heavy oak paneling. Sharkface's cloak fluttered hard as it went backward—the freaking thing was cushioning his impact, just as it had managed to stop shotgun pellets at short range.

Sharkface bounced off the wall, staggering, and I gave it a left and another right, and then kicked its legs out from underneath it as brutally as I knew how. It went to the floor hard.

Once Sharkface was down I stomped for its head with my hiking boots, going for a quick kill, which was exactly what this asshole had coming to it for messing with my favorite joint—but that stupid cloak got in the way. Strips flew out to gain purchase and hauled him out from beneath my boot. Even as I reacted, moving to follow him up, more of the sackcloth tendrils seized a dozen bottles of liquor from behind the bar—and flung them harshly onto the puddles of vicious blue-white fire still burning upon the floor where Sharkface had deflected them.

I slashed at the tumbling bottles with an effort of will, but I hadn't had a soft-touch spell in mind during the previous seconds. My clumsy grab accomplished nothing but to shatter one of the bottles early, and flames roared up from where the spilled liquor fell.

Alcohol fires are a nasty business. Booze burns a good deal hotter and faster than, for example, gasoline. In seconds it can take the temperature from below freezing to seven hundred degrees, hot enough to turn flesh into briquettes. Mac and Thomas were both down. There was no way I could get them both out of the fire in time—which meant my only option was to stop it from happening.

Sharkface let out an eerie, defiant shriek and suddenly vanished into the writhing mass of his coat again, becoming nothing but flailing cloth and dust and stench. The creature bounded into the air and streaked like a sackcloth comet out the front door—and there was diddly I could do to stop it.

Instead, I turned to the fires just as bottles began to shatter on the floor, just as white-hot flames began to leap. I hurled my will through my body, drawing forth the frigid purity of Winter, calling, *"Infriga!"*

Howling wind and cold engulfed the nascent fires. And the floor around where the fires had been. And the walls. And, um, the ceiling.

I mean, pretty much every nonliving surface in the place was completely covered in a layer of frost half an inch thick.

Mac and Thomas started groaning. I gave them a minute to pull themselves together and watched the door. Sharkface didn't show up for a rematch. Maybe he was busy changing into fresh undies because I'd scared him so bad. Right. More likely he was off doing a *Right Stuff* walk and gathering his gang.

The fog lightened and burned off within five minutes or so, and the sounds of the city returned.

The attack was over. Mac stared woozily around the pub, shaking his head. Covered in glittering frost and ice, it looked like the place Santa's elves must go when they finish their shift at the toy shop.

Mac gave me a look and then gestured at the pub, clearly wanting an explanation.

"Hey," I said crossly. "At least it didn't get burned to the ground. Count your blessings, man. That's better than most buildings get around me."

Thomas sat up a moment later, and I helped him to his feet.

"What happened?" he asked blearily.

"Psychic assault," I told him. "A bad one. How you feeling?"

"Confused," Thomas said. He looked around the place, shaking his head. The pub looked like it had just been raided by Super Bowl–berserk Bears fans. "What was that thing?"

I rubbed at my forehead with the heel of my hand. "An Outsider."

Thomas's eyes went wide and round. "What?"

"An Outsider," I repeated quietly. "We're fighting Outsiders."

23

"Outsiders," Thomas said. "Are you sure?"

"You felt it," I said. "That mental whammy. It was exactly like that night in the Raith Deeps."

Thomas frowned but nodded. "Yeah, it was, wasn't it?"

Mac walked silently past us to the ruined door. He bent down and picked something up out of the general wreckage there. It was the Accorded Neutral Territory sign. It was scorched on one corner, but he hung it back up on the wall. Then he leaned his hands against it and bowed his head.

I knew how he felt. Violent encounters tend to be scary and exhausting, even if they last for only seconds. My nerves were still jangling, my legs were trembling a little, and I wanted very badly to just plop down onto the floor and breathe for a while. I didn't. Wizards are stoic about this kind of thing. And my brother would make fun of me.

Thomas exhaled slowly through his nose, his eyes narrowed. "I don't know much about them," he said.

"That's not surprising," I said. "There's not a lot of information on Outsiders. We think that's because most people who run into them don't get a chance to tell anyone about it."

"Lot of things like that in the world," Thomas said. "Sounds like these things are just a little creepier than your average demonic nasty."

"It's more than that," I said. "Creatures out of the Nevernever are a part of our reality, our universe. They can get pretty bizarre, but they have a membership card. Outsiders come from someplace else."

Thomas shrugged. "What's the difference?"

"They're smarter. Tougher. Harder to kill."

"You handled that one pretty well. Didn't look so tough."

I snorted. "You missed out on the end. I hit that thing with my best shot, and I barely made it uncomfortable. It didn't leave because I hurt it. It left because it didn't expect me to fight clear of its whammy, and it didn't want to take any chances that I might get lucky and prevent it from reporting to its superiors."

"Still ran," Thomas said. "Yeah, that mind-meld thing was awful, but the bastard wasn't all *that* bad."

I sighed. "That little creep Peabody dropped *one* Outsider on a meeting of the Council. The best wizards in the world were all in that one room and took it on together, and the thing still managed to murder a bunch of them. It's hard to make magic stick to Outsiders. It's hard to make them leave. It's hard to hurt them. It's hard to make them die. They're insanely violent, insanely powerful, and just plain insane. But that isn't what makes them dangerous."

"Uh," Thomas said. "It isn't? Then what is?"

"They work together," I said quietly. "Near as we can tell, they *all* work together."

Thomas was silent for a moment as he considered the implications of that. "Work together," he said. "To do what?"

I shook my head. "Whatever they do. Their actions are not always predicated on rationality—or at least, that's what the Council thinks."

"You sound skeptical."

"The White Council always assumes that it's at least as smart as everyone else all put together. I know better."

"Because you're so much smarter than they are," Thomas said wryly.

"Because I'm on the street more than they are," I corrected him. "The Council thinks the Outsiders are just a giant box of crazy that can go rampaging in any random direction."

"But you don't think that."

"The phrase 'crazy like a fox' leaps to mind."

"Okay. So what do *you* think these Outsiders are doing?"

I shrugged. "I'm almost certain they aren't selling Girl Scout cookies. But don't quote me."

"Don't worry; I hardly ever want to sound clueless. But the fact that they're working together implies a purpose. A goal."

"Yes."

"So?" my brother asked. "What do they want?"

"Thomas, they're aliens. I mean, they're like super-mega-überaliens. They might not even *think*, at least not in the way we understand it. How the hell are we supposed to make even an informed guess about their motivation—assuming that they have one?"

"Doesn't matter how weird they are," Thomas said. "Moving together implies purpose. Purpose implies a goal. Goals are universal."

"They aren't *from* this universe. That's the point," I said. "Maybe you're right; I don't know. But until I have a better idea, it's smarter to keep reminding myself that I don't know, rather than assuming that I do know, and then translating anything I learn to fit my preconceptions."

"Here's a fact that is no assumption," Thomas said. "They wanted you."

"Yeah," I said.

"Why?" he asked.

"All I can do is guess."

"So guess."

I sighed. "My gut says they're planning a jailbreak."

Thomas grunted. "Might have been smarter for them to have left you alone. Now you know something."

I made an exasperated sound. "Yes. Those fools. By trying to kill me, they've revealed their very souls. I have them now."

Thomas gave me a steady look. "Being Mab's bitch has made you a pessimist."

"I am not a pessimist," I said loftily. "Though *that* can't last."

That made Thomas grin. "Nice."

"Thank you."

At the door, Mac looked up suddenly and said, "Dresden."

Thomas tilted his head, listening. Then he said, "Cops."

I sighed. "Poor guys. Bet last night's watch hasn't even been released to go home yet. They're going to be cranky."

"The explosion thing?" Thomas asked.

"The explosion thing."

We didn't need to be detained and questioned all day, and I didn't need to get into an altercation with the police, either—they've got no sense of humor at all for such things. You always hear about there being no rest for the wicked, but I'm pretty sure cops aren't racking up much extra hammock time, either. Thomas and I traded a look and headed for the door.

I paused by it, and looked at Mac.

"It knew you."

Mac stared at nothing and didn't answer.

"Mac, that thing was dangerous," I said. "And it might come back."

Mac grunted.

"Look," I said. "If my guess is right, that twit and its buddies might wipe out a big chunk of the state. Or possibly states. If you know something about them, I need it."

Mac didn't look up. After several seconds, he said, "Can't. I'm out."

"Look at this place," I said quietly. "You aren't out. Nobody is out."

"Drop it," he said. "Neutral territory."

"Neutral territory that is going to burn with all the rest of it," I said. "I don't care who you are, man. I don't care what you've done. I don't care whether or not you think you're retired from the life. If you know something I need it. Now."

"Harry, we need to move," Thomas said, urgency tightening his voice.

I could hear the sirens now. They had to be close. Mac turned and walked back toward his bar.

Dammit. I shook my head and turned to leave.

"Dresden," Mac called.

I turned to look back at him. Mac was standing behind the bar. As I watched, he took three bottles of beer from beneath the counter and placed them down in a straight line, one by one, their sides touching. Then he just looked up at me.

"Three of them," I said. "Three of these things?" Hell's bells, one of them had been bad enough.

Mac neither nodded nor shook his head. He just jerked his chin at me and said, "Luck."

"We're gonna talk," I said to Mac.

Mac turned a look on me that was as distant and as inaccessible as Antarctic mountains.

"No," he said. "We aren't."

I was going to say something smart-ass. But that bleak expression made it seem like a bad idea.

So instead, I followed my brother up the debris-strewn stairs and into the rainy morning.

We passed the first police car to arrive at the scene on our way out, driving at the sedate pace of upright citizens.

"I love evading representatives of the lawful authority," Thomas said, watching the car go by in his rearview mirror. "It's one of those little things that make me happy."

I paused and thought about it. "Me too. I mean, I know a bunch of these guys. Some of them are good people, some of them are jerks, but most are just guys doing a job. And it's not like sticking us in a room and questioning us is going to accomplish anything to make their day go more smoothly."

"And you enjoy driving authority figures insane," Thomas said.

I shrugged. "I watched *The Dukes of Hazzard* at a formative age," I said. "Of course I enjoy it."

"Where next?" Thomas asked. "Molly's place?"

I thought about it for a minute. I didn't think it would be a great idea to be there when Fix came looking for a fight. Svartalves were a little prickly about territory, and they might not be at all amused if I dragged a personal conflict into their domain. But there were other people I wanted to contact before nightfall, and I needed a phone and some quiet workspace to do it in.

"The Summer Lady has granted your request for an audience," said Cat Sith from the backseat.

Thomas nearly took the Hummer off the street and into a bus stop shelter. My heart leapt into my throat as if it had been given bionic legs and its own sound effects. Thomas regained control of the vehicle almost instantly, letting out a wordless snarl as he did.

"Sith," I said, too loud. My heart was running at double time. I glared at him over the front seat. "Dammit."

The malk's too-long tail flicked back and forth in smug self-satisfaction. "Shall I interpret that as an order to burn something, Sir Knight? If you are to survive long in Winter, you must learn to be much more specific in your turns of phrase."

"No, don't burn anything," I said, grouchily. I thought about giving the malk an order not to sneak up on me like that anymore, but thought better of it. That would be exactly the kind of order that Cat Sith would take grotesque amusement in perverting, and I wanted to avoid putting him into a playful mood. "What did Lily have to say?"

"That she would guarantee your safety from harm wrought by herself, her Court, and any in her employ or influence," the malk said, "provided that you came alone and kept the peace."

I grunted, thinking.

"Why would she want you alone?" Thomas asked. "Unless she planned on doing something to you."

"Because the last time she saw the Winter Knight, he was murdering the previous Summer Knight?" I guessed aloud. "Because the last time she saw the corpse of the Summer Lady, I was the one who'd made it? Because I'm a known thug who wrecks things a lot?"

Thomas bobbed his head slightly to one side in acknowledgment. "Okay. Point."

"Sith," I asked, "where is the meeting?"

"A public venue," Sith said, his eyes half-lidded. "Chicago Botanic Gardens."

"See?" I said to Thomas. "That's not a venue for an assassination—for either of us. There are too many people around. There are plenty of ways out for anyone who wants to leave. That's a viable neutral location."

"If I remember right," Thomas said, "the last time the Summer Lady tried a hit on you, didn't she animate a bunch of plants into a giant monster that tried to kill you in the garden center of a Walmart?"

I rode in silence for a few seconds and then said, "Yeah, but . . . it was dark. Not as many people around."

"Oh," Thomas said. "Okay."

I held the back of my left fist up to him, then used my right fist to make a little circular cranking motion next to it, while slowly elevating the center finger of my left hand until it was fully extended. Then I turned to Sith.

"What do you think? Is the risk acceptable for a meeting in that location?"

"You would be foolish to meet with her at all," Cat Sith replied. "However. Given her promise and her chosen location, I judge it to be at least possible that she may actually intend to treat with you."

"Suppose she's lying," Thomas said.

"She can't," I told him. "None of the Sidhe or the greater powers of either court can tell an outright lie. Right, Sith?"

"Logically speaking, *my* answer to that question would be unsupportable as truth."

I sighed. "Well, that's how it is among them," I said. "No falsehoods. They can twist words around, they can avoid answering, they can mislead you by drawing you to false conclusions, but they can't blatantly tell a lie."

Thomas shook his head as he pulled onto 94 and started north. "I still don't like it. That crowd never gives you what you expect."

"Think how boring it would be if they did," I said.

We both considered that wistfully for a beat.

"You might have to go in alone," Thomas said. "But I'm going to stay close. Things go bad, just make some noise and I'll come in."

"They aren't going to go bad," I said. "But even if they do, I don't want anyone to get hurt. Summer's weird, but they're basically good neighbors. I don't blame them for being jumpy."

Sith made a disgusted sound.

"Problem?" I asked him.

"This . . . compassion," the malk said. "If you prefer, I can slash your throat open now, Sir Knight, and save the vampire the cost of fuel."

"I've got a better idea," I said. "I want you to stay close to Thomas and alert him to any source of danger. If a fight breaks out, your goal is to assist in making sure that both he and I escape, without doing harm to any innocent bystanders, and without killing any mortals."

Sith started making a sound like my cat always did right before he spit out a hairball.

"Hey," Thomas said. "Those are custom leather seats!"

Sith spit out a glob the size of a small plum, but instead of a hairball it was actually a small collection of splintered chips of bone. He flicked his tail in scorn and then leapt lightly into the rear bed of the Hummer.

"Jerk," Thomas muttered.

"Just drive," I said.

He grimaced and did. After a few miles he asked, "You think this is going to work? This peaceful summit thing?"

"Sure," I said. After a second, I added, "Probably."

"Probably?"

"Maybe," I said.

"We're down to maybe now?"

I shrugged. "We'll see."

24

The Botanic Gardens of Chicago aren't actually in Chicago, which always made them seem a little shady to me. Ba-dump-bump.

Rain was coming down in fitful little starts, averaging out to a mild drizzle. The air was cool, in the low fifties, and combined with the rain it meant that the gardens weren't exactly crowded with ardent floraphiles. The weather didn't bother me. In fact, I could have taken the jacket off and felt fine—but I didn't.

My grandfather had taught me that magic wasn't something you used in a cavalier fashion, and it *wasn't* considered to be a seductive, corruptive force, the way black magic and the Winter Knight's mantle were. I had an instinct that the more I leaned on Mab's power, the more of an effect it would have on me. No sense flaunting it.

Once I was inside, I found myself in a setting of isolation that would be hard to duplicate anywhere else this close to the city. The gardens are the size of a moderate farm, more than three hundred acres. That wouldn't mean much to city mice, but to translate that into Chicago units, it was a couple of dozen city blocks' worth of garden. That's a lot of space to wander in. You could walk the various paths for hours and hours without ever visiting the same place.

Most of those paths were grey and empty. I passed a retiree near the entrance, and a groundskeeper hurrying out of the rain toward what looked like a concealed toolshed, and other than that it seemed like I had the whole place to myself.

There were seasonal decorations out here and there—a lot of pump-kins and cornstalks, where they'd been planning on Halloween festivities. Apparently they were going to be hosting some kind of trick-or-treating function that afternoon, but for the time being the place did not teem with costumed children and bedraggled parents. It was a little eerie, really. The place looked like it should have been crowded, and felt like it was meant to be crowded, but my soft footsteps were the only sound other than the whisper of rain.

Yet I did not feel as though I were alone. You hear the phrase "I felt like I was being watched" all the time. There's a good reason for that—it's a very real feeling, and it has nothing to do with magic. Developing an instinct for sensing when a predator might be studying you is a funda-mental survival trait. If you're ever in a spooky situation and have a strong instinct that you are being watched, hunted, or followed, I advise you not to treat those instincts lightly. They're there for a reason.

I walked for about five minutes, and instinct converted into certainty. I was being followed. I couldn't spot who was doing it, exactly, and there were all kinds of plant cover to conceal whoever or whatever was pacing me, but I was confident that they were out there.

Maybe my brother's fears hadn't been entirely without merit.

Lily hadn't said where she intended to meet me, exactly—or rather, I chided myself, I hadn't badgered Cat Sith hard enough for the details. The furry jerk had calmly denied me that rather important piece of in-formation, simply by never mentioning it, and I hadn't questioned him closely enough. My own fault. I'd played the malicious obedience card more than a couple of times in my life, but this was the first time I'd had it played against me.

Man. No wonder it drives people insane.

So I started walking the main paths systematically. The gardens are built on a series of islands in a little lake, joined by footbridges and grouped into themes.

I found Lily waiting on the covered bridge to the Japanese garden.

Her long, fine hair flowed in gentle waves to the small of her back. It was silver-white. Evidently the weather didn't bother her either. She was dressed in a simple green sundress that fell to her knees, the kind of thing you'd expect to see in July. She had a pastel green sweater folded over one arm for appearance's sake. Brown leather sandals wrapped her feet, and their ties crisscrossed around her ankles. She stood very still, her deep green eyes focused on the ripples the little raindrops sent up on the surface of the lake.

And if I hadn't known better, if I hadn't known Lily's features well enough to be sure it was her, I would have sworn that I was looking at Aurora, the Summer Lady I'd murdered at the stone table.

Before stepping onto the bridge, I paused for a moment to look around me, to truly focus my senses. There, in the bushes—something that moved with feline smoothness paced me in utter silence. More presences filled the water, stirring up more ripples than the rain could account for. And on the far side of the bridge, a number of presences lurked, veiled by magic that kept me from knowing anything about them beyond the fact of their existence.

I figured that there were at least twice as many guardians present, the ones I couldn't sense without really buckling down. They would probably be the most capable and powerful of Lily's escort, too.

If Lily meant to do me harm, walking out onto that bridge was a great way to trap myself, and an absolutely fantastic place in which to be shot. The railing on either side was of light, fine material, and would provide no real cover. There were an almost unlimited number of places where a rifleman could be lying in wait. If I went out there and Lily meant to hurt me, I'd have a hell of a time arguing with her.

But she'd given her word that she wouldn't. I tried to look at this from her point of view—after all, I hadn't given my word, and even if I had, I could always break it. Had I intended to attack Lily, the bridge presented her with an opportunity to block me in, to slow me down while she and her people escaped.

Screw this. I didn't have time to waffle.

I hunched my shoulders, hoped no one was about to shoot me again, and strode out onto the bridge.

Lily didn't give any indication that she'd noticed me until I got to within about ten feet of her. Then she simply lifted her eyes from the water, though she never looked at me.

I'd been the one to ask for this meeting. I stopped, gave her a bow, and said, "Thank you for meeting me, Lady Summer."

She inclined her head the slightest visible degree. "Sir Knight."

"Been a while," I said.

"Relative to what?" she asked.

"Life, I guess," I said.

"Much has happened," she agreed. "Wars have raged. Empires have fallen." She finally turned her head to regard me directly. "Friends have changed."

Lily had been gorgeous as a mortal woman. After becoming the Summer Lady, her beauty had been magnified into something that was only barely human, something so tangible and intense that it shone out from her like light flowing out of her skin. It was a different kind of beauty from Mab's or Maeve's. Their loveliness was an emptiness. Looking on them created nothing but desire, a need that cried out to be filled.

By contrast, Lily's beauty was a fire, a source of light and warmth, something that created a profound sense of satisfaction. Looking at Lily made the pains of my heart ease, and I suddenly felt like I could breathe freely for the first time in months.

And some other part of me abruptly filled my mind with a violent and explicit image—my fist tangled in Lily's hair, that soft gentle mouth under mine, her body writhing beneath my weight as I took her to the ground. It wasn't an idle thought, and it wasn't a daydream, and it wasn't a fantasy. It was a blueprint. If Lily was immortal, I couldn't kill her. That didn't mean I couldn't *take* her.

I forgot how to speak for a couple of seconds as I fought the image out of my forebrain. Then I forced myself to look away from her, out to the water of the lake. I leaned down on the guardrail, gripping it with my hands. I was a little worried that if I didn't give them something to do, they might try something stupid. I took a cleansing breath and reengaged my speech centers. "I'm not the only one who's changed since that day."

I could feel her eyes on me, intently studying my face. I had a feeling that she knew exactly what I'd just felt. "True," she murmured. "But we've made our choices, haven't we? And now we are who we are. I am sorry if I made you uncomfortable, Sir Knight."

"What? Just now?"

I saw her nod in my peripheral vision. "A moment ago, you looked at me. I have seen a face with that precise expression before."

"Slate."

"Yes."

"Well," I growled, "I'm not Slate. I'm not some pet monster Maeve made to play with."

"No," Lily said, her voice sad. "You are a weapon Mab made to war with. You poor man. You always had such a good heart."

"Had?" I asked.

"It isn't yours any longer," Lily said quietly.

"I disagree," I said. "Strenuously."

"And the need you felt a moment ago?" she asked. "Did that urge come from your heart, Sir Knight?"

"Yes," I said simply.

Lily froze for a second, her head tilting slightly to one side.

"Bad things are inside everyone," I said. "I don't care how gentle or holy or sincere or dedicated you are. There are bad things in there. Lust. Greed. Violence. You don't need a wicked queen to make that happen. That's a part of everyone. Some more, some less, but it's always there."

"You say that you were this wicked from the beginning?" Lily asked.

"I'm saying I could have been," I said. "I chose something else. And I'm going to continue choosing something else."

Lily smiled faintly and looked back at the lake. "You wished to speak to me about my knight."

"Fix, yeah," I said. "He basically gave me until noon to leave town, or we shoot it out at the OK Corral. I'm busy. I don't have time to skip town. But I don't want either of us to get hurt."

"What do you wish me to do?"

"Tell him to stand down," I said. "Even if only for a few days. It's important."

Lily bowed her head. "It grieves me to say this, Sir Knight. But no. I will not."

I tried not to grind my teeth audibly. "And why not?"

She studied me again, her green eyes intense. "Can it be?" she asked.

"Can it be that you have come so far, have fallen in with your current company, without realizing what is happening here?"

"Uh," I said, frowning. "You mean here, today?"

"I mean here," Lily said. "In our world."

"Yeah, uh. Maybe you haven't heard, but I haven't been in our world much lately."

Lily shook her head. "The pieces are all in front of you. You have only to assemble them."

"Vague much?" I asked. "Why can't you just tell me what the hell you're talking about?"

"If you do know, there is no need to speak. If you truly do not know, no amount of speech will convince you. Some things must be learned for oneself."

I made a disgusted sound and spit into the lake. Take that, lurking bodyguards. "Lily," I said. "Look, this isn't complicated. Fix is about to come at me. I *don't want to hurt him.* So I came here in peace to try to talk it out. What have I done here today that has convinced you that I'm some kind of psychotic maniac who can't be trusted?"

"It isn't anything you've done," Lily said. "It isn't anything you had any control over. You didn't know."

I threw up my hands at that. "Didn't know what?"

Lily frowned and studied me, her expression drawn with worry. "You . . ." She shook her head. "God, Harry. You really mean it. You aren't her creature?"

"No," I said. "Not yet."

Lily nodded and seemed to think for a moment. Then she asked, "Would it pain you for me to touch you?"

"Why?" I asked.

"Because I must know," she said. "I must know if it is upon you yet."

"What?"

She shook her head. "I cannot risk answering any questions until I am sure."

I grunted. I thought about it. Yeah, I could keep my inner caveman on a leash, if it meant getting some answers. "Okay," I said. "Go ahead."

Lily nodded. Then she walked toward me. She reached up and her slender, warm fingers touched my forehead, like a mother checking a child for a temperature. She stayed that way for a long moment, her eyes distant.

Then abruptly she let out a little cry and flung her arms around me. "Oh," she said. "Oh, oh, oh. We thought you taken."

Okay, inner caveman or not, when a girl that pretty is giving you a full-body hug, you don't come up with the wittiest dialogue. "Uh. I haven't had a girlfriend for a while now."

Lily leaned her head back and laughed. The sound of it was like eating hot cookies, melting into a warm shower, and snuggling a fuzzy puppy all at the same time. "Enough," she said. "Enough, come out. He is a friend."

And, just like that, faeries popped out of absolutely *everything* in sight. Elves, tiny humanoids no more than a couple of feet high, rose up out of the bushes. A serpent the size of a telephone pole slithered out of the bridge's rafters. Seven or eight silver-coated faerie hounds emerged from behind a stand of groomed arbor vitae. Two massive centaurs and half a dozen Sidhe of the Summer Court simply blinked into visibility from behind their veils. They were all armed with bows. Yikes. If I'd meant Lily any harm, my body would have resembled a feathery porcupine. The water stirred, and then a number of otters who were all too big to have been born this side of the last ice age came rushing out.

"Ee-aye, ee-aye, oh," I said. "Uh, wow. All this for me?"

"Only a fool wouldn't respect your strength," she said. "Particularly now."

Personally, I thought she'd gotten to overkill about one elf after those bows, but I didn't want her to know that. "Okay," I said. "You touched me. Make with some answers."

"Certainly," she said. Then she moved her hand, and the open air suddenly had the enclosed feeling of a small room. When she spoke, her voice sounded odd, as if it were coming over a radio. She'd put up a privacy spell so that no one could listen in. "What would you like to know?"

"Um, right," I said. "Why did you touch my head like that? What were you looking for?"

"A disease," she replied. "A parasite. A poison."

"Could you repeat that answer, only without the poetry?"

Lily faced me squarely, her lovely face intent. "Sir Knight, you must have seen it. You must have seen the contagion spreading. It has been before your eyes for *years*."

"I haven't seen . . ." Then I paused. My head started adding things together. "You . . . you aren't talking about a physical disease, are you?"

"Of course not," Lily said. "It is a kind of spiritual malady. A mental plague. An infection slowly spreading across the earth."

"And . . . this plague. What does it do?" I asked.

"It changes that which ought not change," she said quietly. "It destroys a father's love for his family by twisting it into maniacal ambition. It distorts and corrupts the good intentions of agents of mortal law into violence and death. It erodes the sensible fear that keeps a weakly talented sorcerer from reaching out for more power, no matter how terrible the cost."

I felt my head rock back as if she'd slammed a croquet mallet into it, and the bottom dropped out of my stomach again.

"Victor Sells the Shadowman," I whispered. "Agent Denton and the Hexenwolves. Leonid Kravos the Nightmare. My first three major cases."

"Yes," Lily whispered. "Each of them was tainted by the contagion. It destroyed them."

I put a hand on the rail and leaned against it. "Fourth case. Aurora. A champion of peace and healing who set out to send the natural world into havoc."

Lily's eyes glistened with tears. "I saw what it did to her," she said. "I didn't know what was happening to my friend, but I saw it changing her. Twisting her day by day. I loved Aurora like a sister, Sir Knight. But in the end, even I could see what she had become." Tears fell, and she made no effort to wipe them away. "I saw. I knew. In the end, you may have killed her, Harry. But you also did her a kindness."

I shook my head. "I . . . I don't understand why you didn't want to tell me about it."

"No one who knows of this speaks of it," Lily said.

"Why not?"

"Don't you see?" Lily said. "What if you had been tainted as well? And I revealed to you that I recognized what was happening?"

I kicked my brain into gear and thought. "Uh . . . then . . ." I felt sick. "You'd be a threat. I'd have to kill you to keep you quiet. Or make you the next recruit."

"Exactly," Lily said.

"But why suspect *me* of being tainted . . . ?" I heard my own voice trail off as I realized the only thing that could have moved Lily against me so strongly.

"Be at ease," Lily said, and beckoned.

And freaking Maeve, the Winter Lady, strolled onto the far end of the bridge and sauntered toward us. She was dressed in leather pants of dark purple and a periwinkle sweater whose sleeves fell past the ends of her fingers, and her mouth was curled into a tiny, wicked smirk. "Hey, there, big guy," she purred. "Lily give you the skinny?"

"Not yet," Lily said. "Maeve, this isn't the sort of thing one should simply ram down another's throat."

"Of course it is," Maeve said, her smile widening.

"Maeve—" Lily began.

Maeve did a little pirouette that wound up with her toes practically touching mine as she smiled up at me, her too-sharp teeth very white. "Do you have a camera? I want someone to get a picture."

"Oh, dear," Lily said.

Maeve leaned in close, her smile widening. "Mab," she breathed, "my mother, the Queen of Air and Darkness, and your liege . . ." She leaned closer and whispered, "Mab has been tainted and has gone utterly mad."

My spine turned to brittle ice. "*What?*"

Lily looked up at me with a sad, sober expression.

Maeve let out a peal of giggles. "It's true," she said. "She means to destroy the mortal world, wizard, and to do it this very night—to unleash chaos and havoc that have not been known since the fall of Atlantis. And make no mistake, she *will* destroy it."

Lily nodded, her eyes pained. "Unless," she began. "Unless . . ."

I finished the thought Lily obviously did not want to complete. "Unless," I whispered, "someone destroys her first."

25

This day had begun so simply: I'd nearly been killed at my birthday party and Mab had ordered me to kill an immortal. I'd survived the first, and if I'd had the good sense to shut up and do the second without asking questions, I might be somewhere reading a nice book or something, and waiting out the clock until it was Maeve-whacking time.

Instead I had this.

"I love watching him think," Maeve told Lily. "You can almost hear that poor little hamster running and running on its wheel."

"You clubbed him over the head with it," Lily said. "What did you expect?"

"Oh, this," Maeve said, her eyes sparkling. "Wizards are always so sure of themselves. I love seeing them off balance. This one in particular."

"Why me?" I said. I wasn't really participating in their conversation.

"You *did* kill my cousin, wizard," Maeve said. "Aurora was a prissy little bint, but she *was* family. It makes me happy when you suffer."

I glowered at Maeve and said, "One of these days, you and I are going to disagree." I turned to Lily. "You say Mab wants to hold an Armageddon-thon, fine. How is she going to do it?"

"We aren't completely certain," Lily said, her eyes earnest.

"It's something to do with that island," Maeve said carelessly.

Gulp.

Wrecking someone's powerful and deadly ritual wasn't such a scary concept. I'd done that before, more than once. But somehow, knowing that it was *Mab's* ritual I was supposed to derail made this situation a whole lot worse. I'd *Seen* Mab before, with the unadulterated perception of my Sight, and I remembered the kind of might she wielded with absolute clarity. Mab had the kind of power you had to describe using exponents. I felt like a man with a shovel and a couple of gunnysacks who has just been told to stop an oncoming tsunami.

And Mab knew the place. She'd taken care of me for *months* there. She knew Demonreach's strengths, its defenses, and its potential. Hell, I'd been her ticket through the door—in fact, I was the *only* one who could have gotten her onto that island.

"You know," I said aloud, "it's just possible that I made a mistake in taking Mab's deal."

The two Ladies gave me level gazes. Neither of them said, "Obviously," but it hung on the spell-muffled air nonetheless.

Then I had a thought. Cat Sith had lied to me very effectively only moments ago, because I assumed reasonable things and he allowed me to charge off down that line of thinking. This was no time to make a rookie mistake like that.

"Okay," I said. "I'm going to do something I know you both hate. I'm going to get direct. And I'm going to get direct answers from you, answers that convince me that you aren't trying to hide anything from me and aren't trying to mislead me. I know you both have to speak the truth. So give me simple, declarative answers, or I assume you're scheming and walk away right now."

That made Lily press her lips together and fold her arms. Her gaze turned reproachful. Maeve rolled her eyes, casually gave me the finger, and said, "Wizards are such weasels."

"Deal with it," I said. "Lily. Are you sure that this contagion you speak of is real, and works the way you say it does?"

Lily looked like opening her mouth exposed her taste buds to something foul, but she answered, "Absolutely."

"Are you sure Mab has been . . . been infected?"

"I am all but certain," Lily said. "But I have not examined her for myself."

"I have," Maeve said calmly. "While you and my people were putting on such a garish distraction at that dreary little celebration of your birth, Sir Knight." She stretched and yawned, making sure to pull her sweater tight against her chest. "That was the purpose of it, after all."

I scowled. "You examined Mab?"

"Yes."

"And you're sure she's infected?" I asked.

For just a fraction of a second, Maeve's smug exterior changed, becoming graver, more somber. In that instant, she and Lily looked as though they might have been fraternal twins. "With absolute certainty."

"And you're sure she means to attack the mortal world as you've described?"

That serious version of Maeve met my eyes. "Yes," she said. "Think, wizard. Remember your godmother, bound in ice at Arctis Tor. That was when my mother trapped her and spread the contagion into her. Think of the creatures of Faerie Wyld who have been behaving irregularly and unpredictably. Think of the strange conduct of some of the Houses of the White Court, changing their diets after centuries of stasis. Think of the Fomor, active and aggressive again for the first time in millennia." She stepped up close to me. "None of these things is coincidence. It spreads, a force that will upend the world and all of us with it. And what has happened until now is *nothing* compared to what will come if Mab is not stopped before the sun rises once more."

Maeve stepped back from me, watching me, her exotic eyes opaque.

Silence fell within the little privacy spell.

Well, crap.

That was pretty much that.

Neither of the Ladies could speak a direct lie. I hadn't left them any room to dance around the truth. They were serious. I guess it was possible that they might have been mistaken, but they were damned well sincere.

"Neither of us can stop her," Lily said into that silence. "Even working together, we do not have anything like the power needed to overcome Mab's defenses, and she would never lower her guard for either of us."

"But for you," Maeve said.

"Her knight," Lily said, "her champion."

"She might not be quite so guarded," Maeve said, her eyes shining fever-bright. "You have power enough to smite her, if you strike when she is unprepared."

"What?" I blurted.

"What we ask you is not fair," Lily said. "We know tha . . ." She glanced at Maeve. "Well. I know that. But we have no other options."

"Uh, yes, you do," I said. "What about Titania? The Queen of Summer is an equal opposite, isn't she? Mab's mirror?"

The two Ladies exchanged a guarded look.

"Out with it," I said. "We're way past word games here."

Lily nodded. "She . . . refuses to act. I do not know why."

"Because she's terrified she'll be infected, too, obviously," Maeve snapped.

"Guys," I said. "I have *seen* what Mab is. Even if I catch her off guard, I don't have the kind of clout it takes to drop someone in her league."

Lily blinked at me several times. "But . . . but you do. You have Winter."

"Which is meaningful because . . . ?"

"Because she *is* Winter," Maeve said. "The Winter within you is Mab and she is it. The one thing you can never protect yourself against is yourself. You of all people should know this, wizard."

I shuddered. I did.

"The Winter Knight is a useful weapon," Maeve said. "But it has ever been one with two edges. Mab stands no mightier than any of the Sidhe against your hand, Sir Knight."

I narrowed my eyes at Maeve. "Wait a minute," I said. "Why in the hell should I think you're trying to help me? Since when have *you* cared about the mortal world, Maeve?"

Her smile widened. "Since I realized that should my mother fall, I will have a very large and very exclusive chair to sit upon back at Arctis Tor, wizard. Do not think for a moment that I do it from the kindness of my heart. I want the throne."

Now, *that* was a scary thought. Mab was a force of nature, sure, but she also acted a lot like one. She rarely took things personally, she didn't play favorites, and she was generally speaking equally dangerous to everyone. Maeve, though. That bitch was just not right. The thought of her with Mab's mantle of power was something terrifying to anyone with half a brain—especially the guy who would be her personal champion.

"I don't dig the idea of serving you, Maeve," I said.

At that, the lazy sex-kitten look came back into her eyes. "I haven't yet begun to persuade you, wizard. But be assured that I would never, *ever* throw away a tool so useful as you would be, should you succeed."

"Even if it might slice into you next?" I asked.

Maeve laughed. "Oh, I am going to love playing games with you, Sir Knight. But first things first. You have no choice but to act. If you do not, millions of your fellow mortals will perish. In the end, you will act to protect them. That is what you are."

"Lady Maeve has a point," Lily said, with evident reluctance. "There is very little time. I understand your trepidation about the consequences of Mab's . . . passing . . . but we have little choice. She is simply too dangerous to be allowed to continue."

I made a low growling sound. "This is insane."

"Fun," Maeve said, her nose wrinkling, "isn't it?"

I eyed both of them. "What are you holding back from me?"

Lily twitched again, and looked displeased at the question. "No one must realize that you know of the contagion," she said. "You cannot know which of your allies or associates it has already taken. If you demonstrate awareness, anyone infected will either remove you or infect you."

"Anything else?" I asked her.

"I will speak to Fix," Lily said. "Otherwise, no."

I nodded at her. Then I eyed Maeve. "What about you? Holding anything back?"

"I want to take you to my bower, wizard," Maeve said, and licked her lips. "I want to do things to you that give you such pleasure your brain bleeds."

"Uh," I said.

Her foxlike smile sharpened. "Also," she said, "my people are about to attempt to kill you."

Lily's eyes snapped toward Maeve, widening.

"*I* promised him nothing," Maeve said with a sniff. "And there are appearances to keep up, after all. I am certain my mother has eyes watching his every move. He can hardly meet peaceably with me without making her suspicious."

"Ah," Lily said, nodding. "Oh, dear."

Maeve leaned toward me, taking a confidential tone. "They don't know of the contagion either, wizard. So their attempts will be quite sincere. I advise you to resist. Strenuously."

Seven figures stepped around a corner of the garden on the far side of the bridge and began striding purposefully toward our little gathering. Sidhe. The Redcap strode along in the center.

"Hell's bells," I snarled, taking an involuntary step back. "Right here? *Now?* You could have given me a couple of minutes to get clear, dammit."

"And what fun would that be?" Maeve asked, pushing out her lower lip in a pout. "I am who I am, too. I love violence. I love treachery. I love your pain—and the best part, the part I love most, is that I am doing it for your own good." Her eyes gleamed white all the way around her irises. "This is me being one of the good guys."

"I'm so sorry, Harry," Lily said. "I didn't want this. I think you should go. . . ." She turned aside to Maeve. "So that the Winter Lady can introduce me to her vassals. This is the first time we've met."

Maeve blinked, and her expression darkened into a scowl. "Oh. *Oh,* you prissy bint."

Lily said, with utmost sincerity, "I regret that this inconveniences your enjoyment, Lady, but protocol is quite clear."

Maeve stomped one foot on the bridge, scowled at me, and then seized Lily by the wrist. She started dragging the Summer Lady toward her oncoming entourage.

Lily gave me a quick wink, the expression as pleasant as the warmth from a cup of hot chocolate, and I started backing off. Once I was off the bridge, I turned and began to run. There was no telling how long Lily's tactic would stall the Redcap and his buddies, and I wanted to be in the truck and gone before introductions were made.

That plan was going pretty well, right up until I passed a huge wall of thick evergreen plants of some kind. Then something small and blurry shot out of the brush about half a step ahead of me. I got a flash impression of Captain Hook in his miniature armor, trailing some kind of heavy cord, and then my feet were tangled in it and down I went.

I tried to be cool and roll into the fall and come back up on my feet, but that works a lot better when you don't have one of your legs abruptly jerked out from beneath you. So mostly I hit the ground in a clumsy sprawl, then slid several feet forward on the damp concrete with my weight on my chest and my cheek.

Ow.

I got back onto my feet, moving as fast as I could. I didn't feel like getting stabbed with more of those steel nails, and my eyes went up to the open sky, scanning quickly for any incoming hostile Little Folk as I got moving again.

So I wasn't as ready as I should have been when a man in biker leathers emerged from the brush at my side and slammed a baseball bat into the base of my skull. My legs turned to jelly and I went down hard, landing on my chin.

I sort of flopped over onto my back, dazed, lifting my hands in a vague and useless defensive gesture. I took the tip of a motorcycle boot directly to the testicles, and my whole world went bright with confusion and pain.

"Yeah," snarled the man. He was of medium height, and had curly dark hair and a short goatee. "That's right, bitch. Who's crawling on the ground now?"

Asking the question seemed to infuriate him. He slammed a kick into my ribs, then another right into the breadbasket, and I curled around myself gasping.

I had to move. The Redcap was coming. I hadn't made any noise to tip Thomas off that I was in trouble—but even as heavily boosted as I was, it wasn't enough to instantly overcome the stunning pain of those blows. Shots like that mess around with your nervous system, disrupting the machinery that sends signals around your body. I wasn't going anywhere for a few more seconds.

"Nail him," the man spat, and those frozen spikes of raw agony I'd felt before blossomed into my body from my right arm, my left calf, and somewhere in my lower back. I heard the buzz of little wings as my attackers zipped past me, driving nails in like harpoons into a floundering whale. It hurt so much that I could barely open my eyes and look up at my attacker.

I recognized him.

Ace, a changeling, one of his parents mortal, the other fae. He was the onetime victim of Lloyd Slate, the onetime betrayer of Fix and Lily and a girl named Meryl. He stared down at me with hate-filled eyes and bounced an aluminum baseball bat a few times in his hand. "I've been waiting *years* for this."

And then he started clubbing me over the head.

26

Taking a beating well is not for amateurs.

You have to get started early, maybe by getting beaten up a lot as a child in school. Then you refine your raw talent by taking more beatings as you get older. Generally, you can seek out almost any crew of athletic types, and you'll find several willing to oblige you, under one guise or another. True craftsmen then seek out gifted individuals with a particular skill set to deliver the most skilled and professional beatings.

That's how you learn to fight, really. You take beatings, and you get tougher, and if you don't start avoiding all the fights, you continue taking beatings until you learn how it's done. Or they kill you.

Some guys are born lucky, with mad natural fighting skills, and they hardly ever take a beating—but that's never been me. I've had to learn the hard way.

Like every other kind of pain, beatings are educational.

Ace started swinging the aluminum bat, and I learned two things about him right away. First, he wasn't any stronger than any other guy about his size—don't get me wrong; that was plenty strong enough to kill me at the moment. But he wasn't going to deliver the coup de grâce by dropping a forklift on my head. Second, he was emotionally invested.

See, beatings have only a couple of purposes. You are either deterring someone from something—flirting with your girl, stealing your wallet, strangling you, whatever—in which case the point of the beating is to convey a very simple message: Stop it. The second "reason" to deliver a beating is to simply inflict pain. There's no actual reason involved, of course. It's all an emotional drive, a need to make someone *hurt*. Sometimes that kind of drive is well justified. Sometimes it's misdirected rage. And sometimes, maybe more often than we really want to believe, people just enjoy making someone else feel pain.

The third motivation for a beating is to kill someone. There's some bleedover, ah hah, between the second reason and the third.

Ace was handing me a beating of the second kind. He wasn't thinking. He had a need to make me feel pain. And I was obliging the hell out of him.

The nails were the worst, like frozen points of pure fire in my flesh. Beside that agony, the first couple of blows from the bat were a dull ache. I got my arms between my noggin and the bat, getting the meat of my forearms in the way wherever I could. Arm bones are considerably less robust than broomsticks, and a solid swing with a club will snap them. Get the muscle and soft tissue in the way, though, and it spreads out the impact, both in surface area and in duration. It disperses the force—and hurts like a son of a bitch.

He swung at me several times. I blocked some. One clipped my forehead. I wriggled out of the way of the rest, the bat throwing up chips from the concrete sidewalk. I kicked at his knees with my feet, though I was in a poor position to do it. That was the part of the conflict that was important to me.

Meanwhile, I gave Ace the part that was important to *him*. I screamed. It didn't take a lot in the way of Method acting to make it convincing. The nails hurt so badly, I was pretty much going to start screaming anyway. So I screamed bloody murder, and he all but frothed at the mouth as he kept after me, swinging faster, more powerfully—and more erratically.

Swinging a club down at a struggling target is harder work than everyone thinks it is, and doing that and dodging clumsy kicks at the same time is the kind of aerobic workout you just don't get at the gym. The longer it went on, the heavier he would be breathing, and the more intently he would be focused on me.

Screaming, howling, very *noisy* me.

See, surprises like this are exactly why you bring backup in the first place. I knew I couldn't last more than a few seconds against Ace's onslaught. I also knew how fast my brother could run.

But someone else got there first.

I heard a pair of light steps and then Ace grunted. I looked up through my impact-numbed arms and saw him swing the bat again, this time at a standing target.

The bat lashed out and never stopped moving in its arc, but suddenly there was a small figure rolling up close to Ace, coming between his chest and the bat in his extended arm. They whirled in a circle, following the spin of the bat, and Ace's heels abruptly flipped up into the air over his head and he landed empty-handed on the concrete with a gasp of pain.

A woman stood over him. She was five nothing, and built with the kind of lithe, solid power that you'd expect in an Olympic gymnast who had stayed fit as she aged. Her blond hair was cut short, to finger-length. She'd had a pert upturned nose the last time I'd seen her. It had been broken since then, and while it had healed, I could see the slight bump the break had left. She had on jeans and a denim jacket, and her eyes were blue and blazing.

Ace started to get up, but a motorcycle boot much smaller than his own slammed down on his chest.

Karrin Murphy scowled at him, tossed the bat into the bushes, and said in a hard voice, "Stay down, creep. Only warning."

It was difficult to translate frantic thought into verbalization through the pain of the cold iron piercing my skin, but I managed to gasp, "Incoming!"

Murphy's eyes snapped around her, scanning in every direction including up, and she saw the first of the armored Little Folk diving down at her. Her hand snatched something out of her jacket pocket, and with a flick of her wrist she snapped out a small, collapsible baton. The Little Folk darted down upon her like a squad of angry wasps.

She didn't try to evade them. She planted her feet and began snapping the little baton with sharp, precise motions. There wasn't really time for her to aim at anything—she was running on pure reflex. Murphy'd been a martial arts practitioner since she was a child, mainly in aikido along with several others. Aikido included all kinds of fun areas of study, and one of them was learning how to handle a sword. I knew that she'd also been spending a lot of time training with a gang of ancient Einher-jaren, postdead Norse warriors of Valhalla. I doubt any of her teachers had trained her for this situation.

But they'd come close enough.

That little baton was a blur as it moved in half a dozen quick, sharp strokes, batting away the incoming Little Folk one by one. There were several sounds of impact and then a sharp *ping* and then a miniature clat-ter as Captain Hook was struck from the air and went into a sprawling crash on the ground. There were a series of high-pitched shrieks of panic, and the Little Folk vanished.

Beginning to end, that little fracas had lasted maybe five seconds.

I started fumbling at the nails still sticking out of me, but Ace and his baseball bat had left my fingers numb and useless. I managed to pull the one in my arm out with my teeth, which was unpleasant in a dimension I hardly knew existed. I spit out the nail and heard myself making short, desperate sounds of pain.

Murphy took several steps back until her heel bumped my shoulder. Then she stepped carefully over my body, never taking her eyes off the downed Ace. "How bad?"

I managed to grate out, "Nails."

The bushes crashed and Thomas appeared from them, pistol in one hand, that insanely big Gurkha knife in the other. His gun tracked to Murphy, then snapped upward, and retrained upon the downed Ace. "Oh, hi, Karrin."

"Thomas," Murphy said shortly. She looked down at me. I tried to gesture at the nails still sticking in me, but given the state of my hands and arms, I managed only to flail around weakly. "Dammit, Harry, hold still."

It didn't take her long. Two quick tugs and the nails were free. The level of pain I was experiencing dropped to maybe a tenth of what it had been. I sagged in relief.

"How bad?" Thomas asked.

"One of these wounds is bleeding, not bad," Murphy reported. "Jesus, his arms."

"We need to get out," I said. My voice sounded raw to me. "Trouble coming."

"No," said a beautiful Sidhe baritone. "Trouble is here."

They appeared from behind their veils, one by one, with so much melodrama that I was mildly surprised that they hadn't each struck some kind of kung fu pose. The Redcap with his red beret was in the center of the group. The others were spread out around us in a semicircle, pinning us against the hedge behind us. They were all holding blades and guns. They looked more like models at a photo shoot than actual warriors, but I knew better. The Sidhe are prancy, but fierce.

Ace let out a croaking laugh. "You see?" he said toward the Redcap. "You needed my help after all."

The Redcap gave Ace a glance and a small shrug that seemed to acknowledge the point. "Well, the vampire and the fallen woman. I cannot comprehend how you manage to convince yourself that you are some kind of heroic figure, Dresden, given the company you keep."

That got a laugh from the other Sidhe, who probably hadn't seen much comedy in the past few years.

I heaved a few times and managed to sit up. Murphy leaned back out of my way. She said to Thomas, "Who are these clowns?"

"Rambo there in the middle is the Redcap," Thomas said. "Pretty big hitter in Faerieland, I guess. The others are his lickspittles."

"Ooh," I said. "Lickspittles, nice."

"Thank you," Thomas said gravely.

"And they have a problem with Dresden, I take it?" Murphy asked.

"Wanna kill him or something. I don't know," Thomas said, nodding. "They tried it on Jet Skis earlier today."

"Roger Moore Bond villains?" Murphy asked, her tone derisive. "Seriously?"

"Be silent, mortal cow," snarled one of the Sidhe.

Murphy tracked her eyes calmly over to that one, and she nodded once, as if memorizing something. "Yeah, okay. You."

The Sidhe fingered his weapons, beautiful features twisting into a scowl.

I tried to rise, but by the time I got to one knee I felt like crawling into a dark room and crying while throwing up. I stopped there and fought back the dizzies that tried to take me back down. I was feeling stronger than before already. If I'd had half an hour, I think I could have been ready to do something vaguely like magical violence. But I didn't have half an hour. I couldn't fight our way out of this, and if they didn't have me supporting them, I was pretty sure Karrin and Thomas couldn't do it either. We needed another option.

"Look, Red," I said. "You made your play at my party and it didn't turn out so well for you. That's fine. No hard feelings. You tried to kill me and my friends out on Lake Michigan this morning, and I can see why you would. That didn't go so swell for you, either. So what makes you think it's going to turn out well for you now?"

"I like my chances," said the Redcap, smiling.

"No reason this has to get ugly," I said in reply.

There was something playful in his voice as he responded, "Is there not?"

"We can stop this right here. Turn around and walk away. We'll do the same. We'll let Ace here go free as soon as we get to our cars."

"Oh, kill him if you wish to," the Redcap said absently. "The half-blood is nothing to me."

Ace let out a hissing sound and stared at the Redcap.

"You aren't," the Redcap said calmly. "I have made that clear several times."

"But I . . . I snared him for you," Ace said. "I slowed him down. If I hadn't, you wouldn't have caught up to him."

The Redcap shrugged without ever glancing at the young man. "And I find that extremely convenient. But I never asked you to help. And I certainly never asked you to be so incompetent as to be captured by the prey."

I was glad Molly wasn't around, because the hate that suddenly flared out from Ace was so palpable that even I felt it. I could hear his teeth grinding, and the sudden flush of anger on his face was like something out of a comic book. Ace's body tensed as though he were preparing to fling himself to his feet.

At that, the Redcap turned, a too-wide Sidhe smile on his face, and faced Ace for the first time. "Ah. There. You may not have talent, but at least you have spirit. Perhaps if you survive the night, we can discuss your future."

Ace just sat there seething, staring daggers at the Redcap, and everyone was focused on the two of them.

Which was why no one but me noticed when the situation silently changed.

The Redcap looked back at me and said, "Have the vampire kill the halfblood if you wish. I'll happily trade my son's life for yours, Dresden. There are Sidhe who get all sentimental about their offspring, but I can't say I've ever been one of them." He focused on me and drew a small knife from his pocket, snapping out the blade. It was an instrument for killing at intimate distance. "Companions," he said, a smug edge to his voice, "with whom should we begin?"

The air crackled with sudden tension. The Sidhe stared with too-bright eyes, their fingers settling on the hilts and grips of various weapons. This was going to be bad. I couldn't fight. Karrin couldn't possibly keep up with attackers who both outnumbered her and operated with superhuman speed and near-invisibility. The Sidhe could defend themselves against my magic, unless I was able to throw absolutely everything at one of them—and I wouldn't get that chance against half a dozen. Physically I was pretty much useless for the moment.

Thomas might make it out, but when this crystalline moment of stillness finally broke, I was pretty sure Karrin and I wouldn't.

Unless someone broke it exactly right.

"Hey," I said innocently. "Weren't there seven of you guys a minute ago?"

The Redcap tilted his head at me and then glanced left and right. Five other Sidhe looked back at him, except on the far side of their line, on my left. The Sidhe warrior who had been there was gone. The only thing remaining where he'd been standing was a single expensive designer tennis shoe.

Right then, in the exact instant of realization, screams, truly agonized *screams* erupted from several yards away in the brush. There was a crystalline, almost bell-like quality to the voice, and the sound was terrifying, nothing that a human would ever make. Then there was a horrible retching sound, and the screams ended.

There was a stunned silence. And then an object came sailing out of the brush and landed at the feet of the Sidhe nearest to the one who had been taken. It was a horrible collection of bloody bone, maybe a foot and a half long—a section of spine, ripped clear of its body, bits of tissue still clinging to it.

That got a reaction from everyone. The Redcap dropped into a crouch, hands up in a defensive posture. Several Sidhe took rapid steps back.

"Holy Mother of God," Murphy breathed.

Everyone's eyes were fixed on the grisly missile lying on the sidewalk, so their heads weren't directed toward the future, weren't able to see that the situation was about to change again.

"Hey," I said, in exactly the same tone. "Weren't there six of you guys a minute ago?"

Eyes swept back up in time to see the brush swaying where something had dragged the Sidhe from the opposite end of the line, on my right side, into the bushes, and more screams erupted, clawing at the rain-drizzled air.

"Sith," hissed one of the female Sidhe, her widened eyes darting everywhere, followed by the barrel of her composite-material pistol. "Cat Sith."

Her attention wasn't on me, and I took the opening. I slammed my will down through my numbed right arm, snarling, *"Forzare!"*

At the same instant, Thomas turned his gun on the Redcap and opened fire.

Invisible force hit the female Sidhe with more or less the same energy as a small car doing twenty-five or thirty. It should have been a lot more than that, and focused on a smaller area, but in my current condition it was everything I had thrown into the best single punch I could throw. She hadn't been able to counter the spell as it struck, and was flung back away from me. She bounced once in a bed of flowers, and then tumbled into the lake.

Meanwhile, the Redcap and the other Sidhe darted in every direction and blurred to near-invisibility behind their veils. Thomas might have hit one of them. It was hard to hear any sounds of impact or screams of pain over the thunder of the ridiculously large rounds used in his Desert Eagle. Other guns went off, too.

Adrenaline surged and I shoved myself to my feet, shouting, "Fall back!"

Something flashed by me, and then Cat Sith appeared from behind his own veil, leaping with all four paws extended, his claws unsheathed. He landed on what looked like empty air, and his legs moved in a blur of ripping, supernaturally powerful strikes. Blood fountained from the empty air, and Sith bounded away, vanishing again, as one of the Sidhe appeared in the space where Sith had been. The Sidhe's upper body was a mass of blood and shredded flesh, his expression shocked. He crumpled slowly to the ground, his eyes wide, as if trying to see through complete darkness. His hands clenched aimlessly a few times, and then he went still.

I turned to run and staggered woozily. Karrin saw it and darted in close to my side, preventing me from falling. She didn't see Ace, behind her, produce a small pistol and aim it at her back.

I shouted and lurched down on top of him. The gun went off once, and then I had his gun arm pinned to the ground beneath both of my forearms and the whole weight of my body. Ace cursed and swung a fist at me. I slammed my forehead into his nose a bunch of times. It took the fight out of him, and his head wobbled dazedly.

There was a high-pitched shriek and a tiny armored form covered in fishhooks hurtled into my face and neck. My injuries swelled into agony again as the damned little metal hooks pierced my skin. I got a quick glimpse of a miniature sword flashing toward my eye. I flinched in a big roll that took me off of Ace, flinging my head in a circle to counter the motion of the little sword with centrifugal force. It cut into my eyebrow and missed my eyeball, and a flood of scarlet blocked out half of my vision.

After that, things were fuzzy. I swatted at Captain Hook with my forearm, and on the third blow the barbed hooks tore free of my skin. A hand with the strength of a hydraulic crane gripped the back of my coat and dragged me to my feet, and then my brother was helping me move. I sensed Karrin on my blind side, shouting something to Thomas, and then the Desert Eagle started thundering on that side of my body.

A Sidhe exploded from the brush, visible and wounded, with Cat Sith in hot pursuit. The Sidhe leapt into the air, shimmered, and transformed into a hawk with golden brown feathers. Its wings beat twice, gaining maybe ten feet of altitude—until Cat Sith sailed through the air in a spectacular pounce, landed on the hawk's back, and they both plunged down into the waters of the lake.

After that, there was a lot of movement that hurt like hell, and I would have fallen a dozen times without my brother's support. Then I was being half thrown into the back of the Hummer, coming down on the custom leather seats hard, and too exhausted to do more than pull my feet in so that they wouldn't get slammed in the door. Both of the front doors opened and closed, and the engine, already running, roared to life, the acceleration pressing me back against the seat for a moment.

We drove for a few minutes before I was able to start sitting up. When I finally did, I found Thomas driving, with Karrin riding shotgun, holding Thomas's Desert Eagle in her hands and turned in the seat to steadily watch the road behind us.

My brother glanced up at me in the rearview mirror and winced. "You look awful."

I could see out of only one eye. I reached up to the other one with my hand and found blood smearing it shut and beginning to dry. I leaned to look in the rearview mirror. I had quite a bit of blood on that side of my head. The hooks had made some messy, if not large holes in my skin when they came out.

Karrin's eyes flicked toward me for just a second, and she might have gotten a little pale, but she didn't let any other emotion touch her face. "Looks like we're clear. No one back there."

Thomas grunted. "They can use magic, and Harry left a bunch of blood on the ground. If they want to follow us, they can."

"Dammit," Murphy breathed. "Castle?"

"And have Marcone's people cleaning the blood off him?" Thomas asked. "Fuck *that*."

"Amen," I agreed woozily.

"Where else, then?" Karrin asked. "Your apartment?"

Thomas shook his head emphatically. "Too many people will see us taking him in. They'll call the authorities. And Lara has eyes on the place. If I take a wounded wizard in there, she'd show up faster than Jimmy John's." He grunted in discomfort as the truck hit a bump in the road.

Karrin turned toward him and leaned over to examine him. "You're hit."

"Only one," Thomas said calmly. "If it was bad, I'd have bled out by now. Gut shot. Don't worry about it."

"Don't be an idiot," Karrin said. "You know how easy it is for these things to go septic? You've got to take care of this."

"Yeah, as soon as we stop somewhere."

"Molly's place," Karrin said. "It's under the aegis of Svartalfheim. No one's getting in there without a major assault."

"Right," I said, the word slurring a little. "There."

"Dammit, Dresden," Karrin said, her voice exasperated. "Just lie down until we can look at you."

I threw her a salute with my right hand and paused, feeling an unfamiliar weight on my arm.

I looked. Captain Hook dangled from it, half a dozen of his armor's barbs caught in the denim of my jacket. I peered at the tiny armored figure and then poked him with a fingertip. He let out a semiconscious little moan, but the hooks had effectively immobilized him.

"Huh," I said. Then I cackled. "Hah. Hah, hah, heh hahhah."

Thomas glanced over his shoulder and blinked several times. "What the hell is that?"

"A priceless intelligence asset," I replied.

Thomas lifted his eyebrows. "You're going to interrogate that little guy?"

"If Molly has a turkey baster, maybe you can waterboard him," Murphy said in an acid tone.

"Relax," I said. "And drive. We need to . . ."

I forgot what I had been about to say we needed to do. I guess all that cackling had really taken it out of me. The world turned sideways and the leather of the backseat pressed up against my unwounded cheek. It felt cool and nice, which was a stark contrast to the waves of pure ache and steady burn that pulsed through my body with every heartbeat.

The world didn't fade to black so much as turn a dark, restless red.

27

I woke up when someone shoved a branding iron into my neck.

Okay, that isn't what happened, but I was coming out of unconscious-ness at the time, and that was what it seemed like. I let out a curse and flailed with my arms.

"Hold him, hold him!" someone said in an intent voice. Hands came down on my arms, pressing them back against a smooth, rigid surface beneath me.

"Harry," Thomas said. "Harry, easy, easy. You're safe."

There were lights in my eyes. They weren't pleasant. I squinted against them until I could see Thomas's upside-down head looming over me.

"There you are," Thomas said. "We were getting worried." He lifted his hands from my arms and gave the side of my face something some-where between a pat and a slap. "You weren't waking up."

I looked around me. I was lying on the table in Molly's apartment, the same spot where we'd seen to Toot's injuries earlier in the day. There was the sharp smell of disinfectant in the air. I felt terrible, but less terrible than I had in the car.

I turned my head and saw a wiry little guy with a shock of black hair, a beaky nose, and glittering, intelligent eyes. He picked up a metal bowl in one hand, and moved a pair of needle-nose pliers in the other, drop-ping something into the bowl with a clink. "And he just wakes up?" Waldo Butters, Chicago's most polka-savvy medical examiner, asked. "Tell me that isn't a little creepy."

"What are you talking about?" I said.

Butters held up the metal bowl, tilting it so that I could see inside. Several tiny, bright, sharp, bloodied pieces of metal were inside. "Barbs from those fishhooks," he said. "Several of them broke off in your skin."

I grunted. My collapse in the car made more sense now. "Yeah," I said. "Any kind of iron gets under my skin, it seems to disagree with the Winter Knight's bundle of awesome. Takes the gumption right out of me." I started to sit up.

Butters very calmly put his hands on my chest and shoved me back down. Hard. I blinked at him.

"I don't do assertive much," he said apologetically. "I don't really like doctoring people who are still alive. But if I'm going to do it, dammit, I'm going to do it right. So. You stay put until I say you can get up. Got it?"

"I, uh . . ." I said. "Yeah, I guess."

"Smart," Butters said. "You have two giant bruises where the lower halves of your arms usually go. You're covered in lacerations, and a couple need sutures. Some are already inflamed. I need to clean them all out. That'll work best if you hold still."

"I can do that," I said. "But I'm feeling all kinds of better, man. Look." I held up my hands and wiggled my fingers. They felt a little tight. I glanced down at them. They were a mottled shade of purple and swollen. My wrists and forearms were blotchy with bruises and swollen, too.

"Harry, I once saw an addict pound his fist into concrete until he'd broken nearly every bone in his hand. He never even blinked."

"I'm not on drugs," I said.

"No? There's damage to your body's machinery. Just because you aren't feeling it doesn't mean it isn't there," Butters said firmly. "I've got a theory."

"What theory?" I asked, as he got to work on the cuts.

"Well, let's say you're a faerie queen with a need for a mortal enforcer. You want the guy to be effective, but you don't want to make him too powerful to handle. It seems reasonable to me that you might fiddle with his pain threshold. He's not actually any more indestructible, but he *feels* like he is. He'll ignore painful things like . . . like knife wounds or . . ."

"Gut shots?" Thomas suggested.

"Or gut shots, right," Butters said. "And most of the time, that is probably a huge advantage. He can Energizer Bunny his way right through your enemies—and then, when it's over, there he is. He feels great, but in reality he's all screwed up and it's going to take his body weeks or months to repair itself. If you don't like the job he's done, well, there he is all weakened and vulnerable. And if you do like it, you just let him rest and use him again another day."

"Wow, that's cynical," I said. "And calculating."

"I'm in the right ballpark, aren't I?" Butters asked.

I sighed. "Yeah, it sounds . . . very Mab-like." Especially if what Maeve had said about me being dangerous to Mab was true.

Butters nodded sagely. "So, as strong or quick or as fast to heal as it makes you, just remember: You aren't any more invincible to trauma than before. You just don't notice it when something happens. . . ." He was quiet for a moment and then asked, "You didn't even feel that, did you?"

"Feel what?" I asked, lifting my head.

He put the heel of his hand on my forehead and pushed it down again. "I just stitched up a three-inch-long slice over one of your ribs. No anesthetic."

"Huh," I said. "No, I didn't. . . . I mean, I felt something; it just wasn't uncomfortable."

"Supports my theory," he said, nodding. "I already did that cut over your eye while you were out. That's a beauty. Right down to the bone."

"Courtesy of Captain Hook," I said. "He had this bitty sword." I glanced up at Thomas. "We've still got Hook, right?"

"He's being held prisoner on a ceramic-lined cookie sheet in the oven," Thomas said. "I figured he couldn't jigger his way out of a bunch of steel, and it would give him something to think about before we start asking questions."

"That's an awful thing to do to one of the Little Folk, man," I said.

"I'm planning to start making a pie in front of him."

"Nice."

"Thank you."

"How long was I out?" I asked.

"About an hour," Thomas said.

Butters snorted. "I'd have been here sooner but someone broke into my house last night and I was cleaning up the mess."

I winced. "Uh, yeah. Right. Sorry about that, man."

He shook his head. "I'm still kind of freaking out that you're here at all, honestly. I mean, we held your funeral. We talked to your ghost. It doesn't get much more gone than that."

"Sorry to put a speed bump on your mental train track."

"It's more of a roller coaster, lately, but a good mind is flexible," Butters said. "I'll deal with it; don't worry." He worked for a moment more before adding, in a low murmur, "Unlike some other people."

"Eh?" I asked him.

Butters just looked up across the large apartment and then went back to work.

I followed the direction of his gaze.

Karrin sat curled up in a chair beside the fireplace, on the far side of the big apartment, her arms wrapped around her knees, her head leaning against the chair's back. Her eyes were closed and her mouth was open a little. She was evidently asleep. The gentle snoring supported that theory.

"Oh," I said. "Uh. Yeah. She didn't seem to handle it real well when I was ghosting around. . . ."

"Understatement," Butters breathed. "She's been through a lot. And none of it made her a bit less prickly."

Thomas made a low sound of agreement.

"She's run most of her friends off," Butters said. "Never talks to cops anymore. Hasn't been speaking to her family. Just the Viking crew down at the BFS. I'm hanging in there. So is Molly. I guess maybe we both know that she's in a bad place."

"And now here I am," I said. "Man."

"What?" Thomas asked.

I shook my head. "You gotta know Karrin."

"Karrin, eh?" Thomas asked.

I nodded. "She's real serious about order. A man dying, she can understand. A man coming *back*. That's different."

"Isn't she Catholic?" Thomas asked. "Don't they have a guy?"

I eyed him. "Yeah. And that makes it so much easier to deal with."

"Medically speaking," Butters said, "I'm pretty sure you were never dead. Or at least, never dead and beyond revival."

"What, were you there?" I asked.

"Were you?" he countered.

I grunted. "From my end, it went black, and then I woke up. Ghosty. Then it went white and I woke up. Hurting. Then did a bunch of physical therapy to recover."

"Wow, seriously, PT?" Butters asked. "How long?"

"Eleven weeks."

"Yeah, that really leans things toward 'coma' for me."

"And all the angels and ghost stuff," I said. "Which way does that make them lean? In your medical opinion?"

Butters pressed his lips together and said, "No one likes a smart-ass, Harry."

"I never liked him anyway," Thomas confided to him.

"Why don't you do something useful?" I said. "Go outside; see if anyone is lurking out there, waiting to kill us the second we walk out."

"Because Molly has to go with me each and every time or they won't let me back in, and she's out dealing with your scouts," Thomas said. "You worried about that faerie crew using your blood to track you?"

"Not sure. Using it is trickier than most people think," I said. "You've got to keep it from drying out, and you've got to get it undiluted. It was raining, so if someone wanted my blood, they'd have had to get to it pretty quick—and it looked like Sith was keeping them busy."

"Sith?" Butters asked.

"Not what you're thinking," I said.

"Oh," he said, clearly disappointed.

"Besides," I said to Thomas, "I'm less worried about them using it to follow me than using it to make my heart stop beating. Or you know . . . explode out of my chest."

Thomas blinked. "They can do that?"

"Oh, my God," Butters said, blinking. "Is *that* what that was?"

"Yes, they can do that, and probably, if you mean all those murders around the Three-Eye drug ring bust," I answered them. "Butters, what's the story here? You done yet?"

"Empty night," Thomas said, his manner suddenly serious. "Harry . . . shouldn't we be putting up circles or something?"

"No point," I said. "If they've got your blood, they've got you, period. Maybe if I ran and hid somewhere in the Nevernever, but even then it isn't certain."

"How much blood do they need?" Butters asked.

"Depends," I said. "Depends on how efficient their magic is—their skill level. Depends on how fresh the blood is. Depends on the day of the week and the phase of the moon, for all I know. It isn't something I've experimented with. The more energy they're sending your way, the more blood they need."

"Meaning what?" Butters asked. "Sit up so I can dress these."

I sat up and lifted my arms out of the way as I explained. "A tracking spell is hardly anything, in terms of energy input," I said. "They wouldn't need much at all for that."

Butters wound a strip of linen bandage around my midsection several times. "But if they want to make your head explode, it takes a lot more?"

"Depends how good they are," I said. "They don't have to crush your head into paste, sledgehammer style. Maybe they put an ice pick up your nose. Less force but concentrated into a smaller area, see?" I shuddered a little. "If they've got my blood and can use it, I'm fucked and that's that. But until that happens, I'm going to assume that I still have a chance and proceed as if I do."

There was a silence then, and I realized that both Butters and Thomas were just staring at me.

"What? Magic is dangerous stuff, guys," I said.

"Yeah, for all of us," Butters said, "but, Harry, you're . . ."

"What? Bulletproof?" I shook my head. "Magic is like the rest of life. It doesn't matter how much a guy can bench-press, or if he can break trees with his hands. You put a bullet through his brain, he dies. I'm pretty good at figuring out where to stand so as to avoid that bullet, and

I can shoot back a lot better than most people—but I'm just as vulnerable as everybody else."

I frowned at that thought. *As vulnerable as everybody else.* Something nagged at me from beneath the surface of my conscious calculations, but I couldn't poke it into visibility. Yet.

"Point is," I said, "if they were going to try to kill me with it, they've had time to do that already."

"Unless they're saving it for the future," Butters said.

I made sure not to growl out loud. "Yes. Thank you. Are you finished yet?"

Butters tore off a final piece of medical tape, stuck the end of the bandage down with it, and sighed. "Yeah. Just try not to . . . well, move, or jump around, or do anything active, or touch anything dirty, or otherwise do anything else that I know you're going to do anyway in the next twenty-four hours."

"Twelve hours," I said, swinging my legs down from the table.

"Oy." Butters sighed.

"Where's my shirt?" I asked, standing.

Thomas shrugged. "Burned it. You want mine?"

"After you got your guts all over it?" I asked. "Ew."

Butters blinked and looked at Thomas. "My God," he said. "You've been shot."

Thomas hooked a thumb at Butters. "Check out Dr. Marcus Welby, MD, here."

"I'd have gone with Doogie Howser, maybe," I said.

"Split the difference at McCoy?" Thomas asked.

"Perfect."

"You've been *shot!*" Butters repeated, exasperated.

Thomas shrugged. "Well. A little."

Butters let out an enormous sigh. Then he picked up the bottle of disinfectant and a roll of paper towels and started cleaning off the table. "God, I hate this Frankenstein-slash–Civil War medicine crap. Give me a second. Then lie down."

I left them to pad across the apartment to my bedroom. To Molly's guest bedroom. I opened the door as quietly as I could so that I wouldn't wake Karrin, and went in to put on another secondhand shirt.

I found one that was plain black, with the Spider-Man emblem on it in white. The black uniform. The one that made Spidey switch teams for a bit, and which eventually gave him all kinds of grief. It seemed fitting.

I slipped into it and turned and nearly jumped out of my boots when Karrin quietly shut the bedroom door behind her.

I stood there for a long moment. The only light was from a single small, glowing candle.

Karrin faced me with an opaque expression. "You don't call," she said, one corner of her mouth quirked into an expression that wasn't a smile. "You don't write."

"Yeah," I said. "Coma."

"I heard," she said. She folded her arms and leaned back against the door. "Thomas and Molly both say it's really you."

"Yeah," I said. "How'd you find me?"

"Scanner. The last time a bomb went off in this town, it was in your office building. I hear another one goes off in the street, and then reports of explosions and gunfire out over the lake just after dawn this morning. Math wasn't hard to do."

"How'd you follow me?"

"I didn't," Murphy said. "I staked out Thomas's place and followed the guy who was following you." She moved a foot absently, touching the back of her other calf with it as if scratching an itch. "His name was Ace . . . something, right?"

I nodded. "You remember."

"I try to keep track of the bad guys," she said. "And on an entirely unrelated note . . . I hear you belong to Mab now."

The words hit me like a slap in the face. Karrin had been a detective for a long time. She knew how to manipulate a suspect.

I guessed I was a suspect, then.

"I'm not a cocker spaniel," I said quietly.

"I'm not saying you are," she said. "But there are creatures out there that can do things to your head, and we both know it."

"You think that's what happened?" I asked. "That Mab's bent my brain into new shapes?"

Her expression softened. "I think she'll do it slower," she said. "You're . . . an abrupt sort of person. Your solutions to problems tend to be decisive and to happen quickly. It's how you think. I'm willing to believe that you found some kind of way to prevent her from just . . . I don't know. Rewriting you."

"I told her if she tried it, I'd start being obstreperous."

"God," Karrin said. "You haven't started?"

She half smiled. For a second, it was almost okay.

But then her face darkened again. "I think she'll do it slower. An inch at a time, when you aren't looking. But even if she doesn't . . ."

"What?"

"I'm not angry at you, Harry," she said. "I don't hate you. I don't think you've gone bad. A lot of people have fallen into the trap you did. People better than either of us."

"Uh," I said. "The evil-Queen-of-Faerie trap?"

"Christ, Harry," Murphy said quietly. "No one just starts giggling and wearing black and signs up to become a villainous monster. How the hell do you think it happens?" She shook her head, her eyes pained. "It happens to people. Just people. They make questionable choices, for what might be very good reasons. They make choice after choice, and none of them is slaughtering roomfuls of saints, or murdering hundreds of baby seals, or rubber-room irrational. But it adds up. And then one day they look around and realize that they're so far over the line that they can't remember where it was."

I looked away from her. Something in my chest hurt. I didn't say anything.

"Do you understand that?" she asked me, her voice even more quiet. "Do you understand how treacherous the ground you're standing on has become?"

"Perfectly," I said.

She nodded a few times. Then she said, "I suppose that's something."

"That all?" I asked her. "I mean . . . is that the only reason you came in here?"

"Not quite," she said.

"You don't trust me," I said.

Her eyes didn't meet mine, and didn't avoid them either. "That will depend largely on the next few minutes."

I inhaled through my nose and out again, trying to stay calm, clear, even. "Okay," I said. "What do you want me to do?"

"The skull," she said. "I know what it is. So does Butters. And . . . it's too powerful to be left in the wrong hands."

"Meaning mine?" I asked.

"I'll tell you what I know. I know you broke into his house when he was at work and took it. I know you left Andi with cuts and bruises. And I know you wrecked the place a bit along the way."

"You think that means I've gone bad?"

She tilted her head slightly to one side, as if considering. "I think you were probably operating under some kind of harebrained lone-hero rationale. Let's say . . . that I'm concerned that you have enough things to juggle already."

I thought about snapping at her but . . . she had a point. Bob was a resource far too powerful to be allowed to fall into the hands of anyone who wouldn't use him responsibly. And I'd been doing the Winter Knight gig full speed for about twelve hours, and I'd already had some disturbing realizations about myself. Twelve hours.

What would I be like after twelve days? Twelve months? What if Karrin was right, and Mab got to me slow? Or worse: What if I was just human? She was right about that, too. Power corrupts—and the people being corrupted never seem to be aware that it's happening. I'd just told Butters that I wasn't magically bulletproof. What kind of arrogant ass would I be if I assumed I was morally infallible? That I would be wise and smart and savvy enough to avoid the pitfalls of power, traps that had turned better people than me into something horrible?

I didn't want her to be right. I didn't like the idea at all.

But denial is for children. I had to be a grown-up.

"Okay," I said, my throat tight. "Bob's in that satchel out in the living room. Give him back to Butters."

"Thank you," she said. "I found where you left the swords."

She meant the two Swords of the Cross, two of three holy blades meant to fill the hands of the righteous in the battle against true evil. I'd wound up babysitting them, being their custodian. Mostly they'd sat around in my place gathering dust. "Yeah?" I said.

"I know how powerful they are," she said. "And I know how vulnerable they are in the wrong hands. I'm not telling you where they are. I'm not giving them back to you. I'm not negotiating."

I exhaled slowly. A slow, hard anger rolled into a knot in my guts. "Those . . . were my responsibility," I said.

"They were," she said. There was something absolutely rigid in her blue eyes. "Not anymore."

The room suddenly felt too hot. "Suppose I disagree."

"Suppose you do," she said. "What would you do if you were in my position?"

I don't remember moving. I just remember slamming the heel of my hand into the door six inches from the side of Karrin's head. It sounded like a gunshot, and left me standing over her, breathing harder, and the difference in our sizes was damned near comical. If I wanted to, I could wrap my fingers almost all the way around her throat. Her neck would break if I squeezed.

She didn't flinch. She didn't move. She looked up at me and waited.

It hit me, what I was thinking, what my instincts were screaming at me to do, and I suddenly sagged, bowing my head. My breath came out in uneven jerks. I closed my eyes, tried to get it under control.

And then she touched me.

She rested her hand lightly on my battered forearm. Moving carefully, as if I were made of glass, her fingers slid down my arm to my hand. She took it gently and lowered it, not trying to force anything. Then she took my right hand in her left. We stood that way for a moment, our hands clasped, our heads bowed. She seemed to understand what I was going through. She didn't push me. She just held my hands and waited until my breathing had steadied again.

"Harry," she said quietly then. "Do you want my trust?"

I nodded tightly, not trusting myself to speak.

"Then you're going to have to give me some. I'm on your side. I'm trying to help you. Let it go."

I shuddered.

"Okay," I said.

Her hands felt small and warm in mine.

"I . . . we've been friends a long time," I said. "Since that troll on the bridge."

"Yes."

My eyes blurred up, stupid things, and I closed them. "I know I've screwed up," I said. "I'm going to have to live with that. But I don't want to lose you."

In answer, Murphy lifted my right hand and pressed it against her cheek. I didn't open my eyes. I couldn't hear it in her voice or her breathing, but I felt a slight dampness touch my hand.

"I don't want to lose you, either," she said. "That scares me."

I didn't trust myself to speak for a long time.

She lowered my hands slowly, and very gently let me go. Then she turned to the door.

"Karrin," I said. "What if you're right? What if I change? I mean . . . go really bad."

She looked back enough for me to see her profile, and a quiet, sad smile.

"I work with a lot of monsters these days."

28

I picked up another jacket hanging in the closet, an old surplus military garment with an eighties-style camouflage pattern—not because I thought I would get cold as much as because I figured maybe the extra pockets would be handy if I found anything for which they would be needed. I didn't have any money or ID. I didn't have a credit card. Hell, I didn't have a *business* card.

What would it say? "Harry Dresden, Winter Knight, Targets Slain, No Barbecues, Waterslides, or Fireworks Displays."

I could joke around with myself all I wanted, but I would be doing it only because I didn't want to face a larger question, a really hard one: How the hell did I put my life back together?

Assuming I could do it at all.

Fortunately, I had dire evil to fight at the moment, which meant that I could think about the life thing later. Thank God for imminent dooms-day. I'd hate to have to face up to the *really* tough stuff so soon after get-ting back into the game.

I heard the front door of the apartment open and close, and some quiet talk. I came out of the bedroom to find that Molly had returned. Toot-toot was riding along on one of her shoulders, hanging on to the top rim of her ear to keep his balance. He looked none the worse for wear.

"Harry," Molly said, smiling. "You look better. How do you feel?"

"I'll do," I said. "Major General, I see you're back on your feet. The last time I saw you, I figured you'd be down for weeks."

Toot stiffened to attention and threw me a salute. "No, my lord! The Little Folk don't have enough time to waste weeks and weeks healing like you big people."

That probably shouldn't have surprised me. I'd seen Toot literally eat half his weight in pizza. And his wings were powerful enough to lift him off the ground into flight. Anything that can put food away that quickly and produce such a prodigious amount of physical power relative to its size must have a ridiculously high-burning metabolism. And with the day I'd been having, it did my heart good to see him upright again.

"Where are we on our scouts?" I asked Molly.

"They're in a food coma," she said. "I ordered twenty pizzas. Must have been five hundred of them in the parking lot. They'll be ready to go as soon as you tell me where you want them to look."

"I need a map," I said.

Molly reached into her back pocket and produced a folded map. "Way ahead of you, boss."

"Soon as they're done, lay it out on the table," I said.

"Got it."

"Major General, I'm glad you're here," I said. "I need you to stay close."

Toot saluted again, and his wings blurred into motion, lifting him up off Molly's shoulder. "Yes, my lord! What is the mission?"

"To prevent a prisoner from attempting escape," I said. "I captured Captain Hook."

"Sort of," Karrin chimed in, her voice amused. She'd returned to her seat by the fireplace.

I gave her a look. "We have him; he's captured; that's the main thing."

Toot put his hand on his sword. "Shall I dispatch him for you, my lord?" he asked eagerly. "Because I totally can."

"If it needs to be done," I said soberly, "I'll make sure it's your hand that does it. But we'll give him a chance to talk first."

"You are a man of mercy and grace, my lord," Toot-toot said, clearly disappointed.

"You bet your ass," I said. "Make sure you're in a good spot to stop our guest from leaving."

"Aye!" Toot said, saluting, and darted across the apartment.

Molly shook her head. "You're always so careful to make him feel involved."

"He is involved," I said, and started back toward Butters's makeshift examination table.

"Of course it hurts," Thomas was saying. Butters was stitching up a small, puckered hole in his lower abdomen. "But not as much as it did before you got the bullet out."

"And you're *sure* you can handle care this crude?" Butters asked. "Because if you were a regular human being, I could pretty much guarantee you that this thing would go septic in a couple of days and kill you."

"Microorganisms aren't a problem to my kind," Thomas said. "As long as I don't bleed out, I'll be fine."

My brother's tone was calm, but the color of his eyes had changed, growing lighter, a shade of fine grey with almost no blue at all in it. A vampire of the White Court had superhuman strength and speed and resilience, but not an infinite supply. Thomas's eyes changed as his personal demon, his Hunger, gained more influence over his actions. At some point, he would need to feed to replenish himself.

"You about done?" I asked him. "I need the table."

"What *is* it with you people?" Butters groused. "For God's sake, these are real injuries here."

"There will be more of them than a thousand reluctant physicians could patch up if we don't get moving," I said. "Today's serious business, man."

"How serious?"

"Can't think when it's been grimmer," I said. "Freaking waste-of-space vampires, lying around on tables you need to use."

"Useless wizards," Thomas said, "jumping on enemy guns and accidentally shooting their allies with them."

"Oh," I said. "That was when I jumped Ace?"

He snorted. "Yeah."

I winced. "Ah. Sorry about that."

"One of these days, Dresden," Thomas drawled, "pow, right in the kisser."

"Talk is cheap," I said. "Table, table, table."

Butters finished patching Thomas up, wrapping a long strip of gauze bandage around his middle. Thomas leaned back on his elbows as the doctor worked. The pose made his muscles stand out sharply beneath pale skin—but then, most poses seemed to do that with Thomas. His pale eyes lingered on Molly for a long moment, and my apprentice abruptly turned away with spots of color high up in her cheeks.

"I, uh," Molly said. "Wow."

"Thomas," I said.

"Sorry," he said. He didn't sound sincere. He got up off the table with lazy grace. "Say, Harry, do you have any more shirts back there? I bled, nobly and sacrificially, all over mine."

"They're Molly's," I said.

He looked at my apprentice. "Oh? What do I have to do to get one?"

"Go ahead," Molly said. Her voice was not quite a squeak. "Take one."

"Appreciate it," Thomas said, and sauntered into the spare bedroom.

Murphy watched him walk by, openly, then gave me a rather challenging look. "What?" she asked. "He's pretty."

"I heard that," Thomas said from the other room.

"Map," I said, and Molly hurried over to the table. Butters got his stuff off of it in rapid order. He'd evidently pulled the slug out of Thomas's guts without making a horrible bloody mess of things. The bullet had to have been close to the surface. Ace's gun must have been fairly lightweight, a .25 or a .22. Maybe he'd been using cheap ammo and the round had been short on powder. Or maybe Thomas's super-abs had stopped the bullet before it could sink in.

After the table was clean, Molly spread the map out on it. It was a map of Lake Michigan and the shores around it, including Chicago and Milwaukee and on up to Green Bay. Molly passed me a pen, and I leaned over and started making marks on the map with my swollen fingers. It hurt but I ignored it. Karrin got up and came over to watch. Thomas joined us a moment later, freshly attired in a plain white T-shirt, which looked like it had been made to fit him. He's a jerk like that.

"What I'm doing here," I said, "is marking out all the nodes I remember."

"Nodes?" Butters asked.

My clumsy fingers made it a little hard to put the marks exactly where I wanted them. "The meeting points of one or more ley lines," I said. "I got to know all about them a few years ago."

"Those are like magical power cables, right?" Karrin asked.

"More or less," I said. "Sources of power that you can draw on to make major magic. And there are a *lot* of them in the Great Lakes region. I'm drawing from memory, but I'm pretty sure these are right."

"They are," Molly confirmed quietly. "Auntie Lea taught them to me a few months ago."

I looked up at her, eyed my battered fingers, and said, "Then why am I doing this?"

Molly rolled her eyes and took the pen. She started marking nodes rapidly and precisely on the map, including the Well on Demonreach (though the island didn't appear on the map).

"Whoever is going to attempt the spell on Demonreach has to do it from somewhere near the shore of the lake," I said. "They're almost certainly going to be at one of these nodes—the closer to the edge of the lake, the better." I pointed out several nodes near the shore. "So we need to send the guard out to check these six locations near the edge of the lake first. After that, they go after the next nearest and so on."

"Some of those are a good way off," Karrin noted. "How fast can these little guys move?"

"Fast," I said. "Faster than anyone gives them credit. They can fly and they can take shortcuts through the Nevernever. They can get to the sites and back before sundown."

Sundown. Which was when the big, bad immortals would come out to play.

"Any questions so far?" I asked, looking at Murphy.

She jerked her chin toward my brother and said, "Thomas filled me in."

"Good," I said. "Exposition gets repetitive fast. A spell like this takes time to set up, and they won't really be able to hide it if we can get eyes on the site. Once we know which of the sites shows signs of use, we can get to it and thwart whatever lunatic is using it."

"Do we know who it is yet?" Murphy asked.

"Answer unclear," I said.

"It's got to be those Outsiders, right?" Thomas asked.

"Stands to reason. But the real question is, who is helping *them*?"
I got a bunch of looks at that.

"Outsiders can't just show up in our reality," I said. "That's why
they're called Outsiders in the first place. Someone has to open the door
and let them in." I took a deep breath. "Which brings me to the next
twist. I talked to Lily and Maeve, and they tell me that Mab is the one
planning to tinker with the island."

Silence followed that.

"That's . . . a lie, right?" Butters asked.

"They can't lie," I said. "They physically can't. And, yes, I got them to
speak directly about it. There's no confusion of signals, no room for ob-
fuscation."

Thomas whistled quietly.

"Yeah," I said.

"Uh," Molly said. "We're up against Mab? Your boss?"

"Not necessarily," I said. "Lily and Maeve may not be lying but they
could still be wrong. Lily has never been a cerebral titan. And Maeve
is . . . maybe 'insane' is the only word that really describes it, but she's
definitely firing on an odd number of cylinders. It's possible that they've
been deceived."

"Or," Thomas said, "maybe they haven't."

"Or maybe they haven't," I said, nodding.

"What would that mean?" Molly asked.

"It would mean," Karrin said quietly, "that Mab sent Harry to kill
Maeve because either she wanted Maeve out of the way or she wanted
Harry out of the way. Which is good, because it means that she's worried
that there's someone who could stop her."

"Right," I said. "Or maybe . . ." I frowned, studying a new thought.

"What?" Thomas asked.

I looked slowly around the room. If Mab had been taken by the contagion, which really needed a better name, that certainly meant that Lea

had been taken as well—and Lea had been tutoring Molly. If it had spread into the White Court, my brother could have been exposed. Murphy was maybe the most vulnerable—she was isolated, and her behavior had changed radically over the past couple of years. Hell, Butters was the person in the room least likely to have been exposed or turned or whatever—which made him the most ideal candidate for being turned.

Paranoia—because why should the conspiracy theorists get to have all the fun?

I just couldn't see any of these people turning on me, no matter the influence. But if you could see treachery coming all that easily, Julius Caesar might have lived to a ripe old age. I'd always been slightly inclined to the paranoid. I had a sinking feeling I was going to start developing my latent potential.

I picked my words very carefully.

"Over the past several years," I said, "there have been several conflicts between two different interests. Several times, events have been driven by internal conflicts within one or both of those interests."

"Like what?" Butters asked.

"Dual interests inside the Red Court, for one," I said. "One of them trying to prevent conflict with the White Council, one of them trying to stir it up. Multiple Houses of the White Court rising up to vie for control of it. The Winter and Summer Courts posturing and interfering with each other when Winter's territory was violated by the Red Court." I didn't want to get any more specific than that. "Do you guys see what I'm getting at here?"

"Oh!" Butters said. "It's a phantom menace!"

"Ah!" Molly said.

Thomas grunted.

Karrin glanced around at all of us and then said, "Translate that from nerd to English, please."

"Someone is out there," I said. "Someone who has been manipulating events. Playing puppet master, stirring the pot, stacking the deck—"

"Mixing metaphors?" Thomas suggested.

"Fuck off. I'm just saying that this situation has the same shape as the others. Mab and Maeve at each other's throats, with Summer standing by ready to get involved, and Outsiders starting to throw their weight around."

"The Black Council," Molly whispered.

"Exactly," I said, which it wasn't. Up until earlier today, I had known someone was covertly causing the world a lot of grief—and due to their connections with some grim events within the White Council I had assumed it was a group of wizards, which was both naturally arrogant and extremely nearsighted of me. But what if I'd been wrong? What if the Black Council was just one more offshoot of one enormous, intangible enemy? If what I'd gotten from Lily was accurate, the problem was a hell of a lot bigger than I had realized.

And I did not want that problem to know that I had spotted it.

"The Black Council," I said. "A group of practitioners using dark magic to influence various events around the world. They're powerful, they're bad news, and if I'm right, they're here. If they're here, I figure it's a good bet that Sharkface and his chums—"

"Shark," Butters said. "Chums. Funny."

"Thank you for noticing," I said, and continued the sentence. "—are working for the Black Council."

"The theoretical Black Council," Karrin said.

"They're out there, definitely," I said.

Karrin smiled faintly. "If you say so, Mulder."

"I'm going to ignore that. The only question is whether or not they're here now."

Molly nodded seriously. "If they are? How do we find them?"

"We don't," I said. "There isn't enough time to go sniffing around methodically. We know someone's going to mess with the island. It doesn't really matter who's pressing the button that sets off the bomb. We just have to keep it from getting pressed. The Little Folk find us that ritual site, and then we go wreck it."

"Um," Butters said. "Not that I lack confidence in you guys, but shouldn't we be calling in the cavalry? I mean, doesn't that make more sense?"

"We *are* the cavalry," I said in a flat tone. "The White Council won't help. Even if I knew the current protocols to contact them, it would take them days to verify that I am in fact alive and still me, and we only have hours. Besides, Molly's on their most-wanted list."

I didn't add in the third reason not to contact the Council—when they found out about my relationship with Mab, the monarch of a sovereign and occasionally hostile supernatural nation, they would almost certainly panic and assume that I was a massive security risk. Which would, for a variety of reasons and to a variety of degrees, be an accurate assumption. And now that I thought about it, given how my, ah, induction had been psychically broadcast to all of Faerie, there was no chance whatsoever that the Council didn't know. Knowing stuff is what they do.

Butters frowned. "The Paranetters?"

"No," I said. "The last thing we need is a small army of newbies floundering around and stumbling into us. That's asking for trouble in the short term, the long term, and every other term there might be. We can go to them for information only. We aren't dragging them in."

The little ME took off his glasses and cleaned them absently with the hem of his scrubs. "What about Lara's team? Or the Einherjaren?"

Thomas shrugged. "I could probably convince Lara to send the team somewhere."

"Ditto," Karrin said, "only with Vikings."

"Good," I said. "We might need more bodies, and we might need to cover multiple sites. Can you two get that lined up when we break?"

They nodded.

"Molly," I said. "You'll take the map up to our little scouts and tell them where to look and what to look for. Keep it simple and promise an entire pizza to whoever finds what we're after."

My apprentice grinned. "Drive their performance with competition, eh?"

"Millions of abusively obsessed sports parents can't be wrong," I said. "Butters, you'll go to the Paranetters and ask if anyone's seen or heard anything unusual anywhere even close to Lake Michigan. No one investigates anything. They just report. Get me all the information you can about any odd activity in the past week. We need to collect data as quickly as possible."

"Right," Butters said. "I've got some now, if you want."

I blinked. I mean, I knew the Internet was the fast way to spread information, but . . . "Seriously?"

"Well," Butters hedged. "Sort of. One of our guys is a little, um, imaginative."

"You mean paranoid?"

"Yes," Butters said. "He's got this Internet lair in his mother's basement. Keeps track of all kinds of things. Calls it observing the supernatural through statistics. Sends me a regional status update every day, and my spam blockers just cannot keep him out."

"Hngh," I said, as if I knew what a spam blocker was. "What's he got to say about today?"

"That boat rentals this morning were four hundred percent higher today than the median for this time of year, and dark forces are bound to be at work."

"Boat rentals," I muttered.

"He's a little weird, Harry," Butters said. "I mean, he has a little headshot photo tree of the people responsible for the Cubs' billy goat curse. That kind of odd. He blows the curve."

"Tell him to take the tree down. The billy goat curse was a lone gunman," I said. "But paranoid doesn't necessarily equal wrong. Boats . . ."

I bowed my head and closed my eyes for a moment, thinking, but if Butter's paranoid basement freak was right, then the puzzle piece he'd handed me was woefully unhelpful. I needed more pieces. "Okay," I said. "Right. Get more data." I looked up, jerked my head at Thomas, and headed for the kitchen. "Let's go talk to our guest about his boss."

I leaned down to look into the oven through the glass door. There was no light inside, but I could make out Captain Hook's armored form huddled disconsolately on a coated cookie sheet. I knocked on the glass, and Captain Hook's helmet turned toward me.

"I want to talk to you," I said. "You're my prisoner. Don't try to fight me or run away or I'll have to stop you. I'd rather just have a nice conversation. Do you understand me?"

Hook didn't give me any indications either way. I took silence as assent.

"Okay," I said. "I'm going to open the door now." I cracked open the oven door and opened it slowly, doing my best not to loom. Tough to do when you're the size of a building relative to the person over whom you are standing. "Now just take it easy and we will—"

I'd opened the door maybe six inches when Captain Hook all but vanished in a blur of speed. I swiped an arm at him about a second and a half too late, but I didn't feel too bad about missing, because *Thomas* tried to snatch the little maniac, too, and missed completely.

Hook, who worked for our enemies, and who had been right there in the kitchen the whole time we'd been scheming, shot toward a vent on one wall, crossing the room in the blink of an eye, and none of us could react in time to stop him.

29

None of us but the major general.

Toot dropped down from where he'd been crouched atop a bookcase, intercepting Hook's darting black form, and tackled the other little faerie to the floor in the middle of the living room. They landed with a thump on the carpeting, wings still blurring in fits and starts, and tumbled around the floor in irregular bursts and hops, sometimes rolling a few inches, sometimes bounding up and coming down six feet away.

Toot had planned for this fight. He'd tackled Hook into the carpet, where the hooks on his armor would get tangled and bind him, slowing him down. Furthermore, Toot's hands were wrapped in cloth until it looked like he was wearing mittens or boxing gloves, and he managed to seize Hook by the hooks on the back of his armor. He swung the other little faerie around in a circle and then with a high-pitched shout flung him into the wall.

Captain Hook slammed into the wall, putting gouges in the freshly painted drywall, then staggered back and fell to the ground. Toot bore down with a vengeance, drawing his little sword, and the armored figure held up a mailed fist. "Invocation!" he piped in a high, clear voice. "I am a prisoner! I invoke Winter Law!"

Toot's sword was already in midswing, but at those last two words he checked himself abruptly, pulling the weapon back. He hovered there over Hook with his feet an inch off the ground, gritting his teeth, but then he buzzed back from Hook and sheathed the sword.

"Uh," I said. "Toot? What just happened?"

Toot-toot landed on the kitchen counter next to me and stomped around in a circle, clearly furious. "You opened your big fat mouth!" he screamed. After a moment, he added, sullenly, "My lord."

I frowned at Toot and then at Hook. The enemy sprite just sat there on the floor, making no further effort to escape. "Okay," I said. "Explain that."

"You offered to take him prisoner," Toot said. "By Winter Law, if he accepts your offer he may not attempt escape or offer any further resistance to you for as long as you see to his needs. Now you can't kill him or beat him up or anything! And I was winning!"

I blinked. "Yeah, okay, fine. So let's make with the questions already."

"You can't!" Toot wailed. "You can't try to make him betray his previous covenants or terror-gate him or anything!"

I frowned. "Wait. He's a *guest*?"

"Yes!"

"By Winter Law?" I asked.

"Yes! Sort of."

"Well," I said, starting toward Hook. "I never signed on to that treaty. So screw Winter Law—"

And abruptly, as if someone had just slammed a row of staples into my skin, the mantle of the Winter Knight vanished completely. Pain soared back into my body, inflamed tissue crying out, my bruises throbbing, the edemas beneath my skin pounding with a horrible tightness. Fatigue hit me like a truck. The sensations were so intense, the only way I could tell that I had fallen to the floor was by looking.

And my body abruptly went numb and useless from my stomach down.

That scared the hell out of me and confirmed one of my worst fears. When I'd consented to serve Mab, my back had been broken, my spine damaged. Taking up the mantle had covered what would probably have been a crippling and long-term injury. But without it, my body was only mortal. Better than most at recovering over time, but still human. Without the mantle, I wouldn't have legs, bladder or bowel control, or, most important, independence.

I was on the ground like that for a subjective week, but it could have been only a few seconds before Thomas reached my side, with Murphy, Butters, and Molly right behind him. I knew they were there because I could see them, but their voices swam down to me from what seemed like a great distance among the cacophony of raking sensations scouring my nervous system. They lifted me to a sitting position—and then abruptly the pain was gone, and my legs started moving again, jerking in a single, gentle spasm.

The mantle had been restored.

"Okay," I said in a ragged voice. "Uh. Maybe we *won't* screw Winter Law."

"Harry," Thomas said, as if he'd said my name several times already. "What happened?"

"Uh," I said. "I think it's . . . a side effect. Fallout from defying the order of things."

"What?" he asked.

"Faeries," I said. "They're kind of insane, and mischievous, and dangerous as hell, but they all share one trait—they're good to their word. They obey what they recognize as law. Especially Mab."

"You aren't making much sense right now," Thomas said.

"The mantle of power comes from Mab. And now it's in me. But it's still a piece of *her*. If I go violating her own realm's laws, it looks like the mantle isn't going to have my back."

"Meaning what?"

"Meaning I'd better figure out what the laws are pretty damned quick," I replied. "Help me up."

Thomas hauled me to my feet and I looked at Toot. "You know the Winter Law?"

"Well," Toot said as if I were an idiot, "of course."

"Where can I learn it?"

Toot tilted his head. "What?"

"Winter Law," I said. "Where can I learn it?"

"I don't understand," Toot said, tilting his head the other way.

"Oh, for the love of . . ." I pinched the bridge of my nose between my thumb and forefinger. "Toot. Can you read?"

"Sure!" Toot said. "I can read 'pizza' *and* 'exit' *and* 'chocolate'!"

"All three, huh?"

"Absolutely."

"You're a scholar and a gentleman," I said. "But where did you learn Winter Law?"

Toot shook his head as if mystified. "You don't *learn* it, Harry. You just . . . *know* it. Everyone knows it."

"I don't," I said.

"Maybe you're too big," Toot said. "Or too loud. Or, you know—too human."

I grunted. Then I eyed Hook, who had continued to sit in the same spot during the entire conversation. "So I've gone and made him my guest, eh?"

"Well. More like your vassal."

I frowned. "Uh? What?"

"That's what surrender is, duh," Toot said. "His life is yours to do with as you please. And as long as you don't starve him or make him an oath-breaker, you can tell him to do whatever you want. And if his liege wants him back, he has to pay you for him."

"Ah. Medieval-style ransom."

Toot looked confused. "He did run some, but I stopped him, my lord. Like, just now. In front of you. Right over there."

There were several conspicuous sounds behind me, the loudest from my apprentice, and I turned to eye everyone else. They were all either covering smiles or holding them back—poorly. "Hey, peanut gallery," I said. "This isn't as easy as I'm making it look."

"You're doing fine," Karrin said, her eyes twinkling.

I sighed.

"Come on, Toot," I said, and walked over to Hook.

The little faerie sat there, apparently ignoring me, which took considerable nerve. If I fell or stepped on him, it would be like a tree falling on a lumberjack. If I were trying to hurt him, physically, I could twist him up like Stretch Armstrong.

On the other hand, Hook was a faerie. It probably never even occurred to him that I might violate Mab's laws.

"The prisoner will stand and face the Za Lord!" Toot shrilled.

Hook obediently got up and turned to face me.

"Identify yourself, please," I said. "I don't want your Name. Just something to call you."

"By some I am called Lacuna," he replied.

"Suits me, Lacuna," I said. "Remove the helmet, please. I want to see who I'm supporting."

Lacuna reached up and removed the face-shrouding helmet.

She was gorgeous.

Fine black hair bound into a braid at least a foot long spilled down out of the helmet when she did. Her skin was paper white, her huge eyes black all the way through. There were small markings or tattoos of some kind in deep purple ink on her skin, but they shifted slightly as I watched, some fading from sight, others appearing. Her features were long and very lean. She had a straight razor's elegant, dangerous beauty.

Toot's jaw just about dropped off of his head. "Wow!"

"Hmmm," Karrin said. "That's the one who beat you up last night, is it?"

"And tripped him this morning," Thomas reminded her.

"And tripped me this morning," I growled. I turned back to Lacuna and studied her for a moment. She looked back at me without blinking. Actually, she didn't move at all—except for her braid, which drifted upward like cobwebs over a heating vent.

"Huh," I said. "Was not expecting that."

Lacuna stared, her eyes flat.

"I won't ask you to break your word," I told her. "And I will treat you with respect and provide for your needs in exchange for your service. Do you understand?"

"I understand," Lacuna said.

"Wow!" said Toot.

"Without breaking any oath, I would like to know," I said, "whatever you can tell me about the person you were serving until you were taken prisoner."

She stared.

I caught my mistake and rolled my eyes. "Let me rephrase that. Tell me whatever you can about the person you were serving until you were taken prisoner without breaking any word you've given him."

Lacuna nodded at that and frowned pensively. Then she looked up and said in a serious, confidential tone, "He does not seem to like you very much."

I took a slow, deep breath. There were more titters behind me.

"I noticed that, too," I said. "Tell me what you know about what's happening tonight."

"Children," she said in a sepulchral voice, and her little face twisted up with unmistakable fury. "And candy. Lots and lots of candy."

"Wow!" Toot said. He zipped away in a flutter of wings.

"Without breaking your word, tell me everything else you know about Ace," I said.

"He owes me," Lacuna replied grimly, "for services rendered."

I sighed. "I don't suppose you'd like to volunteer to offer me some more useful information?"

The armored faerie stared at me without blinking. It was a little creepy.

"Nah, I didn't think so," I said. "Are you hungry?"

She seemed to consider that for a moment, then said, "Yes."

"Do you want some pizza?"

Lacuna's face twisted up in disgust. "Ugh. No."

My eyebrows went up. That was a grade-A first. The Little Folk would quite literally go to war over pizza. They liked it that much. "Uh. What would you like to eat, then?"

"Celery," she replied promptly. "Cheese. Green tea. But mostly celery."

"How random," I said. I looked over my shoulder. "Molly?"

"I've got those," she said, and went to the kitchen.

"Okay, Lacuna," I said. "We've got a bunch of business to take care of. I want you to eat, get some rest, and make yourself comfortable. You aren't to leave this apartment. Understood?"

Lacuna nodded somberly. "Yes." Her wings blurred and she darted across the apartment to the kitchen, where Molly was preparing a plate with Lacuna-chow on it.

"Good. I'll figure out what to do with you later." I rubbed the back of my neck and went back over to the others. "Well. That was a little frustrating."

"Why'd you take her prisoner then?" Thomas asked.

I glowered at him. "Don't you have a squad of mercenaries to round up? Or a bridge to jump off?"

"I guess so."

"Okay, everybody," I said. "You've got your assignments. Let's get them done. Molly, you've got the apartment and the phone, so after you send the search parties, you're coordinating. Anyone learns something, call Molly with it. Otherwise, meet back here by five."

There was a round of nods and agreements, and Butters, Thomas, and Karrin headed out into the city.

Once they were gone, Molly asked, "Why'd you ditch them like that?"

I lifted my eyebrows again. The grasshopper just kept getting cleverer. "I wasn't ditching them," I said.

Molly arched an eyebrow. "You weren't?"

"Not entirely," I said. "That stuff needs doing, too."

"While you go somewhere dangerous all by yourself. Am I right?"

I didn't answer her right away, and she finished making Lacuna's meal. She put the plate on the counter and the serious little faerie fell upon it like a ravening wolf.

"Something like that," I said. "Don't you have a job to do, too?"

Molly eyed me. Then she picked up the map on the table, folded it, and walked toward the door. "I'm not going to fight you about it. I just wanted you to know that I knew."

Just then, Toot buzzed back into the apartment from somewhere. He zipped in frantic, dizzying circles, starting at the point he'd last seen Lacuna, until his spiral search pattern took him to the kitchen. Then he swooped down to Lacuna, landing neatly on the counter.

I peered at the two little faeries. Toot held out to Lacuna a wrapped watermelon Jolly Rancher, as if he were offering frankincense and myrrh to the Christ child. "Hi!" he said brightly. "I'm Major General Toot-toot!"

Lacuna looked up from her food and saw Toot's gift. Her eyes narrowed.

And then she sucker punched Toot-toot right in the face.

My little bodyguard flew back a couple of feet and landed on his ass. Both of his hands went up to his nose, and he blinked in startled bewilderment.

Toot had dropped the Jolly Rancher. Lacuna calmly kicked it into the disposal drain of the kitchen sink. Then she turned her back on Toot, ignoring him completely, and went back to eating her meal.

Toot's eyes were even wider as he stared at Lacuna.

"Wow!" he said.

30

The Montrose Point Bird Sanctuary has a second name—the Magic Hedge. There are about fifteen acres of trees, brush, and winding trails. It's been an established bird sanctuary for decades, and is a major port of call for birds migrating south for the winter. If you read some flyers about the place, they'll tell you all about how the Magic Hedge is chock-full to bursting with the magic of birds and nature.

But the folks who live here also call it the Magic Hedge because it's a fairly well-known hangout for men who are hoping to hook up with other men. The ratio of cruisers to bird-watchers (and don't think I didn't consider an ironic joke about binoculars and watching birds) varies depending on the time of the year. When there are tons of birds and bird lovers around, that means lots of people with binoculars and cameras. That kind of thing really cuts down on the romantic mystique.

The place sticks out like a hook, almost totally enclosing Montrose Harbor, which is mostly a place for boats that are a lot less grubby than the *Water Beetle*. There's a yacht club in there, and a fairly busy beach nearby. So occasionally non-bird-watching, noncruising people wander through the Magic Hedge, too.

People like me.

At the end of October, most of the migrating flocks had already gone by, but the Hedge was still a rendezvous for leftover flocks of sparrows, which would gather together over a few days, then merge and leave in an enormous cloud. I spotted two dozen species on my walk in, without binoculars. I knew most of them, if I had bothered to dig their names out of my memories. I didn't. Ebenezar, when he taught me, had been very serious about making sure I learned the proper names of things.

The park was mostly empty today, under the cold grey drizzling sky. On the way in to where I wanted to go, I passed a man dressed all in black, with a black hat and black sunglasses—sunglasses, for crying out loud—who tracked me with his needlessly cool gaze as I went by.

"Not here for that," I said. "Making a long-distance call. Be gone in half an hour. One way or another."

He didn't say anything, and as I passed he faded back into the brush. There's a community here. Spotters, runners. The police run stings sometimes. Seems like an awful lot of fuss and trouble for everyone involved, to me, especially in the modern world.

Bob wasn't in my shoulder bag anymore, but I'd replaced him with what I'd need. The lake nearby and the falling rain would do for water. Earth was there in plenty, and I used a garden spade to dig a small pit. The fitful cold winds from the northwest would do for air, and once I got the few pounds of kindling I'd brought piled into a small, hollow pyramid, it didn't take me long to get a tiny fire going, even in the rain.

I waited until it had begun to blaze up, building it to make it burn hotter and faster. I didn't want to cook on it. A few minutes were all I needed. I stayed low and moved as little as possible. The song from hundreds of gathered sparrows was enthusiastic, pervasive.

Once the fire was burning, I used the trowel to cut a circle into the soft earth around me. I touched it with my finger and invested a minor effort of will, and the magic of the circle snapped up around me. It was a mystic barrier, not a physical one, something that would contain and focus magical forces, and generally make it easier to do what I was about to do. It couldn't be seen or touched but it was very, very real.

A lot of important things are like that.

I gathered my will, sinking into pure focus. People think wizards use magic words, for some reason. There aren't any magic words, really. Even the ones we use in our spells are just symbols, a way to insulate our minds from the energies coursing through them. Words have a power every bit as terrible and beautiful as magic, and they don't need a special effects budget to do it, either.

What drives magic is, at the end of the day, sheer will. Emotions can help reinforce it, but when you draw on your emotions to fuel magic, even that is simply a different expression of will, a different flavor of your desire to make something happen. Some things you do as a wizard require you to set any emotion you have aside. They're good in a crisis, but in a methodical, deliberate effort they can wreak havoc with your intentions. So I blocked out all my confusion, doubt, and uncertainty, along with my perfectly intelligent terror, until all that remained was my rational self and my need to reach a single goal.

Only then did I lift my head and speak, infusing every word with the power of my need, casting the summoning forth into the universe. The power made my voice sound strange—louder, deeper, richer.

"Lady of Light and Life, hear me. Thou who art Queen of the Ever-Green, Lady of Flowers, hear me. Dire portents are afoot. Hear my voice. Hear my need. I am Harry Dresden, Winter Knight, and I needs must speak with thee." I lifted my joined voice and will and thundered, "Titania, Titania, Titania! I summon thee!"

The last syllable rebounded from every surface in sight with booming echoes. It panicked the sparrows. They flew up in a cloud of thousands of wings and little bodies, gathering in a swarm that raced wildly in circles around the meadow.

"Come on," I breathed to myself. "Come on already." I stood in silence for a long, long minute, and I was starting to think that nothing was going to happen.

And then I saw the clouds begin to rotate, and I knew exactly what it meant.

I've lived in the Midwest for most of my life. Tornadoes are a fact of life out here, part of the background. People think they're scary, and they are, but they're very survivable, provided you follow some fairly simple guidelines: Warn people early, and when you hear the warning, head for the safest space you can reach quickly. That's usually a basement or root cellar. Sometimes it's beneath a staircase. Sometimes it's in an interior bathroom. Sometimes the best you can hope for is the deepest ditch you can find.

But basically it all amounts to "run and hide."

Years of life in the Midwest screamed at me to do exactly that. My heart started speeding up and my mouth went dry, while the clouds overhead—and when I say "overhead" I mean *directly* over *my* head—turned faster and faster.

Birds exploded into the sky from all over the Magic Hedge, joining the sparrows in their wild circling. The air suddenly became close, and the drizzling rain cut off as if a valve had been closed. Lightning with no thunder flickered weirdly through the clouds, which turned every shade of white and blue and sea green as the water vapor separated the light into the visible spectrum.

Then I felt it—a warmth like that I'd felt in Lily, only a hundred times hotter and brighter and more intense. The clouds started to lower, and the frantic birds tightened their circle, until they were a wall of shining feathers and glittering eyes around the meadow. Then there was a flash of light, a toll of thunder that sounded weirdly musical, like the after-tone of some vast gong, and a shower of earth and glowing bits of charred autumn grass flew into the air. I threw up an arm to shield my eyes—but I kept my feet planted.

When the dirt settled and the dust and ash cleared, the Lady of Light and Life and Monarch of the Summer Court stood about fifteen feet away from me.

She was breathtaking. I don't mean beautiful, because she was that, obviously. But it was the kind of beauty that had so much scope, so much depth, so much power that it made me feel dwindling, insignificant, and very, very temporary. You feel it the first time you see the mountains, the first time you see the sea, the first time you see the vast, bleak majesty of the Grand Canyon—and every single time you look at Titania, the Summer Queen.

I'd say that the details of her appearance were unimportant, except that they weren't—particularly for me.

Titania was dressed for a fight.

She wore a gown of mail made from some kind of silvery metal, the links so fine that at first it looked like woven cloth. It covered her like a second skin, all the way to the top of her throat. Over that she wore a long robe of silk that shifted in colors from the yellow of sunlight to the green of pine needles in a slow strobelike pattern. Her silver-white hair had been braided into a tail and then fixed in coils at the base of her neck. Upon her head was a crown of what looked like twisted vine with still-living leaves. She carried neither weapon nor shield, but her wide Sidhe eyes stared at me with the absolute certainty of one who knows she is armed well beyond the ability of her enemy to withstand.

Oh, and if I hadn't known better, I would have sworn to you that it was Mab standing there. Seriously. They didn't look like sisters. They looked like clones.

I started off by bowing to her, deeply. I held it for a beat before rising again.

She was a statue for a few seconds. She didn't so much as nod back to me, to any measurable degree, but some microchange in her body language indicated acknowledgment.

"You who slew my daughter," Titania said quietly. "You dare summon *me*?"

The last word slashed through the air, its fury palpable. It struck the circle surrounding me and broke into a shower of gold and green sparks that vanished almost instantly.

I've had some experience with the Queens of Faerie. When they get angry and start talking to you, you freaking *hear* them. And then if you survive it, you hope you can make it to the emergency room in time. I just hadn't seen any scenario in which my talking to Titania wouldn't make her furious—so I'd drawn the circle as a precaution.

Sometimes I use my brain.

"Crazy, right?" I said. "But I needed to speak to you, O Queen."

Her eyes narrowed. The curtain-cloud of birds continued their circling around us, though they had fallen eerily silent. The clouds overhead continued to spin. We were as isolated from the rest of the world as if we stood in a private garden. "Speak, then."

I thought about my words and picked them carefully. "There are events in motion. Very large events, with serious ramifications for basically the whole world. I mean, I thought the war between the White

Council and the Red Court was a big deal—but now it looks to me like it was more or less an opening act for the real band."

Her eyes narrowed. She nodded her head a fraction of an inch.

"Something is going to happen tonight," I said. "The Well will come under attack. You know what could happen if it is opened. A lot of people would get hurt in the short term. And in the long term . . . well, I'm not sure I know what would happen, but I'm almost certain it wouldn't be good."

Titania tilted her head slightly to one side. It reminded me of an eagle considering its prey and deciding whether or not it was worth it to swoop down on it out of nowhere.

"I'm trying to make sure that doesn't happen," I said. "And because of the nature of this . . . problem . . . I can't trust any of the information I get out of the people I'm working for."

"Ah," she said. "You wish me to pass judgment upon my sister."

"I need someone with knowledge of Mab," I said. "Someone who knows the events are in motion. Who would know if she had . . . uh. . . . Changed."

"And what makes you think that I would have the knowledge you seek?"

"Because I Saw you preparing the battlefield at the stone table, years ago. You're Mab's equal. I Saw your power. You don't get power like that without knowledge."

"That is true."

"I need to know," I said. "Is Mab sane? Is she . . . still Mab?"

Titania did a statue impersonation for a long moment. Then she turned her head to one side and stared out toward the lake. "I do not know." She gave me an oblique look. "I have not exchanged words with my sister since before Hastings."

The next-best thing to a millennium's worth of estrangement. Dysfunction on an epic scale. This was exactly the kind of family tension into which sane people do not inject themselves.

"I'm going to inject myself into your family business," I said. "Because I'm scared to death of what could happen if I don't, and because it needs to be done. I understand that you're Mab's enemy. I understand that if she says black, you say white, and that's the way it is. But we're all in a southbound handbasket together here. And I need your help."

Titania tilted her head the other way and took a step toward me. I almost flinched back out of the circle. I didn't want to do that. I didn't think it would keep me safe for long if she decided she wanted to come at me, but as long as it was there, it meant that she would have to spend at least a little time bringing it down—time in which I could attack her. It also meant that if I took the first swing, I'd be sacrificing the circle's protection, and my only current advantage. She looked down at my feet and then back up at me expectantly.

"Uh," I said. "Will you please help me?"

Something flickered over her face when I said that, an emotion that I couldn't place. Maybe it wasn't a human one. She turned abruptly away and seemed to consider her surroundings for the first time. "We shall see," she said. She turned back to me, her eyes intent. "Why did you come here for the summoning?"

"It's a bird sanctuary," I said. "A natural place, intended to preserve life and beauty. And birds seem kind of Summery to me. Following summer to the south over the winter and then returning. I thought that it might be close to some of Summer's lands in Faerie. That you'd have an easier time hearing me."

She turned her head slowly, as if listening. There was no sound but the constant, muffled white noise of thousands of wings beating. "But this place is more than that. It is a location for . . . unapproved liaisons."

I shrugged. "It's just you and me. I figured if you wanted to kill me, you could do it here without hurting anybody else."

Titania nodded, her expression turning thoughtful. "What think you of the men who come here to meet with one another?"

"Uh," I said, feeling somewhat off balance. "What do I think of gay guys?"

"Yes."

"Boink and let boink, more or less."

"Meaning?"

"Meaning it doesn't have a lot to do with me," I said. "It's none of my business what they do. I don't go over in their living room and get my freak on with women. They don't come over and do whatever they do with other guys at my house."

"You don't feel that they are morally wrong to do so?"

"I have no idea if it's right or wrong," I said. "To me, it mostly doesn't matter."

"And why not?"

"Because even if they are doing something immoral, I'd be an idiot to start criticizing them for it if I wasn't perfect myself. Smoking is self-destructive. Drinking is self-destructive. Losing your temper and yelling at people is wrong. Lying is wrong. Cheating is wrong. Stealing is wrong. But people do that stuff all the time. Soon as I figure out how to be a perfect human being, then I'm qualified to go lecture other people about how they live their lives."

"An odd sentiment. Are you not 'only human'? Will you not always be imperfect?"

"Now you're catching on," I said.

"You do not see it as a sin?"

I shrugged. "I think it's a cruel world. I think it's hard to find love. I think we should all be happy when someone manages to do it."

"Love," Titania said. She had keyed on the word. "Is that what happens here?"

"The guys who come here for anonymous sex?" I sighed. "Not so much. I think that part's a little sad. I mean, anytime sex becomes something so . . . damned impersonal, it's a shame. And I don't think it's good for them. But it's not me they're hurting."

"Why should that matter?"

I just looked at Titania for a second. Then I said, "Because people should be free. And as long as something they want to do isn't harming others, they should be free to do it. Obviously."

"Is it?" Titania asked. "It would not seem to be, judging from the state of the mortal world."

"Yeah. A lot of people don't get that," I said. "They get caught up in right and wrong. Or right and left. But none of that stuff matters if people aren't *free*."

Titania studied me intently.

"Why are you asking me about *that*, of all things?" I asked.

"Because it felt appropriate. Because my instincts told me that your answers would tell me something about you that I needed to know." Titania took a deep breath. "What think you of my sister?"

I debated for a second: polite answer or honest one?

Honest. It's almost always best to go with honest. It means you never have to worry about getting your story straight. "I thought Mab's wrath was pretty bad until I found out what her affection was like."

At that, I think Titania almost smiled. "Oh?"

"She nursed me out of bed by trying to kill me every day for eleven weeks. She scares the hell out of me."

"You do not love her?"

"Not by any definition of the word I've ever heard," I said.

"And why do you serve her?"

"Needed her help," I said. "That was her price. Sure as hell wasn't because I like the decor in Arctis Tor."

Titania nodded. She said, "You are unlike the other monsters she has shaped for herself over the centuries."

"Uh. Thank you?"

She shook her head. "I have done nothing for you, Harry Dresden." She pursed her lips. "In many ways, she and I are alike. In many more ways, we are entirely different. Do you know what my sister believes in?"

"Flashy entrances," I said.

Titania's lips actually twitched. "In reason."

"Reason?"

"Reason. Logic. Calculation. The cold numbers. The supremacy of the mind." Titania's eyes became distant. "It is another place where we differ. I prefer to follow the wisdom of the heart."

"Meaning what?" I asked.

Titania lifted her hand and spoke a single word, and the air rang with power. The ground buckled, ripping my circle apart and flinging me from my feet onto my back.

"Meaning," she said, her voice hot and furious, "that you *murdered* my daughter."

Birds flew shrieking in every direction as if released from a centrifuge. Titania raised a hand, and a bolt of lightning fell from the tornadic sky and blew a smoking crater the size of my head in the ground a yard away.

"You *dare* to come here! To ask for me to interfere in my sister's business! You who gave my Aurora an iron death!"

I tried to get up, only to have Titania grab the front of my jacket and lift me off the ground. With one hand. She held me straight up, over her head, so that her fist was pressed against my chest.

"I could kill you in a thousand ways," she snarled, her opalescent eyes whirling with colors. "I could scatter your bones to the far corners of the earth. I could feed you to my garden and make you scream the entire while. I could visit torments on you that would make Lloyd Slate's fate seem kind by comparison. I *want* to *eat your heart*."

I hung there over the furious Queen of Summer and knew, knew for certain, that there was not a damned thing I could do to save my own life. I can do things, sure—remarkable things. But Titania had no more to fear from me than a polar bear does a field mouse. My heartbeat became something close to a solid tone, and it was all I could do not to wet my freaking pants.

And then something really unsettling happened.

Tears filled her eyes. They came forth and spilled over her cheeks. Titania seemed to sag. She lowered me to the ground and released me.

"I could do these things. But none of them," she whispered, "would give me my daughter back. None of them would fill the emptiness within me. It took time, but Elder Gruff's wise counsel helped me to see that truth."

Hell's bells. Elder Gruff had spoken on my behalf? I owed that guy a beer.

"I am not a fool, wizard. I know what she had become. I know what had to be done." More tears fell, shining like diamonds. "But she was mine. I cannot forget that you took her from me. I cannot forgive you for that. Take your life and leave this place."

I sounded a little unsteady to my own ears when I spoke. "If the Well is ruptured, your realm stands to lose as much as the mortal one does."

"The wisdom of my heart tells me to *hate* you, mortal," Titania said, "whatever my reason might say. I will *not* help you."

"No? What does your heart tell you is going to happen if those things in the Well are set free? They're immortals. The fire in the fail-safe might keep them down for a while, but they'll be back."

Titania didn't turn to face me. Her voice was weary. "My heart tells me that all things end." She paused. "But this thing I will tell a Winter Knight who believes in freedom: You must learn greater discretion. The power you have come to know and fear has a name. One should know the proper names of things."

She turned and walked toward me. My body told me to run like hell, but I told it to shut up, that my legs were shaking too hard anyway. Titania leaned up onto her toes and whispered, very close to my ear.

"*Nemesis*," she breathed. "Speak it carefully—or it may hear you."

I blinked. "It . . . it *what*?"

With that she turned and began walking away. "Fare thee well, wizard. You say that people should be free. I agree. I will not shackle you with my wisdom. Make your choices. Choose what the world is to be. I care not. There is little light left in it for me, thanks to you."

A relatively small flock of birds, only a few hundred, blurred by between me and Titania. When they had passed, she was gone.

I stood there, letting my heart rate slow down, along with the spinning clouds. I felt like crap. When I'd killed Aurora, there hadn't been much in the way of a choice—but I'd still taken someone's little girl away from her forever. I felt like a man in a rowboat with only one oar. No matter how hard I worked, I wasn't really getting anywhere.

But at least I had a name now, for the force the Ladies had told me about.

Nemesis.

And it was *aware*.

The rain that had been held back abruptly began to come down in a torrent, and I sourly suspected that Titania had made sure I was going to get drenched. She hadn't killed me, at least not yet. But I knew she sure as hell didn't like me.

Night was coming on fast, and when it got here, all hell was going to break loose. And that was a best-case scenario.

I bowed my head, hunched my shoulders against the rain, and started out of the Magic Hedge.

31

I whistled down a cab and went to my next destination: Graceland Cemetery.

The place was actually kind of busy, it being Halloween and all. Graceland is one of the great cemeteries of the nation, the Atlantic City of graveyards. It's filled with monuments to men and women who evidently had too much money to throw around while they were still alive. There are statues and mausoleums everywhere, made from granite and ornate marble, some of them in the style of ancient Greece, some obviously more influenced by ancient Egypt. There's one that's practically a full-size temple. The actual style of the various monuments ranges from incredible beauty to absolutely outrageous extravagance, with artists and tycoons and architects and inventors all lying silently together now.

Walk in Graceland and you can find yourself lost in a maze of memories, a cloud of names that no one living could attach to a face anymore. I wondered, passing some of the older monuments, whether anyone ever visited them now. If you'd died in 1876, it would mean that your great-great- or even great-great-great-grandchildren were the ones living now. Did people visit the graves of those who had been gone that long?

No. Not for any personal reason. But that was all right. Graves aren't for the dead. They're for the loved ones the dead leave behind them. Once those loved ones have gone, once all the lives that have touched the occupant of any given grave had ended, then the grave's purpose was fulfilled and ended.

I suppose if you looked at it that way, one might as well decorate one's grave with an enormous statue or a giant temple. It gave people something to talk about, at least. Although, following that logic, I would need to have a roller coaster, or maybe a Tilt-A-Whirl constructed over my own grave when I died. Then even after my loved ones had moved on, people could keep having fun for years and years.

Of course, I'd need a slightly larger plot.

My grave was still open, a six-foot pit in the ground. An old enemy had bought it for me as a form of murderous foreplay. That one hadn't fallen out the way she had expected it would. But apparently whatever mechanism she used to secure the grave and to have it (illegally) left open was apparently still in place, because when I got there, I found it just as gaping and threatening as it had always been. A chill rolled up my spine as I read my headstone.

It was a pretty thing, white marble with gold-inlaid letters and a gold-inlaid pentacle:

HERE LIES HARRY DRESDEN.
HE DIED DOING THE RIGHT THING.

"Well," I muttered, "once, sure. But I guess I'll have to go best two out of three."

I looked around. I'd passed several groups that might have been Halloween haunted theme tours, and a gaggle of kids wearing expensive black clothing and grim makeup, smoking cigarettes and trying to look like they were wise to the world. A couple of older people seemed to actually be visiting graves, putting out fresh flowers.

I paused thoughtfully over my own grave and waited until no one was looking. Then I hopped down into it. My feet splashed into an inch of water and another six inches of mud, courtesy of the drizzling rain.

I crouched a little lower, just to be sure no one saw me, and got into my bag again.

My hands were shaking too much to get the bag open on the first try. It wasn't the cold. It wasn't even standing at the bottom of my own grave—hell, when I'd been a ghost, my own grave had been the most restful place in the whole world, and there was a certain amount of that reassurance that was still present. I still had no desire to get dead; don't get me wrong.

The scary thing was imagining what would happen to all the people I cared about if I died in the next few minutes. If I was right, this next interview might get me everything I needed. If I wasn't . . . well, I could hope to wind up dead, I guess. But I had a bad feeling that wizards who pissed off people on this level didn't get anything that pleasant and gentle.

I made my preparations quickly. Earth and water were all around, no problem there. I'd have to hope that what little air I had was right for the calling. Fire would have been an issue if I hadn't planned ahead. I needed to represent one other primal force, too, something that would call to the exact being I had in mind:

Death.

If working the spell from your own grave on Hallo-freaking-ween wasn't deathy enough, I wasn't sure what would be.

I stood on one foot, and with a gesture and a word froze most of the water in the grave. I put my free foot down on the ice and pulled my other foot out of the part I'd left as mostly slush. Then I froze that, too. I didn't have any problems slipping on the ice—or rather, I did slip a little, but my body seemed to adjust to it as naturally as it would have to small stones turning underfoot on a gravel road. No big deal.

Once the water was nice and solid, I got out my other props. A bottle of cooking oil, a knife, and matches.

I took the knife and drew a short cut into the skin of my left hand, in the fleshy bit between my thumb and forefinger, over an old scar where I had been hurt at the bidding of a Queen of Faerie before. While that welled up and began to bleed, I reached up and slashed off a lock of my hair with the same knife. I took the lock and used the freshly shed blood as an adhesive to hold it together, and dropped it onto the surface of the ice. More death, just in case. Then I poured a circle of oil around the hair and the blood and set it quickly alight with the matches.

Fire and water hissed and spit, and wind moaned over the top of my grave. I braced my hands on either side of it, closed my eyes, and spoke the invocation I'd chosen, infusing my voice with my will. "Ancient crone, harbinger!" I began, then raised my voice, louder. "Longest shadow! Darkest dream! She of the endless hunger, the iron teeth, the merciless jaws!" I poured more of my wind and my will into the words, and the inside of my grave rang with the sheer volume. "I am Harry Dresden, the Winter Knight, and I needs must speak with thee! Athropos! Skuld! Mother Winter, I summon thee!"

I released the pent-up power in my voice, and as it rang out I could hear birds erupting up from where they sheltered all over the graveyard. There were shouts and cries of surprise, too, from the tourists or the Gothlings or both. I ground my teeth and hoped that they wouldn't come my way. Getting killed by Mother Winter wouldn't be like being killed by Titania. That might at least have been huge and messy—not really a fight, but at least a proper slaughter.

If Mother Winter showed up and wanted to kill me, I'd probably just fall into dust or something. Mother Winter was to Mab as Mab was to Maeve—power an order of magnitude above the Winter Queen. I'd met with her once before, and she'd literally knitted up some of the most powerful magic I'd ever seen while carrying on a conversation.

The echoes of my summoning bounced around the graveyard over my head a few times and then . . .

And then . . .

And then nothing.

I sat there for a moment, waiting, while the burning oil hissed and sputtered on the ice. A running tendril of oil ran out to my blood and hair, and a tongue of flame followed a moment later. That part was fine by me. It wasn't like I wanted to leave a target that juicy lying around for someone to steal, anyway.

I waited until the fire burned out entirely, and quiet settled over my grave again, but nothing happened. Dammit. I wasn't going to figure out what was really going on tonight by carefully sifting all the facts and analyzing how they all fit together. Not in the time I had left. My only real chance was to get to someone who knew and get them to talk. Granted, going to talk to Mother Winter was about half an inch shy of trying to call up Lucifer, or maybe Death itself (if there was such a being—no one was really sure), but when you need information from witnesses and experts, the only way to get it is to talk to them.

Maybe my summons hadn't been deathy enough, but I hadn't wanted to kill some poor animal just to get the old girl's attention. I might have to, though. There was just too much at stake to get squeamish.

I shook my head, put my tools away, and then the ice just beneath my toes shattered and a long, bony arm, covered in wrinkles and warts and spots, and belonging to a body that would have been at least twenty feet tall, shot up and seized my head. Not my face. My entire head, like a softball. Or maybe an apple. Stained black claws on the ends of the knobby fingers dug into me, piercing my skin, and I was abruptly jerked down into the freaking ice with so much power that for a second I was terrified my neck had snapped.

I thought I would be broken for certain when I hit the ice, but instead I was drawn *through* it and down into the mud, and through that, and then I was falling, screaming in sudden, instinctive, blind terror. Then I hit something hard and it *hurt*, even through the power of the mantle, and I let out a brief, croaking exhalation. I dangled there, stunned for a moment, with those cold, cruel pointed claws digging into my flesh. Distantly I could hear a slow, limping step, and feel my feet dragging across a surface.

Then I was flung and spun twice on the horizontal, and I crashed into a wall. I bounced off it and landed on what felt like a dirt floor. I lay there, not able to inhale, barely able to move, and either I'd gone blind or I was in complete blackness. The nice part about having your bells rung like that is that mind-numbing horror sort of gets put onto a side burner for a bit. That was pretty much the only nice thing about it. When I finally managed to gasp in a little air, I used it to make a whimpering sound of pure pain.

A voice came out of the darkness, a sound that was dusty and raspy and covered in spiders. "Me," it said, drawing the word out. "You attempt to summon. Me."

"You have my sincerest apologies for the necessity," I said, or tried to say to Mother Winter. I think it just came out, *"Ow."*

"You think I am a servant to be whistled for?" continued the voice.

Hate and weariness and dark amusement were all mummified together in it. "You think I am some petty spirit you can command."

"N-n-nngh, ow." I gasped.

"You dare to presume? You dare to speak such names to draw my attention?" the voice said. "I have a stew to make, and I will fill it with your arrogant mortal meat."

There was a sound in the pitch-darkness. Steel being drawn across stone. A few sparks went up, blinding in the darkness. They burned into my retinas the outline of a massive, hunched form grasping a cleaver.

Sparks danced every few seconds as Mother Winter slowly sharpened her implement. I was able to get my breathing under control and to fight past the pain. "Mmm . . ." I said. "M-Mother Winter. Such a pleasure to meet with you again."

The next burst of sparks gleamed off of an iron surface—teeth.

"I n-need to speak to you."

"Speak, then, manling," said Mother Winter. "You have a little time left."

The cleaver rasped across the sharpening stone again.

"Mab has ordered me to kill Maeve," I said.

"She is always doing foolish things," said Mother Winter.

"Maeve says that Mab's gone insane," I said. "Lily concurs."

There was a wheezing sound that might have been a cackle. "Such a loving daughter."

I had to believe that I was going to get out of this somehow. So I pressed her. "I need to know which of them is right," I said. "I need to know who I should turn my hand against to prevent a great tragedy."

"Tragedy," said Mother Winter in a purr that made me think of rasping scorpions. "Pain? Terror? Sorrow? Why should I wish to prevent such a thing? It is sweeter than an infant's marrow."

It is a good thing I am a fearless and intrepid wizardly type, or that last bit of sentence would have set my flesh to crawling hard enough to carry me across the dirt floor.

I was kind of hosed anyway, so I took a chance. I crossed my fingers in the dark and said, "Because Nemesis is behind it."

The cleaver's rasp abruptly stopped.

The darkness and silence were, for a moment, absolute.

My imagination treated me to an image of Mother Winter creeping silently toward me in the blackness, cleaver lifted, and I stifled an urge to burst into panicked screams.

"So," she whispered a moment later. "You have finally come to see what has been before you all this time."

"Uh, yeah. I guess. I know there's something there now, at least."

"So very mortal of you. Learning only when it is too late."

Rasp. Sparks.

"You aren't going to kill me," I said. "I'm as much your Knight as Mab's."

There was a low, quiet snort. "You are no true Knight of Winter, manling. Once I have devoured your flesh, and your mantle with it, I will bestow it upon someone worthier of the name. I should never have given it to Mab."

Uh, wow. I hadn't thought of that kind of motivation. My guts got really watery. I tried to move my limbs and found them numbed and only partially functional. I started trying to get them to flip me over so that I could get my feet under me. "Uh, no?" I heard myself ask in a panicked, cracking voice. "And why is that, exactly?"

"Mab," said Mother Winter in a tone of pure disgust, "is too much the romantic."

Which pretty much tells you everything you need to know about Mother Winter, right there.

"She has spent too much time with mortals," Mother Winter continued, withered lips peeled back from iron teeth as the sparks from her cleaver's edge leapt higher. "Mortals in their soft, controlled world. Mortals with nothing to do but fight one another, who have forgotten *why* they should fear the fangs and the claws, the cold and the dark."

"And . . . that's bad?"

"What value has life when it is so easily *kept*?" Mother Winter spat the last word. "Mab's weakness is evident. Look at her Knight."

Her Knight was currently trying to sit up, but his wrists and ankles were fastened to the floor by something cold, hard, and unseen. I tested them, but couldn't feel any edges. The bonds couldn't have been metal.

And they weren't ice. I didn't know how I knew that, but I was completely certain. Ice would have been no obstacle. But there was something familiar about it, something I had felt before . . . in Chichén Itzá.

Will.

Mother Winter was holding me down by pure, stark will. The leaders of the Red Court had been ancient creatures with a similar power, but that had been a vague, smothering blanket that had made it impossible to move or act, a purely mental effort.

This felt like something similar, but far more focused, more developed, as if thought had somehow crystallized into tangibility. My wrists and ankles wouldn't move because Mother Winter's will said that was how reality worked. It was like magic—but magic took a seed, a kernel of will and built up a framework of other energies around that seed. It took intense practice and focus to make that happen, but at the end of the day anyone's will was only part of the spell, alloyed with other energy into something else.

What held me down now was pure, undiluted will—the same kind of will that I suspected had backed up events presaged by phrases like "Let there be light." It was far more than human, beyond simple physical strength, and if I'd been the Incredible Hulk, I was pretty sure there was no way I'd have been able to tear myself free.

"Ahhh," said Mother Winter, during one last stroke of the cleaver. "I like nice clean edges to my meat, manling. Time for dinner."

And slow, limping steps came toward me.

32

A slow smile stretched my lips back from my teeth.

Mortals had the short end of the stick on almost any supernatural confrontation. Even most wizards, with their access to terrific forces, had to approach conflicts carefully—relatively few of us had the talents that lent themselves to brawling. But mortals had everyone else beat on exactly one thing: the freedom to choose. Free will.

It had taken me a while to begin to understand it, but it had eventually sunk into my thick skull. I couldn't arm wrestle an ogre, even with the mantle. I couldn't have won a magical duel with Mab or Titania—probably not even against Maeve or Lily. I couldn't outrun one of the Sidhe.

But I could defy absolutely anyone.

I could lift my will against that of anything, and know that the fight might be lopsided, but never hopeless. And by thunder, I was *not* going to allow *anyone's* will to stretch me out on the floor like a lamb for slaughter.

I stopped pressing at my bindings with my limbs and started using my mind instead. I didn't try to push them away, or break them, or slip free of them. I simply *willed* them not to be. I envisioned what my limbs would feel like coming free, and focused on *that* reality, summoning up my total concentration on that goal, that ideal, that *fact*.

And then I crossed my fingers and reached into me, into the place where a covert archangel had granted me access to one of the primal forces of the universe, an energy called soulfire. I had no idea how it might interact with the Winter Knight's mantle on an ongoing basis. I mean, it had worked out once before, but that didn't mean that it would keep working out. I felt certain that I was pretty much swallowing bottles of nitroglycerin, then jumping up and down to see what would happen, but at this point I had little to lose. I gathered up soulfire, used it to infuse my raw will, and cast the resulting compound against my bonds.

Soulfire, according to Bob, is one of the fundamental forces of the universe, the original power of creation. It isn't meant for mortals. We get it by slicing off a bit of our soul, our life energy, and converting it into something else.

Bob is brilliant, but there are some things that he just doesn't get. His definition was a good place to get started, but it was also something that was perhaps too comfortably quantifiable. The soul isn't something you can weigh and measure. It's more than just one thing. Because soulfire interacts with souls in a way that I'm not sure anyone understands, it stands to reason that soulfire isn't just one thing, either.

And in this case, in this moment, I somehow knew exactly what the soulfire did. It converted me, my core, everything that made me who I was, into energy, into light. When I turned my joined will and the blazing core of my being together, I wasn't supercharging a magical spell. I wasn't cleverly finding a weak point in an enchantment. I wasn't using my knowledge of magic to exploit what my enemy was doing.

I was casting everything I had done, everything I believed, everything I had chosen—everything I *was*—against the will of an ancient being of darkness, terror, and malice, a fundamental power of the world.

And the bonds and the will of Mother Winter could not constrain me.

There was a sharp, shimmering tone, like metal under stress and beginning to fail, but more musical, and a blinding white light that washed away the darkness and dazzled my eyes. There was a thunder crack, and a terrible force erupted from my wrists and ankles, throwing a shock wave of raw kinetic energy—a mere shadow of the true forces at work, a by-product—out into the space around me. In that whiteness, I caught an image of a shrouded, hunched dark form, flung from her feet to impact something solid.

And then I was free and hauling myself up onto my feet.

I backed up, hoping I hadn't gotten turned around in the flash, and a surge of relief went through me when my back hit a stone wall. I felt out along on either side of me, and my hand brushed something solid, maybe a small shelf made from a wooden plank. I knocked it off its peg. It fell to the dirt floor with a clatter and a clink of small, heavy glass jars.

I leaned against the wall, dazed, panting, and gasped, in my deepest and most gravelly voice, "No one can chain the Hulk!"

I heard a stir of cloth in the darkness then, a slight grunt of effort, the faintest whistle in the air. I can't claim credit for being smart or cool on this one. Some instinct pegged which way the cleaver was coming and I flung my head sharply to one side. Sparks flew as the cleaver struck the wall where my skull had been and sank into it as if it had been made of rotten pine, not stone. It stayed there, making a faint vibrating sound as it quivered.

I have got to learn to keep my freaking mouth shut. I clenched my teeth together and stayed still, giving no indication of where I might be in the darkness.

For a long time there was quiet, except for the breathing I fought to slow and silence. And then a horrible, slithering sound went through the blackness. It caught in Mother Winter's ancient throat, clicking like the shells of swarming carrion beetles. It wormed its way through the air like a swarm of maggots burrowing through rotten meat. It brushed against me, light and hideous, like the touch of a vulture's lice-infested feather, and I struggled to press myself back a little closer to the stone at the sound of it.

Mother Winter was cackling.

"So," she said. "So, so, and so. Perhaps thou art not entirely useless after all, eh, manling?"

For all I knew, Mother Winter had a whole cutlery set over there. I gathered my will into a shielding spell, but I didn't release it. Magic was like air and water to the fae. I had a feeling Mother Winter would have been able to home in on it.

"That was a test?" I whispered—behind my hand, so that it might not make it utterly obvious where I was standing.

"Or a meal," she rasped. "Either would suffice."

And then brightness flooded the room.

I thought some massive force had inundated the area I stood in, but after a second I realized that it was a door. The light was sunlight, with the golden quality that somehow felt like autumn. I had to shield my eyes against it, but after a moment I realized that I was standing in a small, simple medieval-looking cottage—one in which I had been before. Everything in it was wooden, leather, clay, and handmade. The glass in the windows was wavery and translucent. It was a neat, tidy place—apart from one corner with a large, ugly, raw-looking rocking chair. Oh, and a spilled shelf of small clay pots with wax-sealed mouths.

"You can be so overly dramatic, betimes," complained an old woman's voice, as gentle and sweet as Mother Winter's was unpleasant. She came into the house a moment later, a grandmotherly matron dressed in a simple dress with a green apron. Her long hair, silver-white and thinning, was done up in a small, neat bun. She moved with the slightly stiff, bustling energy of an active senior, and if her green eyes were framed by crow's-feet, they were bright and sharp. Mother Summer carried a basket in one arm filled with cuttings from what must have been a late-season herb garden, and as I watched, she entered, muttered a word, and a dozen tiny whirlwinds cleaned thick layers of soot from the many-paned windows scattered around the cottage, flooding it with more warm light. "We'll need a new cleaver now."

Mother Winter, in her black shawl and hood, bared her iron teeth in a snarl, though it was a silent one. She pointed one crooked, warty finger at the window nearest her, and blackened it with soot again. Then she shuffled over to a chair beneath the window, and settled into the resulting shadow as if it were a comforting blanket. "I do what must be done."

"With our cleaver," Mother Summer said. "I suppose one of our knives wouldn't have done just as well?"

Mother Winter bared her teeth again. "I wasn't holding a knife."

Mother Summer made a disapproving clucking sound and began unloading her basket onto a wooden table near the fireplace. "I told you," she said calmly.

Mother Winter made a sour-sounding noise and pointed a finger. A large mug decorated with delicately painted flowers fell from a shelf.

Mother Summer calmly put out a hand, caught it, and returned it to the shelf.

"Oh, uh, Mother Summer," I said, after a moment of silence. "I apologize for intruding into your home."

"Oh, dear, that's very sweet," Mother Summer said. "But you owe me no apology. You were brought here entirely against your will, after all." She paused for a beat and added, "Rudely."

Mother Winter made another displeased sound.

I looked back and forth between them. *Centuries of dysfunction in this family, Harry. Walk carefully.* "I, uh. I think I'd prefer to think of it as a very firm invitation."

"Hah," said Mother Winter, from her hood. Her teeth gleamed. "The Knight knows his loyalties, at least."

Mother Summer somehow managed to inject her voice with profound skepticism. "I'm sure he's overjoyed to owe loyalty to you," she said. "Why did you bring him here now, of all times?"

More teeth showed. "He summoned me, the precious thing."

Mother Summer dropped her herbs. She turned her head toward me, her eyes wide. "Oh," she said. "Oh, dear."

Mother Winter's rocker creaked, though it didn't really seem to move. "He knew certain names. He was not wholly stupid in choosing them, or wholly wrong in using them."

Mother Summer's bright green eyes narrowed. "Did he . . . ?"

"No," croaked Mother Winter. "Not that one. But he has seen the adversary, and learned one of its names."

Calculation and thought flickered through those green eyes, faster than I could follow. "Ah, yes. I see," Mother Summer said. "So many new futures unwinding."

"Too many bright ones," Mother Winter said sullenly.

"Even you must think better that than empty night."

Mother Winter spit to one side.

It started eating a hole in the dirt floor a few inches from one of my feet. I'm not kidding. I took a small sidestep away, and tried not to breathe the fumes.

"I think," Mother Winter said, "that he should be shown."

Mother Summer narrowed her eyes. "Is he ready?"

"There is no time to coddle him," she rasped. "He is a weapon. Let him be made stronger."

"Or broken?" Mother Summer asked.

"Time, time!" Winter breathed. "He is not *your* weapon."

"It is not *your* world," Summer countered.

"Excuse me," I said quietly.

Green eyes and black hood turned toward me.

"I don't want to be rude, ma'am," I said. I picked up the fallen wooden shelf from where I'd knocked it down, and put it back on its pegs. Then I bent and started putting the sealed jars back onto the shelf. "I'm still young. I make mistakes. But I'm not a child, and I'm not letting anyone but me choose which roads I'll walk."

That made Mother Winter cackle again. "Precious little duck," she wheezed. "He means it."

"Indeed," Mother Summer said, but her tone was thoughtful as she watched me restore the fallen shelf to order.

I kept on replacing jars, lining them up neatly, and spoke as gently and politely as I knew how. "You can take my body and run it like a puppet. You can kill me. You can curse me and torture me and turn me into an animal."

"Can," said Mother Winter, "and might, if you maintain this impertinence."

I swallowed and continued. "You can destroy me. But you can't make me *be* anything but what I *choose* to be, ma'am. I don't know exactly what you both are talking about showing me, ma'am. But you aren't going to shove it down my throat or put it up on a shelf out of my reach, either one. I decide for myself, or I walk out the door."

"Oh, will you?" said Mother Winter in a low, deadly whisper. Her overlong nails scraped at the wood on her chair's arms. "Is that what you think, my lamb?"

Mother Summer arched an eyebrow and eyed Mother Winter. "You test his defiance against his very life, and yet when he passes you are surprised he does not leap to do your bidding?" She made another disapproving clucking sound. "He is brave. And he is courteous. I will show him what you ask—if he is willing."

Winter bared her teeth and spit again, into the same hole, and more earth hissed and melted away. She started rocking back and forth, slowly, and turned her gaze elsewhere.

I picked up the last fallen pot and was about to put it away when I frowned. "Oh. I'm sorry, but there's a crack in this one."

I never heard or saw any movement, but suddenly Mother Summer was there beside me, and her bony, capable hands were wrapping warmly around mine. Her touch was like Lily's but . . . gentler and more vast. It made me think of miles and miles of prairie soaking up the summer sun's heat, storing it through the day, only to give it back to the air in the long hours of twilight.

As gently as if handling a newborn, she took the little clay pot from me and turned it slowly in her fingers, examining it. Then she exhaled slowly, closed her eyes for a moment, and then put it reverently back onto the shelf.

When she took her hands from the little pot, I saw letters written in silvery light upon it and upon neighboring pots, as if the letters had been awakened by the warmth of her hands.

The writing on the cracked pot said simply, *Wormwood.*

The letters began to fade, but I saw some of the others: *Typhos. Pox. Atermors. Choleros. Malaros.*

Typhus. Smallpox. The Black Death. Cholera. Malaria.

And Wormwood.

And there were *lots* of other jars on the shelf.

My hands started shaking a little.

"It is not yet the appointed time for that one to be born," Mother Summer said quietly, and her hard eyes flicked toward Mother Winter.

She didn't look back toward us, but her teeth gleamed from within her hood.

Mother Summer slipped her hand through my arm. I gave it to her more or less out of reflex, and walked across the cottage. She picked up her basket and then we went to the door. I opened it for her and offered her my arm again, and we walked together out of the cottage and into a modest clearing surrounded by ancient forest with trees the size of redwoods. They blazed with the colors of fall, their leaves carpeting the forest floor in glorious fire as far as the eye could see. It was gorgeous, but it wasn't anywhere on Earth.

"I think she likes you, young man."

"Yes, ma'am," I said. "I could tell, because of the cleaver."

"It is her way," Mother Summer said, smiling. "She rarely leaves our cottage anymore. She lost her walking stick. While your summons was impertinent, it was a necessity and you had the right. But it is terribly painful for her to travel, even briefly. You, a mortal, hurt her."

Mother Summer's words made the whole chopped-up-for-stew-meat situation more understandable. Beings like Mother Winter tormented mortals—not the other way around. I'd injured her pride along with the rest of her, and in the supernatural world such insults were rarely forgiven and never forgotten.

"She was balancing the scales," I said quietly. "Is that what you mean?"

Mother Summer nodded approval. "You phrase it simply, but not incorrectly." She stopped and turned to look up at me. "She cannot take you to the places we must walk if you are to understand."

"Understand what?" I asked.

Her green eyes reflected the colors of the autumn forest. "What is at stake," she said. "If you choose to walk with me, what is seen cannot be unseen, and what is known cannot be unknown. It may harm you."

"Harm me how?" I asked.

"You may never know a night's peace again. Knowledge is power, young man. Power to do good and power to do harm. Some knowledge can hurt. Some can kill."

"What happens if I don't have it?"

Mother Summer smiled, a gentle sadness in her eyes. "You keep the bliss of ignorance—and consign our fates to fickle chance. Do not choose lightly."

I pondered it for, like, ten whole seconds.

I mean, come on.

I'm a freaking *wizard*, people.

"It's better to know than not know," I said quietly.

"Why?" Mother Summer challenged.

"Because you can't truly make a choice without knowledge, ma'am."

"Even if it may haunt you? Harm you? Isolate you?"

I thought about it some more and then said, "Especially then. Show me."

An emotion flickered across Mother Summer's face—gentle pain and regret.

"So be it," she said quietly. "Come with me."

33

I walked into the ancient forest with Mother Summer on my arm, following a wide, meandering footpath.

"Do you mind if I ask you a question while we walk?" Mother Summer asked.

"Not at all, ma'am," I said.

"What do you suppose will happen to you if you do not heed Mab's command?"

"Command?" I asked.

"Don't be coy, child," Mother Summer sniffed. "What my counterpart knows, I know. Mab commanded you to slay Maeve. What do you think will happen if you disobey her?"

I walked for a while before I answered, "It depends whether or not Mab's still around when the smoke clears, I guess," I said. "If she is . . . she'll be upset. I'll wind up like Lloyd Slate. If she isn't . . ."

"Yes?"

"Maeve assumes Mab's mantle and becomes the new Winter Queen."

"Exactly," Mother Summer said. "In time, the difference will hardly show. But in the immediate future . . . how do you think Maeve will treat you?"

I opened my mouth and closed it again. I could imagine that vividly enough—Maeve, high as a kite on her newfound power, giggling and tormenting and killing left and right just because she could do it. Maeve was the sort who lived to pull the wings off of flies.

And I was pretty sure whose wings would be the first to catch her eye.

"Well, crap," I said.

"Quite so," said Mother Summer. "And if you do heed Mab's command?"

"Maeve's mantle gets passed on to someone else," I said. "And if . . . the adversary? Can I say that safely?"

Mother Summer smiled. "That's why we use that word rather than a name, Sir Knight. Yes."

"If the adversary has taken Mab," I said, "then it gets to choose an agent to take the Winter Lady's mantle. Two-thirds of the Winter Court will be under its influence." I looked back toward the cottage. "And that seems like it might be bad for Mother Winter."

"Indeed," said Mother Summer. "We are all vulnerable to those who are close to us."

"I never figured Granny Cleaver was close to anyone, ma'am."

The lines at the corners of Mother Summer's eyes deepened. "Oh, she . . . What is the phrase? She talks a good game. But in her own way, she cares."

I may have arched a skeptical eyebrow. "Kind of like how, in her own way, she likes me?" I asked.

Mother Summer didn't answer that, as our steps carried us into a more deeply shadowed section of the forest. "It is at times very difficult to be so closely interwoven with mortals," she said.

"For you?"

"For all of Faerie," she replied.

"What do you mean?"

She gestured at herself. "We appear much as humans, do we not? Most of our folk do—or else they resemble another creature of the mortal world. Hounds, birds, stags, and so forth."

"Sure," I said.

"You are endlessly fascinating. We conceive our children with mortals. We move and sway in time to the mortal seasons. We dance to mortal music, make our homes like mortal dwellings, feast upon mortal foods. We find parts of ourselves becoming more like them, and yet we are not like them. Many of the things they think and feel, and a great many of their actions, are inexplicable to us."

"We don't really understand ourselves all that well yet," I said. "I think it would be very difficult for you to do it."

Mother Summer smiled at me, and it felt like the first warm day of spring. "That's true, isn't it?"

"But you've got a point to make, ma'am," I said. "Or you wouldn't have brought up the subject."

"I do," she said. "Winter is cold, Sir Knight, but never so cold that it freezes the heart altogether."

"You've got to have a heart before it can freeze, ma'am."

"You do."

I walked for a little while, considering that. "You're saying that I have a chance to stay me."

"I'm saying many things," Mother Summer said. "Do you have a chance to remain yourself despite the tendency of the mantle to mold your thoughts and desires? All Knights, Winter and Summer, have that chance. Most fail."

"But it's possible," I said.

She looked up at me and her eyes were deeper than time. "Anything is possible."

"Ah," I said, understanding. "We're not really talking about me."

"We are," she said serenely, turning her eyes away. "And we are not."

"Uh," I said. "I'm getting a little confused here. What are we talking about, exactly?"

Mother Summer smiled at me.

And then she just clammed up.

We *are*? We're *not*?

I kept a straight face while my inner Neanderthal spluttered and then went on a mental rampage through a hypothetical produce section, knocking over shelves and splattering fruit everywhere in sheer frustration, screaming, "JUST TELL ME WHOSE SKULL TO CRACK WITH MY CLUB, DAMMIT!"

Flippin' *faeries*. They will be the death of me.

"In the spirit of balanced scales," I said, "would it be all right if I asked you a question, ma'am?"

"I welcome the question. I make no promises as to the answer."

I nodded. "Who are you, really?"

Mother Summer stopped in her tracks and turned to look at me. Her eyebrows slowly lifted. "That is a very significant question."

"I know," I said. "Blame it on Halloween."

"Why should I do that?"

I shrugged, and we began walking again. "It's just got me thinking: masks. I know of one figure from ancient tales who is alive and well and incognito. Why shouldn't there be more?"

Mother Summer inclined her head, more a gesture of acknowledgment or admission than agreement. "Things change," she said. "Immortals deal poorly with change. But it comes to everyone."

"I called Mother Winter by the names Athropos and Skuld because they seemed to fit her," I said. "I mean, she likes her sharp implements, apparently."

Mother Summer's smile appeared for a moment, dazzling me, and then was gone again. "It was not an imbecilic guess," she said. "And, yes, she has been known by such names before. But you've only guessed the name of one of her masks—not our most powerful name."

"Our?" I said. "Wait. I'm confused."

"I know," she said. "Here we are."

We stopped in the middle of a forest path that didn't look any different from anything around it. Mother Summer stopped and frowned at me. "You really aren't dressed for the climate."

"Don't worry about it," I said. "I can handle cold."

She let go of my arm, looked me up and down, then put a hand on the handle of the basket she carried over one arm and said, "Something a little less . . . informal would be appropriate, I think."

I've played Ken doll to a faerie fashion adviser before, so I wasn't entirely shocked when my clothing began to writhe and simply *change*. When the Leanansidhe had done it, I'd sat in the car for half an hour suffering through one fanciful and undignified outfit after another. Not this time.

My clothes transformed from cloth into custom-fitted steel. Well, probably not steel, but whatever the equivalent was that the Sidhe used in their armor. The armor was plain and functional with no ornaments on it—a breastplate, vambraces, and large pauldrons for my shoulders. Heavy tassets hung from the bottom of the breastplate, protecting my thighs. My lower legs were covered with greaves, front and back. The armor was black and gleaming, and where light fell directly on it, you could see shades of deep purple and dark blue.

I realized that I was holding a helmet under my left arm, and I took it in both hands to look at it. It was a Corinthian helm, like they wore in that movie about the Spartans, only without the fancy tail. It was padded on the inside. I slipped it on, and it fit perfectly.

"Much better," said Mother Summer. "Stay near me at all times."

I looked around the perfectly serene forest. It was a bit of an effort, since the helmet kept me from turning my head very smoothly. I looked up, too. I'm sure the armor made me look goofy. "Uh, okay."

Mother Summer smiled, took my arm again, and stretched out one foot. She used it to brush a layer of dirt and fallen leaves from the pitted surface of a flat stone, like a paving stone, maybe three feet square. She tapped it three times with her foot, whispered a word, and drew me along with her as she stepped onto it.

No drama ensued. The landscape simply changed, as swiftly and drastically as when you turn on a light while in a darkened room. One second we stood in an autumnal megaforest. The next . . .

I've seen movies and newsreels about World War I. They didn't cover it as thoroughly in my schools, because America didn't have a leading role in it, and because the entire stupid, avoidable mess was a Continental clusterfuck that killed millions and settled nothing but the teams for the next world war. But what they did show me I remembered. Miles and miles of trenches. A smoke-haunted no-man's-land strung with muddy, rusty barbed wire and lined with machine guns and marksmen. There was a pall of smoke that turned the sun into a dully glowing orb.

But the movies couldn't cover all the senses. There was a constant rumble in the sky, thunder born of violence, and there was everywhere the smell of feces and death.

We stood atop a small, barren mountain, looking down. Near us, only a few hundred yards away, was an immense wall, the kind you'd use to hold out the Mongols if they were the size of King Kong. It was built entirely from ice or some kind of translucent crystal. Even from here, I could see that there were chambers and rooms in the wall, rooms containing barracks, hospitals, kitchens, you name it. There were dim and indistinct forms moving around in them.

The walls were lined with what had to be tens of thousands if not hundreds of thousands of soldiers. I peered, trying to get a better look, and then realized that they were armored Sidhe.

All of them.

They all wore armor similar to mine, its highlights throwing back the cool, muted shades of Winter.

Out beyond the wall was a land made of dust and mud and loose shale. It was covered in hillocks and steep gullies, and the only plants that grew there looked like they were certain to poke, scratch, or sting you. Though the land was somehow lit, the sky was as black as Cat Sith's conscience, without a single star or speck of light to be seen—and it was an overwhelming sky, enormous, like in the open, rolling lands of Montana and Wyoming.

There were more bodies of troops moving out there. Some of them looked like they might have been giants, or maybe trolls. Larger groups containing smaller individuals were likely Winter's gnomes. Things flew in the air. Bands of what appeared to be mounted cavalry rode back and forth. Some of the soldiers looked suspiciously like animated snowmen.

From this vantage point, I could see two major engagements happening, each containing maybe forty thousand Winter troops. And they were fighting. . . .

I couldn't make out the enemy. There didn't seem to be any unity of form. They were creatures—creatures whose physiologies made no sense, were utterly without order. I saw what appeared to be tentacles, enormous mandibles, claws, fangs, clublike limbs and tails. They weren't bipedal. They weren't quadrupeds. In fact, they seemed to have no regard for bilateral symmetry at all.

I peered a little closer and felt a sudden, horrible pressure inside my head. I felt dizzy for a second, nauseated, and at the same time part of me was screaming that I needed to ditch my escort and go look at these things for myself, that there was something there, something I wanted to see, something I wanted to stare at for a while. A cold, somehow greasy tendril of energy slithered around inside my head, something I had felt before when . . .

I jerked my eyes away with a short grunt of effort, closed them, and left them closed. "Holy . . . Outsiders? Mab's fighting *Outsiders?*"

Mother Summer said nothing.

"I don't . . . I don't understand," I said finally. "White Council intelligence always estimated Mab's troop count at around fifty thousand. There are freaking formations out there with more troops in them than that."

Mother Summer said nothing. But she did lift a finger and point off to the left. I looked, and saw a pair of towers the size of the Chrysler Building rising up over the wall. Between them was a pair of gates.

The gates were something amazing to look at. They were huge, bigger than most Chicago apartment buildings. They were made of a darker shade of the same ice or crystal, and there were designs and sigils carved into them, layer after layer after layer. I recognized a couple of the ones I could see clearly. They were wards, protective enchantments.

There was a sudden sound, a rising moan, like the wind shaking trees or surf striking a cliff wall—and the horizon outside the walls was suddenly lined with dark, grotesque figures, all of them charging forward, toward the Winter troops.

Faint horn calls sounded, clear and valiant. Winter's troops began to retreat back toward the gates, gathering into a great arch on the ground outside them, locking their formation into place while cavalry harassed the oncoming Outsiders, slowing their advance. Then the cavalry streaked from their engagement, passing safely through the lines of infantry to come riding back through the gates.

The Outsiders came on and crashed against the Winter lines. Battle ensued. From this far away, it just looked like a big, confusing mess, with everyone jostling for a better position, but I could see a few things. I saw an ogre go down when an Outsider spit acid that started eating through his eyes into his skull. I saw the Winter lines falter, and the Outsiders began pouring reinforcements into the weakness.

Then a small crew of goblins exploded out of a pile of shale at precisely the right moment, when the Outsiders were pressed almost into the Winter lines, but before reinforcements arrived. The surprise attack drove the Outsiders forward, when I could see that the "weak" regiment had been playing the Outsiders for suckers, falling back, but doing so in good order. The Outsiders had overreached themselves, and were now surrounded on all four sides by the savage troops of Winter.

The would-be invaders didn't make it.

And that was only a tiny fraction of the battle. My senses and mind alike simply could not process everything I was seeing. But my heart was beating very swiftly, and frozen fear had touched my spine like Mab's fingers.

The Outsiders wanted *in*.

"When?" I asked. "When did this start?"

"Oh, Harry," Mother Summer said gently.

"What?" I asked. But I had noticed something. Those layers and mounds of shale? They weren't shale.

They were bones.

Millions and millions and millions of fucktons of bones.

"What the hell is going on here?" I breathed. "Where are we?"

"The edge of Faerie," she said. "Our outer borders. It would have taken you a decade to learn to travel out this far."

"Oh," I said. "And . . . and it's like this?"

"In essence," Mother Summer said. She stared sadly out over the plain. "Did you think Mab spent all her days sitting in her chair and dealing with her backstabbing courtiers? No, Sir Knight. Power has purpose."

"What happens if they get in?" I asked.

Mother Summer's lips thinned. "Everything stops. Everything."

"Holy crap," I muttered. "Does Summer have a place like this, too, then?"

Mother Summer shook her head. "That was never its task. Your Council's estimate was fairly close, counting only those troops protecting the hearts of Winter and Summer. Mab has more than that. She needs them—for this."

I felt like I'd been hit repeatedly in the head with a rubber hammer. "So . . . Mab's troops outnumber yours by a jillion."

"Indeed."

"So she could run you over at any time."

"She could," Mother Summer said, "if she were willing to forfeit reality."

I scanned the length of the wall nervously. It looked like it went on forever—and there was fighting all along its length.

"You're telling me that *this* is why Mab has her power? To . . . to protect the borders?"

"To protect all of you from the Outsiders, mortal."

"Then why does Titania have hers?" I asked.

"To protect all of you from Mab."

I swallowed.

"Titania cannot match Mab's forces, but she can drag Mab personally into oblivion with her—and Mab knows it. Titania is the check to her power, the balance."

"If Mab dies . . ." I began.

She swept a hand along the length of the wall. "A spoiled, sadistic, murderous, and inexperienced child will have control of all of that."

Hell's bells. I rubbed at my eyes, and as I did, I connected some dots and realized something else.

"This is a siege," I said. "Those guys out there are attacking the walls. But there are others trying to dig their way in so that they can open the gates for their buddies. That's what the adversary *is*. Right? A sapper, an infiltrator."

Mother Summer said, "There, you see? You possess the potential to be quite intelligent. Do stay beside me, dear." And she started walking firmly toward the massive gates.

It didn't take us long to get there, but as we came up to the base of the wall and walked along it, we started drawing the eyes of the wall's defenders. I felt myself growing tenser as a marching column of armored Sidhe soldiers came stepping lightly along the ground behind us, catching up quickly.

Mother Summer guided me slightly aside so that we weren't in the column's way, and they started going by us. I didn't think much of it until someone at the front of the column called out in a clear voice, and as one the Sidhe came to a halt with a solid, simultaneous stomp of a couple of hundred boots. The voice barked another command, and the Sidhe all turned to face us.

"Uh-oh," I said.

Mother Summer touched my hand with hers, and reassurance bathed me like June sunshine. "Shhh."

The voice barked another command, and as one the Sidhe lowered themselves to one knee and bowed their heads.

"Good morrow, cousins," Mother Summer said, her voice solemn. She took her hand off my arm and passed it in a broad, sweeping arch over the kneeling soldiers. Subtle, *subtle* power thrummed delicately in the air. "Go forth with my blessing."

One of the soldiers in the lead of the column rose and bowed to her, somehow conveying gratitude. Then he snapped out another loud command, and the column rose, turned, and continued its quickstep march.

"Huh," I said.

"Yes?" asked Mother Summer.

"I was sort of expecting . . . something else."

"Winter and Summer are two opposing forces of our world," she said. "But we are *of* our world. Here, that is all that matters. And showing respect to one's elders is never unwise."

"Yes, ma'am," I said.

Mother Summer gave me a small, shrewd smile.

We continued our walk in their wake, and soon reached the gates. There I saw a smaller set of gates—sally ports—built into the main gates. They were the size of the garage doors on a fire station. As I watched, someone shouted a command and a pair of heavily armored ogres each grabbed one of the sally ports and drew it open. The column that had passed us stood waiting to march out, but they did not immediately proceed. Instead, a column of carts and litters entered, bearing the groaning wounded of the fighting outside, being watched over by several dozen

Sidhe dressed in pure white armor, marked with bold green and scarlet trim—Sidhe knights of Summer. Medics. Despite the massive numbers of troops I'd seen moving around, there were fewer than a hundred casualties brought back to the gates. Evidently the Outsiders were not in the business of leaving enemies alive behind them.

A lean figure came down a stairway built within the walls framing the gates, at first a shadowy blur through the layers and layers of crystal. He was a couple of inches taller than me, which put him at the next-best thing to seven feet, but he moved with a brisk, bustling sense of energy and purpose. He wore a dark robe that looked black at first, but as he emerged into the light, highlights showed it to be a deep purple. He carried a long pale wizard's staff in one weathered hand, and his hood covered up most of his face, except for part of an aquiline nose and a long chin covered in a grizzled beard.

He spoke to the Summer and Winter Sidhe alike in a language I didn't understand but they evidently did, giving instructions to Summer's medics. They took his orders with a kind of rigid, formal deference. He leaned over to scan each of the fallen closely, nodding at the medics after each, and they would immediately carry the wounded Sidhe in question back behind the wall, into what looked like a neat triage area.

"Rashid," I murmured, recognizing the man. "What is he doing here—"

I froze and stared up at the massive gates rising above us.

Rashid, a member of the Senior Council of the White Council of Wizards, had another title, the name he went by most often.

The Gatekeeper.

He finished with the last of the wounded, then turned and approached us with long, purposeful strides. He paused a few steps away and bowed to Mother Summer, who returned the gesture with a deep, formal nod of her head. Then he came the rest of the way to me, and I could see the gleam of a dark eye inside his hood. His smile was wide and warm, and he extended his hand to me. I took it and shook it, feeling a little overwhelmed.

"Well, well," he said. His voice was a deep, warm thing, marked with an accent that sounded vaguely British seasoned with plenty of more exotic spices. "I had hoped we would see your face again, Warden."

"Rashid," I replied. "Uh . . . we're . . . they're . . ."

The Gatekeeper's smile turned a bit rueful. "Ah, yes," he said. "They're impressive the first time, I suppose. Welcome, Warden Dresden, to the Outer Gates."

34

"The Outer Gates aren't real," I said numbly. "They're a . . . They're supposed to be a metaphor."

Mother Summer smiled very faintly. "I'll leave mortal business to mortals," she said. "I'll be nearby, young wizard."

"Um," I said. "Thank you."

She nodded and walked away toward the wounded Sidhe.

"Well," the Gatekeeper said to me. He seemed . . . if not precisely cheerful, it was something that lived on the same block—positive, confident, and strong. "You've managed to travel a very long way from home."

"Mother Summer drove," I said.

"Ah," he said. "Still, I can't recall the last time a wizard of your age managed the trip, however it was done. You take after your mother."

I blinked. "You knew her?"

"Those of us who spend any amount of time walking the Ways tend to develop a certain amount of camaraderie. We would have dinner every so often, compare notes of our walks. And there were several of us who were friends of Ebenezar who . . . took it upon ourselves to watch over her."

I nodded, keeping my face as blank as I could. It was not general knowledge that Maggie LeFey had been Ebenezar's daughter. If Rashid knew, it was because my grandfather trusted him.

The fresh armored column of Sidhe began to move out, and as they did, horns began to call in the land beyond. Rashid turned his head toward them, listening as if to a spoken language, and the smile faded from his mouth.

"They're massing again," he said. "I have little time." He reached up and did something I'd seen him do only once before.

The Gatekeeper lowered his hood.

He had short hair that was still thick and gleamed silver, but his features were weathered, as if from long years under harsh sunlight. His skin was paler now, but there was still something of the desert on his skin. His face was long, his brows still dark and full. He had a double scar on his left eyebrow and cheek, two long lines that went straight down, a lot like mine, only deeper and thicker and all the way to his jawline, and they were much softer with long years of healing. Maybe he hadn't been as good at flinching as I was, because he'd lost the eye beneath the scar. One of his eyes was nearly black, it was so dark. The other had been replaced with . . .

I looked around me. Yes, definitely. The other eye had been replaced with the crystalline material that was identical to that which had been used to create the gates and the walls around them.

"Steel," I said.

"Pardon?" he asked.

"Your, uh, other eye. It was steel before."

"I'm sure it looked like steel," he said. "The disguise is necessary when I'm not here."

"Your job is so secret, your false *eye* gets a disguise?" I asked. "Guess I see why you miss Council meetings."

He inclined his head and ruffled his fingers through mussed, tousled hood-hair. "It can be quiet for years here, sometimes. And others . . ." He spread his hands. "But they need a good eye here to be sure that the things that must remain outside do not slip in unnoticed."

"Inside the wounded," I guessed. "Or returning troops. Or medics."

"You've become aware of the adversary," he said, his tone one of firm approval. "Excellent. I was certain your particular pursuits would get you killed long before you got a chance to learn."

"How can I help?" I asked him.

He leaned his head back and then a slow smile reasserted itself on his face. "I know something of the responsibilities you've chosen to take up," he said, "to say nothing of the problems you've created for yourself that you haven't found out about yet. And still, in the face of learning that our world spins out its days under siege, you offer to help me? I think you and I could be friends."

"Wait," I said. "What problems? I haven't been trying to create problems."

"Oh," he said, waving a hand. "You've danced about in the shadows at the edge of life now, young man. That's no small thing, to go into those shadows and come back again—you've no idea the kind of attention you've attracted."

"Oh," I said. "Good. Because the pace was starting to slow down so much that I was getting bored."

At that, Rashid tilted his head back and laughed. "Would you be offended if I called you Harry?"

"No. Because it's my name."

"Exactly," he said. "Harry, I know you have questions. I can field a very few before I go."

I nodded, thinking. "Okay," I said. "First, how do you know if the adversary has . . . infested someone?"

"Experience," he said. "Decades of it. The Sight can help, but . . ." Rashid hesitated. I recognized it instantly, the hiccup in one's thoughts when one stumbled over a truly hideous memory gained with the Sight, like I'd had with—

Ugh.

—the naagloshii.

"I don't recommend making a regular practice of it," he continued. "It's an art, not a skill, and it takes time. Time, or a bit of questionable attention from the Fates and a ridiculously enormous tool." He tapped a finger against his false eye.

I blinked, even though he didn't, and looked up at the massive gates stretching overhead. "Hell's bells. The gates . . . they're . . . some kind of spiritual CAT scanner?"

"Among many other things," he said. "But it's one of their functions, yes. Mostly it means that the adversary cannot use such tactics effectively here. As long as the Gatekeeper is vigilant, it rarely tries." The horns sounded again, and the muscles in his jaw tensed. "Next question."

I hate trying to be smart under time pressure. "This," I said, pointing up at the gates. "What the hell? How long has this attack been going on?"

"Always," he said. "There are always Outsiders trying to tear their way in. There are always forces in place to stop them. In our age, it is the task of Winter to defend these boundaries, with the help of certain others to support them. Think of them as . . . an immune system for the mortal world."

I felt my eyes get wide. "An immune system . . . What happens if it . . . you know, if it breaks down for a bit?"

"Pardon?" the Gatekeeper asked.

"Uh, it gets a glitch. Like, if somebody new took over or something and things had to reorganize around here . . ."

"Most years, it would pose no major difficulty," he said.

"What about this year?"

"This year," he said, "it could be problematic."

"Problematic."

"Rather severely so." Rashid studied my face and then started to nod. "I see. There are things happening back in Winter. That's why Mother Summer brought you here. To show you what was at stake."

I swallowed and nodded. "No pressure or anything."

Rashid's face reacted at that. I couldn't say what the exact mix of emotion on it was, though one of them was a peculiar kind of empathy. He set his staff aside and gripped my upper arms with his hands. "Listen to me, because this is important."

"Okay," I said.

"You get used to it," he said.

I blinked. "What? That's it?"

He tilted his head to look at me obliquely with his good eye.

"I'll get used to it? That's the important pep talk? I'll get used to it?"

His mouth quivered. He gave my arms a last, maybe affectionate squeeze and released them. "Pep? What is needed in the Warden is far more than *pep*, Harry."

"What, then?" I asked.

He took up his staff and poked my chest with it gently. "You, it would seem."

"What?"

"You," he repeated firmly. "What we need is *you*. You have what you have for a reason. Unwitting or not, virtually your every action in the past few years has resulted in a series of well-placed thumbs in the adversary's eye. You want to know how you can help me, Harry?"

"Engh," I said, frustrated. "Yeah."

"Go back to Chicago," he said, turning away, "and keep being yourself."

"Wait," I said. "I need *help*."

At that, he paused. He looked back at me and gave me a quiet smile. "I know precisely how it feels to be where you are." He gestured back toward the battleground. "Precisely." He seemed to think about it for a moment, and then nodded. "I will do what I can. If we both survive the next several hours, I will settle matters between you and the Council, which knows only as much about our roles as it needs to—and that isn't much. I will verify your return and that you are indeed yourself, and will see to it that your back pay as one of the Wardens is forwarded to you. There's some paperwork to fill out to get the Council's office to reestablish your official identity with the government, but I'll see to it that it happens. I think I remember all the necessary forms."

I stared at him for a second and said, "You'll . . . you'll help me with White Council *paperwork*."

He held up a finger. "Do not underestimate the depth of this favor," he said soberly, but his eye was twinkling. "And on a similar note, do not underestimate yourself. You haven't been given the power and the knowledge and allies and the resources you possess for no reason, Harry. Nothing I have to say can possibly make this task any easier for you. The only way to do it is to do it." He lifted his chin. "You don't need help, Warden. You *are* the help."

"We're in trouble," I said.

He winked at me, restored his hood to its usual position, and said, "We always are. The only difference is, now you know it. God be with you, my friend. I will cover this end. You see to yours."

He took several rapid paces out from under the towering gates and gestured. A second later, I kid you not, a freaking woven carpet, maybe ten feet by twenty, came sailing neatly down out of the sky, coming to hover about six inches off the ground beside him. Rashid stepped onto the carpet, slipped his boots into some kind of securing straps on it, and then lifted his staff. The carpet and the Gatekeeper rose serenely up out of sight, and a second later went streaking out over the storm-lit battle-field in a howl of whirling winds.

And that's when it hit me. I mean, when it really, really hit me.

It was up to me.

There wasn't a backup plan. There wasn't a second option. There wasn't any cavalry coming over the hill. The White Council was the next-best thing to clueless about what was happening, and would never in a zillion years admit that they were.

Tonight, a catastrophe that could kill millions of people, including my daughter, was going to happen unless I stopped it. And on top of that, there was a deadly turbulence happening inside the Winter Court, and depending on which side I threw in on, I could save or destroy the world as we knew it. Walking away from this one was not an option.

No dodges, no delays, no excuses. It would happen or it wouldn't, depending on me.

I looked down at my bruised hands. I slowly closed them into fists and then opened them again. They were battered hands, and they didn't have anywhere near as much skill as I could have wished were in them—but they were what I had. I had earned the scars on them. They were mine.

I'd done this before. Never on this scale, maybe, but I'd done it before. I'd saved the day, mostly, more or less, on several occasions. I'd done it before, and I could do it again.

There wasn't any other way it was going to happen.

The only good thing about having your back to the wall is that it makes it really easy to choose which way you're going to go.

I felt like throwing up. But I stiffened my back and straightened my shoulders and walked quickly over to Mother Summer as she finished standing up from tending to the last of the wounded Sidhe.

"Ma'am," I said quietly. "I'd appreciate it if you could take me home. I have work to do."

35

With all the benevolence she'd had going on, I sort of forgot that Mother Summer wasn't human. She took me from the gates back to her cottage in silence, smiled, touched my head with her hand—and sent me back to my freaking grave.

I landed on my ass in the muddy broken ice—and could still hear the echoes of the crackling detonation when Mother Winter's ugly mitt had smashed up through it and grabbed my noggin. I could still hear the raucous cawing of startled crows. Time had all but stopped while I was gone—or, more accurately, time had flown by extremely swiftly where I had been, in the Nevernever, relative to Chicago. I'd been on the other side of that kind of time dilation while dealing with beings of Faerie before, but this was the first time I'd actually benefited from it, gaining time rather than losing it.

Which I hadn't even considered until now. If things had gone the way they usually did when one got pulled into Faerie business, I could have been gone for an hour and come back a year later, to what would presumably have been a blasted wasteland. The thought made my stomach churn with anxiety.

But I suppose I hadn't exactly volunteered for the trip. It wasn't like I'd taken a hideous risk on that score—it had been something entirely outside of my control.

That was scary, too.

While I was sitting there wondering whether that meant that I was a control freak or just sane, a Goth kid poked her head into view atop my grave and peered down at me. She took a cigarette in one of those long holders out of her mouth, exhaled smoke through her nose, and said, "Dude. That is pretty hard-core down there. Are you, like, gonna cut yourself or something?"

"No," I said, self-consciously hiding my hand behind my back. I looked down and only then did I realize that my outfit had changed from the Sidhe armor back to the secondhand clothes I'd been wearing before. "I fell."

Other Gothlings appeared. The girl repeated herself, and the others agreed that I was hard-core down there.

I sighed. I gathered my things and clambered out with some reluctantly offered help. I didn't need it, but I thought it might be good for some kid's self-esteem. Then I looked around at all the people staring at me, hunched my shoulders up around my head, and hurried out of the graveyard before anyone else could become helpful.

When I got back to Molly's place, she asked, "Why do you smell like cloves?"

"Kids today," I said. "I'm just glad they weren't smoking marijuana."

"Ah," Molly said. "Goths. So I guess that's grave dirt on you?"

"Stop Sherlocking me," I said. "And, yes, it is, and I'm showering. Any word?"

"Not yet," Molly said. "Toot's waiting outside for his crew to get back. I had to promise him extra pizza to keep him from going out to look himself. I figured we needed him to coordinate the guard."

"Good thinking," I said. "One sec."

I went into my temporary quarters and got clean. It wasn't just because I had mud from a century-old graveyard on me, along with an open wound on my hand, and because I feared about a million horrible things that could be made from those ingredients. The whole wizard-metabolism thing means that our immune systems are pretty much top-of-the-line. I doubted the Winter Knight's mantle was slouchy in defending against such mundane threats, either.

It was mostly because I'd been up close and personal with some extremely powerful creatures, and such beings radiate magic like body heat. It's the sort of thing that can cling to you if you aren't careful, maybe coloring the way you think a bit, and definitely having the potential to influence anything you do with magic. (It happens with people, too, but with people, even wizards, their aura is so much less powerful that the effect is negligible.) Running water cleanses away the residue of that kind of contact, and I wanted to be sure that whatever happened tonight, I wasn't going to be handicapped by any mystic baggage from today's visits.

I hit the shower, bowing my head under the hot water, and thought about things. The Mothers had been trying to tell me something, something they hadn't said outright. Maybe they hadn't wanted to just give me what I wanted—but, way more likely, maybe they were incapable of it.

I had bullied Maeve and Lily into straight talk, such as it had been, and it had obviously been uncomfortable for them. I would never have tried the same thing on Titania or Mab. For whatever reason, it seemed that the essential nature of the Queens of Faerie was to be as indirect and oblique about things as possible. It was built into them, along with things like not being able to tell a direct lie. It was who they were. And the farther up the chain you went, the more steeped in that essential nature the Queens became. Maybe Titania or Mab could be a little bit straightforward at times, but I doubt they could have laid out a simple declarative statement about the issue at hand without a major effort. And if that was true, then maybe the Mothers couldn't have done it even if they *wanted* to.

There'd been a message in all their talk, especially Mother Summer's. But what the hell had it been?

Or maybe this wasn't a human-faerie translation problem at all. Maybe this was a male-female translation problem. I read an article once that said that when women have a conversation, they're communicating on five levels. They follow the conversation that they're actually having, the conversation that is specifically being avoided, the tone being applied to the overt conversation, the buried conversation that is being covered only in subtext, and finally the other person's body language.

That is, on many levels, astounding to me. I mean, that's like having a freaking superpower. When I, and most other people with a Y chromosome, have a conversation, we're having a conversation. Singular. We're paying attention to what is being said, considering that, and replying to it. All these other conversations that have apparently been going on for the last several thousand years? I didn't even know that they *existed* until I read that stupid article, and I'm pretty sure I'm not the only one.

I felt somewhat skeptical about the article's grounding. There were probably a lot of women who didn't communicate on multiple wavelengths at once. There were probably men who could handle that many just fine. I just wasn't one of them.

So, ladies, if you ever have some conversation with your boyfriend or husband or brother or male friend, and you are telling him something perfectly obvious, and he comes away from it utterly clueless? I know it's tempting to think to yourself, "The man can't possibly be that stupid!"

But yes. Yes, he can.

Our innate strengths just aren't the same. We are the mighty hunters, who are good at focusing on one thing at a time. For crying out loud, we have to turn down the radio in the car if we suspect we're lost and need to figure out how to get where we're going. That's how impaired we are. I'm telling you, we have only the one conversation. Maybe some kind of relationship veteran like Michael Carpenter can do two, but that's pushing the envelope. Five simultaneous conversations? *Five?*

Shah. That just isn't going to happen. At least, not for me.

So maybe it was something perfectly obvious and I was just too dumb to get it. Maybe the advice of someone less impaired than me would help. I went back into my head and made sure that I remembered the details of my recent conversations, putting them in order so that I could get a consult.

Once my brain had resolved that, it went straight down a road I'd been trying to detour around.

If I blew it tonight, people I loved were going to die. People who weren't involved in the fight. People like Michael, and his family and . . .

And my daughter, Maggie.

Should I call them? Tell them to hit the road and start driving? Did I have the right to do that, when so many other people's loved ones were at risk, too, with no possible way to get them out of reach of harm? Did that matter?

Was I going to be responsible for my daughter's death, the way I was for her mother's?

The lights didn't waver, but it got really, really dark in that shower for a minute.

And then I shook it off. I didn't have time to waste moaning about my poor daughter and my poor life and, gosh, do I feel bad about the horrible things I've done. I could indulge my self-pity after I'd taken care of business. Scratch that. After I'd taken care of bidness.

I slammed the water off hard enough to make it clack, got out of the shower, dried, and started getting dressed in a fresh set of secondhand clothes.

"Why do you wear those?" asked Lacuna.

I jumped, stumbled, and shouted half of a word to a spell, but since I was only halfway done putting on my underwear, I mostly just fell on my naked ass.

"Gah!" I said. "Don't *do* that!"

My miniature captive came to the edge of the dresser and peered down at me. "Don't ask questions?"

"Don't come in here all quiet and spooky and *scare* me like that!"

"You're six times my height, and fifty times my weight," Lacuna said gravely. "And I've agreed to be your captive. You don't have any reason to be afraid."

"Not *afraid*," I snapped back. "*Startled*. It isn't wise to startle a wizard!"

"Why not?"

"Because of what could happen!"

"Because they might fall down on the floor?"

"No!" I snarled.

Lacuna frowned and said, "You aren't very good at answering questions."

I started shoving myself into my clothes. "I'm starting to agree with you."

"So why do you wear those?"

I blinked. "Clothes?"

"Yes. You don't need them unless it's cold or raining."

"You're wearing clothes."

"I am wearing armor. For when it is raining arrows. Your T-shirt will not stop arrows."

"No, it won't." I sighed.

Lacuna peered at my shirt. "Aer-O-Smith. Arrowsmith. Does the shirt belong to your weapon dealer?"

"No."

"Then why do you wear the shirt of someone else's weapon dealer?"

That was frustrating in so many ways that I could avoid a stroke only by refusing to engage. "Lacuna," I said, "humans wear clothes. It's one of the things we do. And as long as you are in my service, I expect you to do it as well."

"Why?"

"Because if you don't, I . . . I . . . might pull your arms out of your sockets."

At that, she frowned. "Why?"

"Because I have to maintain discipline, don't I?"

"True," she said gravely. "But I have no clothes."

I counted to ten mentally. "I'll . . . find something for you. Until then, no desocketing. Just wear the armor. Fair enough?"

Lacuna bowed slightly at the waist. "I understand, my lord."

"Good." I sighed. I flicked a comb through my wet hair, for all the good it would do, and said, "How do I look?"

"Mostly human," she said.

"That's what I was going for."

"You have a visitor, my lord."

I frowned. "What?"

"That is why I came in here. You have a visitor waiting for you."

I stood up, exasperated. "Why didn't you say so?"

Lacuna looked confused. "I did. Just now. You were there." She frowned thoughtfully. "Perhaps you have brain damage."

"It would not shock me in the least," I said.

"Would you like me to cut open your skull and check, my lord?" she asked.

Someone that short should not be that disturbing. "I . . . No. No, but thank you for the offer."

"It is my duty to serve," Lacuna intoned.

My life, Hell's bells. I beckoned Lacuna to follow me, mostly so I would know where the hell she was, and went back out into the main room.

Sarissa was there.

She sat at the kitchen table, her small hands clutched around one of Molly's mugs, and she looked like hell. There was a dark red mouse on her left cheekbone, one that was swelling and beginning to purple nicely. Her hands and forearms were scraped and bruised—defensive injuries. She wore a pale blue T-shirt and dark blue cotton pajama pants. Both were soaked from the rain and clinging in a fashion that made me want to stare. Her dark hair was askew, and her eyes were absolutely haunted. They darted nervously toward me when I appeared, and her shoulders hunched slightly.

Molly said something quiet to her and rose from the table, crossing the room to me.

"She said you knew her," Molly said.

"I do. She all right?"

"She's a mess," Molly said. "Showed up and begged security to call me before they called the cops. And it isn't the first time this has happened to her. She's terrified to be here—terrified of you personally, I think."

I frowned at my apprentice.

Molly shrugged. "Her emotions are *really* loud. I'm not even trying to pick anything up."

"Okay," I said.

"Is she on the level?"

I thought about it for a second before I answered. "She's Mab's BFF."

"So that would be a no, then," Molly said.

"Probably so," I said. "There's bound to be an angle here, even if she doesn't know that there is one. She's a pawn in Winter. Somebody has got to be moving her."

Molly winced.

"She's also a lifelong survivor in Winter, so don't let your guard down.

The last creature who did wound up as frozen kibble." I jerked my head toward the exit. "Heard anything from the scouts yet?"

She shook her head.

"Okay. We'll talk to her. Stay close. I might need to pick your brain about something later."

"Right," Molly said, blinking a little. Then she followed me back over to Sarissa.

She gave me a nervous smile, and her fingers resettled on the mug a couple of times. "Harry."

"I didn't realize you made house calls all the way to Chicago," I said.

"I wish it were that," she said.

I nodded. "How did you know where to find me?"

"I was given directions," she said.

"By who?"

She swallowed and looked down at the tabletop. "The Redcap."

I sat back slowly in my seat. "Maybe you'd better tell me what happened."

"He came for me," she said quietly, without meeting my eyes. "He came this morning. I was hooded, bound, and taken somewhere. I don't know where. I was there for several hours. Then he came back, took my hood off, and sent me here. With this."

She reached down to her lap and put a plain white envelope on the table. She pushed it toward me.

I took it. It wasn't sealed. I opened it, frowned, and then turned it upside down over the table.

Several tufts of hair bound with small bits of string fell out, along with a small metal object.

Molly drew in a sharp breath.

"He said to tell you that he's taken your friends," Sarissa said quietly.

I picked up the tufts of hair one at a time. Wiry black, slightly crinkled hairs, sprinkled with silver ones. Butters. Red hairs, luscious and curly. Andi. And a long, soft, slightly wavy lock of pure white hair. I lifted it to my nose and sniffed. Strawberries. I let out a soft curse.

"Who?" Molly asked, her voice worried.

"Justine," I said.

"Oh, God."

I picked up the metal object. It was a plain bottle cap, slightly dented where it had been removed.

"And Mac," I said quietly. "He had someone following me everywhere I went. He took someone from each place."

"He told me to tell you," Sarissa said, "that he'll trade them all for you, if you surrender to him before sundown."

"And if I don't?" I asked.

"He'll give their bones to the rawhead," she whispered.

36

Silence fell.

"Okay," I said into it. "I've just about had enough of that clown."

Molly looked up at me, her eyes worried. "You sure?"

"Guy gets his jollies dipping his hat in people's blood," I said.

"You can bargain with the Sidhe sometimes," Molly said.

"But not this time," I said, my voice hard. "If we do, he'll keep the letter of his word and he'll make sure they don't make it out anyway. The only way we're getting our friends back is to take them away from him."

Molly grimaced, but after a moment, she nodded.

I picked up the clumps of hair and put them in a neat row on the table. "Molly."

"On it," she said, collecting them.

"What are you doing?" Sarissa asked, her eyes wide.

"The jerk was kind enough to give me some fresh cuttings from my friends," I said. "I'm going to use them to track him down and thwart him."

"Thwart?" Sarissa asked.

"Thwart," I said. "To prevent someone from accomplishing something by means of visiting gratuitous violence upon his smarmy person."

"I'm pretty sure that isn't the definition," Sarissa said.

"It is today." I raised my voice. "Cat Sith. I need your assistance, please."

Sarissa went completely still when I spoke, like a rabbit who has sensed a nearby predator. Her eyes widened, then flicked around the room, seeking escape.

"It's okay," I told her. "I'm getting along with him."

"You're a wizard and the Winter Knight," Sarissa hissed. "You have no idea how vicious that creature is, and I don't have the Queen's aegis protecting me."

"You have mine," I said. I raised my voice, annoyed. "Cat Sith! Kittykittykittykitty!"

"Are you *insane*?" Sarissa hissed.

"He might not be able to get through, Harry," Molly said. "It's not just a threshold here. The svartalves have wards over the building as well."

"Makes sense," I said. "Be right back."

I went out and looked around, but Sith didn't appear. I called his name a third time, which as we all know is the charm. With beings of the Nevernever it's a literal truth. I mean, it's not an irresistible force, like gravity—it's more like a kind of obsessive-compulsive disorder that happens to be present, to varying degrees, in most of them. They respond, strongly, to things that happen in threes, be they requests, insults, or commands. So in a way, three really is a magic number.

Hell. Just ask ménage-à-Thomas. Jerk.

I waited for a while, even going so far as to turn about and take a few steps backward before turning forward again, just to give Sith some really rich opportunities to appear abruptly and startle me.

Except he didn't.

I got a slow, squirmy feeling in the pit of my stomach. The rain was still falling in spits and showers, but the clouds had begun to gain the tint of a slow autumn sundown. Sith had always appeared almost instantly before.

Had Mab been setting me up? Had she given me the eldest malk's assistance so that she could pull the rug out from under me when I needed Sith the most? Had she gotten the Nemesis brainmold?

I hadn't seen Sith since the confrontation at the gardens. Had the enemy Sidhe brought him down?

Or worse, the adversary?

I felt actively sick to my stomach. If Cat Sith had been turned, there was no telling how much damage he might cause. Especially to me.

I felt a little stupid about the kittykittykitty thing. Hopefully, he hadn't been listening.

I went back into the apartment, pensive.

Molly gave me an inquiring look.

I shook my head.

Molly frowned at that; I could see the gears whirling in her brain.

"Okay," I said. "Plan B. Lacuna, come here, if you please."

After a moment, a little voice said from the direction of my room, "What if I don't please?"

"You come here anyway," I stated. "It's a human thing."

She made a disgusted noise and came zipping out of the room on her blurring wings. "What do you want me to do?"

"You can read," I said. "Can you read a map? Write?"

"Yes."

"You're on house duty, then," I said. "If any of the Little Folk come back with a location where a rite is taking place, I want you to write down their descriptions and mark the location on the map. Can you do that?"

Lacuna looked dubiously at the maps spread out on the table. "I think so. Probably. Maybe."

"And no fighting or duels."

"What about when I'm done writing things?"

"No."

Lacuna folded her little arms and scowled at me. "You aren't fun at all."

"Your breath smells like celery," I replied. "Molly, how are those spells coming along?"

"I think there's some kind of counterspell hiding them," she said. "It's tricky, so stop bumping my elbow. I'm concentrating over here."

I let out an impatient breath and fought against a surge of anger. She was the apprentice and I was the wizard. There were wizards who would have beaten unconscious any apprentice who spoke to them like that. I'd always been kind to her—maybe too kind—and this disrespect was what I got in return? I should educate her to respect her betters.

I made a low growling sound in my chest and clenched my fists. That impulse wasn't mine. It was Winter's. Molly and I had a relationship built on structure, trust, and respect—not fear. We had always bantered back and forth like that.

But something in me wanted to . . . I don't know. Put her in her place. Take out my frustrations on her. Show her which of us was the strongest. And it had a really primitive idea of how to make that happen.

But that was unthinkable. That was the mantle talking. Loudly.

Hell's bells. As if I didn't have enough trouble thinking my way past the influence of my own glands already.

I heard a slight sound behind me and turned in time to see Sarissa vanish into the bathroom, moving in absolute silence. The rabbit had given up the statue routine and bolted.

Sarissa had good instincts when it came to predators.

I turned back to Molly to find her looking at me, her eyes wide. Molly was a psychic sensitive. She could feel emotions the way most of us can feel the temperature of a room. Sometimes she could even pluck someone's thoughts out of the air.

She knew exactly what I was feeling. She had all along.

And she hadn't run.

"Are you okay?" she asked quietly.

"It's nothing," I said. I forced myself to think my way past the mantle's influence. "Find a steel needle to use as the focus," I said. "Should give you an edge against whatever magic the Sidhe are using."

"Should have thought of that," Molly chided herself.

"That's why they pay me the big bucks." I turned and walked away from my apprentice to let her work without the distraction of my tangle of Winter's urges blaring into her skull like an airhorn.

I rummaged around in her fridge and made a sandwich from a bagel I split down the middle and a small mountain of two different-colored deli meats. I wolfed it down. Less than five minutes later, Molly tied a needle onto a piece of wood with one of each of the human hairs. She then placed it gently into a bowl of water, and performed the tracking spell without a hitch.

The needle slowly swung around to point east, directly toward my abducted friends. Probably. There were ways to futz about with tracking spells, but it appeared that the addition of steel to our own spell had overcome whatever the Redcap had cooked up. I extended my senses and checked the tracking spell. It was as solid as one of my own.

"Good work," I said. Then I walked over to the bathroom door and knocked gently. "Sarissa," I said. "Can you hear me?"

"Yes," she answered.

"We're going out," I said. "I hope we won't be gone long. You should be safe here, but you're free to leave if you want to do so. I think you might be followed if you do, but you aren't a prisoner or anything. Okay?"

There was a hesitant moment of silence and then she said, "I understand."

"There's food in the fridge," Molly called. "And you can sleep in my room if you're tired. The door has a lock."

There was no answer.

"Let's get moving," I said to Molly. "I want to make a stop before we track them down."

The svartalves' security guy stopped us before we could leave and informed us that my car had been repaired and delivered, and that they would bring it around for me. Molly and I traded a glance.

"Um. How sure are you that the vehicle is secure?" Molly asked.

"Mr. Etri personally requested a security sweep," the guard said. "It's already been screened for weapons, explosives, toxins, and any kind of enchantment, Miss Carpenter. Right now, they're running it under a waterfall to wash away any tracking spells that might be on it. It's the same procedure Mr. Etri uses to secure his own cars, miss."

"Who brought it?" Molly asked.

The guard took a small notebook from his pocket and checked it. "A local mechanic named Mike Atagi. Think there's a picture . . ." He thumbed through the pages, and then held up a color printout that had been folded into the notebook. "This is him."

I leaned forward to peer at the photo. Well, son of a gun. It was my old mechanic, Mike. Mike had been a miracle worker when it came to repairing the *Blue Beetle*, working with a talent that was the next-best thing to sorcery to bring the car back from the dead over and over again.

"Did he say who delivered it to him?" I asked.

The guard checked his notes. "Here. That it was waiting at his shop when he got there, along with a deposit and a rush order, reading, 'Repair this for Harry Dresden and return it to the following address or suffer, mortal smith.'"

"Cat Sith," I said. "Well, at least he was on the job while we were out at the island."

There was a low growling sound and the *Munstermobile* came gliding up out of the parking garage, dripping water from its gleaming surface like some lantern-eyed leviathan rising from the depths. There were still a few dents and dings in it, but the broken glass had all been replaced, and the engine sounded fine.

Okay, I'm not like a car fanatic or anything—but the guitar riff from "Bad to the Bone" started playing in my head.

"Wheels," I said. "Excellent."

The *Munstermobile* came gliding up to us and stopped, still dripping water, and another security guy got out of it, left the driver door open, and came around to open the passenger door for Molly.

I touched Molly's shoulder to stop her from moving to get in immediately, and spoke to her very quietly. "How much do you trust your friend Mr. Etri?"

"Etri might oppose you," Molly said. "He might break your bones. He might cut your throat in your sleep or make the ground swallow you up. But he will never, ever lie about his intentions. He's not a friend, Harry. But he *is* my ally. He's good at it."

I wanted to say something smart-ass about not trusting anyone who lived anywhere near the Faerie realms, but I held back. For one thing, svartalves take paranoia to an art form, and I had no doubt they would be listening to everything everyone said on their own property while not in private quarters. It would have been stupid to insult them. For another thing, they had an absolutely ironclad reputation for integrity and neutrality. No one crossed a svartalf lightly—but on the other hand, the svartalves rarely gave anyone a good *reason* to cross them, either. That garnered them a boatload of respect.

They also had a reputation for rigid adherence to promises, to bargains, and to the law, or at least to the letters it consisted of. "What are the terms of your alliance?" I asked, walking around the car toward the driver side.

"I get the apartment," Molly said. "I mean, it's mine. I own it. They handle any maintenance for the next fifty years, and as long as I'm on their property, they consider me to be a citizen of their nation, with all the rights and privileges that entails."

I whistled as we got in and shut the doors. "And what did you give them for that?"

"Their honor. And there might have been this bomb problem I handled for them."

"Hell's bells," I said. "Look at you, all grown-up."

"You have been," Molly said. "All day."

I tried not to give her a guilty glance as we pulled out. "Um."

"I feel it, you know," she said. "The pressure inside you."

"I've got it buttoned down," I said, and started driving. "Don't worry. I'm not going to let it make me . . . take anything away from you."

Molly folded her hands in her lap, looked down at them, and said in a small voice, "If it's given, freely offered, you can't really take it away. All you're doing is accepting a gift."

Part of me felt like something had torn in my chest, so deep was the ache I felt at the hope, the uncertainty in the grasshopper's voice.

And another part of me wanted to howl and attack her. Take her. Now. It didn't even want to wait to stop the car. If I went purely by the numbers, there was no reason at all not to give in to that urge—except for the car crashing, I mean. Molly was an adult woman now. She was exceptionally attractive. I'd seen her naked once, and she was really good at it. She was willing—eager, even. And I trusted her. I'd taught her a lot over the years, and some of that had been extremely intimate. Master-apprentice relationships were hardly unheard-of in wizarding circles. Some wizards even favored that situation, because on the spooky side, sex can be a whole hell of a lot more dangerous than recreational. They regarded the teaching of physical intimacy as something as inextricably intertwined with magic as it is with life.

It's possible that, from a standpoint of pure, unadulterated reason, they might even have a point.

But there was more to it than reason. I'd known Molly when she was wearing a training bra. I'd hung out in her tree house with her after she'd come home from high school. She was the daughter of the man I respected most in this world and the woman whom I least wanted to cross. I believed that people in positions of authority and influence, especially those in the role of mentor and teacher, had a mountainous level of responsibility to maintain in order to balance out that influence over less experienced individuals.

But mostly, I couldn't do it because Molly had been crushing on me since she was about fourteen years old. She was in love with me, or at least thought she was—and I didn't feel it back. It wouldn't be fair to her to rip her heart out that way. And I would never, ever forgive myself for hurting her.

"It's okay," she almost-whispered. "Really."

There wasn't anything much to say. So I reached over, took her hand, and squeezed gently. After a while, I said, "Molly, I don't think it's ever going to happen. But if it ever does, the first time damned well isn't going to be like that. You deserve better. So do I."

Then I put both hands back on the wheel and kept on driving. I had someone else to pick up before I gave the Redcap my version of a hostage crisis.

We got to Chez Carpenter around five, and I parked the *Munstermobile* on the street. It was the single gaudiest object for five miles in every direction, and it blended in with the residential neighborhood about as well as a goose in a crowd of puffer fish. I turned off the engine and listened to it clicking. I didn't look at the house.

I got out of the car, shut the door, and leaned back against it, still not looking at the house. I didn't need to. I'd seen it often enough. It was a gorgeous Colonial home, complete with manicured landscaping, a pretty green lawn, and a white picket fence.

The grasshopper got out of the car and came around to stand beside me. "Dad's at work. The sandcrawler is gone," Molly noted, nodding toward the driveway where her mother always parked their minivan. "I think Mom was going to take the Jawas trick-or-treating at the Botanic Gardens this afternoon. So the little ones won't be home."

Which was Molly's way of telling me that I didn't have to face my daughter right now, and I could stop being a coward.

"Just go get him," I said. "I'll wait here."

"Sure," she said.

Molly went up to the front door and knocked. About two seconds after she did that, something huge slammed against the other side of the door. The heavy door jumped in its frame. Dust fell from the roof over the porch, dislodged by the impact. Molly stiffened and backed away. A second later, there was another thump, and another, and the sound of the frantic scratching of claws on the door. Then more thumping.

I hurriedly crossed the street to stand beside Molly on the lawn, facing the front door.

The door wiggled, then opened unsteadily, as if being manipulated by someone with his hands full. Then the storm door flew open and something grey and shaggy and enormous shot out onto the porch. It cleared the porch railing in a single bound, hurtled across the ground and the little picket fence, and hit me in the chest like a battering ram.

My dog, Mouse, is a temple dog of Tibet, a Foo dog of a powerful supernatural bloodline, though he could have passed for an exceptionally large Tibetan mastiff. Mouse can take on demons and monsters without batting an eye, and he checks in at about two fifty. He knocked me down as easily as a bowling ball does the first pin. And, superdog though he may be, he's still a dog. Once I was down, he planted his front paws on either side of my head and proceeded to give me slobbery dog kisses on the face and neck and chin, making happy little sounds the whole time.

"Ack!" I said, as I always did. "My lips touched dog lips! Get me some mouthwash! Get me some iodine!" I shoved at his chest, grinning, and managed to lever myself out from underneath him and stand.

That didn't diminish Mouse's enthusiasm in the least. He cut loose with a series of joyous barks so loud that they set off a car alarm on a vehicle a hundred feet away. Then he sprinted in a tight circle, came back to my feet, and barked some more. He did that over and over for about a minute, his tail wagging so hard that it sounded like a helicopter might have been passing in the distance, *whup-whup-whup-whup-whup*.

"All right," I said. "Enough. Come on, it's not like I died or anything, boy."

He quieted, his jaws parted in a canine grin, tail still wagging so hard that it pulled his hindquarters left and right with it. I knelt down and put my arms around him. If I'd been an inch or two shorter, I doubt I could have done it. Damn pooch is huge, and built like a barrel. He laid his chin on my shoulder and panted happily as I hugged him.

"Yeah," I said quietly. "I missed you, too, buddy." I nodded toward the house. "Anyone home?"

He tilted his head to one side slightly, one ear cocked at a slightly different angle from the other.

"He says no," Molly said.

I blinked at her. "First Sherlock, now Dolittle?"

She blushed slightly and looked embarrassed. "It's just something I picked up. A dog's thoughts and emotions are a lot more direct and less conflicted than a human's. It's easier to listen for them. It isn't a big deal."

Mouse came over to greet Molly by walking back and forth against her legs, nearly knocking her down. He stopped and looked fondly up at her, tail wagging, and made a little woofing sound.

"You're welcome," she said, and scratched his ears.

"I need your help, boy," I said. "Bad guys took Butters, Andi, and Justine."

Mouse shook his head vigorously and half sneezed.

"Mouse thinks Andi should be locked in the garage at night, until she learns not to get abducted."

"Once we get her back, we'll start calling her Danger-prone Daphne," I promised him. "She's even got the hair for it. You in, Scoob?"

In answer, Mouse hurried to the street, looked both ways, then crossed it to sit down at the back door of the *Munstermobile*. Then he looked at me, as if asking me why I wasn't opening it for him.

"Of course he's in," Molly translated, smiling.

"Good thing you're here," I said. "He's tough to read."

37

We used the spinning needle in the bowl of water like a compass, driving north to south first, to let us triangulate on our friends' location. As tracking spells went, this one was a little clumsier than most. We had to pull over the *Munstermobile* and let the water settle to use it—but hey, nothing's perfect.

We tracked our friends, and presumably the Redcap and company, to the waterfront. The sun was setting behind us, and had briefly appeared from behind the clouds. The city's skyline cast deep, cold shadows over us.

"Harry," Molly said. "You know that this—"

"Is a trap," I said. "Yep. The Redcap knew exactly what I would do with those bits of hair."

Molly looked a little relieved. "Okay. Then what's the plan?"

"Once we are sure where they are," I said, "I'm going to go in the front door."

"That's the plan?"

"I'm going to be very, very noisy," I said. "Meanwhile, you and Supermutt are going to sneak in the back, all sneaky-like, neutralize any guards that aren't watching me, and get our crew out."

"Oh," Molly said. "Are you sure you don't want me to be the distraction?"

It was a fair question. Molly's One-woman Rave spell could get more attention than a crash at an airshow. "The Sidhe know all about veils," I said. "Mine aren't good enough to get anywhere near them. Yours are. It's that simple."

"Right," she said, and swallowed. "So we're . . . going to depend on me for the important part. Saving people."

"You've been playing Batman for a while now, kid," I said. "I think you've got this."

"Mostly I was the only one in danger if I screwed up," Molly said. "Are you sure this is the right plan?"

"If you think you can handle it," I said. "Or if you don't."

"Oh."

I put a hand on her shoulder. "We don't have time to dance around on this one. So we go dirt simple. When it starts, if someone gets in your way, I want you to hit them with everything you've got, right in the face. Mouse will be with you as muscle."

"Shouldn't he be with you? I mean, if you're going to fight . . ."

"I'm not going to fight," I said. "No time to prepare, no plan, I'd lose a fight. I'm going to be a big noisy distraction."

"But what if you get in trouble?"

"That's my part. You do your part. Keep focused on your objective. Get in, get them, get out, signal. Then we all run away. Got it?"

She nodded tightly. "Got it."

"Woof," said Mouse.

"Huh," I said a few moments later. We had triangulated with the tracking spell and narrowed down their location to one building, and we now lurked in an alley across the street. "I've actually been in there before."

"You have?"

"Yeah," I said. "Client had lost a kid or something to some half-assed wannabe warlock. He had the cheesy dialogue and everything, was gonna sacrifice the kid with this big cheap, spiky knife."

"How did it turn out?"

"If I remember it right, I got beat up," I said. "Didn't make much money on it, either. The bad guy ran away, and the client walked out threatening a lawsuit. Except she left the kid. Turns out, she wasn't even his mom, and his real parents tried to have me arrested. Never heard from her again. No clue what it was about. Chalk."

Molly reached into her bag and came out with a stick of chalk, which she passed to me. I crouched and quickly sketched a diagram of the rectangular warehouse. "Here's the front door. Office door. Back door. There're some windows up high, but you'd have to be a bird to get there. The rear of the warehouse actually protrudes over the water, but there's a wooden deck around the back. That's where you'll go in, at the back door. Watch for trip wires. Mouse can help with that. Trust him. We're basically blind and deaf by comparison."

"Right," Molly said, nodding. "Okay."

"Don't get hung up on what could happen if it goes wrong," I said. "Focus, concentrate, just like we do for a spell. Get in. Get them. Get out."

"Let's just do it," she said, "before I throw up."

"I'll give you five minutes to get into position. Don't go in until I get noisy."

"Right," Molly said. "Come on, Mouse."

The big dog came up beside Molly, and she didn't even have to bend to slip the fingers of one hand through his collar. "Stay this close to me, okay?" she said to Mouse.

He looked up at her and wagged his tail.

She gave him a shaky smile, nodded at me, then spoke a word and vanished.

I started counting to three hundred and briefly wondered why I kept running into repeat uses of various locations around town. This wasn't the first time I'd dealt with the bad guys choosing to reuse a location different bad guys had used before them. Maybe there was a Villainous Time-share Association. Maybe my life was actually a basic-cable television show, and they couldn't afford to spend money on new sets all the time.

Or—and this seemed more likely—maybe there was a reason for it. Maybe the particular vibe of certain spots just felt more like home to predators. Predators like to lair in a place with multiple ways in and out, isolated from casual entry, near supplies of whatever it was they like to eat. Supernatural predators would also have some level of awareness of the nature of the Nevernever that abutted any given part of our reality, even if it was only an instinct. It would make sense that they would be more at ease in places that joined parts of the Nevernever where they would be comfortable. I mean, everyone likes to eat somewhere that feels like home.

If I lived through the next day or so, I needed to start keeping track of where these jokers liked to get their bloodthirsty freak on. It might give me an edge someday. Or at least a list of places that could use a nice burning down. I hadn't burned down a building in ages.

Two ninety-nine. Three hundred.

"Ready or not," I muttered, "here I come."

I strode out of the alley across from the warehouse, gathering my will into a shield around my left hand, and readied a lance of force in my right. Hell's bells, I missed my equipment. Mab had forced me to learn how to do without, but that didn't mean I could do it as *well*. I missed my shield bracelet. I missed my blasting rod. I missed my spell-armored coat. With that gear, this would be pretty simple. I could protect myself better from every direction and have a lot more range on my spells to make the bad guys keep their heads down. But it would take me weeks to build new ones, and I had to work with what I had—which was pretty much just me.

My shields would be as strong, but I couldn't sustain them for as much time, or in every direction—so I couldn't walk in with a nice comfortable bubble of force around me. Without the bracelet or a tool like it, I could protect myself only from the front, and only for a few seconds at a time. My offensive spells would hit just as hard, but they'd have a shorter range, and they would take a few more crucial fractions of a second to enact.

Man, I missed my toys.

The warehouse had a little fence covered in plastic sheeting and topped with barbed wire. There was a gated area in front of the main entryway, though the gate had been blasted off its hinges by some deranged ruffian who did not look like me, no matter what the witnesses said, and apparently no one had replaced it since.

Awful lot of open space out there. I'd be a really juicy target. Which was sort of the point: Make myself so attractively vulnerable that no one was watching the back door. It wasn't the best idea in the world to walk out into that, but Halloween night was maybe an hour away, and there wasn't time to be smart.

That said, there's a difference between being reckless and being insane. I didn't especially like the idea of stumbling over a trip line tied to, let's say, an antipersonnel mine, so before I went in, I flung my right arm forward in a large sweeping underhand motion, as if I were trying to throw a bowling ball at the pins two lanes over from where I was standing. I muttered, *"Forzare!"* as I threw the spell, focusing on shaping the force I'd released into what I needed.

Energy rippled across the ground in a shock wave that threw up dust and bits of gravel and irregular chunks of broken asphalt. It rippled across the ground to the warehouse and landed against its front doorway with a giant, hollow boom.

"Say, 'Who's there!'" I shouted at the warehouse, already walking forward rapidly, while the dust still hung in the air—it would make it more possible, if not likely, to spot any of the Redcap's Sidhe buddies who might be hiding under a veil inside it. "I dare you! I double-dog dare you!"

I hurled another blast of force at the big loading doors in the front of the warehouse, something meant to make a lot of noise, not to tear them down. It succeeded. A second enormous concussion made the building's steel girders and metal walls ring like some vast, dark bell.

"The furious wizard, that's who!" I shouted. "You've got ten seconds to free my friends, unharmed, or I'm going to fucking smite every last mother's son of you!"

I had maybe half a second's warning, and then a streaking black form dived down from above me and raked at my eyes with its talons. I snapped my head back out of the way, only to see a hawk beating back up out of the nadir of its dive. It rolled in the air, and as it did it shimmered, and in an instant the hawk was gone and one of the Sidhe was there in its place, arcing through the air in free fall, holding a bow and an arrow in his hands. He drew and shot in the same instant he shifted, and I barely caught the arrow on my shield. Before he could begin to fall, he completed the roll and shifted again, back into hawk form, then beat his wings and continued rising into the sky.

Hell's bells. That looked *awesome*. It took a serious mastery of shapeshifting to bring equipment and clothes and things with you when you changed form, but that guy had made it look as easy as breathing.

I mean, say what you will about the faeries, but they've got style. Not so much style that I didn't hurl another bolt of force after the flying archer, but I missed him and he winged away with a mocking shriek.

Then I felt a small, sharp pain in my left leg.

I looked down to see a little wooden dart sticking out of the back of my calf. It was carved, perfectly smooth and round, and fletched with a few tiny slivers of scarlet feather. I snapped my gaze around behind me, and caught a single glimpse of the Redcap poised in a crouch atop the fence surrounding the warehouse, balancing his weight with apparent effortless ease along a strand of barbed wire that had to have been a sixteenth of an inch wide.

His mouth was spread in a wide, manic grin. He held a short silvery tube in one hand, and as my eyes found his face, he touched two fingertips of his other hand to his lips, blew me a kiss, and plummeted back off of the fence and out of sight.

I whirled toward him and brought up my shield, then spun around and angled it that way, then jittered about, rubbernecking everywhere at once. But that was it. Assuming the Sidhe weren't simply undetectable to my senses, they were gone.

A slow burning sensation began to spread from the wound in my leg.

A cold shiver oozed down my spine. I tugged the dart out of my calf. It hadn't done much—the slender spear of wood had penetrated maybe a quarter inch into my skin—but when I rolled up my pant leg to look, I found an inordinately large trickle of blood coming from the tiny wound.

And that burning sensation became an almost infinitesimally greater presence with each heartbeat.

This hadn't been a hostage crisis at all.

It had been an assassination. Or . . . or something.

"God*dammit*!" I snarled. "I just got played *again*! I am so sick and tired of this backstabby bullshit!"

I more or less stormed into the warehouse, shoving open the office door and stalking out onto the main floor. The place was just as empty as I remembered, give or take the leavings of several apparent transients between the present and the past. Molly was at the very rear of the warehouse, near the door. She was helping Justine to sit up. Mac was there, too, and he and Butters were between them helping a wobbly-looking Andi to remain on her feet. Mouse was standing guard between the group and the front of the warehouse, and he started wagging his tail when he saw me.

"Clear," I called out to them, hurrying over. "Or at least clearish. What happened?"

"They were under a sleeping enchantment," Molly reported. "Pretty standard stuff. I woke them up."

"Everyone okay?"

"Andi got hit on the head when they took her," she said. "Other than that, I think we're good."

When she spoke, Molly's voice never quavered, but her eyes flickered uncertainly toward Mac. I took a closer look at everyone. Andi, Butters, and Justine had all been bound. Justine was only now getting the ropes cut off of her wrists, and as Molly sawed them away with a pocketknife, I could see the deep red marks they'd left on Justine's slender wrists. Butters and Andi had them, too, visible even in the dimness of the warehouse.

Mac didn't.

That was interesting. Why hadn't Mac been tied up? Or if he had, how come there wasn't a mark to show for it? Either way, that was odd.

My first instinct was to grab him and demand answers—but the direct approach hadn't gotten me anything but more confused as I went through this stupid day. I might have been a better thug than at any point in my life, but that wouldn't matter if I couldn't figure out where to apply my muscle. And I was damned tired of being sneaked up on. So it was time to get sneaky.

I ground my teeth and pretended that Molly hadn't clued me into anything. "All right, people," I said. "Let's move. I think they're gone but they could be back."

"That's it?" Molly asked. "I was expecting more trouble than th—" She broke off, staring at the floor behind me.

My leg throbbed and burned a little more, and I glanced down at it in irritation. To my shock, I saw a long line of small smears of my blood on the tile floor. The little wound had continued bleeding, soaked through my sock and my shoe, and dribbled down onto my heel.

"What happened?" Molly asked.

"It was another stupid trick," I said. "The point wasn't to hold them for ransom. It was to get me here, under pressure, and too keyed up to defend myself from every direction." I held up the dart. "We'd better find out what this thing is and what kind of poison is on it."

"Oh, my God," Molly breathed.

"I'll take whatever help I can get," I said. "Let's g—"

But before I could finish the sentence, there was a loud crunching *whoomp* of a sound, and the entire warehouse shook. I barely had time to think *demolition charges* before there was a deafening crack, and the floor tilted.

And then the back twenty feet of the warehouse, including all of us, fell right off of the street and into the cold, dark water of Lake Michigan.

38

We didn't drop straight down. Instead, there was a scream of shearing bolts, and our part of the building lurched drunkenly and then plunged into the water at an oblique angle.

The confusion of it was the worst part. The loud noise, the disorientation inherent in the uneven motion, and then the short surge of terror as gravity took over all served to create a panic reaction in my head—and I'm not a guy who panics easily.

That's what most people don't understand about situations like this one. People are just built to freak out when something goes wrong. It doesn't matter if you're a kindergarten teacher or a Special Forces operator—when life-threatening stuff happens, you get scared. You freak out. That's just what happens. When it's because you've woken up to a hungry bear in your camp, that's usually a pretty good mechanism.

But being dropped into black water in an enclosed area is *not* a place where panicked adrenaline is going to help you out. That's when you have to somehow set that fear aside and force yourself to use your rational mind to guide you out of the situation. There are two ways to get yourself into that terrified-but-rational state of mind. First is training, where you drill a reaction into yourself so hard and so many times that it becomes a form of reflex you can perform without even thinking. And the other way you get there is to have enough experience to have learned what you need to do.

So the first thing I did as the cold water swallowed me was to close my eyes for a second and focus, just as I would if I were preparing a spell, relaxing my limbs and letting them float loosely in the water. I gathered my thoughts and laid out my options.

First, I had time, but not much of it. I had gotten a good breath before I went under. The others might or might not have done the same. So I had about two minutes to act before people started trying to breathe Lake Michigan. Two minutes doesn't sound like long, but it was enough time to spend a few seconds thinking.

Second, we were surrounded by steel siding. I wasn't getting through that with anything short of a full-power blast, and that wasn't going to happen while I was surrounded by water. Water tends to disperse and ground out magical energies just by being nearby. When water is all around you, it's all but impossible to direct any energy out of your body without it spreading out and diluting to uselessness.

The edges of the building might or might not have grounded themselves into the mud at the bottom of the lake, trapping us all like bugs under a shoe box lid. There wasn't time to search through them systematically, not before people started drowning. That meant that we had to go out through the only way I could be sure was available—the back door.

Except that everyone was spread out in the blackness now, and at least one person, Andi, was already disoriented from the blow to her head. It was possible others had been hurt in the fall, or would get hurt as they struggled to get out. There seemed to be very little chance that I could find the door, then find all of them in the dark, then get them pointed at the door and out. It seemed just as unlikely that everyone would stop to think and come to the same conclusion I had. There was a very real chance that one or more of my friends might be left behind.

But what other options did I have? It wasn't as though I could lift the entire thing out of the water—

No. I couldn't.

But Winter could.

I opened my eyes into the darkness, made a best guess for down, and swam that way. I found mud within a few feet. I thrust my right hand into the mud, thrashing rather awkwardly to get it done. Then I went limp again, floating a bit weirdly, tethered by my hand in the mud, and focused my mind.

I wasn't going to try to lift the freaking building. That was just insane. I'd known things that might have been able to pull it off, but I was certain I wasn't one of them, not even with the power of the Winter Knight's mantle.

Besides, why do it the stupid way?

I felt myself smiling, maybe smiling a little too widely, in the dark water, and unleashed the cold of winter directly into the ground beneath me, through my right hand. I poured it on, holding nothing back, reaching deep into me, to the source of cold power inside me, and sending it out into the muck of the lake bottom.

Lake Michigan is a deep lake, and only its upper layers ever really warm up. Beyond a few feet of the surface, the cold is a constant, an absolute, and the mud at the bottom of what I was guessing to be fifteen or twenty feet of water, at the most, was clammy. As the power poured out of me, the water did what it always did with magic—it began to diffuse it, to spread it out.

Which was exactly what I was going for.

Ice formed around my hand and spread into a circle several feet wide in the first instant, conducted more easily through the mud than through the water. I poured more effort in, and the circle widened, more ice forming, spreading out. I kept up the cold, and the water touching the bottom began to freeze as well.

My heart began to beat harder, and there was a roaring sound in my ears. I didn't give up, sending more and more cold into the lake around me, building up layer after layer of ice across the entire bottom of the lake beneath the collapsed warehouse. At sixty seconds, the ice was three feet deep, and forming around my arm and shoulder. At ninety seconds, it had engulfed my head and upper body, and had to have been five or six feet deep. And when my internal count reached a hundred and ten, the entire mass of ice tore loose from the lake's bottom with a groan and began to rise.

I never let up on it, building it into a miniature iceberg, and the steel beams and walls of the warehouse moaned and squealed as the ice began to lift them free. I felt it when my feet came out of the water, though most of the rest of me was still stuck in the ice. I tore and twisted and seemed to know exactly where to apply pressure and torque without being told. The ice crackled away and I slipped out of it with a minimum of fuss. When I pulled my head out (go ahead; make a joke), I was sitting in dim light atop a sheet of ice floating several inches out of the waters of the lake.

I was still in the rear section of the warehouse. The back door was open, straight above my head, and was letting in most of the light. The broken ends of the room, the floor, and the two walls had been embedded in ice, but crookedly. The ragged edge of the ceiling was a couple of feet out of the water.

Several very startled-looking people and one fur-plastered dog were shivering on the ice. I took a quick head count. Everyone was there.

I sagged down onto the ice in relief, fatigue making my body feel like it weighed an extra ton, and just lay there for a moment as the wreckage bobbed gently in the water. After a few seconds, I became aware of eyes on me, and I looked up.

My friends were all sitting or kneeling on the ice, damp and shivering, and staring at me with wide eyes. Molly's eyes were bright and intense, the expression on her face unreadable. Justine's mouth hung slightly open, and her big dark eyes looked afraid. Butters stared first at me and then down at the ice, his eyes flicking around, the wheels clearly churning in his head as he calculated how much ice there was and how much energy it would have taken to freeze it. Mac regarded me impassively, still supporting the dazed Andi.

Sweetly curved Andi was the most vulnerable. If I could isolate her from the herd, things could get interesting. I'd just saved her life, after all. She owed me. I could think of a few ways that she could express her gratitude.

I pushed the predator thought out of my head and took a deep breath. When I exhaled, it condensed into a thick, foggy vapor, more so than it ever would have naturally, even on the coldest days. I looked down at my hands and they were covered in frost, and my fingertips and nails were turning blue. I put a hand to my face and had to brush away a thin layer of frost.

Hell's bells. What did I look like, to make my friends stare at me like that?

Time for mirrors later.

I stood up, my feet sure even on the wet ice, and found the nearest point of the shoreline. I extended a hand, murmured, *"Infriga,"* and froze a ten-foot-long bridge from my improvised iceberg to land.

"Come on," I said, as I started walking toward the shore. My voice sounded strange, rough. "We don't have much time."

The sun had slipped below the cloud cover, and the sky was a bank of hot coals, slowly burning down toward ember and ash when we got back to Molly's apartment.

Thomas and Karrin were waiting outside. The two of them were leaning against the wall near the security checkpoint. Thomas had a tall coffee cup in one hand and a bagel in the other. Karrin was staring down at a smartphone, her thumbs flicking over its surface.

Thomas took note of the car as it pulled up, and nudged Karrin. She looked up, then did a double take at the *Munstermobile*. She rolled her eyes, then apparently turned the phone off and slipped it into a case on her belt.

I stopped the car and rolled down the window.

"You've got to be kidding me," Karrin said, eyeing the car. *"This?"*

"I think it's a company car," I said.

Karrin leaned down and looked at everyone in the back. "What happened?"

"Inside—I'll explain."

We got parked and everyone made their way to Molly's place, some of them more slowly than others.

"You're limping," Thomas noted, walking beside me. "And bleeding."

"No, I'm . . ." I began. Then I sighed. "Yeah. Redcap shot me with some kind of dinky dart. Maybe poisoned. Or something."

Thomas made a low growling sound in his chest. "I'm just about done with that clown."

"Tell me about it."

Molly opened the door, and the moment I stepped in, Lacuna came zipping over to me. The little armored faerie hovered in the air near my face, her dark hair flying wildly in the turbulence of her own beating wings. "You can't do it!" she cried. "You can't just give them all that pizza! Do you have any idea how much harm you're doing? Can I *please* fight now?"

"Whoa," I said, leaning back and holding up my hands.

"Hey, shortcake," my brother snapped. "Back off."

"You aren't important," Lacuna declared to Thomas, evidently dismissing him entirely as she turned back to me. "I wrote down everything just like you said and now they're going to get that awful pizza all over themselves without the *least* regard for properly protecting themselves, and I'm going to *fight* them for the pizza!"

"In the first place, that is not a fight you are going to win," I said, "and in the second place—they found something?"

"And I wrote it down like you said and now I want to duel them!"

"No duels!" I said, and headed for the dining table. Sure enough, Lacuna had drawn precise little Xs at all of the sites marked on the map. Most of them had been done with a green pen, but two locations were marked in red. One of them was next to one of the primary sites I'd marked earlier, on this side of the lake, north of town. The next was at one of the secondary sites, a little farther inland and on the far side of the lake.

"Lacuna, were they sure that ritual preparation was under way at both of these locations?"

"And the others were clear," the little faerie replied impatiently. "Yes, yes, yes."

"Crap," I muttered. "Molly, time?"

"Twenty-five minutes to sundown, more or less," she replied. She came to the table with a first-aid kit in her hands. "Waldo, can you take a look at this?"

"The minute I'm sure Andi isn't bleeding into her brain," Butters snapped.

"I've already sent for an ambulance," Molly said back in a calm, iron tone that sounded creepily like her mother. "Andi will die with all of the rest of us if Harry doesn't stop things from going boom, so get over here and see to him."

Butters turned toward Molly with absolute murder in his eyes. But then he looked at me, and back to the dazed Andi in her chair. Mac was supporting her. The bartender looked up at Butters and nodded.

"I hate this," Butters said, his voice boiling with anger. But he came over to the table, grabbed the kit, and said, "Try to hold still, Harry."

I planted my foot and kept standing still as he started cutting away my jeans at the knee. "Okay," I said. Karrin was already standing beside me, and Thomas joined us across the table. "What's the word from Marcone's Vikings?"

"Strike team standing by," Murphy said, "waiting for my word."

I grunted. "Thomas?"

"Lara's team is ready, too," he said.

"Butters, what do we have from the Paranet?"

"Dammit, Dresden, I'm a medical examiner, not an intelligence analyst." He gave the little wound a prod with something and a white-hot needle went up my leg to the hip.

"Nngh," I said. "Nothing?"

He took a wipe to the wound, and that didn't feel very good either. "About half a dozen sightings of the Little Folk all over."

"Aren't those yours?" Murphy asked.

"Some, probably," I said. "But I think they're the rest of Ace's crew."

Murphy grunted. "I thought the prisoner wouldn't tell you anything about him."

I shrugged. "I figure it was Ace who threw the explosives at the *Munstermobile* last night, when the Little Folk jumped me afterward. He showed up right when Lacuna ambushed me at the Botanic Gardens. Then when I go to get my friends back from his dad, something else blows up."

"He's learned to play with explosives," Karrin said.

"Yeah, but you've barely seen this guy," Thomas said.

"It makes sense," I said. "Especially if he's playing smart—which he is, just by rounding up a group of the Little Folk as allies. He knows he couldn't handle a straight fight—so he's kept his distance. We've barely seen him, and he's nearly killed me three times in the past sixteen hours."

"Hngh," Thomas said.

"What's he got against you?" Molly asked.

"He was part of Lily and Fix's crew, back when they were all just folks," I said. "They were friends with Aurora and the last Summer Knight. When Mab hired me to find Ronald Reuel's killer, Ace pitched in with this ghoul hitter and the Winter Knight to stop me. Betrayed his friends. Billy and his crew almost killed him, but I let him skate."

"And he hates you for it?" Molly asked.

"I killed Aurora," I said. "His friend Meryl died in that same fight. And you can be damned sure that Lily and Fix haven't wanted anything to do with him since. So from where he's standing, I killed one of his friends, got another one killed in battle, and took the ones who were left alive away from him. Then I beat him up in front of his dad. Guy's got a forest of bones to pick with me."

"Cheery image," Thomas said.

I grunted. "What about your nutjob, Butters. What's his name?"

"Gary."

"Gary turn up anything else?"

"About twenty updates in all capital letters about boats, boats, boats."

I thought about that one for a moment.

Then I said, "Hah."

"We have to move, Harry," Karrin said.

I grunted. "Gard still have her chopper?"

"Yes."

"Right," I said. I thumped my finger on the site on the far side of Lake Michigan. "Lacuna, what's the word on this one?"

The little faerie was still flitting about in the air around the table, fairly bursting with impatience. "It's behind big stone walls on a human's private land, right where I marked it!"

I nodded. "Vikings get that site then. Get them moving."

"Right," Murphy said, and headed for the door, reaching for her phone on the way.

Thomas frowned. "We're going to depend on Lara's people to back us up?"

"Hell, no," I said. "No offense, but I don't trust your sister. Send her crew to the second site."

"This is damned odd," Butters muttered.

I looked down at him. "What?"

"The bleeding won't stop," he said. "It's not really all that dangerous in a wound this small, but it isn't clotting up. It's like some kind of anti-coagulant was introduced. Do you still have the dart?"

"Dart," I said. I patted my pockets. "I guess not. It was in my hand when the warehouse dropped into the water."

"Bah," Butters said. "Inflammation in the skin around it. This hurt?"

He poked me. It did. I told him so.

"Huh," he said. "I can't be sure without tests but . . . I think this might be some kind of allergic reaction."

"How?" I asked. "I'm not allergic to anything."

"I'm just saying what it looks like on your skin," Butters said. "The trickle factor seems to imply some kind of toxin, though. You need a hospital, tests."

"Later," I said. "Just get it wrapped up and keep it from running down my leg."

Butters nodded.

"So," Thomas asked, "if Lara's crew has one site and Marcone's the other, which one are we going to?"

"Neither."

"What?"

"We're not going to either one."

"Why not?"

"Because all day long," I said, "I've been moving in straight lines and it's gotten me nothing but grief." I pointed at the locations marked on the map. "See those? Those are the perfectly rational places for our bad guy to make something happen."

Thomas rubbed at his chin and narrowed his eyes. "They're a distrac-tion?"

"It's how the Sidhe think. How they move. How they are. They put pressure on you, get you to look over there, and then kapow. Sucker punch."

"What if they're expecting you to expect that?" Thomas asked.

"Gah," I said, waving my hands on either side of my head as if brushing away wasps. "Stop it. If I'm wrong, we've got professional badasses to cover it. But I'm not wrong."

"Didn't you say that they required a ley line site to perform a ritual that big?" Butters asked. He had taped a pad over the little injury and was securing it with a roll of gauze.

"Yes," I said.

"And the Little Folk cleared all of them but those two?"

"No," I said. "They cleared *almost* all of them. There was one place the Little Folk couldn't check."

Thomas's eyes widened as he got it. "Boats," he said.

"Yeah," I said. "Boats."

39

Thomas rose, glancing around the room, and said in a quiet voice, "She needs fuel. And I'd better talk to Lara about the second site." But his eyes had drifted over to where Justine now sat by the fire, basking in warmth after our icy dunk and staring at it with a peaceful expression on her lovely face.

"Get moving," I said. I lowered my voice. "You taking her with you?"

"You kidding? Bad guys have been all over us today. That creep took her right off the street in front of our apartment. I'm not letting her out of my *sight*."

"Look, if you leave her here, the building has security that—"

"So does my building, and Cat Sith breezed right past all of it when he came in," Thomas said. "I'm not letting her out of my sight until this thing is settled."

I grimaced, but nodded. "All right. Go. We'll be right behind you."

My brother arched an eyebrow. "All of you?"

"We'll see," I said.

"Did you talk to her?" Thomas asked.

I gave him a steady look and said, "No. Maggie was out trick-or-treating."

"Right. She's what? Nine years old? She might as well have vanished into the Bermuda triangle. How could you possibly be expected to find her? Magic?" He gave me a sour look. "What about the other one?"

He meant Karrin. "We've both been kinda busy. Maybe later."

"Later. Bad habit to get into," Thomas said. "Life's too short."

"It almost sounded like *you* were attempting to enlighten *me* about bad habits."

"The path of excess leads to the palace of wisdom," he said, and turned for the door.

At the exact moment he moved, even though she was not looking at him, and though he said nothing to her, Justine rose from her seat by the fire and started toward the door. The pair of them met halfway there and she slipped herself beneath his arm and up close to him in a motion of familiar, unconscious intimacy. They left together.

My brother the vampire, whose kiss was a slow death sentence, had a stable and loving relationship with a girl who was crazy about him. By contrast, I could barely talk to a woman, at least about anything pertaining to a relationship. Given that my only long-term girlfriends had faked their own death, died, and broken free of enslaving enchantments to end the relationship, the empirical evidence seemed to indicate that he knew something I didn't.

Keep your life tonight, Harry. Complicate it tomorrow.

Murphy came back in with a pair of EMTs I recognized, Lamar and Simmons. They got Andi loaded up onto a stretcher, and Lamar blinked when he saw me. He didn't look as young as he had the last time I'd seen him—a few threads of silver in his hair stood out starkly against his dark hair and skin.

"Dresden," he said. "That you?"

"Mostly."

"I heard you were dead."

"Close. It didn't take."

He shook his head and helped his partner secure Andi to the stretcher. They picked up the stretcher and toted her outside, with Butters hurrying along beside them, his hand on Andi's arm.

Once they were gone, I stood in the room with the grasshopper, Karrin, and Mac. Mouse dozed on the floor near the door, but his ears twitched now and then and I doubted he was missing anything.

"Molly," I said. "Would you ask Sarissa to join us, please?"

She went off to her room, and returned a moment later with Sarissa.

The slender, beautiful woman came into the room silently, and didn't meet anyone's eyes. Hers were focused in the middle distance, as she tried to keep track of everyone in the room through peripheral vision.

"All right," I said. "Things are about to hit the fan. They're confusing as hell and I'm getting tired of feeling like I have no idea what's going on. There are some unknown quantities here, and some of you aren't telling me everything, but there isn't enough time to pry it all out of each of you." I pointed a finger at Sarissa. "Maybe you really are everything you say you are. Maybe not. But I figure there're about two chances in three that you're playing me somehow, and I think you're way too good at backstabbing to leave you standing around behind me."

"Everything I've told you—" Sarissa began.

I slashed a hand at the air. "Don't talk. This isn't an interrogation. It's a public service announcement. I'm telling you how it's going to be."

She pressed her lips together and looked away.

"Mac," I said. "Much as it pains me to level suspicion at the master-craftsman of the best beer in town . . . you're hiding something. That Outsider talked to you as if it knew you. And I don't think it was an aficionado of your ale. Do you want to tell me who you really are?"

Mac was silent for a moment. Then he said, "No. That's mine."

I grunted. "Didn't think so. I figure it's more likely that you are an ally, or at least neutral, than it is that you're a plant for somebody. But I'm not completely sure about you, either."

I looked at them both and said, "I'm not sure if you're my friends or my enemies, but I heard something once about keeping them close and closer. So until things have shaken out, you're both staying where I can keep track of you. And you both should be aware that I'm going to be ready to smack you down if I pick up on the least little hint of treachery."

"I am not—" Sarissa began.

I stared at her.

She bit her lip and looked away.

I turned my eyes to Mac. He didn't look thrilled about it, but he nodded.

"Okay," I said. "We'll be on the lake. There are a couple more coats in the guest bedroom closet. Better grab one."

Mac nodded and beckoned Sarissa with a tilt of his head. "Miss."

They went to the guest bedroom, and that left me facing Murphy with the grasshopper hovering in the background. I made a little kissing noise with my puckered lips, and Mouse lifted his head from the ground.

"You pick up anything weird about either of them?" I asked.

Mouse sneezed, shaking his head, and laid it back down again.

I grunted. "Guess not." I took a deep breath. "Grasshopper, maybe it's good time to take Mouse for a W-A-L-K?"

Mouse's head snapped up.

Molly looked back and forth between Karrin and me and sighed. "Yeah, okay."

"Maybe take those two with you when you go? And have security bring the car around, too. We'll leave shortly."

"Right," Molly said. She collected Mac and Sarissa, now clad in badly fitting secondhand coats, and they left.

It was just me and Karrin.

The fire crackled.

Karrin said, "You picked up Mouse. Did you get to see Maggie?"

"Christ, everyone wants to know about . . ." I shook my head. "She was out."

She nodded. "Did you get out of the car? Or just wait at the curb?"

I gave her a flat stare. She looked back at me with her cop face. I failed to terrify her off the subject.

"Curb," I said.

She smiled faintly. "I've seen you walk into places that should have killed you seven, eight times? You didn't flinch. But now you're petrified with fear?"

"Not fear," I said, so quickly and with such vehemence that it became immediately clear to me that fear was exactly what I was feeling when I thought of approaching Maggie.

"Sure it isn't," Karrin said.

"Look," I said, "we don't have time for—"

"My dad said that a lot," Karrin said. " 'I can't right now. We'll do that later.' He was busy, too. Then he was gone."

"I am not going to deal with this right now."

Karrin nodded. "Right. Not right now. Later."

"Christ," I said.

Karrin looked down at the floor and smiled briefly, then looked back up at me. "I never liked being shrunk. Had to a couple of times. After I shot Denton. Stuff like that."

"So?" I said.

"Some things can't just sit inside you," she said. "Not when . . ." She spread her hands. "Harry, you're dealing with serious pressures here. With something that could . . . change who you are. I don't blame you for being afraid."

"I've got the Winter Knight thing under control," I said.

"Winter Knight, Mab, whatever," she said, as if it were an everyday annoyance. "Magic stuff, you'll deal with it fine. I'm talking about something real. I'm talking about Maggie."

"Oh," I said.

"I figure it'll take Thomas at least ten minutes to fuel the boat," she said. "It's been about five since he left. Which gives you five minutes with no city to save, no evil queens, and no monsters. No one to protect right in front of you, no apprentices to look strong for."

I looked at her blankly and felt my shoulders sag. I hadn't slept in too long. I wanted to find a nice bed somewhere and pull the covers over my head. "I don't . . . What are you looking for, here? What do you expect from me?"

She stepped closer and took my hand. "Talk to me. Why didn't you go see Maggie?"

I bowed my head and let my fingers stay limp. "I can't. I just can't."

"Why not?"

I tried to speak and couldn't. I shook my head.

Karrin stepped closer to me and took my other hand in hers, too. "I'm right here," she said.

"What if . . ." I whispered. "What if . . . she remembers?"

"Remembers what?"

"She was there," I said. "She was there when I cut her mother's throat. I don't know if she was conscious, if she saw . . . but what if she did? In my head, I've run this scenario about a thousand times, and if she saw me and started screaming or crying . . ." I shrugged. "That would be . . . hard."

"You know what's going to be harder?" Karrin asked quietly.

"What."

"Not knowing." She shook my hands gently. "Leaving a hole in that little girl's life. She's your daughter, Harry. You're the only dad she's ever going to have."

"Yeah, but if I show up and she remembers me, I'm not her father. I'm her father the monstrous villain. I'm Darth Dresden."

"She'll learn better," Murphy said. "Eventually. If you try."

"You don't understand," I said. "I can't . . . I can't do anything that might hurt her. I just can't. I barely know that little girl—but she's mine. And I'd rather double-kneecap myself with a frying pan than bring her an ounce of pain."

"Pain passes," Karrin said. "If you think about it—"

"You don't *get* it," I half snarled. "She's blood, Karrin. She's mine. Thinking has no place in this. She's my little girl. I *can't* see her get hurt again—"

I stopped suddenly with my mouth hanging open.

Hell's bells, how could I have missed what the Mothers were trying to tell me?

I couldn't bear to see my child in pain.

And maybe I wasn't the only one who couldn't.

"Stars and stones," I breathed. "That's what's happening here."

Karrin blinked up at me several times. "Excuse me?"

I kept thinking about it, following the logic. "That's why Mab sent me to kill Maeve. She's no different from Titania. She knew it needed to be done but . . ."

"But what?" Karrin asked.

"Maeve is still her little girl," I said quietly. "Mab isn't human, but there are . . . remnants in all the Sidhe. Mother Winter called Mab a romantic. I think this is why. Mother Summer went on and on about how humans have influenced the Sidhe. That's what this whole thing is about."

"I don't understand," Karrin said.

"Mab loves her daughter," I said simply. "She won't kill Maeve because she loves her." I let out a bitter little laugh. "And there's the kind of symmetry here that the faeries are crazy about. I killed the last Summer Lady. It's only fitting that the same hand deal with the Winter Lady."

My brain was running along with my mouth, and I stopped talking so that I could poke at the logic of the theory that my instincts—or maybe my heart—told me was obviously true. If Mab wasn't out to wreck the world, if she hadn't been taken by the adversary, then someone else had been lying to me. Someone who *shouldn't* have been able to lie.

"Okay," Karrin said. "If not Mab, then who is going to pull off this apocalypse ritual magic?"

I kept following the lines of logic and felt myself grow abruptly cold. "Oh. Oh, God. All this time." I turned and started for the door. "Outsiders. At the end of the day, this is all about the Outsiders. We've got to go. Right now."

"Harry," Karrin said.

I turned to face her.

"Why won't you explain . . . ?" She frowned. "You don't trust me. So you're going to keep me close just like the others."

I looked down at the floor. "Don't take it hard. I don't trust myself right now."

She shook her head. "This is the thanks I get."

"It's Halloween," I said. "It's the night when everyone looks like something that they aren't." I turned toward the door. "But I'm about to start ripping off masks. And we'll both see where everyone stands. Come on."

40

I had a word with Toot-toot once we were outside, and by the time the *Munstermobile* rolled out of the lot, we had a ring of tiny, nigh-invisible escorts pacing us, making it their business to dislodge any enemy tiny observers our foes might have sent to keep tabs on us. It didn't make me think that we would avoid the attentions of enemy Little Folk altogether, but every little thing I could conceal from the people working against me could prove to be a critical edge.

Karrin saw the car's paint job again, rolled her eyes, and declined my offer of a ride. She followed us on her Harley. Molly rode shotgun with me, holding her backpack on her lap. Molly was a big believer in shaping the future by way of carrying anything you might need in a backpack. Tonight it looked particularly stuffed.

As I drove, the burn in my calf continued every time I worked the clutch or pumped the brake, getting slowly worse beneath the layers of gauze Butters had wrapped it in. The rest of my lower leg was tingling and itching, too, but at least the wound wasn't soaking through the bandages.

What the hell had that dart *been*? Why plug me with it, unless the Redcap thought it would kill me?

"I, uh," Molly said as I pulled the Caddy into the marina parking lot. "I got you something."

"Eh?" I asked.

"I had them rush it out this morning and we got it this afternoon. I mean, you know. As long as I was using Thomas's card anyway."

I blinked. "You embezzled funds from the White Court to get me a present?"

"I like to think of it less as embezzling and more as an involuntary goodwill contribution," she said.

"Careful," I told her. "You don't want to get entangled with Lara and her crew. Even owing them money isn't smart."

"I didn't borrow it, boss. I stole it. If they weren't cautious enough to stop me, that isn't my problem. They should be more careful who they hand those cards to. Besides, they can afford it."

"The entitled younger generation, I swear," I said. "Well-done." I found a space big enough for the *Munstermobile* and parked, then set the emergency brake and killed the engine. "What is it?"

Molly got out of the car. "Come see."

I started to, but she hurried impatiently around to meet me, digging into her backpack. I shut the car door behind me and she presented me with a paper-covered package tied with string.

I opened it by tearing paper and snapping string, and a long leather garment unrolled.

"Dunh nuh nah nah nunh," Molly sang, singing the opening riff from "Bad to the Bone."

I found myself smiling and held up a long coat of heavy black leather, like one of those old cowboy dusters, except for the long mantle hanging down over its shoulders. It smelled like new leather and shone without a scuff mark to be seen. "Where the hell did you find an Inverness coat?" I asked her.

"Internet," she said. "Security Guy helped me shop for it."

"You don't know his name?" I asked.

"His name is Guy, and he's building security," Molly said. "Security Guy."

"And he did this for you why?" I asked.

"Because I'm pretty and because he might have gotten a gift certificate out of the deal."

"Remind me to never give you one of my credit cards," I said, and I put the coat on.

The weight of the leather settling around me was familiar and comforting, but this coat wasn't the same as my old coat. The sleeves were a little longer, and fit better. The shoulders were a little narrower, and actually matched up with mine. The mantle hung down a bit more. The pockets were in a slightly different place. Most significantly, it didn't have the layers of protective enchantments that took about half a working week to lay down.

But . . .

Yeah, I decided. I could get used to it.

I looked up to see my apprentice grinning widely.

I put my hand on her shoulder for a moment, smiled, and said, "Thanks, Molls."

Her eyes shone.

Mouse piled out of the car and hurried over to sniff the coat, tail wagging.

"What do you think?" I asked him.

"Woof," he said seriously.

"He thinks it suits you," Molly said, smiling.

"Goofy motorcycle cowboy meets Scotland Yard?"

Mouse wagged his tail.

I grunted as Karrin pulled in and parked her Harley far down the row from the *Munstermobile*, in a motorcycle parking space. She eyed me as she came walking up to us, then Molly, and gave her an approving nod. "That's more like it," she said.

"Feels good," I said. I nodded toward the water, where the *Water Beetle* was chugging slowly back into its berth. Thomas was at the wheel, maneuvering the tub deftly. I waved at him and he replied with a thumbs-up gesture. The boat was ready to go.

I turned to speak to the others, but before I could, I felt my concentration disrupted. An eerie, cool frisson rolled down my spine, all the way down my body to my legs. There was a flicker and a chill from the little wound, and the pain became a little less. At the same moment, I sensed the air grow a fraction of a degree colder, something I would never have noticed on my own.

Sundown.

"That's it," I said a second later. "Sun's down. It's on."

"What if you're too late?" Sarissa asked. "What if they're starting right now?"

"Then we're wasting time talking about it," Molly said. "Let's get to the boat." She beckoned Mac and Sarissa. "This way, please."

I glanced at Mouse and jerked my chin toward Molly. He heaved himself up and went after her, walking just behind our two unknown quantities.

Karrin had opened a storage compartment on her Harley. She shrugged out of her jacket, and then slipped into a tactical harness and clicked it shut around her. She added a number of nylon pouches to it, then took out a gym bag and dropped heavy objects in before shutting the compartment and locking it. She looked up at me and nodded. "All set?"

"I miss my gear," I said. "P90 in there?"

"His name is George," Karrin said. "You want my backup gun?"

"Nah, I've already got the finest killing technology 1866 had to offer on the boat. Glad I didn't name it George. How embarrassing would that have been?"

"George isn't insecure," she said.

"What about, ah . . . ?"

"The Swords?"

"The Swords."

"No," Karrin said.

"Why not?"

She frowned and then shook her head. "This . . . isn't their fight."

"That doesn't make any sense," I said.

"I've wielded one," she said. "And it makes perfect sense to me. To use them tonight would be to make them vulnerable. No."

"But—" I began.

"Harry," Karrin said. "Remember the last time the Swords went to the island? When their actual adversaries were there? Remember how that turned out?"

My best friend, Molly's dad, had been shot up like a Tennessee speed limit sign. The Swords had a purpose, and as long as they kept to it, they were invulnerable, and the men and women who wielded them were avenging angels. But if they went off mission, bad things tended to happen.

"Trust me," Karrin said quietly. "I know it doesn't make sense. Sometimes faith is like that. This isn't their fight. It's ours."

I growled. "Fine. But tell the Almighty that He's missing His chance to get in on the ground floor of something big."

Murphy punched my chest, but gently, and smiled when she did it. The two of us turned toward the dock and began to follow Molly and the others. I was just about to step out onto the dock when I heard something. I stopped in my tracks and turned.

It started low and distant, a musical cry from somewhere far away. It hung in the darkening air for a moment like some carrion bird over dying prey, and then slowly faded.

The wind started picking up.

Again the tone sounded, nearer, and the hairs on my arms stood straight up. Thunder rumbled overhead. The rain, a fitful drizzle most of the day, began to fall in chilly earnest.

And again the hunting horn sounded.

My heart started revving up, and I swallowed. Footsteps approached, and then Thomas was standing beside me, staring out the same way I was. Without speaking, he passed me the Winchester rifle and the ammunition belt.

"Is it . . . ?" I asked him.

His voice was rough. "Yeah."

"Dammit. How soon?"

"Soon. Coming right through the heart of downtown."

"*Fuck*," I said.

Karrin held both hands up. "Wait, wait, the both of you. What the hell is happening?"

"The Wild Hunt is coming," I said, my throat dry. "Um . . . I sort of pissed off the Erlking a while back. He's not the kind of person to forget that."

"The king of earls?" Karrin asked. "Now who isn't making sense?"

"He's a powerful lord of Faerie," Thomas explained. "He's one of the leaders of the Wild Hunt. When the Hunt comes to the real world, it starts hunting prey and it doesn't stop. You can join it, you can hide from it, or you can die."

"Wait," Karrin said. "Harry—they're hunting *you*?"

My heart continued to beat faster, pumping blood to my muscles, keying my body to run, run, run. It was hard to think past that and answer her question. "Uh, yeah. I can . . . I think I can feel them coming." I looked at Thomas. "Water?"

"They'll run over it like it was solid ground."

"How do you know that?" Karrin asked.

"I joined," Thomas said. "Harry, Justine."

I clenched my hands into fists on the heavy rifle. "Get on the boat and go."

"I'm not leaving you."

"Oh, yes, you are," I said. "Raith and Marcone have the other two sites covered, but we are the only ones left to get to Demonreach. If we blow it there, and the ritual goes off, we're all screwed. If I go with you, the Hunt follows me and then goes after whoever is close. We'll never pull off an assault with them on our heels."

My brother ground his teeth and shook his head.

"Let's go, Harry," Karrin said. "If they follow us out over the lake, we'll take them on."

"You can't take them on," I said quietly. "The Hunt isn't a monster you can shoot. It's not some creature you can wrestle with, or some kind of mercenary you can buy off. It's a force of nature, red in tooth and claw. It kills. That's what it does."

"But—" Karrin began.

"He's right," Thomas said, his voice rough. "Dammit. He's right."

"It's chess," I said. "We've been checked, with that ritual on the island. We have no choice but to try to stop it with everything we've got. If that means sacrificing a piece, that's how it has to be."

I put a hand on my brother's shoulder. "Go. Get it done."

He put his cold, strong hand over mine for a second. Then he turned and ran for the boat.

Karrin stared up at me for a second, the rain plastering her hair down.

Her face was twisted with agony. "Harry, please." She swallowed. "I can't leave you alone. Not twice."

"There are eight million people in this city. And if we don't shut the ritual down, those people will die."

Karrin's expression changed—from pain to shock, from shock to horror, and from horror to realization. She made a choking sound and ducked her head, her face turned away from me. Then she turned toward the boat.

I watched her for a second longer. Then I sprinted for the *Munstermobile* as the haunting cry of the Wild Hunt's horn grew nearer. I jammed my key into the door lock and . . .

And it wouldn't fit.

I tried it again. No joy. Half-panicked, I ran to each of the others, but every single one of the locks was out of commission. I was going to bust out a window, but I checked the car's ignition through it first. It had been packed with what looked like chewing gum. The *Munstermobile* had . . .

Had been sabotaged. With gum and superglue. It was a trick I'd had Toot and company play on others more than once. And now what I had done unto others had been done unto me at the damnedest moment imaginable.

"Aggggh!" I screamed. "I hate ironic reversal!"

The Za Lord's Guard had been escorting us along the way, but I hadn't said anything about staying on the job once we reached our destination. Given the distance I'd had them covering today, they'd probably dropped down exhausted the second I'd set the parking brake.

The thunder rolled closer, my unthinking panic rose, and my wounded leg felt like it might burst into flames.

My leg.

My eyes widened with horror of my own. The Redcap had killed me at that ambush, and I was only now realizing it. The trickle of blood flowing steadily from that tiny wound would leave a powerful olfactory and psychic trail behind me. Tracking me would be easier than whistling.

I could run, but I couldn't hide.

Thunder roared, and I saw a cluster of dim forms descend from the cloud cover overhead and into the city light of Chicago. I could run, but the Hunt was moving at highway speeds. I wouldn't even be able to significantly delay the inevitable. Shadowy hounds rushed down at me from the north, along the shoreline, and behind them came a blurry cluster of dark figures on horseback, carrying bows and spears and long blades of every description.

I couldn't beat the Hunt. Not even with Mab's 'roids in my system. But maybe . . .

Then there was another roar—this time not of thunder, but of a hundred and forty horses, American-made.

Karrin Murphy's motorcycle slid to a stop close enough to me to throw gravel over my shoes, and I turned to find her revving the engine.

"Karrin! What the hell are you doing?"

"Get on the bike, bitch!" she called over the next horn blast. "Let's make them work for it!"

She smiled, a fierce, bright smile, and I found my own face following her example.

"Fuck, yeah," I said, and threw myself onto the back of the Harley as darkness, death, and fire closed in around my city.

41

I dropped the cartridge belt for the Winchester over one shoulder and hurried to rake in the tail of my new duster before the motorcycle's rear wheel snagged it and killed me. I damn near fell off as Karrin accelerated, but managed to cling to her waist with the arm holding the rifle.

Karrin scowled at me, grabbed the rifle from my hand, and slipped it down into a little section on the side of the Harley that fit the short rifle suspiciously well. I held on to her with a free hand, and with the other made sure my coat wouldn't get me killed.

"Which way?" she shouted back at me.

"South! Fast as you can!"

She stomped one of her feet onto something, twisted a wrist, and the Harley, which had been doing around fifty, leapt forward as if it hadn't been moving at all.

I shot a quick glance over my shoulder, and saw the nearest elements of the Hunt begin to slowly fade back. I guess maybe the Wild Hunt hadn't ever heard about Harley-Davidson.

But she couldn't maintain the speed, not even on a wide Chicago street in chilly, rainy weather. There were just too many other people around, forcing her to weave between traffic, and she had to slow down to keep from splattering us all over some family's sedan. Indignant car horns began to blare as she slipped in and out of lanes, adding an abrasive harmony to the horns of the Wild Hunt.

"How we doing?" she called.

I looked back. The Wild Hunt was less than a hundred yards away—and they didn't have to contend with traffic. The jerks were racing along fifty feet off the freaking ground, up in the dark and the rain, unseen by the vast majority of people going about their everyday business. "They're cheating! Go faster! Head for the Bush!"

Karrin turned her head enough to catch me in the edge of her vision. "Is there a plan?"

"It isn't a very good plan!" I shouted. "But I need a big open area for it to work, away from people!"

"In *Chicago*?" she shouted. Then her eyes widened. "The mills?"

"Go!" I shouted. Karrin blitzed a red light, narrowly avoiding a left-turning car, and continued her furious rush down Lake Shore Drive.

Chicago is a city of terrific demands. Demand for a military presence helped establish the early Colonial-era forts, which in turn provided security for white settlers, traders, and missionaries. They built houses, churches, and businesses, which accreted over time into a town, then a city. Chicago's position as the great crossroads of the emerging American nation meant that more and more people arrived, building more homes, businesses, and, eventually, heavy-duty industry.

By the end of the nineteenth century, Chicago was a booming industrial city—and its steel mills were nearly legendary. U.S. Steel, Youngstown Steel, Wisconsin Steel, Republic Steel, all thriving and growing on the shore of Lake Michigan, down by Calumet City. The lakefront in that entire area was sculpted to accommodate the steel works, and much of the steel that would fuel the Allied efforts in two world wars was produced in that relatively tiny portion of the city.

But all things wither away eventually. The American steel industry began to falter and fade, and by the end of the twentieth century, all that remained of an ironmongery epicenter was a long stretch of industrial-strength wasteland and crumbling buildings on Lake Michigan's shore. A decade later, the city started trying to clean the place up, knocking down most of the buildings and structures—but here and there, stone and concrete ruins remained, like the bones of some vast beast that had been picked clean by scavengers. Nothing much grew there as the city around it thrived—just weeds and property values.

That portion of the waterfront was slated for renewal, but it hadn't happened yet, and right now it was blasted heath, a flat, dark, empty, and desolate stretch of level land dotted with lonely reminders of former greatness. There was no shelter from rain or cold there, and on a miserable night like this, there shouldn't be anyone hanging around.

All we had to do was make it that far.

We flew by the Museum of Science and Industry on our right, then flashed over the bridge above the Fifty-ninth Street Yacht Harbor, moving into a section of road that had a little distance between itself and the nearest buildings and a decided lack of foot traffic on a cold autumn evening.

As if they'd been waiting for an opening away from so many prying eyes, the Wild Hunt swept down on us like a falcon diving onto a rabbit.

But they were not attacking a rabbit. They were attacking a wabbit. A wascally wabbit. A wascally wabbit with a Winchester.

Something that looked like a great, gaunt hound made of smoke and cinders, with glowing coals for eyes, hit the ground just behind the Harley and began sprinting, keeping pace with us. It came rushing in, dark jaws spread to seize the back tire, the same motion it might have used had it been attempting to hamstring a fleeing deer. Mindless animal panic raged inside my head, but I kept it away from the core of my thoughts, forcing myself to focus, think, act.

I saw Karrin's eyes snap over to her rearview mirror as it closed, and felt her body tensing against mine as she prepared to evade to the left. I gathered my will but waited to unleash it, and as the charhound closed to within inches of the tire, Karrin leaned and took the Harley left. The charhound's jaws clashed closed on exhaust fumes, and I unleashed my will from the palm of my outstretched right hand with a snarl of *"Forzare!"*

Force hit the charhound low on its front legs, and the beast's head went into the concrete at breakneck speed—literally. There was a terrible snapping sound, and the charhound's limp body went tumbling end over end, bouncing up into the air for a dozen yards before landing, shedding wisps of darkness all the way.

What landed in a boneless sprawl on the road was not a dog, or a canine of any sort. It was a young man—a human, wearing a black T-shirt and torn old blue jeans. I barely had time to register that before the body tumbled off the road and was out of sight.

"Good shot!" Karrin cried, grinning fiercely. She was driving. She hadn't seen what was under the hound's outer shell.

So that was how one joined the Wild Hunt. It was a mask, a huge, dark, terrifying mask—a masquerade.

And I'd just killed a man.

I didn't get any time to feel angst over it. Karrin gunned the engine of the Harley and it surged ahead, running along the spit of land that bifurcates Jackson Harbor. Even as she did, two riders descended, one on either side of the road, their steeds' hooves hammering against empty air about five feet up. Like the charhound, the steeds and riders were covered in a smoky darkness through which shone the amber fire of their eyes.

Karrin saw the one on the right and tried to move left again—but the second rider pressed in closer, the dark horse's hooves nearly hammering onto our heads, and she wobbled and gunned the accelerator.

I recognized another hunter's tactic. The first had forced us to close distance with the second. They were driving us between them, trying to make us panic and think about nothing but running straight ahead—in a nice, smooth, predictable line.

The second rider lifted an arm and he held the dark shape of a spear in his hand. He hurled it forward, leading the target perfectly. I flung up my left hand, extending my shield spell. It got mixed results. The spear flew into it and through it, shredding my magic as it went—but instead of flying into my face, the spear was deflected just enough that its blade sliced across the back of my neck, leaving a line of burning pain behind it.

The adrenaline was flowing and the pain didn't matter. Hell, it really didn't matter if the wound had opened an artery—it wasn't as though I could stop to get medical attention if it had. I twisted around to fling another bolt of force at the rider, but he lifted a hand and let out an eerie screech, and my attack was dispersed, doing little more than inconveniencing my target. His horse lost a step or two, but he dug black spurs into the beast's hide and it soon made up the pace.

Big surprise, magic wasn't a big threat to the Huntsmen.

Solution: Winchester.

I drew the rifle from the rack on the Harley, thumbed back the hammer while still holding it in one hand, then twisted at the waist to bring it to bear on the rider, the heavy weapon's forearm falling into my left hand. I didn't have much time to aim, and it might have actually been counterproductive, given our speed, the irregularities of the chase, the darkness, and the rain. Plus, I'm not exactly Annie Oakley. So I made a best guess and pulled the trigger.

The rifle let out a crack of thunder, and a burst of disintegrated shadow flew up from the shoulder and neck and jawline of the rider. I got a look at the armor beneath the mask, and a portion of his face, and realized with renewed terror that I'd just put a bullet into the Erlking.

And an instant later I realized with a surge of incandescent hope that I'd just put a *bullet* into the *Erlking* on *Halloween night.*

The Erlking reeled in the saddle, and his horse faltered and veered away, gaining altitude again. I levered a new round into the chamber, gripped the weapon like a pistol, and whirled it back over Karrin's ducked head to point it one-handed at the rider on the right, who was even now making his own approach, spear uplifted.

I guessed again and shot. I didn't hit him, but the thunder of the gun came just as he flung the spear. I didn't rattle the rider, but the flame-eyed horse flinched, and the spear flew wide of us. The rider was not deterred. He brought his steed under control first—then he let out a weird, bubbling screech and swept a long, dark-bladed sword from the scabbard at his side. He started closing the distance again.

It was impossible to lever another round into the rifle quickly while riding behind Karrin. That thing John Wayne does, whirling the rifle one-handed to cock it? It really helps if you have one of those enlarged, oblong lever handles to do it with, and mine was the smaller, traditional rectangle. Also, it helps to be John Wayne. I had to draw the rifle into my chest and hold it steady with my left hand to get it done. The rider swerved in at us and I shot again—and missed as his steed juked and abruptly changed speed, briefly falling back before boring in again.

I repeated that cycle three times before I realized that the rider was playing me for a sucker. He respected the gun, but knew its weakness: me. He wasn't dodging bullets—he was dodging *me*, tempting me into taking shots with little chance of success in an effort to get me to use up my ammo.

And all the while, the rest of the Hunt kept pace with us: *dozens* of riders like this one, plus maybe twice that many shadowy hounds, all keeping about fifty yards back and up, clearly giving the first two hunters the honor of first attempt.

"His horse!" Karrin screamed. "Shoot the horse!"

I ground my teeth. I didn't want to do that. For all I knew, that thing was only a horse costume—there could be another human being underneath that shadowy outer shell.

The rider screeched again, the sound weirdly familiar and completely hair-raising. Again and again he came in on us, and I kept holding him off as we raced at insane speed through the rainy night, trading bullets for time.

"There!" I shouted suddenly, pointing off to our left. "Over there! The walls!"

We had reached the old steelwork grounds.

Karrin gunned the engine and swept the Harley out onto the open ground, racing frantically toward one of the only structures remaining—a trio of concrete walls maybe thirty or forty feet high, running parallel to one another for at least a quarter of mile—the last remains of U.S. Steel.

As the steed's hooves started hitting the ground, they abruptly threw off clouds of angry silver sparks with every strike. The dark horse screeched in agony and I let out a howl of defiance—after a century of labor in the steel mills, there had to be unreal levels of trace steel and iron in the ground where they had stood—and whatever power sustained the Wild Hunt didn't like it any more than the other beings of Faerie did.

"Between the walls!" I shouted. "Go, go, go!"

"That's crazy!" Karrin shouted.

"I know!"

She guided the Harley around a pile of rubble and raced into the heavy shadows between two of the walls, and the rider was right on us as she did.

"Closer!" I screamed. "Force him to the wall!"

"Why!"

A quarter of a mile goes by *fast* on a roaring Harley—and the only thing in front of us was the cold water of Lake Michigan. "Hurry!" I shrieked.

"Agh!" Karrin howled, and abruptly the Harley slowed and cut right.

In an instant, we were even with the rider, and though no expression could show through the darkness surrounding his face, his body language was one of shock.

Now for the dangerous part, I thought. Which made me start giggling. *Now* it was getting dangerous.

Before the rider could change speed or take on altitude, and while the Harley was still leaning toward the rider, I hauled my left foot up onto the seat and sprang at him, still holding the now-emptied Winchester in one hand.

I slammed into the rider, but whoever he was, he was *strong*. I had the power of the Winter Knight at my disposal, but compared to the rider, my strength was that of a child. He threw a stiff-arm into my chest and nearly sent me tumbling—but I grabbed onto his sleeve, and as he fell I simply hung on. That changed things. It wasn't an issue of strength against strength. This made it a contest of mass and leverage versus muscle, and muscle lost. I dragged the rider from his saddle and we both hit the rough ground at speed.

My hand was torn from his arm on impact, and I remember trying to shield my head with my arms. The Winchester flew clear of me, too. I could see the rider tumbling as well, silver fire blowing up from the shadowy mask around him. I stopped tumbling yards later, and frantically staggered back to my feet. I spotted the Winchester lying a few yards away and leapt for it.

I grabbed the weapon, but before I could load it, I heard a footstep behind me and I spun, raising the gun up over my head, parallel to the ground. It was in the nick of time. I felt the staggering power of an enormous blow, and a sword rang against the steel of the Winchester's octagonal barrel.

Kringle recovered from the block swiftly. Scraps of shadow mask hung from him, but he still wore the armor and a bloodred cloak and hood trimmed in white fur. His sword was silvery and unadorned, and he whipped it through a swift series of strikes. I blocked frantically with the Winchester, but I knew enough about fighting to know that I was utterly outclassed. He'd have that sword in me in a matter of seconds.

So I ducked, sprang back from a backhanded slash, and raised the rifle to my shoulder as if I were about to shoot.

That stopped him, forcing Kringle to twist to one side to avoid the theoretical bullet—and when he did, I slammed every bit of will I had into a lance of magical force. *"Forzare!"*

Kringle slipped aside, incredibly nimble for a man his size, and the strike missed him completely.

It did *not* miss the base of the ruined wall behind him.

What must have been a couple of tons of aged concrete collapsed with a roar. Kringle was fast and skilled, but he wasn't perfect. He kept himself from being crushed, but several large stones clipped him and sent him staggering.

I let out a primal scream and rushed him. I hit him at the shoulders, and he was too off balance to bring the sword into play. We both crashed to the ground, but I wound up on top, kneeling over him, gripping the steel barrel of the Winchester in both hands, holding it like a club.

Kringle froze, staring up at me, and I suddenly realized that the night had gone utterly silent. I glanced around. The Wild Hunt had surrounded us, horses coming to a stop, their riders watching intently. Hounds paced nervously around at the horses' feet, but came no closer. The Erlking was there, too, his shadow mask tattered, greenish blood smearing the visible armor on his shoulder. His right arm hung limply. I turned back to Kringle.

"Join, hide, or die," I growled. "Those are your options when the Wild Hunt comes for you."

Kringle narrowed his eyes. "Everyone knows that's true."

"Not anymore it isn't," I growled. I got to my feet, slowly, and just as slowly I lowered the rifle. Then I extended a hand to Kringle. "Tonight, the *Hunt* is joining *me*." I swept my gaze around the silent assembly, filling it with all the steel and resolve I had. "I just put the Erlking on the bench and laid a beat-down on freaking Santa Claus," I told them. "So you tell me. Who's next? Who comes to make an end of the Winter Knight, a peer of the Winter Court and Mab's chosen? Who is at the top of *this* food chain? Because tonight is Halloween, and I am damned well not afraid of any of you."

Firelight eyes stared at me from all around and nothing stirred.

Then Kringle's chuckle began rumbling up out of his throat, a pulsating sound of deep and hearty mirth. One of his huge hands closed on mine, and I hauled him back to his feet. I glanced over at the Erlking as I did. I could see nothing of his face, but he nodded his head toward me, very slightly. There was something ironic about the way he did it, and I sensed a kind of quiet amusement.

There was a low rumble as the Harley came purring slowly over the ground toward us. Karrin stared at the scene, her eyes wide, and drew the bike to a stop next to me.

"Harry?" she asked. "What just happened?"

"A change of leadership," I said, and swung one leg over the Harley to hop up behind her. Even as I did, shadows began to whirl and slither. They crawled up Kringle's legs, restoring the concealing mask—and as they did, they also started climbing the Harley and both of the people sitting on it.

It was a bizarre sensation. Everything about my physical perception sharpened, and I could suddenly sense the world around me with perfect clarity. I could feel the other members of the Hunt, knew exactly where they were and what they were doing on sheer instinct—an instinct that guided them, as well. The night brightened into a silvery fairyland that remained night while being as bright as the noonday sun. The shadow masks became something translucent, so that if I peered closely enough, I could see what was behind it. I didn't do much peering. I had a feeling that I didn't *want* to know what was behind all of those shadows.

Karrin twisted the throttle on the Harley nervously, gunning the engine—but instead of a roar, it came out as a primal screech. The cry was instantly taken up by every single member of the Hunt, even as Kringle, his shadow mask restored, remounted his steed and whirled it to face me.

"Sir Knight," Kringle said, inclining his head slightly to me, "what game amuses you this fine, stormy evening?"

I started loading shells from the ammo belt into the Winchester, until the rifle was full again. Then I levered a shell into the pipe, slipped a replacement into the tube, shut the breach with a snap, and felt a wolfish smile spreading my mouth. "Tonight?" I asked. I raised my voice to address them all. "Tonight we hunt Outsiders!"

The bloodthirsty screech that went up from the Wild Hunt was deafening.

42

"Pipe down!" I shouted. "We're going quiet until we get there!"

The Hunt settled down, though not instantly. Karrin revved the Harley's engine, and it was completely, entirely silent. I could feel the vibration of the increased revolutions, but they did not translate into sound. The shadows around the Harley shifted and wavered, and after a second I realized that they had taken on a shape—that of an enormous black cat, muscled and solid, like a jaguar. That was astounding to me. Magic was not some kind of partially sentient force that did things of its own volition. It wasn't any more artistic than electricity.

"Okay," I said to Karrin. "Let's move."

"Uh," she asked, without turning her head, "move where?"

"The island," I said.

"Harry, this is a motorcycle."

"It'll work," I said. "Look at it."

Karrin jerked as she noted the appearance of the Harley. "You want me to drive into the lake."

"You have to admit," I said, "it isn't the craziest thing I've ever asked you to do. It isn't even the craziest thing I've asked you to do *tonight*."

Karrin thought about that one for a second and said, "You're right. Let's go."

She dropped the Harley into gear, threw out a rooster tail of dirt and gravel, and we rushed toward the shore of the lake. The steel mills had been engaged in actual shipping traffic in their day, and the level field of construction marched right up to the water's edge and dropped off abruptly, the water four or five feet straight down.

Karrin gunned the engine, covering the last two hundred yards in a flat-out sprint, and the torque on that Harley's engine was something epic, its bellow too loud to be wholly contained by the shadow mask, emerging from the shadow tiger's mouth as a deep-throated roar. Karrin let out a scream that was two parts excitement to one part terror, and we flew twenty feet before the tires crashed down onto the surface of the lake—and held.

The bike jounced a couple of times, but I held on to Karrin and kept from flying off. It was an interesting question, though: If I had, would the water have supported me, like an endless field of asphalt? Or would it have behaved as it normally would?

The entire Hunt swept along behind us, silent but for the low thunder of hooves and the panting of the hounds—when suddenly the silver starlight turned bright azure blue.

"Whoa!" Karrin said. "Did you do that?"

"I don't *think* so," I said. I looked over my shoulder and found Kringle and the Erlking riding along behind me, I jerked my head at them in a beckoning gesture, and they obligingly came up on either side of the Harleytiger.

"What is that?" I asked, pointing at the sky.

"A temporal pressure wave," the Erlking said, his flaming eyes narrowed.

"A wha'?" I asked.

The Erlking looked at Kringle. "This is your area of expertise. Explain it."

"Someone is bending time against us," Kringle said.

I stared at him for a second and then it clicked. "We're being rushed forward so that we'll get there too late," I said. "We're looking at a Doppler shift."

"Is what he said correct?" the Erlking asked Kringle curiously.

"Essentially, aye. We've already lost half of an hour by my count."

"Who could have done this?" I asked.

"You have encountered this before, wizard," Kringle said. "Can you not guess?"

"One of the Queens," I muttered. "Or someone operating on their level. Can we get out of this wave?"

The Erlking and Kringle traded a look. "You are the leader of the Hunt," Kringle said. "What you wright with your power will grace each of us. Would you like to do it?"

Was he kidding me? I had almost as much of an idea of how to screw around with the fabric of time as I did which of my clothes could be safely washed in hot water. "I probably need to save myself for what's coming," I said.

Kringle nodded. "If it is your will," he said diffidently, "we can set our hands against it."

"Do it," I said.

They both nodded their heads at me in small bows, and then their steeds raced out in front of the pack. Sparks began to fly from their horses' hooves, first blue, then abruptly darkening to scarlet. The air seemed to shimmer, and strange, twisted sounds writhed all around us. Then there was a reverberating crash that sounded like something between thunder and the discharge of a blaster. The air split in front of the two of them like a curtain, and as the Hunt hurtled through it, the stars washed out to their normal silver hue again.

"Well-done, I guess!" I shouted—and then I noticed that Kringle was no longer there, though the Erlking still raced along. Over the next few moments he slowed enough to pace Karrin and me. "Hey, where'd Bowl-Full-of-Jelly go?"

"Kringle was our stepping-stone out of the rapids of the stream," he called back. "To lift us out, he had to remain behind. He will rejoin us farther down the shore."

"Harry," Karrin said.

"How much farther down the shore?"

The Erlking shrugged with his uninjured arm. "Time may hold no terror for us immortals, Sir Knight, but it is a massive force, all but beyond even our control. It will take as long as it takes."

"Harry!" Karrin snapped.

I turned my eyes front and felt them widen.

We had arrived at Demonreach—and the island was under attack.

The first thing I saw was the curtain wall around the island's shore-line. It was nothing but a flicker of opalescent light, like a dense aurora borealis, stretching from the water's edge up into the October sky. It cast an eerie glow over the trees of the island, steeping them in menacing black shadow, and its reflection in the waters of the lake was three or four times bigger and more colorful than it should have been.

As the Hunt rushed closer, I could make out other details, too. There was a small fleet of boats surrounding the island—it looked like something out of WWII's Pacific theater. Some of the boats were modest recreational models, several at least the size of the *Water Beetle*, and three looked like tugboat-barge units, the kind that could ferry twenty loaded train cars around the lake.

I could see motion in the waters around the shore. *Things* were swarming up out of the lake, hideous and fascinating—hundreds of them. They smashed into Demonreach's curtain wall. Light pulsed in liquid concentric circles where they touched it, and shrieks of alien agony stretched the air toward a breaking point. The waters within twenty feet of the shore bubbled and thrashed in a demonic frenzy.

I felt a pulse of power stir in the air, and a bolt of sickly green energy lashed across the waters and slammed into the curtain wall. The entire wall dimmed for a second, but then resurged as the island resisted the attack. I tracked the bolt back to the barge and saw a figure in a weird, writhing cloak standing on the deck, facing the island—Sharkface.

As I watched, I saw a Zodiac boat carrying a team of eight men in dark clothing rush in toward the shore. The man in the nose of the boat lifted something to his shoulder, there was a loud *foomp*, and a fire blossomed in the brush, burning with an eye-searing chemical brilliance. Then the Zodiac whirled and rushed back out again, as if to escape a counterstrike—or maybe they just didn't want to stay anywhere close to waters full of piranhalike frenzied Outsiders while sitting in a rubber boat. Half a dozen other boats were doing the same thing, and several other similar craft were sitting still, full of armed men waiting silently for the chance to land onshore.

I stared in shock. The recent rain meant that the island wasn't likely to burst into flame anytime soon, but I had utterly underestimated the scope of tonight's conflict, ye gods and little fishes. This wasn't just a ritual spell.

This was an all-out amphibious assault, my very own miniature war.

"Erlking," I said. "Can you veil the Hunt, please?"

The Erlking glanced at me, and then back at the Hunt, and suddenly the cold, weirdly flat-sounding dimness of a veil against both sight and sound gathered around us like a cloud.

"This doesn't make any sense," I said. "The ritual would still need a platform, and that would take time and work to set up—at least a day. It would show. They haven't even gotten onto the island y—" Then the truth hit me in a flash. "The barges," I said. "They set up a ritual platform on one of the barges. It's the only thing that makes sense."

"The waters of the lake would diminish the power they could draw from the ley lines running beneath it," the Erlking said.

"Yeah," I said. "That's why they're assaulting the shore. They're going to force a breach and then run the barge aground on the island. That'll put them in direct contact with the ley line."

"There are *many* Outsiders here, Sir Knight," he noted. "More than enough to do battle with the Hunt, if we become bogged down in their numbers. They will react to us as one beast, once they know the danger we pose to them. Have a care for where we enter the fray."

"We'd better make the first punch count," I said. "Three barges. Which one has the platform?"

"Why assume there's only one?" Karrin asked. "If it was me, I'd set the spell upon all three of them, for redundancy."

"They might have set the spell up on all three of them for redundancy," I said.

She drove one of her elbows back against my stomach, lightly.

"We start this by sinking a barge," I decided. Then I blinked and looked at the Erlking. "Can we sink a barge?"

The shadow-masked Erlking tilted his head slightly to one side, his burning eyes narrowed. "Wizard, please."

"Right," I said. "Sorry. Eeny, meeny, miney, moe, catch a Sharkface by the toe." I pointed at the barge in the middle, where I'd seen the Outsider a moment ago. "That one. And once it's down, we'll split into two groups. You'll lead half the Hunt for the barge on the far side, and I'll take my half to the nearer one. If we can nix any possibility of the ritual happening, maybe they'll call it a night and go home."

"That seems unlikely," said the Erlking. He slowly flexed the arm I'd shot him in, and I could sense that, while it was not comfortable, the lord of the goblins was already functionally recovered from the injury.

"Never know until you try," I said. I looked back at the Hunt and pointed toward the center barge. I repeated my instructions to them, and soot black hands drew dozens of shadowy weapons.

I leaned into Karrin a little and said, next to her ear, "You ready for this?"

"Only a lunatic is ready for this," she said. I could hear her smile as she spoke. Then she turned her head and, before I could react, planted a kiss right on my mouth.

I almost fell off the Harley.

She drew her head back, flashed me a wicked little smile, and said, "For luck. *Star Wars*–style."

"You are so hot right now," I told her. I lifted my Winchester overhead, then dropped it to point forward, and the Hunt surged ahead at its full, insane speed, silent and unseen and inevitable.

"Go right past its rear end," I told Murphy.

"You mean its stern?"

"Yes, that," I said, rolling my eyes. And then I began to gather in my will.

It was *hard*, a slow strain, like trying to breathe through layers of heavy cloth. It was like holding a fistful of sand—every bit of energy I drew in wanted to slip away from me, and the harder I tried to hold it, the more trickled through my fingers.

So I gritted my teeth, accepted that I wasn't going to have a lot of energy to work with, and tried to hold it loosely, gently, as we closed in on the barge. We were the first to pass it, and as we did I flung out my hand, crying out, "*Forzare!*" Raw will leapt through the air, shattering our concealing veil. The energy was focused into the shape of a cone, needle-pointed at the top, and widening gradually to about six inches across—an invisible lance. I couldn't have done any more with the limited energy I had at my disposal. It hit the hull of the barge with a clang and a shriek of tearing metal, and then we were past it, and Karrin was tugging the Harley into a tight, leaning turn.

I checked over my shoulder and saw the Erlking, his sword in hand, lean over the saddle and strike. There was a hissing sound, and a howl of screeching steel, and, starting at the hole I'd punched in the barge's hull, a straight line of red-hot metal appeared where his sword had simply sheared through it. Behind him, the next riders struck, their weapons carving steel like soft pine, slashing at the weakened section and tearing the original hole I'd made wider and wider.

I heard a howl of rage, and looked up on the deck of the barge to see Sharkface there, already gathering energy to hurl at the riders of the Hunt.

He didn't take the hounds into consideration.

Before he could unleash his power, a dozen of the beasts hit him, all together, in a single, psychotic canine wave. Since they were running fast enough to get themselves a speeding ticket in most of Illinois, the impact was formidable. Hounds and Outsider alike flew out over the rails of the barge and vanished into the waters of Lake Michigan—and somehow, I knew, the fight continued beneath its waves.

The Erlking let out a shriek of encouragement, one that was echoed by the other riders as the tail end of the column passed the barge. As the last rider struck, a column of eerie green fire rose up from the glowing edges of the shredded steel hull, and with a groan of strained seams, the barge started to list badly to the right—starboard, I guess—as water rushed in through the hole the Hunt had made.

Karrin had already wheeled the Harley into a snarling turn, one that let us see the deck of the ship as it began to sink. Smart. She'd been thinking farther ahead than me. I could clearly see the dozens of lines and figures that had been painted onto the barge's deck, along with burning candles, incense, and the small, still remains of animal sacrifices—mostly rabbits, cats, and dogs, it looked like.

Rituals, whatever form they take, always involve the use of a circle, explicit or otherwise—the circle had to be there to contain the energy that they'd been building up with all the sacrifices, if nothing else. This one had been established invisibly, maybe originally set up with incense or something—but as the water lapped over the edge of the circle, it immediately began to disperse the pent-up energy, visible as clouds of fluttering sparks, like static, that danced along the surface of the water.

And for just a second, everything in the night went silent.

Then there was a disturbance in the water, with more ugly green light pouring up from below. Water suddenly rushed up, displaced by something moving beneath the surface, and then Sharkface exploded up from the depths, his freaky rag-cloak spread out around him in an enormous cloud of tentacle-like extrusions. He turned his eyeless face toward me—me, exactly, not Karrin, and not the Erlking—and let out a howl of fury so loud that the water for fifty feet in every direction vibrated and danced in time with it.

And a wave of pure, violent, blinding, *nauseating* pain blanketed the face of Lake Michigan.

43

Suddenly, I wasn't on the bitch seat of Karrin's Harley. I was hanging suspended in midair, and I was in agony.

I opened my eyes and looked wildly around me. Barren, icy earth. Cold grey sky. My arms and legs were stretched out into an X shape, and ice the color of a deep blue sky encased them, holding them stretched out against what felt like an old, knotted tree. Muscles and ligaments from my everywhere were at the trembling breaking point. My own heartbeat was torment. My face burned, exposed to cold so severe that it hurt even me.

I tried to scream, but couldn't. A slow, gargling moan came out instead, and I coughed blood into the freezing air.

"You knew this was coming," said a voice, a voice that still made my entire body thrum in response, something simple and elemental that did not care how long she had held me in torment. "You knew this day would come. I am what I am. As are you."

Mab walked into my vision from the left. I barely had enough strength to keep my eyes focused on her.

"You saw what happened to my last Knight," she said, and began to take slow steps closer to me. I didn't want to give her the satisfaction, but I couldn't help it—I heard myself make a soft noise, felt myself make a feeble effort to move or escape. It made her wide eyes glint for an instant. "I gave you power for a purpose, and that purpose is complete." She turned her hand over slowly, and showed me something she held in it—a small metal spike, too large to be a needle, too small to be a nail. She walked closer to me, rolling the fine-pointed etcher between two fingers, and smiled.

Her fingertips traced over my chest and ribs, and I shuddered. She'd carved the word *weak* upon my body in dozens of alphabets and hundreds of languages, etching it into my flesh, the palms of my hands, the soles of my feet, with miles upon miles of scars.

I wanted it to be over. I wanted her to kill me.

She leaned close to my face. "Today," she breathed, "we start carving your teeth."

Cold enveloped me, and water slithered into my mouth though I tried to keep it out. Some seeped through my cracked lips. More went up my nostrils and took the long way around—and then it froze into ice, slowly forcing my jaws apart. Mab leaned in close to me, lifting the etcher, and I caught the faint scent of oxidation as the instrument began scratching at my incisors. . . .

Oxidation. The smell of rust.

Rust meant steel—something no Faerie I'd ever seen, apart from Mother Winter, could touch.

This wasn't actually happening to me. It wasn't real. The pain wasn't real. The tree wasn't real. The ice wasn't real.

But . . . I still felt them. I could feel something behind them, a will that was not my own, forcing the idea of pain upon me, the image of helplessness, the leaden fear, the bitter vitriol of despair. This was a psychic assault like nothing I'd ever seen before. The ones I'd felt before this one were feeble shadows by comparison.

No, I thought.

"Nnngh," I moaned.

And I then I drew a deep breath. This was not how my life would end. This was not reality. I was Harry Dresden, Wizard of the White Council, Knight of Winter. I had faced demons and monsters, fought off fallen angels and werewolves, slugged it out with sorcerers and cults and freakish things that had no names. I had fought upon land and sea, in the skies above my city, in ancient ruins and in realms of the spirit most of humanity did not know existed. I bore scars that I'd earned in dozens of battles, made enemies out of nightmares, and laid low a dark empire for the sake of one little girl.

And I would be *damned* if I was going to roll over for some punk Outsider and his psychic haymaker.

The words first. Damned near everything begins with words.

"I am," I breathed, and suddenly the ice was clear of my mouth.

"I am Harry . . ." I panted, and the pain redoubled.

And I laughed. As if some freak who had never loved enough to know loss could tell *me* about pain.

"I AM HARRY BLACKSTONE COPPERFIELD DRESDEN!" I roared.

Ice and wood shattered. Frozen stone cracked with a sound like a cannon's blast, a spiderweb of tiny crevices spreading out from me. The image of Mab flew away from me and blew into thousands of crystalline shards, like a shattering stained-glass window. The cold and the pain and the terror reeled away from me, like some vast and hungry beast suddenly struck on the nose.

The Outsiders loved their psychic assaults, and given that this one happened about two seconds after Sharkface came up out of the water, it was pretty clear who was behind it. But that was fine. Sharkface had chosen a battle of the mind. So be it. My head, my rules.

I lifted my right arm to the frozen sky and shouted, wordless and furious, and a bolt of scarlet lightning flashed from the seething skies. It smashed into my hand and then down into the earth. Frozen dirt sprayed everywhere, and when it had cleared, I stood holding an oaken quarterstaff carved with runes and sigils, as tall as my temple and as big around as my joined thumb and forefinger.

Then I stretched my left arm down to the earth and cried out again, sweeping it up in a single, beckoning gesture. I tore metals from the ground beneath me, and they swirled like mist up around my body, forming into a suit of armor covered in spikes and protruding blades.

"Okay, big guy," I snarled out at the dark will that even now gathered itself to attack again. "Now we know who I am. Let's see who you are." I took the staff and smote its end down on the ground. "Who *are* you!" I demanded. "You play in my head, you play by my rules! Identify yourself!"

In answer, there was only a vast roaring sound, like an angry arctic wind gathering into a gale.

"Oh, no, you don't," I muttered. "You started this, creep! You want to get up close and personal, let's play! Who *are* you?"

A vast sound, like something you'd hear in the deep ocean, moaned through the sky.

"Thrice I command thee!" I shouted, focusing my will, sending it coursing into my voice, which boomed out over the landscape. "Thrice I bid thee! By my name I command thee: Tell me who you are!"

And then an enormous swirling form emerged from the clouds overhead—a face, but only in the broadest, roughest terms, like something a child would make from clay. Lightning burned far back in its eyes, and it spoke in the voice of gale winds.

I AM GATEBREAKER, HARBINGER!

I AM FEARGIVER, HOPESLAYER!

I AM HE-WHO-WALKS-BEFORE!

For a second, I just stood there, staring up at the sky, shocked.

Hell's bells.

It worked.

The thing spoke, and as it did, I *knew*, I knew what it was, as if I'd been given a snapshot of its core identity, its quintessential self.

For one second, no more than that, I *understood* it, what it was doing, what it wanted, what it planned and . . .

And then that moment was past, the knowledge vanished the way it had come—except for one thing. Somehow, I'd held on to a few crumbling fragments of insight.

I knew the thing trying to tear my head apart was a Walker. I didn't know much about them except that nobody else knew much about them either, and that they were extremely bad news.

And one of them had tried to kill me when I was sixteen years old. He-Who-Walks-Behind had nearly done it. Except . . . from where I stood now, I wasn't sure he'd really been trying to kill me. He'd been shaping me. I don't know for what, but he'd been trying to provoke me.

And this thing in my head, the thing I'd named Sharkface, was like him, a Walker, a peer. It was huge, powerful, and in a way utterly different from the kinds of power I had seen before. This thing wasn't *bigger* than Mab. But it was horribly, unbearably *deeper* than her, like a photograph of a sculpture compared to the sculpture itself. It had power at its command that was beyond anything I had seen, beyond measure, beyond comprehension—just plain beyond.

This thing was power from the Outside, and I was a grain of sand to its oncoming tide.

But you know what?

That grain of sand might be the last remnant of what had once been a mountain, but that which it is, it is. The tide comes and the tide goes. Let it hammer the grain of sand as it may. Let lofty mountains fear the slow, constant assault of the waters. Let the valleys shudder at the pitiless advance of ice. Let continents drown beneath the dark and rising tide.

But that grain of sand?

It isn't impressed.

Let the tide roll in. The sand will still be there after it rolls out again.

So I looked up at that face and I laughed. I laughed scorn and defiance at that vast, swirling power, and it didn't just feel good. It felt *right*.

"Go ahead!" I shouted. "Go ahead and eat me! And then we'll see if you've got the stomach to keep me down!" I lifted my staff and golden white fire began to pour from the carved runes as I gathered power into it. The air grew chill with Winter, and frost formed on the razor-edged blades in my armor. I ground my feet into place, setting them firmly, and the glow of soulfire began to emanate from the cracks in the earth around me. I bared my teeth at the hungry sky, flew the bird at it with my free hand, and screamed, "Bring it on!"

A furious voice filled the air, a sound that shook the earth and sky alike, that made the ground buckle and the swirling clouds recoil.

And then I was back on the Harley, clutching Karrin's waist in one hand and clinging to the Winchester with the other. The motorcycle was still in motion, but it wasn't accelerating. It felt like we were coasting.

Karrin let out a low, gurgling cry, and suddenly sagged forward, panting. I pulled her back against me, helping her to sit up, and after a few seconds she gave her head a few quick shakes and snarled, "I hate getting into a Vulcan mind meld."

"It hit you, too?" I asked.

"It . . ." She cast a look over her shoulder, up at me, and shuddered. "Yeah."

"You okay now?"

"I'm starting to get angry," she said.

A hideously mirthful sound spread over the air—the sound of the Erlking's laughter. His great steed swerved in close to the motorcycle, and he lifted his sword in a gesture of fierce defiance. Then his burning eyes turned to me and he spoke in a voice that was murderously merry. "Well-done, starborn!"

"Uh," I said. "Thank you?"

The lord of the goblins laughed again. It was the kind of sound that would stick with you—and wake you up in the middle of the night, wondering whether perhaps poisonous snakes had surrounded your bed and were about to start slithering in.

I looked back. The Hunt had spread out into a ragged semblance of its former cohesion, but even as I watched, the riders and hounds poured on extra effort to gather together again. I looked around but saw no sign of Sharkface.

I *did* see something else—V-shaped ripples coming toward us through the water. A whole lot of them.

"Here they come!" I shouted to the Erlking. "Good hunting!"

"That much seems certain," he called in that same cheerfully vicious voice, and wheeled his horse to the right. Half of the riders and hounds split off with him, while the other half continued streaming after me.

I pointed at our target as the Erlking headed toward his. "There!" I called. "Let's do it!"

The Harleytiger let out another snarling roar, and Karrin raced toward the second barge. Hellish shrieks went up from both groups of the Hunt—and the oncoming things in the water smoothly split into two elements as they came forward. We raced the enemy toward the barges.

This time we didn't have surprise on our side. It couldn't have been more than a minute or two since the Hunt had announced its arrival, but I saw figures stirring on the deck of the barge ahead of us.

"Gun!" shouted Karrin. "Incoming!"

Crap.

Out over the water like this, I didn't have access to anywhere near enough magic to provide a continuous shield—and I couldn't try to slap down individual bullets, either. By the time I saw the gunfire, the round would already be going through us. Which meant that this was going to happen the vanilla way, the way soldiers worldwide have done it for a few centuries now. Advance, advance, advance, and hope that you didn't get shot.

Then Karrin snatched the rifle out of my hand and screamed, "Take the bike!"

I fumbled for a moment, but found the handlebars, reaching around her to make it happen. I gunned the throttle as Karrin raised the Winchester to her shoulder, half rose, and squinted through the buckhorn sights.

Flashes came from the boat, and something that sounded like an angry hornet flicked past my ear. I saw bits of spray coming up from the water ahead of us as the shooters misjudged their range, and I kept on racing straight ahead.

When we got to within a hundred yards, Karrin started shooting.

The old rifle boomed, and sparks flew up from the barge's hull. She worked the lever action without lowering it from her shoulder and fired again. One of the dark shapes on the deck vanished, and two more flinched away. More gunfire came from the boat—panic fire, splashing wildly everywhere and mostly nowhere close to us. Whoever was over there, they didn't like getting shot at any more than I did.

As we closed the last yards, Karrin fired three more times in a rapid, assured pace. I couldn't see whether she hit anyone else until we went roaring past the barge, no more than ten feet away, when a man holding the distinctive shape of a shotgun rose into sight. Karrin was covering the barge's stern with the Winchester when he popped up. The old gun roared again, and the gunman fell away and out of sight.

We raced by unharmed, but the enemy gunfire had done its work.

The riders and hounds of the Hunt had been distracted by the flying bullets, and they didn't do nearly as much damage to the barge as in the initial attack. Even as I watched, more and more figures with guns appeared on the barge and started shooting.

I checked the oncoming rush of Outsiders.

We weren't going to sink the barge before they got here.

"—to sink it!" Karrin was shouting.

"What?"

"We don't have to sink the barge!" she shouted. "It can't move on its own! We just have to kill the boat that's pulling it!"

"Right!" I said, and leaned the Harley into a turn that would take us arching back toward the barge—this time at its front, or prow, or bow or something, where a rig containing a tugboat a bit bigger than the *Water Beetle* had been built on.

It also brought us closer to the oncoming Outsiders, and I couldn't tell which of us would get there first. As I sped up, Karrin dug into the compartments on the Harley, reaching around me, then said, "Hold it steady!"

Then she stood up, and I couldn't see a damned thing—but I *did* see the way she pulled the pin out of a freaking hand grenade, and let the spoon spin off into the night. The Harley buzzed past the tugboat's rig maybe ten feet ahead of the Outsiders, and Karrin gave the grenade a rather feeble little flick as we went by. I heard it smash into glass, like a stone thrown against a window, and then we were past the barge, and a huge sound thudded through the air, like an entire library of books all dropped flat at the same instant, and an incandescent white light flared from the tug.

I looked back over my shoulder and saw that the tugboat was on fire, pouring out thick black smoke and leaning sharply to one side. Murphy saw it, too, and let out an ululating war cry before she sat back down and pushed my hands off the handlebars, reassuming control of the Harley. "Two down!" she said. "One to go!"

I looked back behind me. The Outsiders had begun swarming at the barge, and one of them actually came out of the water at one of the rearmost riders of the Hunt—this horrible thing that was all pustules and multiple limbs with too many joints. As it leapt, the rider raised a shadowy bow and loosed a darkling arrow. It struck the Outsider and burst into red-amber flame the same color as the burning eyes of the Hunt. The Outsider let out an unearthly wail and plunged back beneath the surface.

"Come on," I said to Karrin. "Head for the other boat."

"Should we?" she asked. "That Erlking guy seems a little . . . do-it-yourselfy."

She was right about that. Like any of the other seriously powerful beings of Faerie, the Erlking had a strong sense of pride—and you crossed that pride at your own risk. If I showed up and the Erlking thought I was making the statement that I judged him unfit to finish the task, it could come back to haunt me. On the other hand, I'd already insulted him once and there was a lot on the line. "If he didn't want me making calls like this, he shouldn't have let me shoot him and take over his Hunt," I said. I turned to beckon the riders and hounds behind me and shouted, "Come on!" My voice came out as both my own *and* in the howling screech of the Hunt, the two interwoven, and the rest of my group joined in the shriek and formed up around the Harley as it raced across the water, toward the third barge.

Where the fight wasn't going well.

There were several long, straight streaks of molten steel where the Erlking and his riders had struck the barge's hull, the edges marked with flickering tongues of eerie green fire, but they had not torn a hole in it like we had the first barge, either, and the Outsiders had gotten to this barge faster than they had to mine. Even as we approached, I saw a racing hound of the Hunt vanish in a spray of water as things, plural, too twisted and too confusing to count, surged up from below and began to drag the hound down.

A shriek loud enough to cause spray to rise from the water shook the air, and the Erlking himself plunged down from overhead, leading a trio of hunters behind him. Blades and arrows struck at the Outsiders in plumes of ember fire. The Erlking seized the hound by the scruff of its neck and dragged it up out of the grasp of the creatures beneath the surface.

The Erlking and his riders had fallen into a formation, a great, tilted wheel. At the far end, the riders were maybe fifty feet above the waves, circling in the air to then charge down at the surface of the water where it met the hull of the barge. The Outsiders would throw themselves up out of the waves, meeting each individual rider. Hounds would, in turn, try to throw themselves on the Outsiders, smothering their defense so that the rider could strike the barge.

Meanwhile, figures aboard the barge fired rifles wildly into the night, though the deck of the thing was actually bobbing with the thrashing of the Outsiders in the water around it. Whoever they were, they struck me as amateurish—though maybe it was only because I'd been exposed to real soldiers before, who were a deadly threat even on the scale of supernatural conflict. These guys weren't the Einherjaren—but at the end of the day, they still had deadly weapons, and more than one rider and hound had been struck by rounds and bled molten light from their shadow-masked bodies. The piercing screech of the Hunt met with the howls of Outsiders and the crack of rifle fire, and bit by bit, the barge's hull bled red-hot steel.

But it wasn't happening fast enough.

With a groan, the barge's tugboat, this one mounted behind it, began shoving the thing forward through the water and toward the shore of Demonreach.

"I shouldn't have split us up," I said. "We didn't cover twice as many targets. We just got twice as half-assed."

Karrin made a sputtering sound, then said, "You and math are not friends. Regret later. Lead now."

"Right," I said. The barge wasn't exactly leaping into motion—but it wouldn't stop on a dime once it got moving, either. "Do you have any more grenades?" I asked Karrin.

"I used them a couple of weeks ago," she said.

"With Kincaid?" I asked. There was an edge to it. She and the assassin were kind of an item, the last time I looked.

"Harry," she said, "focus."

Hell's bells, she was right. I didn't need the Winter mantle turning me into a territorial alpha dick right now. I stared at the barge for a long second, pushing that instinct away, and then said to the Hunt, "Join the Erlking! Attack the barge!"

Hounds and riders streamed past us, joining the madman's wheel of death in the sky, and I lowered my voice, speaking only to Karrin as I reloaded the Winchester. "Get me to the tugboat."

She gave me a quick, wide-eyed glance, and then seemed to get it. She gunned the motor, sending the Harley shooting past the Erlking's very large, very threatening, and very *distracting* formation, as we raced alone toward the chugging tugboat.

She brought us right alongside it, and once again I leapt from the back of the Harley. I hit the side of the tug pretty hard, but was able to get the fingers of my left hand around the top of the rail, and with a few kicks managed to swing myself up onto the deck. I landed in a crouch, clutching the rifle, got my bearings, and headed toward a stairwell that would lead me to the boat's bridge.

I went up it as quietly as I could, which is pretty damned quiet for a guy my size, Winchester at the ready. The bridge of the tug was big enough to merit its own enclosed space, and I slipped up to the door, took a breath, then ripped it open, lifting the Winchester as I did.

The bridge was empty, the wheel secured with a pair of large plastic ties. There was a piece of paper taped to the wheel, and on it was written in large black marker, LOOK BEHIND YOU.

I started to turn, but a cannonball hit me between the shoulder blades. I flew forward onto the bridge and slammed my head against the Plexiglas forward windows. I fell back from that, stunned, and a heavy weight hit me from the side, slamming me into a bulkhead, which felt almost exactly like being slammed into a steel wall.

I wound up prone, my face to the deck, and once more the heavy weight slammed into me, landing on my back.

And Cat Sith, who had told me not to turn my back on anyone, purred, "Wizard, Knight, fool. Too ignorant even to know how to die properly." His skin-crawling voice came out in a throaty buzz next to my ear. "Allow me to educate you."

44

The reasonable thing to do would have been to whimper or flinch or just freak out and look for the nearest exit. But instead of doing any of those things, I felt a chill settle over my brain, and a very cold, calm part of me studied the situation objectively.

"Join, hide, or die," I said. I heard the faint echo of the Wild Hunt's screech in my voice.

"Excuse me?" Cat Sith said.

"You have excellent hearing," I said. "But I will repeat myself. Join. Hide. Or die. You know the laws of the Hunt."

"I do know them, wizard. And once I have slain you, the Hunt will be mine to do with as I please."

"The real Cat Sith wouldn't be having this conversation with me, you know. He'd have killed me by now."

A blow struck the back of my head, sharp, painful, but not debilitating. "I *am* Cat Sith. The one. The only."

I turned my head slightly and said, "So why do I still have a spine?"

And I threw an elbow at the weight on my back. I connected with something, hard, and slammed it off me. It hit the other wall of the bridge, and I flung myself to my feet in time to see the large, lean form of Cat Sith thrash his tail and bound at me.

I ducked him, moving forward under his leap, and spun, and it left the two of us facing each other across the full length of the bridge.

"Slow," I said. "I've seen him move. Cat Sith is faster than that."

A hideous growling sound came from the form of the malk. "I *am* he."

"Get me a Coke," I snarled.

"What?"

"You *heard* me, Mittens. Get me a freaking Coke and do it *now*."

Sith remained in place, as if locked to the floor, though his whole body was quivering, his claws sheathing and unsheathing in rhythm. But he didn't fly at me, ripping and tearing, either.

"You see," I said, "Cat Sith is a creature of Faerie, and he swore an *oath* to Queen Mab to obey her commands. She commanded him to obey mine. And I just gave you a command, kitty. Did Mab release you from her command? Did she suspend the duties of her vassal?"

Sith snarled again, his eyes getting wider and rounder, his tail thrashing around wildly.

"They got to you, didn't they?" I said. "They jumped you back at the Botanic Gardens while you were covering my exit. Freaking Sharkface was watching the whole thing and he got you."

Sith began quivering so hard that he was jitterbugging back and forth in place on the floor, his head twitching, his fur standing on end and then abruptly lying flat again.

"Fight it, Sith," I urged him quietly. "It doesn't have to win. *Fight* it."

For a second, I thought I saw something of Cat Sith's smug, contemptuous self-assurance on the malk's face. And then it was gone. Just gone. Everything went away, and the malk stood for a second with its head down. Then it lifted its head and the motion was subtly wrong, something that simply didn't have the grace I'd seen in the elder malk before. It faced me for a moment and then it spoke, its voice absent of anything like personality. "A pity. I would have been more useful to them as an active, covert asset."

I shuddered at the utter absence in that voice. I wasn't talking to Sith anymore.

I was speaking with the adversary.

"Like Mab wouldn't have figured it out," I said. "Like she did when you infected Lea."

"Further conversation is not useful to our design," Not-Sith said, and then the malk's form flew at me in a blur.

It was a testament to the power of the Winter Knight's mantle and the Wild Hunt's energy that I survived that first leap at all. Sith struck straight at my throat. I got my arms in the way. The black shadow mask of the Hunt over my arms and chest blew apart into splinters, dispersing some of the impact energy of the malk's spectacular leap, and instead of pulping me against the wall behind me, he just pounded me into it with tooth-rattling force.

Sith bounced off me, which was what I had hoped would happen. In my line of work, I've dealt with more than one critter that is faster than fast. When they've got their feet underneath them, it's the next-best thing to impossible to land anything on them—but when they're in the air, they're moving at the speed gravity and air resistance dictate, like everybody else. For that one portion of a second, Sith was an object moving through space, not a blindingly fast killing machine. Someone who didn't know that wouldn't have known to be ready for it.

But I did. And I was.

The blast of raw force I summoned wasn't my very best punch—but it was the best I was going to get out here over the lake. It slammed into the creature that had been Cat Sith and plowed it out through the Plexiglas window. The plastic didn't break. It came entirely out of its housing, and the malk and a slab of Plexiglas the size of a door went whirling out into the madness of the night. Sith flew out over the bow of the tugboat and plunged down into the water through the open spaces of the pipe-steel rig between it and the barge.

I stared hard after the departed malk for a few seconds, to be sure he wasn't going to bounce right back into my face somehow. As I did, I watched in the other half of the bridge's forward window while the shadow mask of the Hunt slithered back up over my arms and face. I gave it to a three count, nodded, and then went to the tug's wheel. I snapped the plastic ties securing it with a pair of fast jerks, then started rolling the wheel as far as it would go to the right. There was a big lever that looked like a throttle, and when I pushed it forward, the boat's engines started to roar with effort.

The barge groaned as the tug changed the direction in which it applied force, and the barge's back end began slowly slewing out and to the left. That drew shouts of consternation from the deck of the barge. I didn't feel like getting shot in the face, so I knelt down, out of sight, while I pulled the secondhand belt off of my old jeans and used it to secure the wheel in position. Then I recovered the Winchester and backed out of the bridge, hurrying away from it as quietly as I could.

What I'd done was a delaying tactic at best. It wouldn't turn the barge around—but it *would* set it to spinning in place, and maybe cost the enemy time to turn it around if they took control of it again. But that was exactly what the Hunt needed to sink her—time. The longer the barge played sit-and-spin, the better. So I found a nice quiet patch of shadow where I could see the stairs leading up to the tug's bridge, and where I could stand behind a very large steel pipe. I rested the Winchester on the top bend of the pipe, sighted on the doorway, and waited.

It didn't take long for the first couple of crewmen to arrive. I wasn't sure whether they came up from belowdecks or somehow swarmed over from the barge, but two men in dark clothing, carrying pistols at the ready, came hurrying along and started up the stairs.

I'm not a great shot. But when you're resting a rifle on a solid surface, one that is perfectly still (at least relative to all the solid surfaces around it), and when the range is about forty feet, you don't have to be an expert. You just have to take a breath, let it out, and squeeze.

The Winchester cracked with thunder, and the first man arched into a bow of agony just as he reached the top of the stairs. That ended up working in my favor. He fell back into the second man, just as the second guy spun and raised his pistol. The first man fell into the second, sending his first shot wild, and knocked him about halfway over. The second man couldn't hold the gun with both hands, but he kept pulling the trigger as fast as he could.

At forty feet, terrified, in the dark, unsure of his target's exact location, and sprawled out with the deadweight of another man flopping against him, the poor bastard didn't have a chance. He got off seven or eight rounds, none of them coming anywhere close. I worked the action on the Winchester, took a breath, let half out, and squeezed the trigger.

It wasn't until the flash of light from the shot illuminated him that I recognized Ace, his expression panicked, his gun aimed at a point ten feet to my left. The light flashed and burned his face into my retina for a moment as the dark returned.

And the tugboat was silent again.

It didn't take long for the Erlking to finish his work. Maybe three minutes later, a chorus of hideous screams went up from the lake's surface, and the Hunt howled its triumph and circled into the sky, horns blaring, hounds baying. I saw green fire burning fiercely from the spot the Hunt had started carving, and then the barge started to list toward that side as the water poured into her. Barges aren't warships, or even maritime vessels. If they have belowdecks spaces at all, they generally aren't fitted with flood compartments and sealable doors. They sure as hell don't have automatic systems. They're just soup bowls. Poke a hole in the bottom, and a bowl isn't gonna hold much soup.

I didn't feel like getting *Titanic*ked, so I hustled over to the spot where I'd boarded the tug. There was a roar from the shadow-tiger mask around the Harley, and Murphy swept up alongside the boat. I leapt down onto the back of the bike in a single smooth motion, which I felt was cool, and landed with way too much of my weight on my genitals, which I felt was not.

"Go, go, go," I gasped in a pained falsetto, and Murphy peeled away from the doomed ships.

Within moments, the Hunt had fallen into formation around me again, and the Erlking was laughing maniacally, whirling his sword over his head. The shadow mask over one leg and a section of his ribs had been torn away, and I could see wounds beneath—but already the shadows were stretching over them again. "I love nights like this!" he bellowed. "I *love* Halloween!"

"Yeah, it's pretty badass," I said in my wobbling, creaky voice.

"Sir Knight," he said, "that was passably done, but from here I believe it shall take more experience and expertise than you possess to continue the Hunt. Do I have your leave to resume command and pursue these Outsider vermin in a more appropriate fashion?" he asked me.

"Uh," I squeaked. "You aren't going to come after *me* with it, are you?"

He broke into laughter that could have been heard for miles. He was smiling so hard, it went right through the shadow mask, turning his face into a crazed jack-o'-lantern of soot and fire. "Not this night. I give you my word. Have I your leave?"

Rather than answer the Erlking in my Mickey Mouse voice, I gave him the thumbs-up.

The Lord of the Goblins threw back his head and let out another screech, and his steed began to gain altitude. The rest of the Hunt followed him.

"Uh, Harry?" Karrin said.

"Yeah?"

"This is a *motorcycle*."

It didn't register for a second, and then I blinked.

We were cruising down the surface of Lake Michigan, and it was chock-full of monstery goodness—and we had just *left* the Wild Hunt.

"Oh, *crap*," I said. "Head for the island! Go, go, go!"

Murphy leaned hard into a turn and opened up the throttle. I looked over my shoulder at the Erlking, wheeling in the skies above the lake, spiraling higher and higher, the Hunt following after. We went by a couple of Zodiacs so fast that their occupants didn't have time to shoot at us before we were gone.

Then the motorcycle slowed.

"What are you doing?" I screamed.

"We can't hit the beach at this speed," Karrin shouted back. "We'll pancake ourselves into those trees!"

"I don't really feel like taking a swim tonight!"

"Don't be such a pussy," Karrin snapped. She leaned the bike into another turn, one that angled our direction to run parallel to the shore, and cut out the accelerator.

I felt the Harley slowing, and for a second I thought I felt it beginning to sink.

Then the Erlking cried out again and dived, his horse sprinting straight *down*, trailing the fire of the Hunt from its hooves. The rest of the hounds and riders followed in formation, and their horns and cries rebounded around the night.

Then, maybe a second before they hit the water, the Hunt *changed*.

Suddenly the Erlking wasn't mounted on a horse, but on a freaking killer whale, its deadly-looking black-and-white coloration stark in the night. Behind him, the other steeds shifted, too, their riders screeching with excitement. The hounds changed as well. Their canine bodies compressed into the long, lean, powerful shape of large sharks.

Then the whole lot of them hit the water in a geyser of spray, and the Harley promptly fell into the water of the lake—

—and onto sand just under its surface. The bike slowed dramatically, pushing me up against Karrin, nearly pushing her over the handlebars, but she locked her arms straight and held, drawing the bike up onto the shore of the island. She rode the brake until we'd come to a halt, about five feet short of hitting one of the big old trees on the island.

"See?" Karrin said.

"You were right," I said.

She looked back up at me, her eyes twinkling. "You are so hot right now."

I burst out into a hiccuping laugh that felt like it could have veered off into manic or depressive at any second, the pressure and terror of this entire stupid, ugly day finally getting to me—but it didn't. There were no enemy ships right on hand, and no one had launched grenades at the island since the Wild Hunt's attack had begun. There might have been Outsiders in the water, but apparently the Hunt was occupying their total attention. For the moment, we were alone, and Karrin started laughing, too. We laughed like that for several moments. We each tried to speak, to say something about the day, but it kept getting choked off by the half-hysterical laughter.

"Grenades," I said. "As if a date has to have—"

". . . look on Molly's face . . ."

". . . know he's a dog but I swear that . . ."

"Santa Claus smackdown!" Murphy gasped finally, and it set us both into gales of laughter that had no wind to support them, until finally we were just sitting with her small warm form leaning her back against my chest, in the darkness.

Then she turned her head, slowly, and looked up at me. Her eyes were very blue. Her mouth was very close.

Then I noticed something.

The second barge, whose tug Murphy had torched with her grenade, was *moving*.

I stood up and climbed off the bike, my eyes widening. "Oh, *crap*," I said.

From there, I could see that Sharkface stood calmly on the surface of the lake at the rear of the barge, his cloak twining and writhing all around him. His arms stretched forward in what was clearly a gesture of command. The waters at the rear of the barge boiled with Outsiders, most of them at least partly out of the water, and it took me only a second to work out what was happening.

They were doing an Evinrude impersonation, slamming their combined mass and preternatural strength against the rear of the barge. The burning tug was still a massive column of smoke and flame in front of the barge, but the barge was definitely moving—and it was close to shore.

Eerie green and scarlet light flashed in the depths of the lake, soundless and random. Sharkface had been smart. When the Hunt entered the water, he must have sent the lion's share of his Outsiders against them—while he and a few others came back up to the surface to ruin the crap out of my potential romantic moment.

"Oh, stars and stones," I breathed. "If they get that boat to shore . . ."

"The Harley can't get us there," Karrin said. "Not through this terrain and brush."

"You can't keep up with me here," I said.

Murphy gritted her teeth at that, but nodded. "Go," she said. "I'll come as fast as I can."

And then I thought to myself that if I kept on waiting for things to quiet down and be more appropriate and safer before I took action, I was never going to get anywhere in life.

So I slipped a hand behind her head, leaned down, and kissed her on the mouth, hard. She didn't stiffen. She wasn't surprised. She leaned into it, and her mouth tasted like strawberries.

I gave it two heartbeats, three, four. Then we both drew away at the same time. Her eyes were slightly wide, her cheeks high with color.

"I'm not going anywhere," I told her.

Then I turned and sprinted toward the stretch of shore at which Sharkface had pointed the last barge.

45

For me, running across the island wasn't a physical effort. It was mostly a mental one.

My awareness of the place was bone-deep, a total knowledge that existed as a single, whole body in my mind—a kind of understanding that some medieval scholars had called intellectus. It came to me on the level of reflex and instinct. When I ran, I knew where every branch stood out, where every stone lay ready to turn beneath my foot. Moving happened as naturally as breathing, and every step seemed to propel me forward a little faster, like running across the surface of one of those bouncy cages at a kid's pizza place.

I didn't have to run across the island. I just had to think about it and let my body effortlessly follow my mind.

I came out of the woods on the beach above where the barge was headed, which was roughly twenty-three yards, one foot, and six and one half inches from the nearest edge of the Whatsup Dock. One of the three major pulsing ley lines ran out from the island at almost that exact point, and if the barge managed to ground itself in contact with the line, Chicagoans were going to have a really rough morning commute.

Now that the Hunt and the Outsiders had taken their fight mostly below the waves, it was quiet enough to hear the barge approaching. Someone had already begun chanting on the deck of the barge. I couldn't see them through the smoldering wreckage of the tug out in front of the barge, but voices were certainly being raised in unison in a steady chant of some language that sounded as if it were meant to be spoken while gargling Crisco.

"Whatever happened to *Ia, Ia, Cthulu fhtagn*?" I muttered. "No one has a sense of style anymore."

Behind the chanting, I could hear the bubbling, sloshing water as the Outsiders pushed the barge nearer and nearer.

I rested the butt of the rifle on the ground next to my foot, crouched down, and squinted out at the boat. It was going to be here shortly, but not instantly, and I was pretty sure I'd get only one chance to stop it. I started gathering power to myself, an action I'd done so many times over the years that it was all but a reflex now, and squinted at the barge.

If the ritual was already in progress, then there was a chance that they were simply in a holding pattern, maintaining the skeleton of the spell with their own limited energy and waiting until the right moment. Once they were close enough to use it, they'd drop their circle and channel the energy of the ley line, shaping it into the spell's muscles and organs, filling out the frame that was prepared to accomodate it. I had to make sure they never got that chance.

A hole in the hull would work, but by the time the barge came within my limited range, it would be too late to drown it. I'd already tried killing its engine once, so I wasn't terribly excited about the prospect of taking out the creatures pushing it.

I had to *stop* it.

"For destruction," I said aloud, "ice is also great, and would suffice." I nodded once to myself, rose, and said, "Okay, Harry. Get this one right."

I went down to the shore. Using the butt of the rifle, I inscribed a circle in the mud, and closed it with a touch of my hand and a whisper of will. Once I felt its presence snap into place, I took the will I'd been gathering, reached down into the earth, and gathered more, drawing it up like water from a well.

I could feel the seething power of the ley line beneath me, could feel how close I came to it in my quest to gather as much energy as I could before I unleashed my attack. The earth trembled with a subterranean river of dark power, the spirit of violence, havoc, and death expressed as energy, and if I tapped into it, I could potentially direct its terrible strength at the enemy. There would be consequences to an action like that, chain reactions and fallout I couldn't predict, but it would sure as hell get the job done.

For a second, I almost did it. There was so much on the line. But you can't go around changing your definition of right and wrong (or smart and stupid) just because doing the wrong thing happens to be really convenient. Sometimes it isn't easy to be sane, smart, and responsible. Sometimes it sucks. Sucks wang. Camel wang. But that doesn't turn wrong into right or stupid into smart.

I'd kinda gotten an object lesson in that.

So I left that power alone.

The magic continued to pour into me, more than I usually used, more than was comfortable. After thirty seconds, I felt as if my hairs were standing on end and sparks were shooting between them. I ground my teeth, dug into the cold power of Winter, and kept drawing more. I began directing it down toward my right hand, and cold blue-white fire abruptly wreathed my fingers like the flame from a newly lit gas burner.

The burned tug was only about a hundred yards away when I lifted my hand, stepped forward out of the circle, and cried out, *"Rexus mundus!"*

And a globe of blindingly intense blue light the size of a soccer ball flew out into the night. It spewed mist from every inch of its surface, and flashed through the night like a dying comet. It landed in the water twenty yards in front of the slow-moving barge.

There was an abrupt screech as the sphere of condensed, absolute-zero cold hit Lake Michigan. Ice formed almost instantly, and large crystals of it shot out in every direction, sharp as spears, kind of like Superman's Fortress of Solitude. One instant it was clear sailing for the barge—the next, the mutant spawn of an iceberg and a giant porcupine bobbed in the water directly in front of it, a barrier of ice the size of a tractor trailer.

I could have gone bigger, but there just wasn't enough *time*. I'd needed it to happen fast, to get that weight into position—but I wasn't a complete dummy. My pointy iceberg was the size of a semi, but the barge could have carried twenty of them. I just had to get the first piece into the right spot.

Again I reached for Winter, and again I lifted my hand, howling, "*Infriga!*"

Pure cold screamed from my hand into the air, spreading over the surface of the lake in a field shaped like a folding fan. The surface crystallized and froze, and I poured more and more into it, thickening the ice, spreading it toward the little iceberg. The wreckage of the tugboat hit my obstacle first, and the spears of ice punched through the weakened wooden hull of the tug, nailing the iceberg to it. The barge slowed, and pieces of the tug's rig screamed and bent in protest. Then, as it approached, it started hitting the thinnest ice at the edge of the fan—but as it kept coming, the ice got thicker and thicker, providing increasing resistance to the barge's forward motion. It began to grind to a halt.

A furious shriek ripped the air. Sharkface. I'd just pissed the Walker off big-time. It probably says something about my maturity level that it made me grin from ear to ear.

I saw him jump into the air—not like a bunny hop, but a full-on Kung Fu Theater leap, way up over the barge. His rag-strip cloak spread out like dozens of little wings as gravity turned his jump from an ascent into a dive. I was starting to feel the effort of using so much brute-power magic in such a short amount of time, but I had enough left to handle this thing. I prepared a blast of force, ready to swat him away from my barrier of ice and unleash it on him the moment he came within range.

I missed. Well, I didn't *miss*, exactly. But just before the bolt slammed home, Sharkface split into *dozens* of identical shapes that splintered off in every direction. So one of those shapes got hit with a slap of force that would have rocked a car up onto two wheels, and that one went soaring away.

But the other forty or fifty crashed down onto my field of ice like cannonballs, smashing through in most places, in some only sending wide cracks through the ice. When that happened, the copies of Sharkface just started tearing it apart with their claws. Thick ice is no joke as an obstacle—unless you're a Walker of the Outside, I guess, because these things ripped it apart like it was Styrofoam.

There were so damned *many* of them. I started slamming more of them, but it was heavy work, and there were just too many targets. While some of them ripped apart the remaining ice, others began to tear apart the iceberg and the tugboat, rending them into scrap with an inexorable strength and claws like steel knives. I might have hit seven or eight of them, but it just didn't matter. I was the wrong tool for the job, so to speak. This was a much larger problem, and I had no idea how to solve it.

The chanting on the barge rolled upward an octave, gaining frenzied volume. Outsiders thrashed through the water, pushing the barge, surging ahead of it to push pulverized chunks of ice out of its way, their howls and weird clicks and ululations like their own horrible music. Other Outsiders came rushing toward me, on the shore—only to smash uselessly against the glowing barrier of Demonreach's curtain wall. They couldn't get to me. Which seemed fair enough, because I couldn't seem to get to *them*, either. I'd slowed them down, cost them maybe a couple of minutes, and that was all.

The water near me stirred and then a Sharkface rose up out of it as if on an elevator, slow, his mouth tilted up into a small smile. He stood there on the water perhaps five feet away from me. His eyeless face looked smug.

"Warden," he said.

"Asshat," I replied.

That only made his smile wider. "The battle is over. You have failed. But you need not be destroyed this day."

"You're kidding," I said. "You're trying to recruit me?"

"The offer is made," the Walker said. "We always appreciate new talent."

"I'm no one's puppet," I said.

The Walker actually barked out a short laugh. "At what point have you been anything *else*?"

"You can forget it," I said. "I'm not working for you."

"Then a truce," Sharkface said. "We do not need you to fight our battles for us. But if you stand aside, we will accord you respect and leave you in peace. You and those you love. Take them to a safe, quiet place. Stay there. You will not be molested."

"My boss might not go along with this plan," I said.

"After tonight, Mab will no longer be a concern to anyone."

I was going to say something badass and cool but . . .

Take the people I love somewhere. Take Maggie. Somewhere safe. Somewhere without mad Queens or insane Sidhe. And just get out of this entire thankless, painful, hideous business. Wizarding just isn't what it used to be. Not so many years ago, I'd think it was a busy week if someone asked me to locate a lost dog or a wedding ring. It had been horribly boring. I'd had lots and lots of free time. I hadn't been rich, but I'd gotten to buy plenty of books to read, and I'd never gone hungry. And no one had tried to kill me, or asked me to make a horrible choice. Not once.

You never know what you have until it's gone.

Peace and quiet and people I love. Isn't that what everyone wants?

Ah, hell.

The Outsider probably wasn't good for it anyway. And I did have one more option.

I had been warned not to use the power of the Well. But . . .

What else did I have?

I might have done something extra stupid at that moment if the air hadn't suddenly filled with a massive sound. Two loud, horrible crunching sounds, followed by a single, short, sharp clap of thunder. It repeated the sequence, again and again. Crunch, crunch, crack. Crunch, crunch, crack.

No, wait. I *knew* this song.

It was more like: stomp, stomp, *clap*. Stomp, stomp, *clap*.

What else did I have?

I had *friends*.

I looked up at Sharkface, who was scanning the lake's surface, an odd expression twisting his unsettling face.

I smiled widely and said, "You didn't see this coming, didja?"

STOMP, STOMP, CLAP!

STOMP, STOMP, CLAP!

This was somebody's mix version of the song, because it went straight to the chorus of voices, pure, human voices, loud enough to shake the ground—and I lifted my arms and sang along with them.

"Singin' we will, we will rock you!"

The Halloween sky exploded with strobes of scarlet and blue light, laser streaks of white and viridian flickering everywhere, forming random, flickering impressions of objects and faces, filling the sky with light that pulsed in time with the music.

And as it did, the *Water Beetle*, the *entire* goddamned *ship*, exploded out from under a veil that had rendered it and the water it had displaced and every noise it had made undetectable not only to me, but to a small army of otherworldly monstrosities and their big, bad Walker general, too.

The Walker let out another furious shriek, his hideous features twisted even more by the frenetic explosion of light in the sky, and that was all he had time to do—the *Water Beetle* slammed into the last barge at full speed.

The mass differential between the two ships was significant—but this was different from when the barge had hit my iceberg. For one thing, it was almost entirely still, having only barely begun to pick up speed again. For another, the *Water Beetle* didn't hit it head-on. Instead, it struck the barge from the side, and right up by its nose. With less than ten yards to spare before the barge's prow ground up onto Demonreach's shore, the *Water Beetle* brutally slammed her nose away from contacting the power of the outgoing ley line.

I couldn't hear the collision over the thunder of Queen's greatest hit, but it flung objects all over both ships around with the impact—more so on the *Beetle* than on the barge. The barge wallowed, stunned, its nose turned away from the beach, its long side being presented to the island, while the *Water Beetle* rebounded violently, drunkenly, and crunched up onto her hull in the shallows, listing badly to one side.

Mac and Molly were up at the wheel. She had nearly been thrown from the craft, but Mac had grabbed my apprentice around the waist and kept her from getting a flying lesson. I'm not sure she even noticed. Her face was contorted in a concentration so deep, it was practically dementia, her lips moving frantically, and she held a wand in either hand, moving them in entirely disconnected movements, as if directing two different orchestras through two different speed-metal medleys.

And as I watched, two other forms bounded up onto the *Water Beetle*'s rail, then into graceful leaps that carried them over onto the barge—

directly into the center of the ritual that was still running at a frantic pitch.

Thomas had gone into the fight with his favorite combination of weapons—a sword and a pistol. Even as I watched, my brother whirled into a mass of figures on the deck, blade spinning, blood flying out in wide, clean arcs. He moved so swiftly that I could barely track him, just a blur of steel here, a flash of cold grey eyes there. His gun fired in quick rhythm between strokes of his falcata, scything down the Outsiders' mortal henchmen like sheaves of wheat.

The second figure was grey and shaggy and terrifying. Mouse's lion-like ruff of fur flew out like a true mane as he whirled and lunged into the ritual's participants wherever Thomas hadn't. I saw him rip a shotgun from the hands of a stunned guard and fling it with a snap of his head into another one before bounding forward and bringing half a dozen panicked men to the deck under his weight—and smashing them through the circle that had surrounded the ritual.

The reduced energy the ritual had been able to use, the framework that the ley line would have turned into a deadly construction, vanished, released into the night sky to be shaken to pieces by the music. *We will, we will, rock you.*

"Hey, Sharkface!" I shouted, stepping forward, gathering Winter and soulfire as I went.

The furious Walker whirled back to me just in time to have the heavy, octagonal barrel of the Winchester slam *through* the ridge of bone that he had instead of front teeth, and drive all the way to the back of his mouth.

"Get rocked," I said, and pulled the trigger.

Along with the .45-caliber bullet, I sent a column of pure energy and will surging down the barrel and into the Walker's skull. His head exploded, literally exploded, into streamers and gobbets of black ichor. His cloak of rags went mad, throwing the headless body into the air and sending it thrashing through the shallow water like a half-squashed bug. Dark vapor began issuing from the frantically twitching body—then suddenly gathered into a single cloud, all in a rush, and shot away, emitting a furious and agonized and terrorized scream as it went, alien but unmistakable.

Then the body went limp in the water. The cloak continued flopping and thrashing for a few seconds before it, too, went still.

A unified howl of dismay rose from the surface of the lake, from the Outsiders, and V-shaped wakes appeared on the surface, retreating from the island in every direction, chased by flickering spears of light and music—and the horns of the Hunt began to blare in a frenzy, ringing up from the water's quivering surface. I saw a massive black-and-white form seize a fleeing Outsider and roll, while a shadow-masked rider lashed out over and over with a long spear. In another place, a shark exploded from the waves, hanging against the sky for a second, jaws gaping, before plunging down directly atop another Outsider, driving it beneath the waves where a dozen wickedly sharp fins abruptly converged.

The woods stirred behind me and Murphy came panting out of them, her P90 hanging from its sling. She came to my side, staring at the chaos.

I couldn't blame her. It was horrible. It was unique. It was glorious. It was . . .

Suddenly it felt like my heart had stopped.

It was distracting.

"Molly!" I screamed. "Molly!"

Mac heard me through that mess, and shook Molly. When she didn't react, he grimaced and then delivered a short, sharp smack to her cheek.

She gasped and blinked her eyes, and the sky show and sound track abruptly vanished, right in the middle of the guitar solo.

"Get them out of the water!" I screamed. "Get onto the shore! Hurry!"

Molly blinked at me several times. Then she seemed to get it and nodded her head quickly. She and Mac hurried down to the *Beetle*'s slanted deck, to the door to below. She called out and Sarissa and Justine appeared, both looking terrified. Molly pointed them at the island, and the three jumped from the ship to the waist-deep water and started wading ashore.

Mouse caught what was happening and let out a short, sharp bark.

Mouse doesn't bark often, but when he does he can make bits of spackle fall from the ceiling. He and Thomas plunged from the bloodied deck of the barge into the water, and began swimming swiftly toward the island.

The cries of the Hunt and frantic Outsiders filled the air now, and even as they did, I forced myself to calm my thoughts, to take slow breaths, to focus on my intellectus of the island. I couldn't sense anything specifically, but an instinct dragged my chin around, turning me to stare up toward the crest of the island, where the old ruined lighthouse stood among the skeletal forms of the late-autumn trees.

Then it hit me. I shouldn't have been able to see the lighthouse or the trees from down here, not on a cloudy night, but their silhouettes were clear.

There was light up there.

And as my friends reached the shore and hurried over to me, I realized that there was an empty place in my awareness of the island. I would never have sensed it if I hadn't been looking. I couldn't feel anything from around the top of the hill.

"The Walker was just the distraction," I breathed. "Dammit, they're not pulling that same trick on me this time." I turned to them and said, "I think someone's up at the top of the hill, and whatever they're doing, it ain't good. Stay right behind me. Come on."

I was pretty sure I knew who was up there, and I wasn't about to do this alone.

So I started toward the top of the hill, taking the agonizingly slow route that I knew would enable my friends to keep up with me.

46

Whoever was up at the top of the hill had things ready to stop me from getting there. It didn't work out well for them.

I knew about the trip lines that had been strung up between the trees at ankle level, and knew where the gaps were—more harassment-level opposition from the enemy Little Folk, I was guessing. The people with me didn't even realize that there *were* any trip lines.

After that was a trio of particularly vicious-looking fae hounds, the little cousins of Black Dogs. I had taken a Black Dog on once, in my calmer days, and didn't care for a rematch. I clipped one of the hounds with a shot from the Winchester while it was crouching in the brush ahead, waiting for me to come a few steps closer, and I set on fire a thicket where another one hid before we got within thirty feet. Ambush predators become unnerved when their would-be prey spots them. Fae hound number three hustled out of a hollow log where he'd been planning to rush out and attack with his buddies, and retreated with the two wounded hounds to the far side of the island.

"How did they get on the island?" Molly asked as we kept moving. She was breathing hard, both from her efforts on the lake and from the hike up. "I thought it kept everyone away."

Demonreach was meant to keep things *in*, not out, but I didn't want to blab about that in front of mixed company. "It encourages everyone to stay away, and turns up the heat slowly for anyone who doesn't," I said back. "But that's when it isn't being attacked by an army of cultists and a horde of howling freaks from beyond reality. It was busy making sure none of the Outsiders could come up onto shore—and none of them *could*. It just outmuscled an army led by something that could go toe-to-toe with Mab. Everything has its limits." I checked with my intellectus and realized that Mac and Sarissa were bringing up the rear. That wouldn't do. I still didn't know the role they were playing in this game. "Mouse," I called. "Take rear guard, in case those hounds circle around and try to sneak up on us."

The big furball made a huffing sound, an exhalation somewhere between a bark and a sneeze, but chewier. Heh. Chewie. I reminded myself to keep track of Mac and Sarissa as we went, but I felt better once Mouse was back there. Intellectus was handy as a reference guide, but not as an early-warning system. If either of them tried anything shady, the shaggy Tibetan guardian was probably the one most likely to notice first, anyway. Might as well have him close.

"Who's up there?" Karrin asked, her voice low and tense.

"Faerie Queens, I think. Plural."

"Whoa," Thomas said. "Why?"

"Complicated, no time," I said. "No one does anything until I do. Don't even talk. If the balloon goes up, go after whoever I light up first. After that, improvise."

Then I continued, increasing the pace a little. The trees near the crown of the island were older, thicker, and taller. The spreading canopy of their branches had shaded out most of the brush beneath them, and the ground was easier to move across, being mostly an irregular, soggy carpet of years and years' worth of fallen leaves. The scent of molds was thick as we went through, disturbing them.

We emerged into the clearing at the top of the hill, and I stopped in my tracks six inches before I would have come out of the shadow of the forest. Thomas bumped into me. I looked partly over my shoulder with a little push of air through my teeth. He elbowed me in the lower back.

The hilltop had been closed in a circle of starlight.

I didn't know how else to describe it. I didn't know what I was looking at. Twelve feet off the ground was a band of illumination, glowing rather than glaring, something that filled the hilltop with gentle light, like an enormous ring floating above the earth. It was of precise width, as if drawn with a compass, and I knew that it was exactly one foot thick—twelve inches. The color was something I had never seen before, changing subtly moment to moment, holding silver and blue and gold, but it wasn't any of those things and . . . and words fail. But it was beautiful, like love, like music, like truth, something that passed through the eyes and plunged straight to the soul. Gentle, softly glowing light slid from the outer edge of the circle like a sheet of water from an elegant fountain, falling to the ground in a slow-motion liquid curtain of pure light, hiding what was behind it.

I felt the grasshopper move up beside me, her eyes wide. "Boss," she whispered. "This would make my mom talk in her church voice. What are we looking at?"

"Merlin's work, I think," I breathed. "That circle. I think it's part of the island's architecture."

"Wow."

"I . . . It's beautiful," Sarissa murmured. "I've never seen anything like it. And I've been looking at incredible things my whole life."

I spoke something I was certain was true in the same moment that I understood it. "It had to be beautiful. It had to be made from beauty. There is too much ugly inside for it to be made of anything else."

"What do you mean, ugly?" Karrin asked, her voice hushed.

"Later," I said. I shook my head and blinked my eyes several times. "City to save." I tried to find something about the circle in my intellectus, but I had apparently already learned everything I could learn about it that way. I knew its exact dimensions; I knew it was part of the structure of the massive spell that made the Well exist. And that was it. It was like the entire thing had been . . . classified, top secret, need-to-know only—and apparently I didn't need to know.

Which, I supposed, made sense. We were talking about a massive security system.

Molly stooped and picked up a rock. She gave it a gentle underhand toss at the wall of light and it passed through without making a ripple. "Safe?" she asked.

"I doubt it. Give me something that isn't a part of the island," I said.

I heard her slip her backpack off her shoulder and open a zipper. Then she touched my arm and passed me a granola bar wrapped in plastic. I tossed it at the wall, and when it touched, it was destroyed. It didn't go violently. It simply became a flicker of softly glowing light in the precise shape of the bar of "food."

Then it was gone.

"That also was pretty," Thomas noted. "In a completely lethal kind of way."

"Look who's talking," Molly said.

"It's not all that high," he said. "Maybe I could jump it."

"Molly," I said.

She passed me another granola bar, and I threw it over the wall.

The wall destroyed it in midair.

"Maybe not," Thomas said.

"Okay," Karrin said. "So . . . How do we get through it?"

I thought about it for a second. Then I licked my lips and said, "We don't. I do."

"Alone?" Thomas said. "Sort of defeats the point of bringing us. Also, death. Bad plan."

"I think it will let me through," I said.

"You *think?*"

"Look," I said. "Me and the island are . . . kind of partners."

"Oh, right," Thomas said. He looked at Karrin and said, "Harry's a geosexual."

Karrin arched an eyebrow and gave me a look.

"You can't go alone," Molly said, her voice worried.

"Looks like it's the only way I can go," I said. "So we do this Ulysses-style. I go in, I figure a way to let down the gate and then we sack Troy."

"Can you do that?" Karrin asked.

I licked my lips and looked at the wall of light. "I'd better be able to."

"You're tired," Molly said.

"I'm fine."

"Your hands are shaking."

Were they? They were. "They are fine also."

I didn't *feel* tired. Given how much magic I'd been throwing around this day, I should have been comatose with fatigue hours ago, but I just didn't feel it. That wasn't a good sign. Maybe Butters had been right: No matter how much juice I got from the mantle of Winter, bodies have limits. I was pushing mine.

I passed the Winchester to Thomas and took off my new duster. At his lifted eyebrow, I said, "Not of the island. Hold 'em for me."

He exhaled and took them. "No reruns, okay?"

"Pfft," I said. "Be like sneaking into the movies."

Karrin touched my arm. "Just don't say that you'll be right back. You'll jinx it."

"I am a professional wizard," I said. "I know all about jinxes."

Having said that, I checked to make sure my shirt wasn't red. It wasn't. Then I realized I was putting this off because if I was wrong, I was about to go join Yoda and Obi-Wan in blue-light country. So I took a deep breath and strode forward into the beautiful, deadly barrier.

47

I lived.

Just in case anyone was wondering.

I stepped through and the liquid light poured over me like warm syrup. There was a little bit of a tingle as it passed over the surface of my body, and then it was gone.

As were my clothes. Like, completely.

I had sort of hoped that they would stay—the way Superman's unitard stays mostly invincible because it's really close to his skin. Plus I hadn't felt like stripping in front of everyone for something so relatively trivial as preserving my garage-sale wardrobe and, more important, I didn't think I had time to start playing Mr. Rogers while someone screwed around with my island. City to save. Check out my focus.

Of course . . . going into battle full commando could be problematic.

On the other hand, every single time Mab had come at me during my recovery—*every time*—I'd been just like this, without resources of any kind except what I carried within me. I wasn't a big believer in coincidence. Had she been trying only to strengthen me generally? Or had she been preparing me for this exact situation?

Could Mab see that far ahead? Or was this simply a case of superior preparedness proving itself in action? What was it I'd heard in a martial arts studio at some point? Learn to fight naked and you can never be disarmed. Which is fine, I guess, as long as there aren't mosquitoes.

I got low and stayed still and opened my senses.

First thing: I was inside a ritual circle, one that was currently functioning, being used for a spell. It wasn't the cheap and quick kind I was used to, I guessed, or it would have been broken when I crossed it. Maybe it had kept its integrity because as part of the island, I already existed on either side of the circle. There were certain creatures who could move back and forth across boundaries like that without disturbing them in the slightest—most notably the common cat. It was one reason practitioners so often kept cats as house pets. From a technical standpoint, they are very magic-friendly. Maybe I hadn't broken it because it had been set up in such a way as to consider the island's Warden one of those creatures. Or maybe it was the continual, rippling, liquid nature of the circle itself.

Whatever the case, I was standing inside an active circle. Possibly the most active circle I had ever seen. Magic hummed through the air and the ground, so much that I felt my hair standing on end, and some primitive instinct-level awareness from the Winter Knight's mantle, the same part that had given me so much trouble all day, started advising me to get the hell out of there along with the rest of the island's animals. That was why my intellectus hadn't been able to tell me what was happening here. As a form of magical awareness, an active circle had blocked my intellectus out. Now it worked just fine for what was inside the circle—it was everything *outside* of it that it could no longer touch.

I learned all of that at the same time my regular old five senses registered what was happening: I was not alone. The crown of the hill was covered with faeries.

All right, that wasn't literally true. There were twenty of them, plus one other mortal.

And Demonreach.

The island's spirit made manifest stood in the ruins of the lighthouse, in the opening in the wall that led to the entrance to the stairs down to the Well. Its vast form was planted, braced like a man standing against a strong wind, hunched, bent forward slightly, but not in a stance of battle. The spirit did not exist for such things. Instead, I realized, it did only what it always had: It endured. But even as I watched, I saw bits of Demonreach flying backward, away from its mass, but slowly, as if a current of thick syrup flowed past the spirit, slowly wearing it away.

The spirit stood at one point of an equilateral triangle.

At one of the other points stood Lily, the Summer Lady. She stood with her right arm, the arm that projects energy, upraised. She wore the same simple dress I'd seen her in earlier. It was pressed against the front of her body, and her silver-white hair was blown back as if in a strong wind. There was no visible display of energy coming from her other than that, but the ground between her and Demonreach was covered in fresh green grass, and I could feel that she was pouring out power against spirit.

Behind her stood a pair of Sidhe of the Summer Court, each with a hand on her shoulder. Behind them were three more, and four more were behind them, each with their hands on the shoulder of someone in front of them, forming a pyramid shape. They were all projecting power forward, focusing it through Lily, making her even stronger than she already was.

Maeve stood at the third point of the triangle, with her own pyramid of supporters. She wore leather short-shorts, military boots, and a bikini top, all of midnight blue. She stood in the same stance as Lily, the same unseen power flaring from her outstretched hand, but her face was set in a wide, manic smile, and the ground between her and Demonreach was covered in a layer of frost.

The Redcap stood at her right hand, one hand on her shoulder. The massive rawhead from my birthday party was there, too, and its bony claws, drenched in and dripping fresh blood, rested on her other shoulder. Eight other Winter Sidhe were behind them, forming a power pyramid of their own.

Then I heard footsteps, and a second later Fix, the Summer Knight, stepped around the corner of my partially completed cottage and walked toward me. He was wearing faerie mail, gleaming, draping over a wiry, hard-muscled frame, and he carried his sword in his hand. Fix stopped between me and the triangle at the top of the hill.

"Hey, Harry," he said quietly.

"Hey, Fix."

"Cold?"

"Not so much. You know what's happening here?"

"What must happen," he said.

"According to whom?"

"My Lady."

"She's wrong."

Fix stood there for a time, quiet. Then he said, "Doesn't matter."

"Why not?"

"Because she is my Lady. You will not raise your hand against her."

I stared at Fix, who had suffered under the office of Lloyd Slate, and behind him at Lily, who had been Slate's frequent victim. I wondered how many times, back then, Fix had ached to be able to save her, to have the power to stand up to the Winter Knight.

And now he did.

There comes a time when no amount of talk can change the course of events—when people are committed, when their actions are dictated by the necessity of the situation their choices have created. Fix had put his faith in Lily, and would fight to the death to defend her. Nothing I had to say would change that. I could see that in his face.

"Go back," he said.

"Can't. Stand aside?"

"Can't."

"So it's like that?" I said.

Fix exhaled. Then he nodded. "Yeah."

And for the first time in a decade the Winter Knight and Summer Knight went to war.

Fix hurled a bolt of pure Summer fire that scorched the ground beneath it as it flew at me.

I didn't have time to think, but some part of me knew this game. Dodging the bolt wouldn't be enough—the bloom of heated air coming off that fire would burn me if it even came close. That was why Fix would have the advantage in this match if he kept the distance open and just threw bolt after bolt. So I called upon Winter to chill the air around me as I ducked to one side. Fire and cold met, clashed, and filled the air with mist—mist that would give me the chance to close to grips with my foe.

Part of me, the part of me that I was sure *was* me, viewed these tactics with alarm. I was freaking naked and unarmed. Fix had the mantle of the

Summer Knight, and it made him just as strong and fast and tough as I was. He was armored and toted a freaking sword, and he'd had ten years of training with the Summer Court to learn how to fight and use the mantle. Plus, he presumably hadn't spent all day pushing his abilities to the limit.

But the Winter mantle didn't *care* about that. It simply saw its enemy and wanted to destroy it. The best way to do that was to get in close and rip out Fix's throat.

Except that wasn't how the last Winter Knight had killed the last Summer Knight. Lloyd Slate had iced the stairs underneath the other guy's feet and pushed him down. And Slate had been young and in good shape, whereas the other Summer Knight had been an old man. So I thought it would be smart to assume that the instinctual knowledge of the Winter mantle, while it could be handy, was basically that of a starving predator, a wolf in winter—it wanted blood, lots of it, now.

And if I played it like that, Fix was going to leave my guts on the ground.

Instead of charging ahead, I veered to one side for several steps and then froze. An instant later, another bolt of fire lit up the mist, right through where I would have been if I'd followed the mantle's instinct.

Of course—it had to be that way. Winter's Knight was the mountain lion, the wolf. Summer's was the stag, the bison. Winter was oriented to stalking, hunting, and killing prey. Summer to avoiding a confrontation until an advantage could be had, then savagely pressing that advantage for all it was worth. Fix would have a wealth of instinctive knowledge to draw on if I went after him Winter's way, and would be at his most dangerous the same way as, for example, a student of pure aikido. He would use the strength of an attack to assist his own defense, turning it back on the attacker. But if I didn't *give* him that kind of aggressive assault, I would rob him of his instinctive advantage.

Screw being the Winter Knight. Before everything else, I was a wizard.

So I flicked my wrist, whispered, *"Obscurata,"* and vanished behind a veil.

My veils aren't much good compared to the grasshopper's, or almost anyone else's, really, but when you're standing in a giant fog bank they don't need to be very good to make you effectively invisible—and I know how to move *very* quietly. I wouldn't have trusted them against one of the Sidhe, but Fix wasn't one. He was a changeling, with one mortal parent and one fae one, but except for the Summer mantle, he was as human as the next guy.

I prowled ahead, Listening, sharpening the acuity of my ears to a far greater level than that of which they were normally capable, and heard Fix's smooth breathing before I'd taken a dozen steps. I froze in place. I couldn't locate him exactly, but—

I kept myself from making an impatient sound and consulted my intellectus. Fix was standing thirty-six feet, four inches away, about twenty-two degrees to the left of the way my nose was facing. If I'd had a gun, I was pretty sure I could have shot him.

Fix had frozen in place, too.

Bah. His mantle was probably advising him to be patient, just as mine was screaming at me to stop waiting, stalk him, and pounce. I took advantage of it for maybe a minute, consulting my intellectus and moving fifty feet to one side, where I could pick something up off the ground. Then I went back and waited—but he still hadn't stirred.

This wouldn't work if he stood his ground. I had to make him move.

I retreated a few more steps into the mist and spoke away from him, hoping the lousy visibility and my veil would confuse the exact origin of my voice. "I get Lloyd Slate a little better now, you know," I said. "The mantle. It drove him. Made him want things."

"Lloyd Slate was a monster," came Fix's voice.

I hated to do it but . . . I had to push his buttons. "He was as human as the next man," I said. "It just . . . made his desires louder and louder. There wasn't anything he could have done about it."

"Do you hear yourself, Harry?" Fix called. There was an edge in his voice. "You sound like a man making excuses—or justifications."

"Yeah, but I'm not Slate," I shot back, my voice hotter. "Slate was some pathetic bully. I had as much power as a hundred Slates way before I cut his throat."

Fix's breathing came faster. He had it under control—but he was scared. "The Harry Dresden I knew never would have said something like that."

"That was ten years, a persecution complex, and a war ago, Fix," I told him, "and you haven't got room to get all righteous with me. I know you're feeling things, too, just like I am." Time to sink the right barb, to goad him into movement, aggression. "What do you see when you look at Lily, man? She's gorgeous. I have a hard time thinking about anything else when she's there."

"Shut up," he said in a quiet voice.

"Seriously," I continued. The dialogue came easily—too easily. The Winter mantle was talking to a part of me that did not have much in the way of restraint. "That hot little ass? I mean, gosh, just thinking about it . . . If you could see me now, I'd be a little embarrassed."

"Shut up," he said again.

"Come on, bros before hos, man. That Summer mantle got a herd instinct going? 'Cause for something as sweet as that, I'm thinking we could share i—"

If my intellectus hadn't been focused on him, to let me see what was coming, I'd have been burned alive. I flung myself to one side as he turned and hurled another bolt of fire at me. I had to gather more Winter around myself to protect my vulnerable hide, thickening the mists even more—and Fix seemed to key on the surge of cold. He pivoted toward me, took two steps, and leapt with his sword held in both hands.

Thirty-seven feet. That was how far he jumped, and it had come effortlessly—he could have done more. I knew exactly how much force he pressed the ground with when he left it, exactly what angle he'd jumped at. My intellectus could track the air and the mist he was displacing as he leapt through it.

I took two steps away just as he leapt.

I felt sick, like I was fighting a blind man.

Fix landed exactly two feet short of where I'd been, and his sword came down through the space where I'd been standing. If I'd still been there, he would have split me into two gruesome halves.

But I wasn't. I was standing behind him, within inches of his back, and before he could rise, I struck. A moment before, I'd used my intellectus to locate an old nail on the ground, about four inches long, partly coated in rust. Thomas or I must have dropped it while walking to or from the cottage, back when we'd been beginning repairs on it and building the Whatsup Dock. The nail had lain out through several seasons, only lightly touched by them.

I put my thumb behind its head, used the strength of the Winter mantle, and drove it straight through mail that had never been designed to stop such a small point, and two inches into the muscle of Fix's shoulder blade.

Fix let out a scream of shock and pain and swung his sword at me—but with cold steel piercing his skin, and his access to the Summer mantle disrupted, he had only his own reflexes, strength, and skill to rely on. He hadn't trained in them without the power of the Summer Knight to back them up, and he hadn't learned in the brutal school of hard knocks that Mab had put me through. The sword's slash was slowed and clumsy, and I struck him twice—once on the wrist, breaking it with a clear snap, sending the sword tumbling away, and once on the jaw, not quite as hard, sending Fix to the ground in a senseless heap.

"Knight takes Knight," I called into the cloudy night air. "Check."

The struggle between the Queens and Demonreach had already been a silent one, but now the air abruptly went still. I couldn't see them, but I knew that Lily had turned her body partly away from Demonreach, toward me, breaking her connection with one of the two Sidhe supporting her. Demonreach, for its part, had altered its facing to square off against Maeve. I could sense that the little bits of its body that had been eroding away were now moving in the opposite direction, reaccruing to its main mass.

"Fix?" the Summer Lady called, her voice vaguely confused. Then it was touched by sudden, cold fear. "*Fix!*"

"What are you doing?" Maeve snarled. "You stupid cow! I cannot defeat the guardian alone!"

Lily ignored her. I sensed her move her hand, an almost absent gesture.

And a sudden wind brushed the fog Fix and I had created from the hilltop as easily as a young mother sweeping fallen Cheerios from a toddler's tray.

Holy crap.

I knew the Ladies were powerful, but I hadn't realized what that meant in practical terms. Making that much air move that precisely and that suddenly is *hard*, and it would take a serious investment of energy to make it happen. I could have done it, but it would have been enough heavy lifting to make me want a cold beer and a nice sit-down when I was finished. If I'd had to do it two or three times in a row, I'd have been too tired to lift the beer.

Lily had done it with a comparative flick of her fingers.

And there I was, standing naked on the hilltop over the unmoving form of Fix. I still had my veil up, but it was so rudimentary as to be useless against someone as savvy as the Sidhe. I shouldn't have bothered to hold on to it at all, but some irrational instinct made me condense it instead to a small field of blurry energy around my hips.

"He's alive, Lily," I said, quickly. "We need to talk."

The whites showed all the way around Lily's eyes. "What?" she demanded, fury swelling in her tone. "What did you say to me?"

Whoa. On my worst diplomatic day, I still shouldn't have garnered a reaction like that from what I'd said. "Lily, calm down. Fix is alive. But I think you're still you over there, and I don't think you've been given the whole truth. Let's talk before things happen that everyone regrets."

"How dare you!" she snarled, her rage turning incandescent. Literally. Fire burst from her hands and wreathed her forearms. "How *dare* you!"

I held up my own hands in front of me, empty. I was pretty sure I looked confused. "Hell's bells, Lily, what the hell? I do *not* want a fight here!"

Lily screamed, and Summer fire engulfed her, causing her courtiers to leap away. Gold and green and starlight silver, the fire danced around her, mesmerizing—and swelling. Suddenly I saw the same rage that I'd seen in Titania's eyes, but that had been the smoldering coals left over after the passing of years, after mourning and grief had eased. The power Lily held on to now came from the same kind of passion—but it was fresh and white-hot, and it wasn't going to cool anytime soon.

Then I realized what was going on. Maeve had extended her other hand toward me, and her fingers were dancing merrily. She gave me the briefest flash of a look, and it was poisonously amused. I reached into the air in front of me and felt it there, an elegant little glamour, simple enough that Maeve could have done it in her sleep, complex enough to slip by anyone not looking for it, even one of the Sidhe. I'd been talking, but it hadn't been my words getting to Lily. Maeve had chosen my words for me.

I don't know what she'd said, but she'd picked something exactly right to drive her Summer counterpart mad with rage. Lily's gentler, more compassionate nature had been used against her. Maeve had employed her simple little glamour with exquisite timing, at the one instant when there was no way the relatively inexperienced Lily would have expected it—when she was full of concern for the fallen Fix. With a sinking feeling I realized that the passionate young Lady of Summer was no Titania. She had all the heat, but none of the restraint, the balance, and there was no way in hell that she was going to be able to think, to reason, to hold back her fury.

"Destroy him!" she screamed. Trees shook and rocks cracked as she spoke. The sound of it ripped at my ears, and I felt a sudden hot wetness in them. "Destroy Harry Dresden!"

She threw forth her hands and a wall of fire twenty feet high and as wide as a football field roared toward me.

48

For a fraction of a second, my brain squealed like the last little piggy running all the way home, a spinal-level fear reaction. I had an experience with fire once. It's the kind of memory that sticks pretty hard.

Fire's tough to defend against. That's one of the reasons it's always been my favorite form of attack. Even if you don't actually set your target on fire, you can still roast it by heating up the air around it, unless it just throws away everything to get out of your way, in which case it isn't thinking about doing anything back to you. As weapons go, fire is top-drawer.

But.

Fire's tricky and fickle. Without focus, it's just chaos, the random release of stored chemical energy. It isn't enough to just have fire. You've got to know when and where and how to use it to best effect—and Lily didn't.

I threw myself down over the unconscious Fix and focused, thrusting my hands out to either side, shouting, *"Defendarius!"*

As I formed a shield around us in a bubble, the firestorm roared down onto us, washing over us like an ocean tide. My shield held the fire back, but it couldn't stop it entirely, and heat began to burn through. That was why I reached for Winter and filled the little bubble around us with the cold. That wave of fire was too massive for me to overcome—but I didn't have to overcome it. It was spread out over such a huge area that all I had to do was beat a relatively tiny portion of it, to hold out against it like a large stone on a beach. I didn't have the strength to beat it—but I did have the strength to hold it away, and to keep just the air within my shield from becoming an oven.

The fire washed over us, and I held on to the shield for a few seconds more, as long as I thought I could. Without my bracelet or my staff to help direct the energy, a few seconds were all I could do—but it was enough to survive. It left me on my hands and knees, gasping, on a small circle of frost-covered earth, but I made it, and so did Fix.

Go, me.

Maeve's mocking laughter rang out over the hilltop.

Hot air touched the side of my face and grew gently, along with an approaching light. I looked up to see Lily walking toward me over the scorched earth, naked now but for the flames curling around her body, her own clothing burned away in the firestorm. Her eyes weren't there. There were only a pair of searing fires burning where they had been, wisps of orange and scarlet flame rising up from them as she came closer. Her silken white hair rose into a wavering column like a flame itself, lifted by the hot air and colored golden green and orange by the light of her fiery nimbus.

Behind her, the other Summer Sidhe were shadows, with fire dancing in the reflection of silvery weapons, and with the echoes of it flickering in their hands and upon their brows, power and weapons alike spreading out around me to leave me no escape—but at the flick of a hand from Lily, they stopped and withdrew, back to their original positions near the tower.

I guessed that she didn't want to incinerate her Summer buddies along with me. I started to lift my hand, to ready another shield, but my other arm couldn't take the weight of my body and I nearly collapsed.

That was it, then.

I was out of gas.

I managed to get myself up onto my knees and sat back on my heels, panting. Then I tugged the nail out of Fix's back, gripped it grimly, and faced Lily.

She stopped about six feet away from me, covered in living fire, and stared down, her eyes like spotlights.

"He's okay, Lily," I said. "Fix is okay. God, Lily. Can you even hear me?"

Evidently she could not. Lily lifted a hand, and a minuscule sphere of white-hot light formed in the air above it, a tiny star.

Now there, that was focus. I couldn't have stopped something that concentrated without a major amount of preparation. I could appreciate it in a professional sense, even if it was about to kill me horribly.

And suddenly I felt very stupid. What the fuck had I been thinking? The Queens of Faerie, even the least of them, were elemental powers, something that was simply out of the league of any mortal. I should have tried to contact my grandfather and the Grey Council, should have at least put out a scream to the White Council, even if they were less likely to help.

And I should have sent Michael and his family—and Maggie—out of town the second I'd realized the danger. I'd saved the day before, maybe often enough to make me overconfident. I sneer about the White Council being arrogant all the time, but I'd walked into the exact same stupid trap, hadn't I? Confident of my ability to handle anything that came along, I'd gathered together my little band of enablers and cruised right into this disaster.

"Lily," I said wearily. "Listen to me. We've both been set up by Maeve."

White fire stared at me.

"The adversary," I said. "It's in her. It's been in her for a long time. Think. It makes the things it takes act against their natures. And you know what it's done for Maeve?" I leaned forward, holding my weary hands palms up. "It's let her *lie*. She can lie her ass off and never blink an eye. *Think*. How much of your trust in her, of your awareness of what's going on in the world is based on knowing that she can't speak an untruth?"

Fire stared—and did not consume me. So I kept talking.

"Don't take me at my word," I said. "Just look at what she is *doing*."

And Lily spoke, her voice burning with the unleashed power of Summer. "We are working together. We are destroying the largest source of dark energy and corruption in this world. The source *you* are so desperate to protect that you call Outsiders to defend it!"

Oh, God.

Lily didn't *know* what was in the Well. She understood that it was a source of dark energy, but not *why*.

I kept forgetting that she had had the job for only a comparatively tiny amount of time. Before I'd killed Aurora and left poor Lily holding the mantle of the Summer Lady, she'd been a young woman, no older than Molly, only without Molly's skills and training. She'd been putting her life back together while dealing with the massive power of her mantle, taking a crash course in faerie leadership, struggling to learn.

And if someone had been there to feed her lies as part of her basic education in the supernatural, someone whose word she had trusted, God only knew how much her knowledge had been twisted and colored.

"Who told you I called up Outsiders?" I asked. "Maeve?"

"So arrogant," Lily said. "You reek of arrogance and deception, like all wizards. Even the famous Merlin, who built this abomination." Her eyes narrowed. "But as complex as it is, it is still made of mortal magic. This circle that we used to stop your interference—it's a part of the architecture here. All we had to do was feed power into it to close this place against your allies while we tore it down from inside."

"If you keep going," I told her, "you are going to destroy yourself, Lily, and everyone you brought with you, and a lot of innocent people are going to *die*."

"Finish it, Lily," Maeve called. "I told you they would lie. Mortals *always* lie, and that is why we must stand together. We cannot allow ourselves to be divided. Put him down and we will complete what we have begun."

"Lily, please," I said. "Don't take my word for it. Don't believe me. But be certain. Find out for yourself. Then you'll know. You don't have to do this."

The Summer fire vanished abruptly.

Lily stood over me, her hair mussed, her naked body so beautiful, it hurt. She spoke in a quiet, dreadfully numb voice. "You can't tell me that," she said. "Not you. Do you think I wanted this? Do you think I wanted pain and death and fear and war? Do you think I wanted this mantle, this responsibility?" Her eyes welled, though her expression didn't change. "I didn't want the world. I didn't want vast riches, or fame, or power. I wanted a husband. Children. Love. A home that we made together. And that can never happen now." The tears fell, and as the heat, the fury, came back into her voice, the fire gathered around her again. "Because of you. Because you killed Aurora. Because you *made* me into *this*. You raise your hand against my champion, my *friend*, and when you are defeated you *dare* tell me what I must and must not do?"

"Lily, please," I said. "You have a choice."

Maeve was laughing again in the background, an Arkham Asylum kind of laugh that echoed across the bare, burned ground.

"Now," Lily said, her burning voice bitter. "*Now* you give me a choice." The ministar flared to life in her palm again. "*Thus* do I choose, you son of a bitch. Knight of Winter, burn and die."

I got it, I think. Or at least, I got most of it. Lily had spent her life a victim because of her luminous beauty. Lloyd Slate had been the last man to abuse her, but I doubted he was the first. All her life, she had been shut away from making choices, but she clearly had not wanted to be part of the world of Faerie; as a changeling, she could have Chosen to become a full faerie being at any time—and she hadn't. Then when I killed Aurora, I had even taken the choice to remain human away from her.

I hadn't meant to do that when I killed Aurora, but that fact made no difference in the outcome. I hadn't just killed Aurora that night. In many ways, I'd effectively killed Lily, too. I'd thrown her into a world where she was lost and afraid. A grieving and furious Titania had doubtless not been the supportive mentor figure Lily had needed. And even if she'd been a newly minted immortal, she must have been horribly angry, and sad, and afraid—and lonely.

Easy prey for Maeve. Easy prey for Nemesis. I wasn't sure whether there was anything about that entire situation that I could have changed, even if I'd known that it needed changing, but I still felt like I was the one at fault. Maybe I was. It had been my choice that changed everything.

Maybe it was fitting that Lily kill me, in turn.

Her fiery eyes seared into mine as she launched the little star at my heart.

49

There was a flash of silver, and the little star bounced off of the mirror-bright flat of Fix's long sword.

It soared into the earth a dozen yards away and hit the ground with a flash and a howl of heated air, creating a brief column of white flame that, presumably, had been intended to replace my head and neck.

Fix was holding himself up on one elbow, and held the sword in his left hand. He looked like hell, but he made a single deft rolling motion and came onto his feet as if he didn't weigh anything.

And he came to his feet between Lily and me.

"Lily!" Fix said. "What is *wrong* with you?"

Eyes of flame regarded him. "You . . . you're all right?"

"I *said* that," I said. My voice might have squeaked a little. My heart rate was up.

"Harry, shut up," Fix said. "Lily, *look* at him. He isn't a threat to anyone."

I guess I must have looked kind of bad, but still . . . "Hey," I said.

Fix twitched his hips and kicked me in the chest. It wasn't hard, but in my condition it didn't need to be. It knocked me over.

"Sir Knight . . ." Lily said. "I . . . Fix, it *burns.*"

"Stop this," he urged quietly. "Let's get out of here, find someplace quiet for you to meditate until you've got it under control again."

"I *need* to . . . He tried to *hurt* you."

Fix's voice hardened. "The ground is burned black, Lily," he said.

"And there's frost all over my mail. There are burns all over his arms and shoulders, but I wake up fine, lying in the only grass left on the hilltop." He held up his sword. The last six inches or so of the blade were simply gone, ending in a melted mess. The point must have been lying outside the area my shield had covered. "But it was hot enough to do this. Forget what anyone *said*. Who was protecting me, Lily?"

She stared at Fix, the furious fire still curling around her, lifting her hair, burning from her eyes. Then she closed them with a groan, and the fires went out. Lily turned her head sharply away from me. "This is too much," I heard her whisper. "I'm going to fly apart."

"My lady?" Fix asked.

Lily made a snarling sound, turning eyes that still flickered with embers toward me. "Stay where you are, Sir Knight," she said, spitting the last word. "If you move or lift weapon or power against our purpose, I will not show mercy a second time." Then she turned and swept back toward the pyramid formation of Sidhe assaulting Demonreach. Her feet left clear imprints in the soot and ash on the ground, and little fires flickered up in the wake of her steps, dying away again when she had passed. She did not say a word, just lifted her hand and again something like an invisible sandblaster started pouring into Demonreach.

I watched, too drained to move more. I did, I noted, have burns on my arms. I didn't feel them. They didn't look like anything epic, but they were there.

"Fix," I said. "Thank you."

He looked at me, his expression guarded, but nodded his head slightly. "It seemed I was in your debt, Winter." His eyes sparkled, just for a second. "Couldn't have that."

I found myself laughing weakly. "No. No, it might break something."

"It broke my damned wrist." He snorted. "My jaw isn't happy either. Good punch."

"I cheated," I said.

"Our business, there's no such thing," he said. "I should have known you were goosing me, talking like that. Most of the fighting I've done, there hasn't been much in the way of taunt and insult."

"Raise your standards. There's almost always time for an insult or two."

He smiled, though it was a bit pained. He waggled the fingers of his right hand experimentally. "Are you done?"

I exhaled slowly, and didn't answer.

"How much of what you told her is true?" he asked.

"What did you hear?" I asked him.

"Pretty much everything after you took the knife out of me."

"Nail," I corrected him, and held it up so he could see. It still had his blood on it.

He looked a little pained. "Harry, would you mind?"

"No," I said, and wiped the blood into the earth, scrubbing it off the nail.

"Thanks," he said. He squinted at the wall and then at me. "How the hell did you get in here?"

"Trade secrets," I said. "How did you guys get here? I know you didn't take a boat."

"Flew in," Fix said. "Shape-shifters. I dropped from a hang glider over the lake and parachuted in."

"Damn. You got extreme."

"I'm getting there," he said.

"So you landed here and put the circle up?"

"Trade secrets," he said cautiously. "You realize we still aren't sitting in the same dugout, right? I can do the frenemies thing. It's kind of traditional. But we are not on the same side."

"No. You're on the wrong side," I said. "Maybe more than one."

"That's what every conflict sounds like," he said. "Not everyone can be equally right, Harry."

"But believe you me, everyone *can* be equally wrong," I said. "Fix, this is about more than Winter and Summer."

He frowned at that.

"Tell me this," I said. "I'm not asking for anything specific, anything that I might be able to use against you later." As if Maeve would let me have a later. "Just tell me: Has Maeve ever asked you to take something at her word. And just *told* you something was true? Straight up?"

Fix's frown deepened.

"And you thought to yourself, 'Hey, that's odd. She never just *tells* anyone anything straight up.'"

His lips parted slightly, and his eyes fixed on Maeve.

"And you thought that if anyone but one of the Ladies had said it, you would wonder if she was lying. But she didn't leave any wiggle room, so it *had* to be the truth."

"So?" he asked, very quietly.

"So let me ask you this," I said. "If you assume that she *can* lie, even if it was just that once—how does it change the picture?"

Fix might have had some foolish idealism going, but he'd never been anywhere close to stupid. "Oh," he breathed. "Um."

"Remember when Lily opened the door to Arctis Tor for us, back when?"

"Sure."

"When we got inside, the Leanansidhe was popsicled in Mab's garden," I said. "Because something had invaded her and influenced her actions. Mab was in the middle of some kind of exorcism based on the model of an ice age."

"And?"

"And what if this invader got into the water before Mab caught it?" I asked. "What if it got into Maeve?"

"That's crazy," he said. "Mab's the one who's gone mental."

"Is she?" I asked him. "Is it so crazy? Remember that meeting at Mac's? Remember how we found out that Mab had cracked a gasket?"

"Maeve told . . ." He stopped speaking suddenly.

"Yeah," I said. "A minute ago, you told Lily to ignore the words and look at the actions. You know as well as I do which speaks louder. You know who I am and what I've done. So I'm going to ask one more question," I said. "Whose idea was it to be here tonight? Lily's? Or Maeve's?"

The blood drained from his face. "Oh. Fuck."

I bowed my head. Then I said, "Fix, I saved you because you're a decent guy, and I don't care if we're on different teams. I don't want you dead."

"Yeah," he said quietly. "It . . . speaks pretty loud. But maybe you knew I'd think that. Maybe you did it so that you could play me."

"Maybe you're giving me way more credit for cunning than I'm due. You know how I work. How often do I get to a neat, elegant solution that ties everything up? Can you look at me right now and honestly say to yourself, 'Dresden, that wily genius! This must be a part of his master plan'?"

I spread my hands and looked up at him expectantly.

Fix looked at me, dirty, naked, shivering, burned, bruised, covered in soot and ash.

"Fuck," he said again, and looked back at the Ladies.

"I don't think Maeve did anything to Lily's head," I said. "I don't think she needed to. I think Lily was insecure and lonely enough that all Maeve needed to do was act sort of like a person. Give Lily someone who she felt understood what she was going through. Someone she thought would have her back."

"A friend," Fix said.

"Yes."

"Everyone wants to have a friend," he said quietly. "Is that so bad?"

"Thelma and Louise were friends," I said. I pointed at the triangle. "Canyon."

The muscles along his jaw jumped several times. "Even if . . . even if you're being honest, *and* you're right—and I'm not copping to either—so what? Those coteries with them are their inner circles. They'll obey without question. You've got nothing left to fight with. And I sure as hell can't take them all on alone."

I didn't want to say it, to give away anything to a potential enemy. Nemesis could have taken Fix, for all I knew. It could be there inside him right then, smirking at the rapport it was establishing with me. That was the ugly fact.

But sometimes you have to ignore the math, and . . .

And follow the wisdom of your heart.

My heart told me that Fix was a decent guy.

"Fix, I know about this island. It's kind of my stomping grounds.

That's how I got through. And I know that if Maeve has her way, this island is going Mount Saint Helens, and taking Chicago with it."

He stared at me, frowning, pensive.

"My daughter is in town," I said in a whisper. "She'll die."

He blinked. "You have a . . . ?" Then he rocked back a little, as he realized what I'd entrusted him with. "Oh. Christ, Dresden."

I took a deep breath and pressed on. "The Hunt is out there taking it to the Outsiders right now," I said. "And they're winning. And my crew is here, outside the circle. Murphy, Molly, Thomas, Mouse. If I can take the circle down, we aren't alone."

"When did 'we' happen?" he asked in a flat, hard tone.

I looked up at him and saw laughter at the corners of his eyes.

Sometimes the wisdom of the heart is not at all a bad thing.

"I won't let anything hurt Lily," he said. "For any reason. Period."

"Agreed," I said. "Maeve's the bad guy."

He tested his right hand again and got a little more motion out of it before he winced. "I don't know where this will get you," he said, "but as far as I could tell, this was just a ritual circle, like any other."

"How so?"

"When we landed, Maeve sent some hounds and some Little Folk after you and went straight for that lighthouse—and the guardian just popped up out of the ground, where it is now. Maeve assaulted the spirit, just like right now. She kept it busy while Lily walked a circle of the hilltop, singing. I've seen her set up circles like that a thousand times. But once she'd gone all the way around, kaboom, up came the wall."

I grunted. "Then . . . it's a preinstalled defense that can be triggered like . . . Hell's bells, not *like* a ward. It *is* a ward. A huge one. But if anything of the island passes through the circle without disturbing it, and anything that isn't of the island is destroyed . . ." I followed the logic through and sagged.

"What?" Fix asked.

"Then there's no way to break the circle," I breathed. "It's like a timelock safe. It isn't coming down until sunrise."

"Meaning what?"

I swallowed. Sunrise was too late. So I gathered whatever scraps of strength I had left in me and pushed myself slowly, wearily to my feet.

"Meaning," I said, "we're on our own."

Fix eyed the center of the clearing. He passed me a silvery knife he drew from his belt and said, "There you go with that 'we' again."

50

I started walking. It was iffy for a couple of steps but I got the hang of it.

"Is there a plan?" Fix asked, keeping up with me.

"Maeve. I kill her."

Which had been Mab's freaking order in the first place.

He glanced aside. "You know she's an immortal, right?"

"Yeah."

His eyes narrowed. "What do I do?"

"They've got the guardian pinned down," I said. "I think one of those crews has *got* to stay on it, or it will break loose. Otherwise, Maeve would have been stomping on me right next to Lily."

Fix nodded. "She never passes up the chance to tear the wings off a fly." He frowned. "What happens if the guardian gets loose?"

I wasn't sure. Demonreach had enormous power, an absolute dedication to purpose, and no sense of proportion. I had very little idea of its tactical capabilities. It might or might not be able to help in a fight. Actually, I was sort of hoping it wouldn't—imagine trying to kill specific ants, in a crowd of ants, with a baseball bat. I was pretty sure that if Demonreach ever started swinging at someone, I wanted to be over the horizon at the very least.

In fact, I realized, that was probably the problem here. Demonreach existed on an epic scale. It was neither suited to nor capable of effectively dealing with beings of such relative insignificance. Standing off a Walker and a small army of Outsiders had not been a huge problem for the island. But Maeve and Lily had slipped inside its guard. They and their personal attendants were sparrows attacking an eagle. The eagle was bigger and stronger and capable of killing any of them, and it didn't matter in the least.

Not only that, but Demonreach was a genius loci, a nature spirit. The fae were intimately connected to nature on a level that no one had ever been able to fully understand. One could probably make an argument that Demonreach *was* one of the fae, or at least a very close neighbor. Either way, the mantles of the Ladies of Winter and Summer would carry a measure of dominion and power over beings like Demonreach. Clearly they were not sovereign over the guardian spirit, because it was withstanding them. Just as clearly, they had *something* going for them, because it wasn't trying to crush them, either.

"I'm not sure," I answered. "But the point here is that if we jump Maeve, Lily is going to be too busy keeping a lid on the guardian to get involved."

"The two of us," Fix said, "are going to take on all ten of them?"

"Nah," I said. "I take Maeve. You get the other nine."

"What if they don't cooperate?"

"Chastise them."

Fix snorted. "That'll be quick. One way or the other. And . . . it's going to mean war if the Summer Knight assaults nobles of the Winter Court."

"Not at all," I said. "They aren't nobles. They're outlaws. I just outlawed them by the authority invested in me and stuff. I also hereby declare us a joint task force."

"We're a task force?"

"As of now," I said.

Fix bobbed his head amiably. "If we dance fast enough, maybe we can sell that. Then what?"

"If we're both alive, we'll figure it out."

We took a few more steps before Fix said, "You can't take Maeve, wizard. Not in the shape you're in. Not even if she was alone."

"No," I said. "I can't."

But maybe the Winter Knight could.

Ever since I'd gotten out of my bed in my quarters in Arctis Tor, I'd felt the power of the Winter mantle inside me, and held it back. I'd felt the primal drives that were its power, the need to hunt, to fight, to protect territory, to kill. Winter's nature was beautiful violence, stark clarity, the most feral needs and animal desires and killer instinct pitted against the season of cold and death—the will and desire to *fight*, to *live*, even when there was no shelter, no warmth, no respite, no hope, and no help.

I'd fought against that drive, repressed it, held it at bay. That savagery was never meant for a world of grocery stores and electric blankets and peaceable assembly. It was meant for times like this.

So I let Winter in, and everything changed.

My weariness vanished. Not because my body was no longer weary, but because my body was no longer important—only my will. My fear vanished, too. Fear was for prey. Fear was for the things I was about to hunt.

My doubts vanished as well. Doubt was for things that did not know their purpose, and I knew mine. This *was* a Winter matter, a Faerie matter, a family matter, and it was precisely correct that only beings of Faerie resolve it. I knew exactly what I had to do.

There was a throat that needed ripping.

"Harry?" asked Fix. "Uh. Are you okay?"

I looked aside at him. As hunting partners went, Fix didn't look like much, but I'd seen him in action before. He was no one to underestimate. And I needed him. Once I didn't, things might change, because he was on my island and that wasn't something I could let slide. But for now I could do worse than to have him at my side.

"I'm a little hungry," I said, and smiled. "Here. Don't need it." I tossed the knife to him, point first.

He caught it deftly by the handle. I saw the minor shifts in shadow on his neck as his shoulders tensed up. "Remember. You've got iron."

I didn't sneer at him, because what would be the point? But I did roll the nail back and forth between my fingers, and heard it scraping on ice.

I looked down and found that ice had condensed out of the water in the air and formed over my fingertips. I put the nail between my teeth so that I could hold up my fingers. As I watched, icicles began to form, guided by raw instinct, stretching out from my fingertips. I flexed my fingers a few times, and saw the edges form, the ice hard and razor sharp. Nice.

I debated. Armor, too? Too heavy. This needed to happen fast. Besides, I wouldn't want the armor to be in the way for what would come after. That was going to be the good part.

"Time to play," I said around the nail. I took four steps, building up to a run, and leapt into the air toward Maeve. Fifty feet. No problem. It was glorious, the freedom, the certainty, and I could not imagine what had made me so squeamish about embracing Winter in the first place.

Bad things kept happening to me. It was high fucking time *I* started happening to *them*.

Maeve must have sensed something at the last instant, despite her focus on Demonreach. I was a fraction of a second away before she moved with the serpentine quickness of the Sidhe, throwing herself to one side. My claws missed her throat by inches. They did slice off one of her dreadlocks, and it whirled through the air as I hit the ground, legs absorbing the shock as my feet dug into the muddy ground near the lighthouse.

There was an instant of complete shock from Maeve's coterie, and I used it to slice at the Redcap's eyes just as Fix landed on the rawhead's shoulders and overbore the creature, sending it toppling forward to the ground.

I felt my claws hit. The Redcap screamed and reeled away from most of the blow, darting back, brushing past one of the Sidhe from the Botanic Gardens, behind him. The Sidhe had a blank, confused look on his face as he tried to fight his way out of the concentration of supporting Maeve in her suddenly interrupted spell. No time to think. Claws of bloody ice flashed at him, and I opened his throat to the windpipe. He went down with a choked scream, and I stepped on his chest to fling myself at the two behind him, one a twisted figure inside a droopy grey cloak and hood, the other a lean, gangling thing with the head of a boar, covered in tattoos and bone beads.

I stomped a foot down onto the cloak, slammed my clawed hand into the body behind it, and ripped out something ropy and hot and slippery. The boar-headed thing tore at my body with its tusks, and I felt bright, distant pain on my ribs. I drove a foot up between its legs in a kick that lifted it six inches off the ground, and took off an ear and half its face with my claws.

I sensed Fix at my back and heard him grunt, "Down!"

I dropped to my knees and bounced back up again. In the time I was down, his sword flicked out over my head, drove into the chest of the boar thing, and whistled out again, taking heart's blood with it.

Then there was a roar, a sound that came from something truly enormous, and someone slammed a tree trunk into my lower back. It took me off my feet and sent silver pain through my body. I landed in a roll and came up to mostly steady feet, one hand supporting some of my weight, the other up in a defensive posture.

It was the rawhead.

Rawheads are parasites, creatures that assemble bodies for themselves out of the bone and blood of freshly dead beings. They were more common when every farm and village did some slaughtering each day, back before grocery stores and fast food. As I noted before, this one was enormous, bigger than a couple of large steers, twelve feet tall and weighing at least a ton. The cloak had been torn from it, and now it looked like a bizarre sculpture of bones of various creatures, drenched in fresh blood. It had the skull of something big, maybe a hippo or a rhino, and luminous lights danced in the empty eye sockets. It drew in a huge, wheezing breath and roared again.

Fix was picking himself up off the ground, bounding up as if he hadn't been hurt at all—but the Redcap and four other Sidhe were stalking toward him with weapons drawn. Fix faced them squarely, blade in hand, a small smile on his plain face.

"My, my, *my*," Maeve said. She stepped around the leg of the rawhead into sight, giving me a frankly appraising stare. "Who would have thought you would dirty up so well, wizard? I mean, the claws, the blood, the eyes." She shivered. "It gets to me. I've always had a thing for bad boys."

I smiled around the nail. "Funny. Because I've got something for you, too."

"Yeah?" she asked, and licked her lips. "You finally gonna nail me, big guy? You've been so coy."

"I'm done teasing," I said.

Maeve slipped both hands behind her back, arching her body, thrusting her chest toward me. It wasn't a particularly impressive chest, but it was well formed, and pale, and lovely, and hidden beneath entirely too much bikini for my taste. A snarl bubbled up out of my throat.

"That's right," Maeve said, her wide eyes unblinking. "I know what you're feeling. The need to fight. To kill. To take. To fuck." She took a pair of slow steps toward me, making her hips shift back and forth. "This is right. It's exactly what you should be feeling."

I flexed the fingers of my free hand and prepared to strike. She just had to come a little closer.

"Can you imagine this all the time, wizard?" Maeve purred. Steel began to ring out, back where Fix was. But I ignored it. Two more steps. "Can you imagine feeling this strong all the time? Can you imagine being so hungry?" She took another step, and another deep breath. "And feeding that hunger. Sating it. Quenching it in flesh and screams."

She slid her left hand out from behind her back and ran her palm slowly over her stomach and side. "This flesh. I would not give it to you. I would fight, dare you to do your worst. You could unleash your every aching need. And that would just be the beginning."

I was breathing hard now, though I hadn't been a moment before. My eyes had locked onto the interplay of muscle and skin over her vulnerable belly. The claws would tear through her guts so easily there. Or I could use my teeth. Or just my tongue.

"Sex and violence," Maeve purred. She had taken a couple more steps toward me, but I wasn't sure when. Or why it mattered. "Hunger and need. Take me, here, on this ground. Don't give me pleasure, wizard. Just take. Let it out, the beast inside you. I wish you to. I dare you to." Her fingers popped the snap on the little shorts. "Stop denying yourself. Stop thinking. This *feels* right."

Hell, yeah, it did. Maeve might have been one of the Sidhe, and fast, and have all kinds of magic powers, but she wasn't stronger than me. Once I took her to the ground, I could do as I pleased with her. I felt my mouth water. Some might have come out of one corner.

Maeve stepped closer yet and breathed, "You came for my throat, didn't you?" She let her head tilt bonelessly to one side, and slid her hand up her lithe body to push her hair back and away from her neck. Her hips were making small, slow shifts of her weight, a constant distraction. Her throat was lean and lovely. "Here it is. Come to me, my Knight. It's all right. Let it out, and I will make everything worth it."

Her throat. I had wanted it for something, I thought. But now I just *wanted*. That would be how to do it. Set my teeth on her throat while I took her. If she struggled—or didn't struggle enough—I would be able to start ripping my way toward the blood.

"This is how it is supposed to be," Maeve purred. "Knight and Lady, together. Fucking like animals. Taking what we please." Her mouth turned up into a smile. "I thought you'd never let it in. Let it in deep, where I could touch." Her lovely face took on a feigned, youthful innocence. "But I can touch it now, can't I?"

I growled. I'd forgotten how to do whatever that other thing was. All I could think about was the need. Claim her as a mate. Take whatever I pleased from her. Make her mine.

Except . . .

Wait.

A fluttering surge of pure terror went through me, and it was energy enough to let me rip the Winter from my thoughts, to push it back. It didn't want to go. It fought me every inch of the way, howling, filled with raw lust for flesh and for blood.

My ribs suddenly ached. My head spun a little. I suddenly needed that hand on the ground to keep my balance.

Maeve saw it the second I regained control. Her eyelids lowered almost closed, and she breathed, "Ah. So close. But perhaps there is still time. Is that your staff, wizard, or are you just happy to see me?"

I bared my teeth and said, "Maeve . . ."

"This is perfect," she said. "In one night I'm going to unleash the

Sleepers, slay a starborn, put an end to this troublesome mortal city, and begin a war between Summer and Winter. By the time the real assault on the Gates begins, Winter and Summer will be hunting one another in the night, and be so busy gouging out one another's eyes that they'll never see what is coming—all thanks to me. And you, of course. I couldn't have done this at *all* without you."

She leaned a little closer as she spoke that last, and I ripped at her throat with my ice claws.

I was exhausted, and it was slow, entirely lacking in the focused power and precision I'd felt under the influence of Winter. She bobbed her head back a fraction of an inch, and the swipe missed and sent me down into the dirt.

Maeve let out a little peal of laughter and clapped her hands. Then she flicked a couple of fingers negligently toward me and said to the rawhead, "Tear him to pieces."

The rawhead took two lumbering steps forward and reached down toward me with bony, bloody claws.

But before it could grab me, there was a rush of footsteps, and a four-legged form consisting entirely of what looked like mud slammed into its rearmost leg.

The mud creature hit the rawhead *hard*. The power of its impact cracked bones and blew the leg out from beneath the rawhead. The fae giant bellowed a ground-shaking roar. A ton of bloody bones fell, and the mud creature, white teeth flashing, kept after it.

Snarling.

And a nimbus of blue light gathered around its muddy jaws.

I looked up to see more mud creatures rushing up the hill, though the others were bipedal, of various sizes and shapes. The first one to reach me drew a steel sword from a muddy scabbard and went after the raw-head as well, falcata being used with the brutal power strikes normally employed with a freaking ax. Silver eyes flashed in the blobby, mud-covered face.

Thomas.

Maeve snarled and stepped toward me, bringing her right hand out from behind her back. She gripped a tiny little automatic in her fingers, though God only knew where she'd been concealing it. She half lifted it, but before she could shoot, gunshots rang out, sharp and clear. One of them hit the ground maybe three feet away, and Maeve bolted aside, vanishing behind a veil as she went.

The smallest mud figure came to my side, lowering a mud-covered P90. She hooked a little hand beneath one of my arms, her blue eyes reddened and blinking rapidly. With surprising strength, she dragged me back from the rawhead while Thomas and Mouse fought it.

The others hurried up to join Karrin, and while Karrin covered us, muddy Mac got a shoulder underneath me and with a grunt of effort picked me up in a fireman's carry.

"Come on," Karrin said. "The cottage."

While she kept her P90 at the ready and Mac toted me, the other two mud figures, Sarissa and Justine, hurried along beside us. A moment later Mac dumped me gently, more or less, onto the floor of the cottage. Karrin kept her gun pointed at the door.

"Karrin," I managed to gasp.

Her eyes didn't waver from the door. "Got tired of waiting on you. I'm here."

I spit the nail out of my mouth and into my hand. *"How?"* I asked. Then I eyed them all and said, "Mud. You covered yourselves in mud."

"Everywhere," she confirmed. "Nostrils, eyes, ears, everywhere the light could touch. We figured out that if you completely covered something, it could make it through that wall. God, I'm going to shower for a week."

Oh, that was clever. The defense mechanism wasn't a thinking being, capable of making judgment calls. It was simply a machine, albeit one made of magic, a combination detector and bug zapper. By covering themselves with mud, they'd tricked it into thinking they were of the island.

Outside the cottage, the rawhead bellowed, and Mouse's snarling battle bark rang out defiantly.

"This is insane," Sarissa breathed.

"The stones of the cottage have protections on them," I said. "Not sure how well they work, but they should help." I looked back at Karrin. "Where's Molly?"

"Out there, playing Invisible Girl."

There was the sound of a heavy impact, and Mouse let out a terrible, pained-sounding yelp.

Then it was quiet.

Karrin's breathing started coming faster. She resettled her grip on the weapon.

"Oh, God," Sarissa said. "Oh, God, oh, God, oh, God."

I would have gotten terrified, too, but I was just too tired for it to stick.

There was no warning, nothing at all. The rawhead shoved its arm into the cottage, seized Karrin by the gun, and hauled her out. The weapon barked several times as she went.

And then it got quiet again.

"We have to run," Sarissa said in a whisper. "Harry, please, we should run. Open a Way into the Nevernever. Get us out of here."

"I've got a feeling we wouldn't like the part of the Nevernever this place borders," I said.

"Oh, Sir Knight," Maeve called from outside. "Come out, come out, wherever you are, you and everyone with you. Or I'm going to start playing with your friends."

"Hey, why don't you come in here, Maeve?" I called back. "We'll talk about it."

I waited for an answer. I got one a minute later. Karrin let out a pained, gasping sound.

"Dammit," I muttered. Then I started to climb to my feet again. "Come on."

"What?" Sarissa asked. "No. I can't go out there."

"You're about to," I said quietly. "Mac."

"We go out," Mac said, "she'll kill us."

"If we don't, she'll kill us anyway. Starting with Karrin," I said. "Maeve likes hurting people. Maybe we can string her along until . . ."

"Until what?" Sarissa asked. "Sunrise? That's hours away."

Justine put her hand on Sarissa's shoulder. "But we'll stay alive a little longer. Where there's life, there's hope."

"You don't understand," Sarissa said. "Not for me. Not for me."

Karrin let out another gasp of pain and I ground my teeth.

"Sarissa," I said, "we don't have a choice. Lily just about roasted the top off the hill in a moment of pique. Maeve can do worse. If we stay in here, she will."

"Die now, or be tortured to death in a few hours," she said. "Those are our choices?"

"We buy time," I said. "We buy time so that I can think and maybe figure some way for us to get out of this clusterfuck. Now get up, or so help me I'll carry you out there."

A flash of anger went through Sarissa's eyes. But she got up.

"All right, Maeve!" I called. "You win! We're coming out!"

I held up my hands, palms out, and walked out of the meager makeshift protection of the ruined cottage.

51

Maeve was enjoying her victory tremendously.

She stood on a pile of stone fallen from the lighthouse, next to the Summer Lady and her coterie, who were still focused upon restraining Demonreach. On the ground in front of her lay Thomas, Karrin, and Mouse. Mouse had been hog-tied and his muzzle held shut with thick bands of what looked like black ice. He wasn't struggling, but his deep, dark eyes were tracking everyone who moved. Karrin sat with her hands tied behind her back, scowling so ferociously that I could see the expression even through the mud. And my brother lay on the ground, bound up like Mouse was, but it didn't look like he was conscious.

The rawhead loomed over them, minus one of its arms. The arm lay over on the ground, a jumble of brittle, cracked bones held together by withered strands of some kind of reddish fiber. The rawhead didn't have an expression to read, but I thought the glow of its eyes looked sullen and satisfied. The Redcap was standing off to one side. Half of his face was a bloody mess, and he had only one good eye now. He was holding Karrin's P90 casually, with much of the mud knocked off of it. Next to him, two of the Sidhe held Fix's arms behind his back. The Summer Knight had a bruise blackening the entire left side of his face, running right to the hairline.

But Molly was not visible.

So. I might have been dealt a bad hand, but I still had a hole card out there somewhere.

Maeve hopped down from the fallen stones, still holding that little automatic in her hand, and smiling widely. "You made it interesting, Dresden. I'll give you that. Your merry band is just so"—she kicked Karrin in the small of the back, drawing nothing but a hard exhale—"feisty." She eyed the people standing with me. "Now let's see. Who do we have here?"

Maeve made a gesture with one hand, and the air suddenly felt thick. Mud started plopping off of everyone covered in it, as if it had begun to rain again and gotten wetter and runnier. "Let's see, let's see," she murmured. "Ah, the bartender. Irony, there. Getting a good view, are you?"

Mac stared at Maeve without speaking.

"Please allow me to make sure you don't get bored. This is a participation sport," Maeve said, and shot him in the stomach.

Mac grunted and rocked back onto his heels. He stared at Maeve, his expression completely impassive. Then he exhaled a groan and fell to one knee.

"Oh," Maeve said, her eyes glittering. "That just never gets old."

Justine made a quiet sound and went to Mac's side.

Maeve's eyes fastened on her. "And the vampire's crumpet. Luscious little thing, aren't you? And so close to Lady Raith. You and I are going to have a long talk after this, darling. I just know you're going to start to see things my way."

Justine didn't look at Maeve, and didn't answer. She didn't look frightened—just concerned for Mac. Maybe because Justine was not the most balanced and danger-aware person I knew. Or maybe her poker face was just way better than mine.

Maeve's eyes stopped on the last person with me and her smile became positively vulpine. "Well, well, well. Sweet little Sarissa. Isn't this luscious? There's nothing I have that you don't want to ruin, is there?"

"Maeve," Sarissa said. She didn't seem frightened either. Just tired. "Maeve, for God's sake, how many times have we had this talk?"

"And yet you keep spoiling things for me!"

Sarissa rolled her eyes and gave a helpless little lift and fall of her hands. "Maeve, *what* could I *possibly* have ruined for you? Did *finally* moving out of that studio apartment destroy your life? Did getting my nursing degree somehow diminish your power? Did I steal some boyfriend of yours that you accidently left breathing after the first night?"

"It always goes back to that, doesn't it?" Maeve said, her tone waspish. "How important you think men are. And here you are trying to impress Mother by bedding this one."

"It was *work*, Maeve. Therapy."

"I could see how therapeutic that dress was at his party."

"*My* dress? You were wearing *rhinestones*. And nothing else!"

Maeve's face contorted in rage. "They. Were. *Diamonds*."

Karrin looked back and forth between them with an expression of startled recognition. "Harry . . ." she said quietly.

"Yeah, I got it," I said. I turned to Sarissa, who looked younger than Molly. "Mab's BFF, eh?" I asked her.

"You said that, not me," she said quickly.

"Right," I said. "You're just a young, single rehabilitative health professional."

"This decade," sneered Maeve. "What was it last time? Mathematics? You were going to describe the universe or some such? And before that, what was it? Environmental science? Did you save the Earth, Sarissa? And before that, an actress? You thought you could create art. Which soap opera was it again?"

"It doesn't matter," Sarissa said. She saw me staring at her and said, "It was before your time."

I blinked. "What?"

She looked embarrassed. "I told you I was older than I looked."

"Finally I realize who you remind me of." I sighed, looking back and forth between Sarissa and Maeve. "It must have been the scrubs that threw me off. Maeve is always dressed like a stripper, and she's always had the piercings and the club lighting and the crazy Rasta hair." I looked back and forth between the two. "Hell's bells, you're identical twins."

"Not identical twins," they both said at exactly the same time, in the exact same tone of outrage. They broke off to glare at each other.

"How does that work, exactly?" I asked. I was curious, but it was also an effort to buy time. I've yet to meet a megalomaniac who doesn't love talking about him- or herself, if you give them half a chance. Especially the nonmortal ones. To them, a few minutes of chat in several centuries of life is nothing, and they let things build up inside them for decades at a time. "You two . . . were born changelings, weren't you? What happened?"

"I Chose to be Sidhe," Maeve spat.

"And you Chose humanity?" I asked Sarissa.

Sarissa shrugged a shoulder and looked away.

"Hah," Maeve spat. "No. She never Chose at all. Just remained between worlds. Never making anything of herself, never committing to anything."

"Maeve," Sarissa said quietly. "Don't."

"Just floating along, pretty and empty and bored," Maeve went on in a sweet, poisonous tone. "Unnoticed. Unremarkable."

"Maeve," said Lily in a harsh voice, looking up from where she stood. The Summer Lady kept a hand extended toward Demonreach, and her face was covered in sweat, and she seemed to be leaning back against the hands of the Sidhe behind her to stay upright. "I can't hold the spirit alone all night. We have to talk about this before it gets any more out of control. Hurry, and let's finish this."

Maeve whirled toward Lily, stamping her foot on the ground. "This is *my* night! Do *not* rush me, you stupid cow!"

"Always so charming," Sarissa noted.

Maeve turned back to Sarissa, and her right arm, the one holding the gun, twitched several times. "Oh, keep it up, darling. See what happens."

"You aren't going to let me live anyway, Maeve," Sarissa said. "I'm not stupid."

"And I am not *blind*," Maeve spat back. "Do you think I did not know about all the time she has been spending with you? All the intimate talk, the activity together. Do you think I don't know what it means? She's doing with you what she always meant to do with you—using you as a spare. Preparing you as a vessel for the mantle. Preparing my replacement. As if I were a broken piece of a machine."

Sarissa looked pale and nodded slowly. "Maeve," she said, her voice very soft. "You're . . . you're sick. You've got to know that."

Maeve stopped, tilting her head, and her hair covered most of her face.

"Somewhere, you have to realize it. She wants to help you. She cares in her way, Maeve."

Maeve moved her left arm alone, pointing a finger straight at me. "Yes. I can see how much she cared."

"It isn't too late," Sarissa said. "You know how she lays her plans. She prepares for everything. But it doesn't have to happen that way. The Leanansidhe was sick and Mother helped her. But her power alone isn't enough to heal you. You have to want it, Maeve. You have to want to be healed."

Maeve quivered where she stood for a moment, like a slender tree placed under increasing strain.

"We need the Winter Lady now," Sarissa said. "We need you, Maeve. You're a vicious goddamned lunatic and we *need* you back."

Maeve asked in a very small voice, "Does she talk about me?"

Sarissa was silent. She swallowed.

Maeve said, her voice harsher, "Does she talk about me?"

Sarissa lifted her chin and shook her head. "She . . . won't say your name. But I know she fears for you. You know that she never lets things show. It's how she's always been."

Maeve shuddered.

Then she lifted her head and stared venomously at Sarissa. "I am *strong*, Sarissa. Stronger than I have ever been. Here, now, stronger than *she* is." Her lips quivered and twitched back from her teeth into a hideous mockery of a smile. "Why should I want to be *healed* of that?" She cut loose with one of her psychotic laughs again. "I am about to unmake every precious thing *she* ever valued more than her own blood, her own *children*. And where is she?" Maeve stuck her arms out and spun around in a pirouette. Her voice became pure vitriol. "Where? I have closed the circle of this place and she may not enter. Of course, these stupid primates sussed out a way through it, but she, the Queen of Air and Darkness, could not possibly stoop to such a thing. Not even if it costs her the lives of her daughter and the mortal world, too."

"Oh, Maeve," Sarissa said, her voice thick with compassion and something like resignation.

"Where *is* she, Sarissa?" Maeve demanded. There were tears on her cheeks, freezing into little white streaks, forming white frost on her eyelashes. "Where is her *love*? Where is her *fury*? Where is her *anything*?"

While that drama was going on, I thought furiously. I thought about the mighty spirit who was my ally, who was being held immobile and impotent. I thought about the abilities of all of my allies, and how they might change the current situation if they weren't all incapacitated. Molly was the only one at liberty, and she had worn herself out over the lake. She wouldn't have much left in her—if she appeared now, the fae would defeat her handily. She couldn't change this situation alone. Someone would have to set things into motion, give her some chaos to work with.

I just didn't have much chaos left in me. I was bone-tired, and we needed a game changer. The mantle of the Winter Knight represented a source of power, true, but Maeve had damned near talked me into joining her team when I'd let it have free rein. I wasn't going to help anyone if I let myself give in to my inner psycho-predator.

If we weren't all inside the stupid circle, at least I could send out a message, a psychic warning. I was sure I could get it to my grandfather, to Elaine, and maybe to Warden Luccio. But while I was sure a mud coating could get us out of the circle, there was no way the fae would give us time to coat ourselves and do it. We were effectively trapped in the circle until sunrise, just like a being summoned from the Nevernev—

Wait a minute.

Circles could be used for several different things. They could be used to focus the energy of a spell, shielding it from other energies. They could be used to cut off energy flows, to contain or discorporate a native being of the Nevernever.

And if you were a mortal, a genuine native of the really real world, they could be used for one thing more: summoning.

The hilltop was one enormous circle: one enormous *summoning* circle.

"She is not here," Maeve was ranting. "She sends her hand to deal with me? So be it. Let me send her a message in reply!" The little automatic swiveled toward my head.

I shouted as swiftly as I could, putting whatever will I had left into the shortest and most elemental summons there is: "Mab! Mab! Mab! I summon thee!"

52

It's impossible to know how something is going to arrive when you summon it.

Sometimes it's huge and dramatic, like it was with Titania. Sometimes they come in a burst of thunder or flame. Once, this thing I'd summoned arrived in a shower of rotting meat, and it took me a month to get the smell out of my old lab. Less often, they simply appear, like a slide-show image suddenly projected on the wall, drama-free.

Mab came in a bell tone of sudden, awful, absolute silence.

There was a flash—not of light, but of sudden snow, of frost that abruptly blanketed everything on the hilltop and gathered thick on my eyelashes. I reached up a hand to flick the snowflakes out of my eyes, and when I lowered it, Mab was there, again in her crow black dress, with her midnight eyes and ebon hair, floating three feet off the ground. The frost was spreading from her, covering the hilltop, and the temperature dropped by twenty degrees.

In the same instant, everything on the hilltop ceased moving. There was no wind. There were no fitful drops of rain. Just pure, brittle, crystal-line silence and a sudden bleak black presence that made me feel like hiding behind something, very quietly.

Mab's dark, bleak gaze took in the hilltop at a glance, and stopped on Lily and her supporting coterie. Mab's left eye twitched once. And she spoke in a low, dreadfully precise voice. "Cease. This. Rudeness. At once."

Lily suddenly stared at Mab with wide eyes, like a teenager who had been walked in upon while making out in the living room. The confidence of her stance faltered, and she abruptly lowered her hand. There was a sigh, as of completed labor, from her crew. I checked Demonreach. The guardian spirit had ceased to look slow-motion windblown, and simply stood in the opening to the lighthouse, motionless.

Lily stared at Mab for a few seconds. Then she lifted her chin in defiance and took a few steps, until she stood shoulder to shoulder with Maeve.

Mab made a low, disgusted sound and turned to face me. "I have heeded your summons; yet I would not enter this domain unless specifically bidden. Have I your permission to do so?"

"Yes," I said. "Yes, you do."

Mab nodded her head slightly, and descended to the ground. From me, she turned to Demonreach. "I thank you for your patience and your assistance in this matter. You could have reacted differently but chose not to. I am aware of the decision. It will not be forgotten."

Demonreach bowed its head, barely, a gesture of acknowledgment, not cooperation or compliance.

Once she had seen that, something seemed to ease out of Mab. It was hard to say what gave me that impression, yet I had the same sense of relief I would have felt upon seeing someone remove his hand from the grip of a firearm.

Mab turned back to me and eyed me up and down. She quirked one eyebrow, very slightly, somehow conveying layers of disapproval toward multiple aspects of my appearance, conduct, and situation, and said, "Finally."

"There's been a lot on my mind," I replied.

"It seems unlikely that your cares will lighten," Queen Mab replied. "Improve your mind."

I was going to say something smart-ass, but said mind noted that maybe I could wait until my bacon was entirely out of the fire before I did. I decided to pay attention to my mind and bowed my head in Mab's direction instead. I felt like I'd gotten a little smarter already. Baby steps.

Then Mab turned to Maeve.

The Winter Lady faced the Queen of Air and Darkness with cold fury in her eyes and a smile on her lips. "So," Maeve said. "You come in black. You come as a judge. But then, you always did that with me. But it's just a game."

"How a game?" Mab asked.

"You have already judged. Passed sentence. And dispatched your executioner."

"You have duties. You have neglected them. What did you expect?"

"From you?" Maeve said bitterly. "Nothing."

"Nothing is precisely what I have done," Mab said. "For too long. Yet to lose you presents a danger of its own. I would prefer it if you allowed me to assist you to return to your duties."

"I'm sure you *would*," Maeve sneered. "I'm sure you would enjoy torturing me to the brink of sanity to make me a good little automaton again."

Mab's reply was a second slower coming than it should have been. "No, Maeve."

Maeve ground her teeth. "No one controls *Maeve*."

Frost formed on Mab's soot black lashes. "Oh, child."

The words had weight to them, and finality—like the lid to a coffin.

"I will *never* be your good little hunting falcon again," Maeve continued. "I will never bow my knee to anyone again, especially not to a jealous hag who envies everything she sees in me."

"Envy?" Mab asked.

Maeve cut loose with another one of those lithium-laced laughs. "Envy! The great and mighty *Mab*, envious of her little girl. Because I have something you will *never* have, Mother."

"And what is that?" Mab asked.

"*Choice*," Maeve snarled.

"Stop," Mab snapped—but not in time.

Maeve bent her elbow to point her little gun casually across her body and, without looking, put a bullet into Lily's left temple.

"No!" Fix blurted, suddenly struggling against the Sidhe holding him.

Lily froze into absolute stillness for a second, her beautiful face confused.

Then she fell like the petal of a dying flower.

"Lily!" Fix screamed, his face contorted with agony. He fought wildly, though he couldn't escape, lunging toward Maeve, paying no attention whatsoever to his captors. For their part, Winter and Summer fae alike seemed stunned into near-paralysis, eyes locked onto Lily's fallen form.

Mab stared at Lily for a long second, her eyes wide with an echo of the same shock. "What have you *done*?"

Maeve threw back her head and howled mocking, triumphant laughter, lifting her hands into the air.

"Did you think I did not *know* why you prepared Sarissa, hag?" she half sang. "You wrought her into a vessel of Faerie. Rejoice! Thy will is done!"

I didn't know what the hell she was talking about for a second—but then I saw it.

Fire flickered to life over the late Summer Lady. It did not consume Lily. Rather, it gathered itself into green and gold light, a shape that vaguely mirrored Lily's own, arms spread out as she lay prostrate upon the frost-covered earth. Then, with a gathering shriek, the fire suddenly condensed into a form, the shape of something that looked like an eagle or a large hawk. Blinding light spread over the hilltop, and the hawk suddenly flashed from Lily's fallen form.

Directly into Sarissa.

Sarissa's eyes widened in horror, and she lifted her arms in an instinctive defensive gesture. The hawk-shaped Summer fire, the mantle of the Summer Lady, plunged through Sarissa's upraised arms and *into* her chest, at the heart. Her body arched into a bow. She let out a scream, and green and gold light shone from her opened mouth like a spotlight, throwing fresh, sharp shadows across the hilltop.

Then her scream faded into a weeping, gurgling moan, and she fell to the earth, body curling into a shuddering fetal position.

"Mantle passed." Maeve tittered. "Nearest vessel filled. The seasons turn and turn and turn."

Mab's eyes were wide as she stared at Maeve.

"Oh, *oh*!" Maeve said, her body twisting into a spontaneous little dance of pure glee. "You never saw that coming, did you, Mother? It never even *occurred* to you, did it?" Her own eyes widened in lunatic intensity. "And how will you slay me now? Whither would *my* mantle go? Where is the nearest vessel *now*? Some hapless mortal, perhaps, ignorant of its true nature? The instrument of some foe of yours, in alliance with me, ready to steal away the mantle and leave you vulnerable?" Maeve giggled. "I can play chess *too*, Mother. Better now than *ever* you could. And I am now less a liability to you alive than dead."

"You do not understand what you have done," Mab said quietly.

"I know *exactly* what I have done," Maeve snarled. "I have *beaten* you. This was never about the sleepers, or this accursed isle, or the lives of mortal insects. This was about beating *you*, you hidebound hag. About using your own games against you. Kill me now, and you risk destroying the balance of Winter and Summer forever, throwing all into chaos."

Sarissa lay on the ground, moaning.

"And it was about taking *her* away from you," Maeve gloated. "How many mortal caterwauls or sporting events will the Winter Queen attend with the Summer Lady? And every time you think of her, you remember her, you will know that *I* took her from you."

Mab's black eyes went to Sarissa for a moment.

"The blame for this lies with me," Mab said quietly. "I cared too much."

I realized something then, in that moment when Mab spoke. She wasn't reacting as she should have been. Cold rage, seething anger, megalomaniacal outrage—any of those would have been something I would have considered utterly within her character. But there was none of that in her voice or face.

Just . . . regret. And resolution.

Mab knew something—something Maeve didn't.

"Remember that when this world is in ashes, Mother," Maeve said, "for you cannot risk my death this night, and I will not lift a *finger* to aid you in the Night to come. Without the Winter Lady's power, your downfall is simply a matter of time—and not much of that. After this night, you will not see me again."

"Yes," Mab said, though to which statement was unclear.

"I have choice, Mother, while you will be destroyed in your shackles," Maeve said. "You will die, and I will have freedom. At *last*."

"To fulfill one's purpose is not to be a slave, my daughter," Mab said.

"And you are not free, child, any more than a knife is free because it leaves its sheath and is thrust into a corpse."

"Choice is *power*," Maeve spat in reply. "Shall I make more choices this night, to demonstrate?"

She lifted the little pistol again and pointed it at me.

Karrin drew a sharp breath.

And I suddenly understood what was happening; I understood what Mab knew that Maeve didn't.

Sarissa wasn't the only Faerie vessel on the hilltop. She was simply the one Maeve had been *meant* to see.

There was one other person there who had been spending time with a powerful fae.

Who had a relationship with one that was deeper and more significant than a casual or formal acquaintance.

Whose life had been methodically, deliberately, and covertly reshaped for the purpose.

Who had been extensively prepared by one of the Sidhe.

"Maeve," I said in a panic. "Don't! You're killing yourself. You haven't won. You just can't see it."

Maeve cackled in delight. "Can't I?"

"Being able to choose to tell lies isn't a freaking superpower, Maeve," I said. "Because it means you can always make the *wrong* choice. It means you can lie to *yourself*."

Maeve's smile turned positively sexual, her eyes bright and shining.

"Two plus two is *five*," she said, and rotated the gun sideways, the barrel still pointed at my eye.

Mab moved her little finger.

Karrin's hands flew out from behind her back in a shower of broken chips of black ice. She tore her little holdout gun from a concealed ankle holster.

"No!" I shouted.

Two shots rang out, almost simultaneously.

Something hissed spitefully past my ear.

A neat, round black hole appeared just to the side of Maeve's nose, at the fine line of her cheekbone.

Maeve blinked twice. Her face fell into what was almost precisely the same expression of confusion Lily's had. A trickle of blood ran from the hole.

And then she fell, like an icicle in a warm sunbeam.

"Dammit, no," I whispered.

Deep blue fire gathered over the fallen Winter Lady. It coalesced with an ugly howl into the outline of a serpent, which coiled and then lashed out in a strike that carried its blazing form fifteen feet, to the nearest corner of the ruined cottage . . .

. . . where Molly, behind her veil, had been crouched and waiting for a chance to aid me.

The serpent of Winter cold plunged into her chest, shattering her veil as it struck, and my apprentice's expression was twisted in startled horror. She didn't even have time to flinch. It struck, and she fell back against the side of the cottage, her legs buckling as if the muscles in them had forgotten how to move.

Molly looked up at me, her expression bewildered, confused, and she barely managed to gasp out, "Harry?"

And then she, too, collapsed to the ground, shuddering and unconscious.

"Oh, God," I breathed. "Oh, God."

Molly.

53

Two Queens of Faerie lay dead.

Long live the Queens.

Everyone was shocked, still.

I turned to the retinues of the fallen Queens and said, "Let Fix go. Now."

They released the smaller man, and he went at once to Lily's side, his face still wrenched with grief.

"You will put down anything you took from my friends," I told the fae in a level voice. "Then you will withdraw as far down the hill as the wall will allow. If I see any of you try anything violent, you will never leave this island. Am I understood?"

I didn't look like much, but Mab was looming right over one of my shoulders, and Demonreach over the other, so they took me seriously— even the rawhead. They all moved away, breaking into two groups as they went.

"Harry," Karrin said. "What just happened? Is Molly all right?"

I stared hard at Mab. "I don't know," I said to Karrin. "Can you and Justine get them both into the cottage? Just . . . make sure they don't swallow their own tongues or something." I looked over at Justine. "How you doing, Mac?"

Mac gave me a weary, shaky thumbs-up.

Justine looked up from tending to him. "I don't think there's too much bleeding. But we need to get this dirt washed off of him."

"There's a pump by the door to the cottage," I said. I looked around and frowned at Demonreach. "Hey, make yourself useful and help them carry the wounded inside."

Demonreach eyed me.

But it did so, lumbering forward to pick Molly and then Sarissa up, very carefully, the way a person would carry an infant, one in each arm. Then it walked over to the cottage, carrying them. Karrin, meanwhile, went to Justine, and between the two of them, they were able to get Mac on his feet and hobbling into the cottage. I went and managed to drag Thomas over my shoulder. I toted his unconscious form to the cottage, too, and told Mouse, "Stay with him, boy."

Mouse made a distressed noise, and looked over at Molly. He sat down on the floor halfway between the two of them, and looked back and forth.

"Just have to have a little campout until dawn," I said. "We'll take care of them."

Mouse sighed.

"Harry," Karrin began.

"Gun," I said quietly, and held out a hand.

She blinked at me, but she checked it, engaged the safety, and handed it over.

"Stay here," I said, moving toward the door.

"Harry, what are y—"

"Stay *here*," I snarled, furious. I took the safety off and left the cottage to stalk over to Mab.

As I crossed to her, her black gown and hair became storm-cloud grey, then silver, then white again.

"Yes, my Knight?" she asked me.

I started walking around the base of the tower, away from the cottage. "Could you please come this way?"

She arched a brow but did, moving over the ground with the same approximate weight as moonlight.

I walked until we were out of sight of the cottage and the fae down the hill. Then I thumbed back the hammer on the little gun, spun, and put the barrel against Mab's forehead.

Mab stopped and regarded me with luminous unblinking eyes. "What is the meaning of this?"

"It's still Halloween," I said, shaking with exhaustion and rage. "And I am in *no* mood for games. I want answers."

"I have turned villages to stone for gestures less insulting than this one," Mab said in a level tone. "But I am your guest here. And you are clearly overwrought."

"You're goddamned right I'm overwrought," I growled. "You set me up. That's one thing. I walked into it with open eyes. I get it, and I'll deal with it. But you set *Molly* up. Give me one good reason not to put a bullet through your head right now."

"First," Mab said, "because you would not survive to finish pulling the trigger. But as threatening your life has never been a successful way to pierce your skull, I will provide you with a second. Miss Carpenter will have difficulty enough learning to cope with the Lady's mantle without you handing her mine as well. Don't you think?"

Right. I hadn't thought about that part. But I wasn't feeling terribly rational.

"Why?" I demanded. "Why did you do it to her?"

"It was not my intention for her to replace Maeve," Mab said. "Frankly, I would have considered her a better candidate for Summer."

"You still haven't told me *why*," I said.

"I meant Sarissa to take Maeve's place," Mab said. "But one does not place all one's hopes with any one place, person, or plan. Like chess, the superior player does not plan to accomplish a single gambit, a particular entrapment. She establishes her pieces so that regardless of what her enemy does, she has forces ready to respond, to adapt, and to destroy. Molly was made ready as a contingency."

"In case something happened to your own daughter?" I asked.

"Something had *already* happened to my daughter," Mab said. "It was my intention to make Sarissa ready for her new role, much as I made you ready for yours."

"*That's* why you exposed her to all of those things alongside me?"

"I have no use for weakness, wizard. The situation here developed in a way I did not expect. Molly had originally been positioned with another purpose in mind—but her presence made it possible to defeat the adversary's gambit."

"Positioned," I spat. "Gambit. Is that what Molly is to you? A pawn?"

"No," Mab said calmly, "not anymore."

That rocked my head back as surely as if she'd punched me in the nose. I felt a little bit dizzy. I lowered the gun.

"She's a kid," I said tiredly. "She had her whole life ahead of her, and you did *this* to her."

"Maeve was always overly dramatic, but in this instance she was quite correct. I could not risk killing her if I did not have a vessel on hand to receive her mantle—and the lack of the Winter Lady's strength would have been critical. It is one of the better plays the adversary has made."

"You don't get it, do you?" I said.

"I do not," she said. "I do not see how what I have done is substantially different from what you have been doing for many years."

"*What?*" I asked.

"I gave her power," she said, as if explaining something simple to a child.

"That is *not* what I have been doing," I spat.

"Is it not?" Mab asked. "Have I misunderstood? First you captured her imagination and affection as an associate of her father's. You made her curious about what you could do, and nurtured that curiosity with silence. Then when she went to explore the Art, you elected not to interfere until such time as she found herself in dire straits—at which point your aid placed her deep within your obligation. You used that and her emotional attachment to you to plant and reap a follower who was talented, loyal, and in your debt. It was actually very well-done."

I stood there with my mouth open for a second. "That . . . that isn't . . . what I did."

Mab leaned closer to me and said, "That is *precisely* what you did," she said. "The only thing you did not do is admit to yourself that you *were* doing it. Which is why you never availed yourself of her charms. You told yourself lovely, idealistic lies, and you had a powerful, talented, loyal girl willing to give her life for yours who *also* had nowhere else to turn for help. As far as your career as a mentor goes, you grew into much the same image as DuMorne."

"That . . . that isn't what I did," I repeated, harder. "What you're doing to her will change her."

"Did she not change after you began to indoctrinate her?" Mab asked. "You were perhaps too soft on her during her training, but had she not already begun to become a different person?"

"A person she *chose* to be," I said.

"Did she choose to be born with her gift for the Art? Did she choose to become someone so sensitive that she can hardly remain in a crowded room? I did not do that to her—you did."

I ground my teeth.

"Consider," Mab said, "that I have done something for her that you never could have."

"What's that, exactly?"

"I have put her beyond the reach of the White Council and their Wardens," Mab said, again as if explaining something to an idiot. "While they might howl and lecture as much as they wish about an apprentice wizard, they can do nothing at all to the Winter Lady."

I took a deep breath.

That . . . was also true.

"You've made her life so much harder," I said quietly. I wasn't saying it to Mab, really. I was just sounding out loud the chain of argument in my head. "But so have I. Especially after Chichén Itzá."

"You trusted her with your mind and your life," Mab said. "I took that as a statement of confidence in her abilities. You will be working frequently with the Winter Lady. It seems to me that this would be a most appropriate match."

"And her duties?" I asked. "What is the purpose of the Winter Lady?"

"That is for her to know," Mab said. "Know this, my Knight: Had I not considered her an excellent candidate, I would never have had her prepared. She has the basic skills she will need to master the power of the mantle—especially if one she trusts is there to advise and reassure her."

"You should have spoken to me about this first," I said. "You should have spoken to her."

Mab moved so quickly that I literally never saw it. The gun was suddenly, simply gone from my hand and was being pushed into my face—in exactly the same spot where Maeve had been shot.

"I," Mab said coolly, "am not *your* servant, Dresden. You are mine."

"Demonreach," I said. "If our guest pulls that trigger, take her below and keep her there."

The guardian spirit's vast shadow fell over us even though there was nothing actually casting it, and Mab's eyes widened.

"Servant," I said. "I don't like that word. I suggest that you consider where you stand and choose a different term. My Queen. And you will be gentle with that girl, or so help me I will make you regret it."

Mab's mouth quirked very slightly—her eyes more so. She looked up at me almost fondly, exhaled, and said, "Finally, a Knight worth the trouble." She lowered the gun and calmly passed it back to me.

I took it from her.

"Have you any other questions?" she asked.

I frowned, thinking. "Yeah, actually. Someone called Thomas and told him to be ready at the boat when I first got back to town. Do you know anything about that?"

"I arranged it, of course," Mab said, in a voice that sounded exactly like Molly's. "As a courtesy to the ancient one, just before your party started."

At that, I shuddered. Molly's voice coming from that inhumanly cold face was . . . just wrong.

"Lily," I said. "She waved her hand over my chest, as if she could detect the influence of the adversary."

Mab's lips pressed into a firm line. "Yes."

"Could she?" I asked.

"Of course not," Mab said. "Were it so simple a task, the adversary would be no threat. Not even the Gatekeeper, at the focus of his power, can be absolutely certain."

"Then why would she think she could?" I asked. Then I answered my own question. "Because Maeve led her to believe that she could. All Maeve had to do was lie, and maybe sacrifice a couple of the adversary's pawns to make it seem real. Then she could have Lily wave her hands at her, and 'prove' to her that Maeve was clean of any taint. And Lily wasn't experienced enough to know any better. After that, Lily would have bought just about anything Maeve was selling."

"Obviously," Mab said, her tone mildly acidic. "Have you any questions you cannot answer for yourself?"

I clenched my jaw and relaxed it a couple of times. Then I asked, "Was it hard for you? Tonight?"

"Hard?" Mab asked.

"She was your daughter," I said.

Mab became very silent, and very still. She considered the ground around us, and paced up and down a bit, slowly, frowning, as if trying to remember the lyrics of a song from her childhood.

Finally she became still again, closing her eyes.

"Even tonight, with everything going to hell, you couldn't hurt her," I said.

Mab opened her eyes and stared down through a gap in the trees at the vast waters of Lake Michigan.

"A few years back, you got angry. So angry that when you spoke it made people bleed from the ears. That was why. Because you figured out that the adversary had taken Maeve. And it hurt. To know that the adversary had gotten to her."

"It was the knife," Mab said.

"Knife?"

"Morgana's athame," Mab said in a neutral tone—but her eyes were far away. "The one given her by the Red Court at Bianca's masquerade. That was how the Leanansidhe was tainted—and your godmother spread it to Maeve before I could set it right."

"Oh," I said. I'd been at that party.

Mab turned to me abruptly and said, "I would lay them to rest upon the island, the fallen Ladies, if that does not offend you."

"It doesn't," I said. "But check with the island."

"I shall. Please excuse me." She turned and began walking away.

"You didn't answer my question," I said.

She stopped, her back straight.

"Was it hard for you to kill Maeve?"

Mab did not turn around. When she spoke, her voice had something in it I had never heard there before and never heard again—uncertainty. Vulnerability.

"I was mortal once, you know," she said, very quietly.

And then she kept walking toward her daughter's body, while I stared angrily . . . sadly . . . thoughtfully after her.

The rest of the night passed without anyone getting killed. I sat down with my back against the outside wall of the cottage, to keep an eye on my "guests" down the hill, but when I blinked a few seconds later, my eyes stuck shut, and then didn't open again until I heard, distantly, a bird twittering.

Footsteps came crunching up the hill, and I opened my eyes to see Kringle approaching. His red cloak and gleaming mail were stained with black ichor, the hilt of his sword was simply missing a chunk, as if it had been bitten away, and his mouth was set in a wide, pleased smile. "Dresden," he said calmly.

"Kringle."

"Long night?"

"Long day," I said. Someone, during the night, had covered me with an old woolen army surplus blanket that had been in a plastic storage box in the cottage. I eyed him. "Have fun?"

A low, warm rumble of a laugh bubbled in his chest. "Very much so. If I don't get into a good battle every few years, life just isn't the same."

"Even if it's on Halloween?" I asked.

He eyed me, and his smile became wider and more impish. "Especially then," he said. "How's the leg?"

I grunted and checked. Butters's dressing had stayed on throughout the events of the night. The constant, burning sting was gone, and I peeled off the dressing to see that the little wound on my leg had finally scabbed over. "Looks like I'll live."

"Hawthorn dart," Kringle said. "Nasty stuff. Hawthorn wood burns hot, and doesn't care for creatures of Winter." His expression sobered. "I've a message for you."

"Ah?" I asked.

"Mab has taken the new Ladies with her," he said. "She said to tell you that the new Winter Lady would be returned safely to her apartment in a few days, after some brief and gentle instruction. Mab is on excellent terms with the svartalves, and anticipates no problems with your apprentice's . . . new position."

"That's . . . good, I guess," I said.

"It is," Kringle replied. "Dresden . . . this is the business of the Queens. I advise you not to attempt to interfere with it."

"I already interfered," I said.

Kringle straightened, and his fierce smile became somehow satisfied. "Aye? Like to live dangerously, do you?" He leaned a little closer and lowered his voice. "Never let her make you cringe—but never challenge her pride, wizard. I don't know exactly what passed between you, but I suspect that if it had been witnessed by another, she would break you to pieces. I've seen it before. Terrible pride in that creature. She'll never bend it."

"She'll never bend," I said. "That's okay. I can respect that."

"Could be that you can," Kringle said. He nodded to me and turned to go.

"Hey," I said.

He turned to me pleasantly.

"The whole Winter Knight thing," I said. "It's made me stronger."

"True enough," he said.

"But not *that* much stronger," I said. "You could have beaten me last night."

"Oh?" Kringle's smile faded—except from his eyes.

"And I've seen goblins move a few times," I said. "The Erlking could have gotten out of the way of that shot."

"Really?"

"You meant me to have the Wild Hunt."

"No one can be given a power like the Wild Hunt, Dresden," Kringle said. "He can only take it."

"Really?" I said, as drily as I knew how.

That got another laugh from Kringle. "You have guts and will, mortal. It had to be shown, or the Hunt would never have accepted you."

"Maybe I'll just punch you out whenever I feel like it, then," I said.

"Maybe you'll try," Kringle replied amiably. He looked out at the lightening sky and let out a satisfied breath. "It was Halloween, Dresden. You put on a mask for a time. That's all." He looked directly at me and said, "Many, many mantles are worn—or discarded—on Halloween night, wizard."

"You mean masks?" I asked, frowning.

"Masks, mantles," Kringle said. "What's the difference?"

He winked at me.

And for the briefest fraction of a second, the shadows falling from the tower and the cottage in the gathering morning behind us seemed to flow together. The eye he winked with vanished behind a stripe of shadow and what looked like a wide scar. His face seemed leaner, and for that instant I saw Vadderung's wolfish features lurking inside Kringle's.

I sat straight up, staring.

Kringle finished his wink, turned jauntily, and started walking down the hill, humming "Here Comes Santa Claus" in a rumbling bass voice.

I stared after him.

"Son of a bitch," I muttered to myself.

I stood up and wrapped the army surplus blanket around myself before I walked into the cottage. I smelled coffee and soup, and my stomach wanted lots of both.

There was a fire going in the fireplace, and my coffeepot was hanging near the fire. The soup kettle was hanging on its swinger, too. The soup would be made from stock and freeze-dried meat, but I was hungry enough not to be picky. Everyone else there probably felt the same way.

Thomas was sacked out on one of the cots, snoring. Justine had spooned up behind him, her face pressed into his back. They both had clean faces and hands, at least. Mac was snoozing on the other cot, bare to the waist, his chest and stomach evidently washed free of any dirt—and any blood or any injury as well.

Sarissa was gone. Molly was gone. Fix was gone. I felt confident they had left together.

Karrin sat at the fire, staring in, a cup of coffee in her hands. Mouse sat beside her. When I came in, he looked over at me and started wagging his tail.

"You leave the blanket?" I asked quietly.

"Once we got the fire going," she said. "I suppose I could go get you your duster now, though."

"I'd look like a flasher," I said.

She smiled, very slightly, and offered me two mugs. I looked. One had coffee, the other very chunky soup. She passed me a camp fork to go along with the soup. "It isn't much," she said.

"Don't care," I said, and sat down on the hearth across from her to partake of both. The heat gurgled into my belly along with the food and the coffee, and I started feeling human for the first time in . . . a while. I ached everywhere. It wasn't at all pleasant, but it felt like something I'd come by honestly.

"Christ, Dresden," Karrin said. "You could at least wash your hands." She picked up a towelette and leaned over to start cleaning off my hands. My stomach thought stopping was a bad idea, but I put the mugs aside and let her.

She cleaned my hands off patiently, going through a couple of towelettes. Then she said, "Lean over."

I did.

She took a fresh towelette and wiped off my face, slowly and carefully. There were nicks and cuts. It hurt when she cleaned one of them out, but it also felt right. Sometimes the things that are good for you, in the long run, hurt for a little while when you first get to them.

"There," she said a moment later. "You almost look human—" She paused at that, and looked down. "I mean . . ."

"I know what you mean," I said.

"Yeah."

The fire crackled.

"What's the story with Mac?" I asked.

Karrin looked over at the sleeping man. "Mab," she said. "She just came in here a few minutes ago and looked at him. Then before anyone could react, she ripped off the bandage, stuck her fingers into the wound, and pulled out the bullet. Dropped it right on his chest."

"No wound now," I noted.

"Yeah. Started closing up the minute she was done. But you remember the time he got beaten so badly in his bar? Why didn't his injuries regenerate then?"

I shook my head. "Maybe because he was conscious then."

"He did turn down the painkillers. I remember it seemed odd at the time," Karrin murmured. "What is he?"

I shrugged. "Ask him."

"I did," she said, "right before he passed out."

"What'd he say?"

"He said, 'I'm out.'"

I grunted.

"What do you think it means?" she asked.

I thought about it. "Maybe it means he's out."

"We just let it go?" she asked.

"It's what he wants," I said. "Think we should torture him?"

"Point," she said, and sighed. "Maybe instead we just let him rest."

"Maybe we should let him make beer," I said. "What about Thomas?"

"Woke up. Ate." She frowned and clarified, "Ate *soup*. Been asleep for a couple of hours. That big bone thing really clobbered him."

"There's always someone bigger than you," I said.

She gave me a look.

"More true for some than others," I clarified.

She rolled her eyes.

"So," I said, a moment later.

"So," she said.

"Um. Should we talk?"

"About what?"

Mouse looked back and forth between us and started wagging his tail hopefully.

"Quiet, you," I said, and rubbed his ears. "Bad guy made of *bones* and he gets the drop on you? Charity giving you too many treats or something? That fight should have been like Scooby-Doo versus the Scooby Snack Ghost."

Mouse grinned happily, unfazed, still wagging his tail.

"Don't be so hard on him," Karrin said. "There's always someone bigger." Then she shook her head and said, "Wow, we are such children. We'll grab at any excuse not to talk about us right now."

My soup did a little flip-flop. "Um," I said. "Yeah." I swallowed. "We . . . we kissed."

"There's a song about what that means," Karrin said.

"Yeah. But I don't sing."

She paused, as if her soup had just started doing gymnastics, too.

Then she spoke very carefully. "There are factors."

"Like Kincaid," I said, without any heat or resentment.

"He's not one of them," she said. "Not anymore."

"Oh," I said, a little surprised.

"It's you, Harry."

"Pretty sure I'm supposed to be a factor."

"Yeah," she said. "Just . . . not against." She took my hands. "I've seen things in you over the past day that . . . concern me."

"Concern you."

"They scare the holy loving fuck out of me," she said calmly, by way of clarification. "This Winter Knight thing. You're not changing. You've already changed."

I felt a little chill. "What do you mean? Tonight? Hell, Karrin, when haven't we done monsters and mayhem?"

"We've done it a lot," she said. "But you've always been scared of it before. You did it anyway, but you thought it was scary. That's the sane thing to think."

"So?" I asked. "What was different about it tonight?"

"The way your erection kept pressing into my back," she said wryly.

"Uh," I said. "Really?"

"Yeah, a woman kind of notices."

I hadn't.

Gulp.

"It's just . . . Karrin, look, that thing hardly ever does something that isn't ill-advised. Doesn't mean it's going to make the calls."

"I will never understand why men do that," she said.

"Do what?"

"Talk about their genitals like they're some other creature. Some kind of mind-controlling parasite." She shook her head. "It's just you, Harry. It's all you. And part of you was really loving everything that was going on."

"And that's bad?" I asked.

"Yes," she said. Then she made a short, frustrated sound. "No. Maybe. It's a *change*."

"Do changes have to be bad?"

"Of course not. But I don't know if this one is bad or not yet," she said. "Harry . . . you are the strongest man I know, in more than one sense of the word. And because you are . . . it means that if you *do* change . . ."

"You think I'd be some kind of monster," I said.

She shrugged, and squeezed my hands with hers. "I'm not saying this right. It's not coming out right. But I *felt* you, when we were with the Hunt. I knew what was driving you, what you were feeling. And in the moment, I was down with it—and that scares me, too."

"So am I too much of a monster or are you?" I asked. "I'm getting confused."

"Join the club," she said.

"You're saying that the problem is, you think I could go bad," I said.

"I *know* you could," she said. "Anyone can. And you've got more opportunity than most. And maybe you shouldn't be rocking your emotional boat right now. When Susan broke your heart, right after she was changed? You went into a downward spiral. If that happened now, with the kinds of things you're facing . . . Harry, I'm afraid you might not be able to pull out of it."

That much sure as hell was true. "You aren't wrong," I said. "But we haven't even gone on a date yet and you've already skipped ahead to the ugly breakup?"

"There are factors," she repeated in a firm, steady voice.

"Like what?" I asked.

"Like this thing with Molly," Karrin said.

"There's no thing with Molly," I said. "There's never going to be a thing with Molly."

She sighed. "You're a wizard. She's a wizard. Now you're the Winter Knight. And she's the Winter Lady."

"Karrin," I began.

"And I'm going to get old and die soon," Karrin said very, very quietly. "Relatively soon. But you're going to keep going for centuries. And so is she. The two of you are close—and even if nothing ever happens . . . it's one more thing. You know?"

We held hands and the fire crackled.

"Oh," I said.

She nodded.

"So there are things stacked against us," I said. "What else is new?"

"You are the captain of disaster in the supernatural world," she acknowledged. "But I'm the one who has repeatedly taken relationships into icebergs. I've done it enough to know that you and I are the *Titanic*."

"We're people," I said. "Not some fucking ship."

"We're also people," she said. "A kiss when we're both ramped up on adrenaline is one thing. A relationship is harder. A lot harder." She shook her head. "If it ends in tears, I'm afraid it could destroy us both. And there's a lot on the line right now. I don't think this is something we should rush into. I need time to think. To . . . I just need time."

I swallowed. She still wasn't wrong. I didn't like what she had to say, not one bit, but . . .

She wasn't wrong.

"Is this where you tell me we need to be friends?" I asked.

She blinked and looked up at me. She touched my face with her fingertips. "Harry, we're . . . We went past that a long time ago. I don't know if we can . . . if we should be lovers. But I'm your friend. Your ally. I've seen what you want, and what you're willing to sacrifice to make it happen." She took one of my hands between hers, pressing hard. "I feel lost since they fired me. I don't know what I'm meant to do or who I ought to be. But what I do know is that I've got your back. Always." Tears fell from her blue eyes. "So goddammit, don't you start taking the highway to Hell. Because I'm going to be right there with you. All the way."

I couldn't see her face after that. I felt her head underneath my chin, and I put my arms around her. We sat together like that for a while.

"Things are going to get bad," I said quietly. "I don't know how or when, exactly. But there's a storm coming. Being near me isn't going to be . . . sane."

"Let's just agree that I'm not all the way together, and save us both some time arguing," she said. "Always, Harry. I'm there. End of story."

"Okay," I said. "One condition."

"What?"

"That's not the end of the story," I said. "I mean, maybe neither one of us is ready. But we could be, one day. And maybe we will be."

"Optimistic idiot," she said, but I could hear the smile.

"And if we get to that place," I said, "you don't chicken out. You don't run away, no matter how it looks to you. We set course for the fucking iceberg, full speed ahead."

She started shaking. She was weeping.

"And the sex," I said. "It will be frequent. Possibly violent. You'll be screaming. Neighbors will make phone calls."

She started shaking harder. She was laughing.

"Those are my conditions," I said. "Take them or leave them."

"You're such a pig, Dresden," Karrin said. Then she drew back enough to give me a look through tearstained blue eyes. "Maybe you'll be the one screaming."

"You sure about this?" asked Thomas. "Out here by yourself?"

"Cold isn't really an issue anymore," I said, untying the first of the lines from the *Water Beetle* to the Whatsup Dock. I was wearing some of his clothes from the ship. The sweats were too short, and the shirt was too tight, but the duster hid most of that. "And I've got supplies for a week or so, until you can make it back. You sure that tub's going to make it back to town?"

"Put three patches on the hull after I got her off the beach, and the pumps are working," Thomas said. "We should be fine. What about you? That thing the island said was in your head?"

"Another reason to stay here," I said. "If Molly's the one who can help me, I'm on my own for now. But Demonreach seems to be able to make it leave me alone, at least while I'm here. Pretty much means I need to stay until Molly gets herself back together."

My brother exhaled unhappily, and squinted up at the noonday sun, south of us, hidden behind grey clouds. "Heard from Lara on the radio."

"And?"

"Both her team and Marcone's found rituals in progress at the two sites. They broke them up. Someone *really* wanted this place to get screwed up."

"Or some*thing*," I said with a melodramatic waggle of my eyebrows.

He snorted. "You joke around. But I can't help but think that Fix is going to hold you responsible for some of what happened last night," he said. "He might show up to explain that to you."

"He shows up here, there's nothing he can do," I said quietly. "I can take him on neutral ground. Here, it won't even be a fight."

"Still," Thomas said. "Out here, alone?"

"I think it's important," I said. "I've got to know more about this place and what it can do. The only way to do that is to invest the time."

"And it's got nothing to do with facing Molly's parents," he said.

I bowed my head. "It isn't my place to tell them. Molly should decide who they hear it from first. Once she has, yeah. There's going to be a really hard talk. Until that time, I need to be here."

"And it's got nothing to do with facing Maggie," Thomas said.

I looked away, out at the grey water of the lake.

Fix knew that Maggie existed. If he wanted to hurt me . . .

"She's with Michael because he's got an NFL lineup of angels protecting his house and family," I said. "And Supermutt, too. Am I going to be able to provide a real home for her, man? An education? A real life? What's her college application going to look like: 'Raised on Spooky Island by wizard with GED, please help'?" I shook my head. "And when the fallout from the White Council about Molly and about this place starts hitting, it's going to be a nightmare. I might as well have a target tattooed on her forehead as keep her near me."

"Michael is awesome," Thomas said. "Hell, I wish he'd raised me. But he isn't her dad."

"I had sex with her mother," I said. "That's not the same as being her father."

Thomas shook his head. "You'd be a good dad, Harry. You'd spoil her and you'd indulge her, and you'd embarrass her in front of her friends, but you'd do right by her."

"This is me," I said. "Doing right by her. For now. Maybe someday things could change."

Thomas eyed me. Then he shook his head and said, "Kids change. Into adults. Way faster than it seems like they should. Don't take too long deciding how much change is enough."

Hell, he was right about that much, at least. I sighed and nodded slowly. "I'll keep it in mind."

"I know," he said, and smiled at me. "Because I'm not going to shut up about it."

I rolled my eyes and nodded. "Good. Don't."

I offered my fist for bumping.

Thomas ignored me and gave me a rib-cracking hug, which I returned.

"Glad you're back," he whispered. "Loser."

"You gonna start crying now, wuss?" I said back.

"See you in a few days," he said. "We'll get the cottage finished off. Make it someplace Maggie won't need to learn shape-shifting to survive in."

"Just don't forget the books," I said. "Or the pizza for the guard."

"Won't." He let go of me and hopped up onto the *Water Beetle*. "Any messages?"

"Molly," I said. "When she gets back, ask her to send Toot and Lacuna to me. And . . . tell her that when she's ready to talk, I'm here."

Thomas nodded, untied the last line, and tossed it to me. I caught it and started coiling it. Thomas climbed up onto the bridge and took the ship out, chugging away at the sedate pace he would use until he cleared the stone reefs around Demonreach.

Karrin came out of the cabin and stood on the deck. Mouse came with her, looking solemn. She leaned back against the cabin's wall and watched me as she went.

I watched, too, until I couldn't see her anymore.

Thunder rumbled over Lake Michigan, unusual in November.

I settled the new black leather duster over my shoulders, picked up the long, rough branch I'd cut from the island's oldest oak tree a few hours before, and started back up the hill, toward the former lighthouse and future cottage. I had preparations to make.

There was a storm coming in.

About the author

A martial arts enthusiast whose résumé includes a long list of skills rendered obsolete at least two hundred years ago, Jim Butcher turned to writing as a career because anything else probably would have driven him insane. He lives in Independence, Missouri, with his wife, his son and a ferocious guard dog. You can visit Jim's website at www.jim-butcher.com

Find out more about Jim Butcher and other Orbit authors by registering for the free monthly newsletter at www.orbitbooks.net